THE SPRING OF
KASPER MEIER

THE SPRING OF KASPER MEIER

BEN FERGUSSON

Little, Brown

LITTLE, BROWN

First published in Great Britain in 2014 by Little, Brown

Copyright © 2014 by Ben Fergusson

The moral right of the author has been asserted.

A CIP catalogue record for this book
is available from the British Library.

HB ISBN 978-1-4087-0504-9
C Format ISBN 978-1-4087-0505-6

Typeset in Garamond by M Rules
Printed and bound in Great Britain by
Clays Ltd, St Ives PLC

Papers used by Little, Brown are from well-managed forests
and other responsible sources.

MIX
Paper from
responsible sources
FSC
www.fsc.org   FSC® C104740

Little, Brown
An imprint of
Little, Brown Book Group
100 Victoria Embankment
London EC4Y 0DY

An Hachette UK Company
www.hachette.co.uk

www.littlebrown.co.uk

For Barbara Fergusson and Katie Thomas

O schöner Tag, wenn endlich der Soldat
Ins Leben heimkehrt, in die Menschlichkeit,
Zum frohen Zug die Fahnen sich entfalten,
Und heimwärts schlägt der sanfte Friedensmarsch.

Die Piccolomini, Friedrich Schiller

Oh glorious day, when the soldier finally
returns home – to life, to humanity –
when the flags unfurl on the jubilant cavalcade,
and the soft peace march beats the way home.

The Piccolomini, Friedrich Schiller

SERGEI IGNATOV

Frau Leibnitz's tiny bar in Prenzlauer Berg was filled with shouting Russian voices and the smell of sweat, cheap schnapps and vomit. The most noise came from a small table in the corner, where four Russian soldiers were singing a series of bawdy songs about German women. Frau Leibnitz stared over their heads with an expression of concentrated sadness. Her gaze was fixed on the building opposite the bar, still in ruins, its brick and plaster shoved into a pile at the side of the road by the rubble women, so that the Russian Jeeps could pass by. The ruins had been sacked, turned, combed over by scavengers searching for hidden treasures to exchange and wood to burn, and their work had exposed a large plaster cornucopia, its yellow paint partially flaked away.

Sergei Ignatov sat in the middle of the group of singing soldiers, the only one not to have taken off his green padded jacket. As they sang, the other men, who were all ten years his senior, would jostle him, ruffle his hair and invite him to stand up and sing. He would laugh shyly and knock away their hands in a friendly, bear-like gesture.

Sergei was watching Frau Leibnitz at the bar. They had been

1

coming here for three weeks and he had hoped each time to ask her to share a cigarette with him, but every time he tried to strike up a conversation he choked on the words and miserably took his drinks back to his table of roaring comrades.

In his bed, early that morning, he had thought about Frau Leibnitz and masturbated quietly under his woollen blanket. He would make love to her gently, his face buried in the soft curls of her brown hair. It would be different from his first time, jeered on by his friends, their hands slapping his back and their cheers as he came into the crying girl. It would be just him and Frau Leibnitz and they would both be completely naked. He had never seen a woman completely naked before; at least not one that was alive.

'I'm going back,' said Sergei. His friends, who were now trying to climb onto the table to dance, didn't hear him. Some schnapps spilled from one of their glasses and wet his leg. He said again, 'I'm going back now,' and he stood up and moved across the bar towards the door. As he opened it, he turned towards Frau Leibnitz, but she didn't notice the teenage boy at the door; she was staring ahead, her fingertips hovering above the stained tablecloth spread across the bar.

The snow was gone, but Sergei could still feel winter in the wind that whipped down the street, flicking up dirt from the ruins opposite. Only four buildings in Frau Leibnitz's street were still standing; in the daytime the rest became a citadel of towering brick walls, thin, burnt, streaked with rain, atop rolling hills of grey stone and dust. But in the meagre light from a half-moon and a few bright stars in an otherwise cloudy sky, the piles of debris rose and fell beside him like the silhouettes of distant mountains.

He walked down towards Schönhauser Allee and soon he could hear his footsteps louder than the Slavic voices coming from the bar behind him and for a second he imagined he was back in Kazan, walking back to his parents' house from the school. Sergei sniffed, shrugged his shoulders and spat onto the floor. He decided that he would bring Frau Leibnitz some sort of gift the following day; some tinned meat perhaps, or maybe something more romantic – some soap or stockings.

He heard a sound – the scrape of a shoe – and put his hand on his gun. He looked down, then back towards the bar and then up the main street, but he saw nothing. He heard the noise again and, turning, he noticed a woman standing in the door-way of a partially collapsed building. Her skin was so pale, and the street so dark, that her head floated dismembered in the black until she stepped out into the street. And then he saw that she was pretty in her way, but thin, and her black hair was cut strangely short, like a boy's. She said something in German that he didn't understand, but he understood what she was propos-ing. He looked back at the bar and then at the woman. She smiled. He took out some cigarettes and showed them to her. She nodded and gestured that he follow her through the door-way. He walked gingerly forward.

The inside of the building was completely black except for a little grey light coming from the entrance into the courtyard behind it, framing an empty, formless space. The smell of burnt wood and mould hung heavy in the still air.

'Hello,' he said in Russian. His voice echoed up the stairwell. He stumbled over the broken brick and plaster on the floor and reached out in the darkness for her. 'Hello?' he said.

There was a white flash, then a crack – Sergei was lying on his back on the rubble. He tried to speak, but he had no air in his lungs and he became aware that the heat on his face was his own blood. He heard the woman's knees cracking as she bent down. She put her fingers on the jugular vein in his throat, his pulse beating up against her fingertips in heavy waves, and then he felt the gun pressed onto his forehead again, the tip levering forward until he felt the cold circle flush to his skin.

3

A LIGHTER WITH A NAKED WOMAN AND A HORSE

In April 1946 Windscheidstraße was still littered with a few strips of intact apartment blocks. The plaster on their frontages was cracked and peppered with scars from bullets and shrapnel, and the glass was often missing from the doors. But there were doors – large handsome wooden doors that rattled and shook as they shut. And beyond the doors the smooth wooden banister snaked up to the apartments in the front of the building, the top matt where the paint or polish had not been renewed for seven years. On the stairs the worn lino was still on the treads, though one now heard the ubiquitous sound of dust crunching underfoot, impossible to get rid of.

Past the staircase, through the back door to the central courtyard, the ground was now ploughed up and planted with vegetables. But it was still surrounded by the apartments to the side and at the back, streaked grey from the dust and ash that had mixed with the rain and the snow and dribbled down the high painted walls, reaching up sheer to the rectangle of sky above.

At Windscheidstraße 53 Frau Sauer was sweeping the courtyard with the thinning brush of an old broom. She regularly
came out of her ground-floor apartment, habitually flicking at
the cracked concrete pathway. She was in fact just showing herself to the other residents and to any visitors, keeping a territorial
eye on the small patch of potatoes growing in her corner of the
courtyard garden. She looked up every now and again to see if
anyone was watching her, but her only regular attendant was
Herr Meier, whose white hand floated behind his kitchen
window, five floors up, his face just out of sight.

At that moment Kasper Meier's hands were engaged in splitting
the tobacco from one black market cigarette into four thin ones,
using the cigarette paper for two and newspaper for the second
pair. This had turned the fingertips and nails of his right hand
permanently black and left a grey smudge on his bottom lip,
where his hand rested when he was thinking. He took pleasure
from the tobacco itself and the fact that the act of smoking was
wholly selfish, but more consciously there was pleasure in the
tradable value of the cigarettes on the black market; so as Kasper
took a first drag he felt as if he was smoking money itself.

The chairs were positioned by his kitchen window and over-
looked the courtyard. When he had taken the top-floor
apartment at the back of the courtyard in 1939 the other residents of Windscheidstraße 53 thought that he was charmingly
confident about the swift success of the war believing as he did
that Berlin was immune to attack. When the first raids began in
1940 and he refused to leave the apartment while the sirens
screamed, they thought he was being stubborn and shrugged
their shoulders. 'Poor old Herr Meier,' they said, 'even if the
Tommies miss him he'll never escape a fire.' When the bombing
began in earnest in 1943, and he still refused to come down to
the bomb shelter in the cellar, the other residents stopped talking to him and told their children to avoid him.

Kasper's only intention in staying in his apartment was to spend as little time with his neighbours as possible, and so this outcome was an unexpected gift. The idea of being blown up, choked to death, or burnt alive, seemed a far more preferable end to him compared to being buried alive in a cellar with the other residents of Windscheidstraße 53, until they gossiped themselves out of air.

And having survived the bombings and the occupation, losing only one windowpane to the butt of a British soldier's gun searching the apartment for illegal goods and the temporary use of the little finger on his left hand to the winter that was finally dying away, his position and the animosity of his neighbours suited him perfectly; he was able to sit undisturbed at his window and see anyone approaching his apartment, knowing that they had five floors of stairs to get up, giving him plenty of time to assess the situation and hide cigarettes, money, scraps of information or himself. And if the stranger had asked someone they bumped into on the way for some information about Herr Meier, he knew they would roll their eyes and say something like, 'Don't waste your time,' or 'I'm glad to know absolutely nothing about that old coot.'

If they said anything, they would resort to gossip, telling the visitor that he was once a very important Nazi, a very important Communist or a Russian, British, American or French spy. The favourite rumour would be told to the visitor conspiratorially, by Frau Sauer or Frau Schwarz, leaning on their brooms and saying quietly, 'His blind eye? I shouldn't say – it's none of my business – but . . . well if you must know, he used to peep through keyholes in his last apartment block. Eventually one of them stuck a skewer through while he was looking.' In her retelling, Frau Schwarz often said that the woman was a prostitute and that she had heated up the skewer over the stove, so that it was red-hot when she jammed it, sizzling, into the jelly of his eye.

Kasper Meier took a second drag on his thin cigarette and the jumpy ball of his seeing eye fixed on a new visitor waiting in the courtyard – a woman who appeared to have come straight from clearing rubble. She was young, dressed in boots, grey men's trousers tied up high on her waist with a length of thin rope, a khaki shirt with cotton epaulettes, and a headscarf from under which half a fringe of blonde hair had escaped. She looked first at the door to the side building and then to Kasper's side of the courtyard before turning her head up to the window, shading her eyes. Spotting Kasper there, she threw her hand into the air and waved at him. He took another, slow drag on his cigarette.

He heard her running up the stairs, but didn't move from his seat. The hinges of the door to the apartment had warped, perhaps from the winter's arctic freeze, or perhaps from the five times it had been kicked in. Whatever the reason, the door now required a careful lifting and pushing movement to get it open. When unexpected guests first arrived they tended to struggle with it for a few minutes, calling through the gap, while Kasper finished off his cigarette. This visitor, however, knocked and cried, 'Hello,' and started immediately to push at the door. Kasper raised his eyebrows and continued to smoke. Instead of the usual intermittent shoving and calling, however, the woman paused for a few seconds, then rammed the door open in a series of rapid bangs that Kasper assumed she'd made by shoulder-barging it and she appeared, a little flushed, but smiling, at the doorway to his kitchen having kicked the door closed again. 'Your door's broken.'

'Evidently,' said Kasper.

'Herr Meier?' she said.

'Yes.'

'Eva Hirsch. Nice to meet you.' She offered up her hand and Kasper waved his cigarette in the air as a reason not to shake it. She was younger than he had first thought – perhaps twenty. She was thin, but not starving, her bare, grubby forearms protruding long and straight from the rolled up sleeves of her baggy shirt.

She pulled off her headscarf and boisterously ran her fingers through her hair, creating a small haze of fine white dust. Some twisting strands of blonde were stuck around her ears and forehead with sweat and dirt; the rest had become a curling mess beneath the cloth, vaguely parted on one side and tumbling down almost to her shoulders. She flattened it a little with a few rough pulls and the early spring sun created a pale white halo from its frizzy ends.

'Well,' she said. Kasper watched her taking in the room, the sooty walls, the sour smell of old ersatz coffee and rancid milk, the cock-eyed shelf containing his rations: a small brick of black bread, two small potatoes, an open shoe-polish tin with three cigarettes and a package of greasy paper, bound with string, containing maybe butter or perhaps a little fatty meat if he had some connections; she would assume he did. And she would wonder what was under the old rug, pushed up against the kitchen wall, covering piles of stacked up items.

'This is all very nice. Look you've even got some drink,' she said. She pointed to a brandy bottle by the leg of his chair with an inch of spirit left in the bottom.

Kasper said nothing. Eva smiled in a supportive way that he recognised from other younger women – and, though she might pity him, he wasn't unhappy with the way he looked. When combined with a stony expression, he invited a certain distance that he enjoyed; that he needed. And pity, the rare moments when it was forthcoming, could be just as useful as fear.

The fear could be engendered by his height – the frightening length of his limbs, which were accentuated by a dark-blue, crumpled suit that hung loose on his bony frame, but was not long enough to cover his wrists or ankles. A height that also gave

9

itself away, in that moment, in the arm that hung down by his side, the hand almost touching the floor. And perhaps there was also something alarming about the unsettling thickness of his straight, white hair, that despite brushing and trimming, stuck up in heavy tufts, yellowing slightly at the fringe, where the smoke from his cigarette curled up after staining the parts of his fingers that weren't already blackened.

The pity didn't come from his age – it was indeterminable, people would guess anywhere between forty-five and fifty-five, perhaps even sixty. In Berlin, a face full of lines carved out by dirt, fear and exhaustion didn't tell you anything about someone's age anymore. There was only pity when they noticed his right eye, which was milky white and immobile. What had once been a shining black pupil, surrounded by a bright green iris, was now a faded blue stain beneath a smooth misty layer, like cooked egg white. And however grave or sure his expression, the eye always seemed desperate to shed its husk, to see again.

'Can I sit down?' said Eva. 'Gosh, I'm sweating like a pig,' she said, pulling at the armpits of her shirt. 'Very ladylike, isn't it? Not much opportunity to be a lady these days, is there?'

'What do you want?' said Kasper.

Eva looked about her, then lifted a pile of newspapers off a crate by the cold iron stove and dropped them onto the floor. She sat down and took two full-sized cigarettes from the breast pocket of her shirt, fanned them out in one hand and reached out to take the thin ember that remained in his.

'May I?' she said. He hesitated for a moment, but then held out his hand and she took the tiny dog-end from him, lit one cigarette from it, then the second. She passed one back to him, tossing the ember onto the floor and putting it out with her boot. He looked at the cigarette he had been given then took a long drag on it with his healthy eye shut, positioning his head so that the blind, white eye continued to stare at her. He blew out the smoke slowly, opened his eye again and said, 'I hope to God you're not here to sell anything.'

'Oh no,' said Eva, 'nothing like that. I'm looking for somebody.' She crossed her legs, so that she was sitting on top of the crate like a Buddha, and rested the elbow of her smoking hand on her knee. A stream of little cuts and bruises, pink, grey, blue and yellow, tumbled down her forearms to her hands where the skin around her fingernails was red and bitten, the nail beds dirty, a thumbnail black. 'I heard that you were good at finding people,' she said.

'You heard wrong.'

'It was a very reliable source.'

'Huh,' said Kasper, flicking ash onto the windowsill, 'there's no such thing as a reliable source in Berlin.'

'He's a pilot.'

'They're the least reliable.'

'No, the person we're looking for is a pilot.'

'Then you've definitely come to the wrong place. I don't do military.'

'Can't really avoid military in Berlin,' she said.

'You just have to try very hard. Who's we?'

'Sorry?'

'You said "we're looking".'

'Gosh, you are good,' she said and briefly nibbled at her cuticle. 'It's for a friend of mine. But she can't come. It's complicated.'

'It's always complicated and it's always a friend.'

'It really is a friend,' she said. 'It's terribly boring and straightforward, I'm afraid. She's pregnant. They had a thing and now she's having a baby and she wants him to know. She liked him and she thinks he'll take her out of Berlin; take him with her. I know it's ridiculous, but . . .'

Kasper laughed, at first lightly to himself and then out loud.

11

He took his legs off the chair opposite him and balanced his elbow on his knee and his chin on his hand. 'That really is a very sweet story, but I don't normally take on teenage romance cases. I would suggest your "friend" cruises the same bars and hangout spots that she picked up her Tommy, Yank or Ivan in and waits it out. I'm sure he'll come sniffing around sometime soon and she can entrap him to her heart's content.'

Eva took a long drag on her cigarette and flicked the ash onto the floor. She looked up at him; her eyes were strange, clear and dark blue – almost purple. He couldn't tell if they were too large for her face or beautiful in their queer magnitude. Despite her slight frame, she seemed rugged, robust somehow – perhaps a physical strength from working the rubble, perhaps something more ephemeral. It made him think of birds, of sparrows. Maybe she is in her twenties, Kasper thought, refusing to look away before she did. She had a confident, adult charm about her. But then the skin of her neck was so smooth and so thin, where the light outdoor-worker's tan faded in his peripheral vision, just beneath the collar of her shirt; where her blue veins appeared as soft aquarelle lines. And then there was her incessant childlike fidgeting and those compulsive fingers – rubbing her eyes, teasing out strands of hair and twisting them into curls, worrying her hairline and the end of her cigarette. A girl that war had made adult.

'They said you'd be difficult.'

'I hate to disappoint,' he said, leaning back in his seat.

'We would obviously make it worth your while.' She took a cigarette case out of her pocket and placed it on the windowsill beside him. It was plated silver, perhaps Russian, with an embossed picture of a bare-breasted woman holding the head of a horse. 'We have a good black market connection. Cigarettes. Or if you want something else. Something special.'

'I have plenty of good black market connection, Fräulein

Hirsch. I am a good black market connection,' Kasper said and pushed the ugly trinket back towards her. 'As I said, I don't think I can help you. And you'll be hard pushed to find anyone who's going to gladly go poking around in military matters, especially to solve a lover's tiff.'

Eva looked at the window, one pane of which had been replaced with a piece of rotting wooden board, and then stared out into the sky above the building – it was bright grey, as it had been throughout February and March. What was that uncomfortable confidence, Kasper thought? And he suddenly concluded that he was being robbed. He jumped off his chair and stumbled quickly to the door, but when he looked out, the corridor was empty. 'What do you really want?' he said, turning back to her. 'What are you doing here?'

'Like I said, I need this information.' She smiled. 'But I thought that would probably be your answer.' Yes she was young and her face almost glowing with youth in the white light, but Kasper could see the lines around her eyes already taking root, carved out by the dust and a year of chipping mortar off brick through a roasting summer and a freezing winter. And her hands were already ten years older than the rest of her body and if he had shaken them, he knew he would have found them to be dry and cracked and powerful like a man's. He wondered if she really was just an over-confident young girl who had come about a pregnant friend. He tried to sound comforting. 'I'm sorry,' he said.

She nodded and stared down at the end of her cigarette.

'Look,' Kasper said, 'maybe I could give you a couple of names – someone else that could help. Or I could point you in the right direction.'

She looked up at him, shocked. 'You don't need to placate me,' she said. 'You shouldn't.' She seemed suddenly confused and her neck and cheeks flushed red. 'No, you have to do it.

You see ...' She stumbled on her words again, but then stared forcefully down at the floor and said. 'This contact that I got your name from. He's called ...' She paused. 'Herr Neustadt. Heinrich Neustadt.' Kasper had learnt to meet any proffered name with a completely blank expression – even a name that caused his gut to contract and a squirt of acid to shoot into his empty stomach. She looked up at him now, warily – not lifting her head. 'So, how do you know each other?' she said quietly.

'I know a lot of people.'

Kasper returned to his chair, feigning nonchalance, and put his forgotten cigarette back between his lips.

She seemed to have regained control of her discomfort and said, 'I was chatting with your landlady and I described him to her. She said she'd seen him here.'

'He visited me once, needing something found. Not that it's any of your business.'

'Well, she wasn't sure exactly – she says she takes little interest in your life – apparently she's not your biggest fan. But she's seen him here at any rate. She could testify to it.'

He felt his anger stinging around the collar of his shirt, in an absence of breath, in an aching pain at the base of his head. And yet he remained impassive. He flicked his cigarette and let his knuckles brush the floorboards beside his chair in a slow, gentle back and forth. 'What are you getting at, Fräulein ...?'

'Hirsch.'

'I thought you weren't one to beat around the bush and yet you seem to have flogged this one almost to death.'

He bit the flesh of his lip. She sighed.

'I need someone's help and no one will help me. I've got ways of paying for it, but still no one wants to take it on and you're my last hope. What I'm saying is that I'll make you a deal. You help me and I'll pay you – simple as that. It's no big issue for you. And if the payment isn't enough of an incentive I promise not to . . . Well, you know – report you and Herr Neustadt.'

Kasper clucked his tongue and scratched the side of his nose. 'Blackmail is a very ugly business, Fräulein Hirsch.'

'So is buggery.'

Kasper looked out of the window, into the courtyard, where Frau Langer was slopping dirty water down the only working drain. 'I don't really see how you would expect to prove your claim.'

'Letters.'

'Letters? You think I would send incriminating letters to this friend of yours?'

'Well you sent this,' she said, fishing a note out of her pocket and reading from it, '"Dear Herr Neustadt, I hope this finds you well. We can meet as planned at 4.40 p.m. in Sybelstraße on Monday the 15th. Yours sincerely, Herr Meier."'

'It's hardly Sodom and Gomorrah.'

'And then I have his reply, which he gave me to pass on, but failed to seal properly. It says, "My dear Kasper, Monday 15th would be perfect. When we are apart I long to see you. All my love, Heinrich Neustadt."'

'That sounds very out of character.'

'Nevertheless he signed it. And,' she said removing another note from her coat pocket, 'I could also say that I had a testimony from another resident, who saw the door to your apartment ajar, walked in, and, unnoticed of course, witnessed you two, you know, at it. Well, it seems rather cut and dried. And I get the impression that with a little fishing around . . . I mean, that it wouldn't take much.'

'What did you offer him to get him to write that?'

Fräulein Hirsch shrugged. 'Honour isn't what it was, Herr Meier.'

Kasper sucked the last out of his cigarette and put it out on the black spot on the leg of his chair that grew and flaked malignantly with every application. 'And what do you think is going to stop me just shooting you now? Or having you shot? Who's going to miss one more little rubble slut?' He regretted using the word the moment it had left his mouth, but it didn't shock her. She threw her cigarette into the small sink that was hung from the wall with wire and hopped off the crate.

'It's a risk, but as I said this is important – it really is,' she said seriously. She tucked the letters back into her top pocket and pulled out a little card. She dropped it onto the windowsill. 'And like most people in Berlin nowadays, I don't really have anything to lose. Luckily you do.'

He stared down at the white dog-eared rectangle. 'Why me?' he said, ashamed that he sounded so pathetic.

'It wasn't you particularly. It's just hard to find anyone in Berlin who's doing anything bad enough for anyone to care about. Luckily everyone still hates queers, so I'm afraid it was just the luck of the draw.'

'Well fortune's always shone on my side.'

'I'm sorry,' she said. 'The card has an address of a bar on it. Meet me there on Tuesday at eight once you've had some time to think it over.' She turned to leave, but paused in the doorway. 'Look,' she said, nodding towards the cigarette case on the windowsill. 'You can keep that for your trouble.' He turned away from her, staring down at his hand resting in his lap. The girl took in a breath, as if to say something, but remained silent. Kasper looked up. She was holding on to the kitchen doorframe, staring down the apartment's dark corridor, her mouth half open. She turned to Kasper, scrutinised his face, then walked back to the passageway. He heard floorboards cracking and the flap of a curtain. She bit her lip, then suddenly fled, frowning, dragging the door shut as she went.

'Shit,' said Kasper to himself and went to the kitchen door.

The corridor was dark and empty. The floorboards creaked again and a heavy curtain in front of a doorway parted. An old man, with a white beard and bare feet, dressed in loose trousers, a cream shirt that may have once been white and an unbuttoned waistcoat, tottered out of the room and leant his hand against the wall.

'Herr Meier,' he said in mock surprise, his voice weak and husky, scraped bare with another cold.

'What did I tell you about coming out of your room? What have I told you time and time again?'

'There's no one here.'

'There was someone here and she just saw you.'

'I don't know what you're talking about.'

'You're lying.'

The old man crossed his arms. 'I needed to use the lavatory.'

Kasper shook his head. 'Papa, we agreed. If someone thinks we're related we'll lose your room. We could have a family of East Prussians in here by tomorrow if this woman decides to report you. Ten of the buggers.'

The old man sighed and shrugged. 'She looked harmless enough to me,' he said.

'More harmless than she thinks she is,' said Kasper.

'And anyway, she doesn't know we're related.'

Kasper looked up at him as if he was looking into a dusky, unflattering mirror. Kasper was his father's image in height, form, posture; in the crazed white hair and the large lobes of his ears. Though deeper, the wrinkles on his forehead, around his eyes, around his mouth were copied line for line, but with a broader brush. Kasper's father had once been a tall, sanguine Victorian, with a broad stockiness that Kasper had never achieved. But he had shrunk over the last ten years, their wartime frames now alike. He still kept his beard trim with a blunt razor and brushed his hair every morning, and managed

17

to retain an air of his once colossal, cheerful dignity. But Kasper didn't see this; he couldn't quite see past what had gone, what once had been. He was the one personal tragedy left that Kasper was unable to ignore and it made him miserable.

'Did she bring anything?'

'A cigarette,' said Kasper, walking back into his room, to his chair and looking out of the window. The old man appeared at the door. 'You shouldn't be trying to make it down to that lavatory the whole time,' said Kasper. 'Call me – when I haven't got company – and I'll empty anything that needs emptying.'

'I'm trying to retain some sense of dignity. And I can get out of bed if I want.'

'You're sick.'

'I'm always sick. I'm bored.'

Kasper turned and stared at him. 'Well there's nothing more exciting to do in the kitchen.'

The old man shook his head. 'What did I do to deserve you?' he said and disappeared. Kasper heard the door opening again and the steps creaking as he made his way downstairs to the working toilet two flights below. He coughed heavily as he went, heaving up all the catarrh that he had saved up while there was a visitor in the next-door room.

Kasper watched the dark stain of water in the courtyard drying around the drain. Now Fräulein Hirsch had two secrets to tell – she had him and she had his father. He had dealt with worse than a little extortion, and yet the interview sat like a stone in his stomach. He thought he'd located the nervous pressure in the oddity of a young woman resorting to blackmail, but was it any more strange than the old mayor's wife in the front building who fixed trousers for cigarettes, the one-armed, legless dentist on the old Adolf-Hitler-Platz or the eight-year-old who had held a knife to his stomach, while his younger brother helped himself to Kasper's rationing coupons? He wondered whether it had more to do with his certainty that she was not working alone – all those 'we's', a nauseous sense that she was just the visible sprout of some tuber lying deep underground, huge and ancient. Because it was impossible that her anodyne story was true. Finally he wondered if it was the girl herself, her physical confidence pocked with embarrassment, her unfinished roughness and – though it seemed ridiculous to allow the word to form in his head and at his lips – her charm.

She reminded him of someone: a cabaret singer he had often seen before the war, perhaps? Was she called Rosa? She had sung 'Pirate Jenny' badly, but eagerly.

> *At midday, it will be quiet at the harbour,*
> *when they ask: Who has to die?*
> *And they'll hear me say: All of them!*
> *And when their heads roll I'll say: Hooray!*

His father walked back past his door. 'I'm getting a migraine,' shouted Kasper as he disappeared out of sight again, back to his room. 'Can you hear me? Papa? You've given me a bloody migraine.'

He rolled back the rug in the kitchen to reveal a single mattress, with a stack of brandy bottles, some packets of cigarettes and three tins of ham beside it; it represented the currency of his payment, for the last few years. He fished a dirty piece of cloth out of the bucket of water by the sink and climbed down onto the mattress, undoing his jacket and laying the wet rag on his forehead.

Kasper remembered Heinrich Neustadt only very vaguely from his bar during the Thirties – a presence on the periphery of things. When he had approached Kasper nervously at Frau Müller's some months earlier, Kasper had talked to him as a stranger, trying to escape the man's inane, uneasy chatter, until

Heinrich had tentatively asked after Phillip. Kasper had sat open-mouthed and then garbled something about him having left. As Heinrich made his apologies, Kasper had studied his face, trying to place him in that lost world. The man's hair was now all but gone, but he managed to draw together the stocky shoulders and barrel chest, the black eyes, the dark, heavy eyebrows into something like a memory of a person. He found it hard to remember his voice from then, but he saw him in dark corners, at the end of the bar, at the edge of other people's tables.

The affair had begun uncomfortably. Almost by invitation. Heinrich had continued to come to Frau Müller's and told Kasper that he had a room in an apartment in Sybelstraße. A locked room in an intact house, a willing, persistent partner, gave the invitation a stronger attraction than it might have otherwise had. And one drunken night at Frau Müller's, after Kasper had spent the afternoon haggling with a ten-year-old girl over the jewellery of her recently dead mother, Heinrich's warm hand pressed onto his was enough of an offer. Kasper did not recall the grateful smile and the sour kisses with pleasure, but sleeping beside someone, two people alone in an apartment, waking in the night with a warm body beside him, was enough to make him return the following week, and in the weeks after that.

He had made it clear a few times that he wanted to break things off, but the last time, just a week earlier, he had forced the issue, he had been cruel. He had tried to remain calm – he had – but Heinrich had begged, and then threatened to cry, and then shouted, pushing him into a corner, touching him – his hands on his wrists, on his chest and neck. 'You're disgusting!' Kasper had shouted. A sad, persecuted little man, and Kasper had told him he was disgusting. Heinrich had shrunk away into the corner of the room and Kasper had left him in there in the dark. And now a bit of revenge that would surely land Heinrich in more trouble than it would Kasper – the thought filled him with the familiar mix of anger and pity that had marked their whole relationship.

Kasper opened his eyes and blinked, trying to shut out those images – to push Eva and Heinrich away. When he closed them again he attempted to just listen to the sounds around him – to his father's coughs and the rustle of his sheets, the scraping of Frau Sauer's broom, a mother's raised voice somewhere else in the block, the barely audible rumble of military vehicles on the ruined streets.

But there was someone else there: he saw Phillip's bloodied eyes. It was as if the girl had brought him with her. And like déjà vu, he felt as if he had known that he would come today – it seemed suddenly inevitable. He shuddered. The eyes melted into a face and a body. Kasper's forehead was still hot. He turned the cloth over on his head. He had begun to shiver.

SEVEN TINS OF HAM

The next morning Kasper put a plate containing a single boiled potato by his father's sleeping head. He watched the light wisp of steam curling up from the vegetable's white flesh and decided that the girl wouldn't have the nerve to make things difficult for him. He wasn't afraid of her, of what she could do – he could find a hook, something to get rid of her – no one had nothing to lose. Last October a boy had threatened to come and shoot him in his sleep, to 'haunt his every waking hour' – a kid from Weißensee, trying to get back British chocolate bars his brother had traded with Kasper a few hours earlier. But the boy had a mother and the mother hadn't been happy to learn that he'd been buying guns from the Russians and suddenly Kasper's problem disappeared. And yet this thought – that Eva Hirsch was as easy to manipulate as any – didn't erase her presence. Even when he focused on something else, visually, mentally, there was a sliver of feeling around the top of his stomach, in his bowels.

He looked down at his father – the high arch of his chest rising and falling in heavy intervals. The winter had taken its toll on the old man – Kasper was surprised he had made it until spring. But it wouldn't be long – he wouldn't see falling snow again, probably not even falling leaves. He saw his own end in the old man's death. Not a decided action, nothing so planned. But it represented in his mind a full stop; a point he didn't see beyond, a release, a time to stop trying to seem alive. The final departure of someone whom he cared to comfort. So whatever Eva Hirsch could muster he could keep it at bay for as long as he needed, he was almost sure.

There was a little life in the street as Kasper left the apartment building and descended the few steps to the crumbling pavement. A line of women and children were queued up in front of the water pump with a ramshackle array of receptacles – buckets, yes, but also cooking pots, jugs and jars, industrial-sized American food cans, with jagged edges around their open tops like teeth, where they'd been prised open. An elderly woman passed him with a sack of branches tied to her back, the ends muddied and distressed to make them look as if she had found them, fallen from the trees, and not hacked them off with her own hands. A group of children were dragging the dead, snaking weight of a tank track past a ruined house opposite his building, and inside its doorway stood a girl and a boy, young teenagers. The boy had small features, a freckled nose and a tight angry mouth. The girl shared the mouth, but not the nose, and Kasper would have assumed that they were siblings on this basis alone; but the fact was made irrefutable by their unnervingly large eyes, the expansive whites and the icy blue irises, as light as a hole made in the snow with a finger, but edged with a grey ring as intense as their black pupils. Accentuated by their tall frames and their thin grubby faces, the eyes were luminous. Kasper was used to people staring at his milky, dead eye, but he was unable to tell if the girl and the boy were staring in disgust, in longing, in anger, in misery – if they were staring at him at all. He nodded at them, in case they had come to sell or buy something, but they didn't move, nor break his gaze. They were mad perhaps, or driven crazy with hunger, thought Kasper, and he turned away from them into the cold sunshine of the street unable to shake the sense that the eyes had turned with him and followed him down the road.

Despite this ominous beginning, the day was successful. Kasper got rid of seven tins of ham for three cheap watches, which he swapped with a Russian soldier for ten packets of cigarettes, two tins of corned beef, woollen socks and a tin of peaches. As he shook the tin, though, to check that there was liquid inside, he recalled Eva Hirsch's 'They said you'd be difficult' and her 'We have a good black market connection' and a vague picture of a group of conspirators formed in his head. He thought of them surrounding Heinrich Neustadt. He thought of the man's nervous, grateful smile as he was paid off and scuttled away like a beetle into the ruined city. He recalled Heinrich's thoughtful questions when they had first met and felt a fresh wave of anger, thinking about the man's sham civilities and phony semblances of friendship and affection. And then he had a vague recollection that Heinrich had once had a wife, that he had confided in Kasper the terrible things he'd seen in France during the war, but which Kasper had forgotten as soon as they were disclosed, and he felt ashamed, realising that he had never asked Heinrich about himself, about his life; that Kasper had no claims on the man, to whom he had been cold and guarded. A man he had cruelly rejected.

Kasper had found the address and regular drinking establishments of a factory owner from Münster who owed money to a group of old industrialists who lived together in Spandau – in return they gave him two bottles of brandy, a hairdryer and ten spools of red cotton. While they were counting the spools out, standing them up on the table like soldiers, he found himself picturing his father being pulled off his mattress and shoved down the stairs, past a family of thin, nervous-looking Pomeranians; their compassion worn to nothing by the ice and snow of a winter spent living in a refugee camp, with freezing winds curling up under the badly staked edges of the canvas. He saw the shame in the old man's eyes – a final, literal fall from grace.

He offered five spools of red cotton to a part-time seamstress in Kreuzberg, who gave him a packet of cigarettes and half a loaf of bread in return. He refused and managed to get rid of all ten spools and the hairdryer to the baker's wife in Neukölln in exchange for corned beef, two pats of butter, a bottle of home-made fruit wine, a pair of men's leather shoes and the address of a man in Friedenau who would sell him a grenade if he needed. As he looked down at the scrap of paper, he thought about the cold walls of a prison. Perhaps it wouldn't be so bad. He'd be fed. Perhaps he would meet Eva Hirsch and tell her that – make her feel powerless. But then he saw his father again, the soldiers checking his papers, seeing that he'd lied about not being related to Kasper in order that they might keep two rooms, instead of one. He saw them pushing the old man out onto the street, his corpse being found in the ploughed mud of the Tiergarten, his white body thrown naked into a burial pit, half submerged beneath a layer of glossy, black water.

While he was waiting for the American doctor to measure out the iodine that he was buying in exchange for the names of three old Nazis with stolen paintings in their houses, Kasper began to think about the teenagers in front of the building that morning. They had held his gaze on purpose – he was suddenly sure of it. And yet they hadn't tried to communicate anything with their eyes – they conveyed neither desire nor hatred, neither an invitation, nor a rebuttal. But the stare was intentional – he was certain.

Overcome with a brief wave of horror, Kasper snatched the iodine off the doctor, a spot of the brown liquid spilling onto his hand. He took a stuffed, clunking tram to Berlin Zoo and ran back to Windscheidstraße. He arrived as the sun was beginning to set, but the siblings were gone. There was only a group of children in front of his building – two girls and young boy – chalking pictures of soldiers onto the broken concrete. Their skin was orange in the fading light, their shadows dark purple. And the spiky ruins at the end of the street, black in front of the powder pinks of the sunset, might have been romantic if they hadn't been unnervingly silent in the windless street.

Upstairs, in the apartment, his father was awake and had propped himself up on his thin stained pillow. He was rereading Kleist's short stories, one of the eleven books he had managed to rescue when he had fled to Kasper's. He read them all in succession, except for the three volumes of Mommsen's *History of Rome*, which were a gift from his wife, but which he hadn't read through since the thirties, when its legions of marching soldiers and standard bearers became troublingly prescient. He finished his page, marked it with his finger, then looked up at the doorway where Kasper stood.

'Well?'

'Well what?' said Kasper.

'You're the one mooching around in my doorway.'

Kasper huffed. 'I've just run halfway across town to make sure you're all right.'

'Why shouldn't I be all right?'

'I don't know why I bothered.'

'You didn't answer my question, Kasper – it's very rude not to answer people's questions.'

'You're ridiculous.'

Kasper left and went into the kitchen where he stood in front of the large stove, a mass of low cold metal. He stood holding onto the rail in front of the hot plates, then took his hat off, threw it onto his mattress and went back to his father's doorway. 'Someone's trying to blackmail me.'

His father shrugged. 'Well, it's hardly surprising, the way you carry on.'

'What do you mean, the way I carry on?'

'All this black market business.'

'Oh, well you can moralise. If you want I can put you on proper rations for the elderly – you'd be dead in a day and—'

Kasper cut himself off. He looked down at the brown veins of cracked leather on the toes of his black shoes.

'Kasper, you're being petulant.'

'I'm not a child. I'm forty-se— I'm fifty, I . . .'

'Then stop behaving like one.'

Kasper made to leave again, but stopped. 'And there were a couple of kids outside – teenagers. I was worried they were mixed up with this girl. That they might do something – something to you. I've been worrying about it all day. I almost ran home, because I was worried about you.'

'You didn't seem that worried at lunchtime. You completely ignored me.'

'What are you talking about?'

'At lunchtime. I heard you clattering around in there.'

Kasper shot into the kitchen and lifted the rug that was pushed against the wall, revealing a small cache of tinned food, cigarettes, bottles of spirits and medicines. He counted each group of items swiftly, whispering beneath his breath . . . *dreißig, fünf und dreißig, vierzig, fünf und vierzig, fünfzig* . . . Everything was still there. Nothing had moved. A cold sweat of terrible possibilities burst across Kasper's back.

28

'I wasn't here at lunchtime, you old fool,' he shouted.

'Who was it then?'

'God knows. You're meant to block the door up after I leave.'

'It's broken!' cried his father from the next-door room, and began to cough.

Kasper turned and saw a small slip of folded yellow paper sitting on the chair by the window. 'It's your responsibility to block it when I'm gone,' he shouted, and picked up the scrap.

'What?' his father shouted back. 'I can't hear you!'

The piece of paper, ripped from a larger sheet, was covered in lists of food items, written in pencil, then rubbed out again, then written over, both horizontally and vertically. Over the top, someone had written in scratchy dry ink,

You would be lucky to go to jail, even luckier to come out alive. Your father will know first. Then the British. Your neighbours too. This is bigger than you. You don't have a choice. Queers still die in Berlin. Find the pilot.

'What?' said his father, much quieter now. He was at the kitchen door, holding himself up on the doorframe.

Kasper looked over at him. 'Did you read this?'

'Of course I didn't read it.'

Kasper looked at it again, then tore it up and threw the pieces into the stove.

'Even you can't go around wasting paper.'

'No,' said Kasper, looking down at the stove top. 'I didn't think.'

'I tried to block the door up, but it's broken. I can't lift those beams you use to wedge it shut at night.'

'I'll fix it tonight.'

'I don't want to be thrown onto the streets or attacked in my bed.'

'I know,' said Kasper. 'I'll fix the door. It was only the girl – the girl from the other night.'

'It's not serious, is it Kasper? This blackmail business?'

'No, it's nothing. It's nothing to worry about. It's just a silly girl . . .'

His father sighed then walked on, past the doorway, towards the stairs. Kasper listened to the steps creaking as his father descended again, step by step, to the toilet. He saw him in his study in the apartment they had owned in Friedenau, turning in his chair as Kasper walked in, before he left for Verdun. His father had laughed, revealing a heavy set of straight, white teeth beneath his large, waxed moustache. He had laughed because Kasper looked so gangly in his baggy uniform. He stood up and Kasper came forward and shook his father's hand. His father gripped Kasper's shoulder. 'You look fine, my boy,' he said. 'If your mother had known she'd had a soldier.' He laughed again. Kasper remembered that this laughter was a peculiarity of his father's, much commented on by friends. But when he tried to recall the withered man laughing now, he only saw him then, in his study, his heavy hand on his shoulder, as if he was still there, left behind on the other side of two wars.

Kasper became aware of a figure in his doorway: a short young man in a shabby brown suit. He had one arm, which was holding a crumpled hat. The empty sleeve of his jacket was tucked into the side pocket and pinned in place, flat. 'Who the bloody hell are you?' said Kasper turning. He reached under the kitchen counter top to locate the folding razor that was slipped into a little sheath made of waxed paper that he had affixed to its underside.

'The door was open,' said the man.

Kasper's fingers found the ivory handle of the blade and his fingertips hovered around it. 'Ever heard of knocking?'

'I did knock,' said the man, 'but you didn't hear me. There was shouting.'

'What do you want? Have you got anything to do with those bloody kids out front? Or Fräulein Hirsch? What do you all want from me? What is this?'

'I ...' the man looked down at his feet and then up at Kasper's chest. 'No, I don't know anything about kids or Fräulein anyone. I don't live here – I live in the French Sector. I ... It's about Herr Schwalbe downstairs – the neighbour under you, that is. My father. And my sister, his daughter.'

'And?'

'They were trading in kerosene – illegally of course.'

'Well, I didn't give to them. I wish I had some bloody kerosene.'

'No, it's not that. It's just that ... there was an accident. A spill in the apartment. They're dead.'

'Oh,' said Kasper. He took his hand out from under the counter and put it on his hip, then on his thigh, then into his pocket. 'I'm sorry. I didn't know them well.'

'Yes. Well, I thought you should know. I knocked on the door of the other apartment – the one opposite.'

'There's no one there – it's ruined. That whole side of the house. There's only me, your father and Frau Langer at the back of the courtyard. Everything else is ruined.'

'Yes,' said the man.

'Someone has to come and deal with the spill,' said the man, 'A fire officer or something. Then they'll move someone else in there, I suppose; probably quite quickly.'

'Yes,' said Kasper. He looked at the man's face – it was dry, but his eyes were red from crying. 'Look, do you want a drink or something?'

The young man shook his head. 'No, I have to get back to my wife. She's pregnant. Stupid, but I ... Well, I'd better be getting back. I just thought you should know.'

31

'Yes,' said Kasper. 'Thank you.' He watched the man turn to leave. 'Here,' said Kasper and knelt down and slipped out a can of tinned ham from beneath the large rug pushed up against the wall. 'Take this.'

'Oh,' said the man. 'That's kind.' He looked around awkwardly for a surface, but finding none nearby, put his hat back on his head and took the can. He looked down at it. 'Thank you,' he said, not taking his eyes off it. 'Shall I give you something for it?'

'No, take it.'

The man nodded.

'Your father and your sister,' said Kasper, 'They were always very friendly, very helpful.'

'Really?' said the man. But of course he knew them better than Kasper did, and so probably knew that they barely talked to their upstairs neighbour, if not actively disliked him. 'Well, good evening,' said the man.

'Yes,' said Kasper. 'Good evening.'

Kasper waited until the man had gone, then sat down by the window, slowly lifting his feet up to rest them on the chair opposite. He looked at his face in the black mirror that the night had made of the window, all the light from the apartments on the other side of the courtyard still blocked from view behind their thick, black-out blinds. He wondered how long Herr Schwalbe and his daughter had been lying below him dead, or when he had last heard any noise from the apartment. Perhaps a week or more. Herr Schwalbe had had the sagging face of a man who had once been overweight, his daughter was a rather plain, but sweet-voiced girl with an overbite. He had barely passed two words with them, but his impression was of a closeness, an openness that he didn't have with his own father. Though they would have slept apart, he somehow saw them lying together on the floor, the father embracing his daughter in death.

What a start to the week, he thought, but then he frowned – he was unsure of what day it was. Perhaps it was already the weekend.

He closed his eyes and concentrated on Phillip – concentrated hard to keep the memory fixed at a comforting moment. When his thoughts were disturbed and his bank of images and senses liable to jump forward in a sickening jerk – forward to later, frightful images – he concentrated on a single moment: Phillip waiting for him by the Märchenbrunnen in Volkspark Friedrichshain. The white stone of the fountain is grey beneath the bright layer of fresh snow that continues to fall from the sky, sitting in a thick layer on the frozen terraced pools. Kasper approaches, but the monument is empty, except for the melancholy sculptures, still in the frozen morning. Kasper stops, considers leaving, but then Phillip appears beneath one of the stone arches, wearing a long black coat and a grey hat. He turns towards Kasper and lifts up an ungloved hand to wave at him – the only colour is the pink of his freezing face and hand.

Kasper felt relief and joy, but when his emotions were even slightly disordered, he never went closer than the first shallow step in front of the fountain. The moment he felt the light stubble on a cold cheek, smelt soap on skin, felt the pressure of being embraced, the image would become unsteady, he would lose control, he would see and feel terrible things.

He opened his eyes and lit a thin cigarette and wondered how much kerosene had spilled, how flammable it was. He thought about the flames climbing up the bare walls of the kitchen as he slept. Perhaps the kerosene would combust before the fire officers arrived, he thought. Not such a terrible way to go. But his usually comforting thoughts of a lost past and of oblivion had been disturbed. It was the girl; it was Fräulein Hirsch. He felt that something was happening; not something good, but something alive, something since she had visited him. The note meant that he would have to see her again, at least once. And yet the thought didn't disturb him as he might have supposed it would. He felt a growing desire. Not sexual, surely – how could it be? But he wanted to see her. Because she liked him, despite herself. He felt it. And behind her cock-sureness, her hardness, there was a warmth and a vulnerability. He realised that he may well not need to catch her out, that he could just appeal to this softness. She was a poor blackmailer – he could charm himself out of this one. He smiled and sucked at the cigarette and listened to the crackling of the burning tobacco and paper in the silent room.

CASH

Kasper knocked on the door of Frau Müller's apartment block. He heard some girlish giggling from the other side and after a minute or so a young man, barely fifteen and with a broken nose, answered the door. He was holding a cheap plastic hairclip in his mouth like a cigarette, rotating it with his tongue. He recognised Kasper, but said, 'Magic word?'

Kasper smiled unconvincingly and pushed past him.

The giggle came from a skinny woman pushing thirty, who was sitting on one of two stools in the gloom of the cold hallway. She had let her hair spill down around her shoulders and was playing self-consciously with the tips. She looked up at him, imitating a coquettish teenager, but seeing how old he was, she looked back down at her shoes. They looked like they might have once been red leather, but were now grey, scratched and heavily repaired at the toes.

'Fräulein,' said Kasper, touching the front of his hat, and the woman giggled, revived, holding the tip of her tongue between her teeth and looking up at the doorman, probably fifteen years her junior. Despite the age difference, she was beautiful, he ugly, but in Berlin healthy young men with four limbs were a rare commodity.

Kasper walked past them, through the front hall and the large opening that had once held a back door. The sky was overcast, so that the courtyard of Frau Müller's building was almost black, save for the little light that escaped through a slit in the curtains of the first floor apartment and lit the treads of the three steps up to the door of the back building a dull orange.

Kasper could hear the light swing of an American jazz record and the gentle mutter of voices punctuated by the odd guffaw. He could also hear Herr Steinmeyer – once a cheerful, fervent Nazi – snoring somewhere near the great dark mountain that sat in the middle of the quad. In the last weeks of the bombing the drains near Frau Müller's building had been destroyed and now the cellars flooded every time it rained – Kasper could smell the damp stink of wet coal dust and rotting wood in the cellar's cold breath, that poured out into the courtyard, in through its low doors and cracked windows. The residents of the building had sat in those cellars during the last days of the war, waiting for the Russians to come, trying to keep their feet out of the water and away from the rats. And once the occupation was complete they emptied the basement, piling what they could save into a giant heap in the middle of their courtyard, like a pyre, covered by a tarpaulin, which the residents took turns guarding. Herr Steinmeyer watched the pile most nights, because he was only fifty and he had nothing left to look after, since his three sons had been killed and his wife had hanged herself when they heard the first punching booms of the Katyusha rockets coming from the East.

Kasper knocked at the door to Frau Müller's apartment. The peephole blackened and the door opened releasing a curling cloud of smoke and hot, sweaty air. Kasper squeezed through the gap sideways, into the corridor of the apartment, and greeted the second doorman with raised eyebrows. The brightest light came from the doorway into the kitchen that shone dimly onto a group of bottles on the bar set up in front of it – an old door balanced on two wooden crates.

'Herr Meier,' said Frau Müller, the once fat, former proprietress of a basement bar near Savignyplatz whose skin now hung about her thin arms in loose flaps, like raw dough, and whose original bar had disappeared with her lover under the very first carpet of British bombs in 1940. She nodded to a girl, who was sitting on a stool by the bar. The girl looked up at Frau Müller, bored, then over at Kasper and then sloped off drunkenly into the darkness of the corridor, towards the muttering in the dim next-door room.

'Frau Müller,' said Kasper, removing his hat and laying it on the bar, over the doorknob. 'A good night?'

'So, so,' said Frau Müller, 'No trouble. What can I get you?'

'Brandy,' he said.

'We have some vodka as well. It's quite good.'

'No thanks. Have the Russians been here?'

'Just one last week. An officer. I don't think he'll be bringing any of his comrades along though. Not after what he took home with him.'

Kasper laughed grimly.

'Rough day?' she said.

'Something like that.' She poured his brandy into a short wine glass with a crack in the lip. 'I'll pay cash today,' he said and handed her a note. She held it under a small table lamp with a dusty, beaded shade, which offered up the only light source in the dirty kitchen.

'Do you want change?'

'No, just tell me when I've used it all up.' She slipped it into a pocket of her apron and made a note on a sheet of grubby paper, headed with the name and address of a firm of solicitors, using a pencil stub that was so short she had to hold it between her thumb and forefinger like a needle.

'Are you wearing lipstick, Frau Müller?' said Kasper, drinking half the glass of brandy in one mouthful.

She put her hand to her mouth, as if she needed to check. 'Not everyone can pay in cash or cigarettes,' she said, 'and sometimes a girl has to get a little something for herself.'

Kasper smiled. He finished the brandy and she refilled the glass. 'Have you seen Heinrich Neustadt?'

'He's not been here tonight,' she said. 'Such a charming gentleman. I'm so glad you two hit it off.'

'He's been causing me trouble.'

'Trouble, Herr Meier? How appalling. I thought . . . Well, I know where my loyalties lie, Herr Meier. I know where they lie and you say the word and he'll never darken my door again. He always seemed such a fine sort.'

'No, just let me know when you've seen him, will you?' Kasper took five cigarettes out of his jacket pocket and left them on the bar.

'Of course, Herr Meier. And, you know, you should keep your cigarettes,' she said, already gathering them up.

Kasper shifted uncomfortably in his seat. He looked down at the bar top, at the old door, and reached forward to touch the brass keyhole. It was dull, full of scratches from years of having a key inexpertly hit into it by someone now scattered across a field in France or the Ukraine. 'Did Herr Neustadt come here before me? Was he ever a regular?'

'Not at all. He's only been around for the last few months. A good customer though. It will be painful to lose him, but I know where my loyalties lie. I'd never seen him until he came in here asking for you.'

'He came in asking for me?'

'I think so. It's a while ago now, Herr Meier. We have so many people through the door, thank God. But while I think about it, there was someone in here just this week asking after you.'

Kasper's finger froze over the small keyhole, but he didn't look up. 'Who?' he said.

'A young man.'

'How young?'

'Very young – I wondered if I should let him in, but since he was looking for you . . . You know I'd never turn away a friend of Kasper Meier's. And there's nothing but very young men and very old men in Berlin nowadays – I don't think I'd recognise a thirty-year-old if I saw one, Herr Meier, I honestly don't.'

'Was he with someone? A girl, the same age?'

'Not that I saw. But he only came in briefly; just to ask after you.'

'He didn't leave anything? Any note?'

'Nothing like that. Surly one. Apologies, of course, if he's a friend.'

'He's not a friend.'

'Oh good. Because he had a queer way about him. I didn't think much of him.'

'If he calls again . . .'

'Yes?'

There was another knock and the door opened, just enough to allow a tall soldier to slip through the gap. Kasper moved from his stool. 'Never mind,' he said.

'Look out for a Herr Schwarzkopf,' said Frau Müller, 'blond, a little shorter than you. He'd be pleased to meet you.' Kasper picked up his hat and turned to walk down the corridor as Frau Müller greeted her new visitor, saying in English, with a heavy Berlin accent, '*Meester Rowjers – Nice to see you agin.*'

Kasper walked into the next room, the smoke thickening and mixing with the smell of hot, infrequently washed bodies and cheap spirits. There were two lamps, one standing on a

39

duck-taped occasional table, the other on an upturned suitcase, the makeshift stands being the only easily identifiable objects in the room. Both were covered with small sheets of cloth, making the light low and brown. The cloth coverings both had maroon burns, like birthmarks, where the fabric touched the bulbs beneath. The rest of the room was a mix of sofas and chairs, bodies, dark corners and muttering voices, making it impossible to guess the dimensions of the space in the dim light.

He felt his way across – stepping on the toes of a woman who was sitting on the floor, muttering into the lap of her suitor – and lowered himself onto a broken sofa in the corner of the room, the springs giving way on one side, causing him to sink down into the rough viscose pile. There was a scratching noise as someone changed the record from one American jazz tune to another. He heard someone singing along gently to it: '*I can't begin to tell you, how happy I would be, if I could speak my mind, like others do . . . '*

As his eyes adjusted to the light he noticed that the warm mass beside him was the bottom of a young woman. She had fallen asleep on the shoulder of a man who had managed to get into the right position to stare down her top as she slept.

Kasper sipped his brandy and thought about leaving. He heard a sickly, pneumonic cough and two men talking in English. There was a conversation going on in Russian somewhere as well, and two German women, one of whom he recognised as Frau Müller's granddaughter Birgit, were whispering about a film they'd seen at the British cinema on Ku'damm.

Kasper put the tips of his fingers up to his lips and wondered about Frau Müller's visitor, about the two youths in front of his building. He shuddered at the thought of them being in the room at that moment, in a corner, waiting for him with their huge, unblinking eyes. He tried to imagine Eva Hirsch being part of some conspiratorial group of juvenile killers – it seemed unlikely. A trickster maybe, but he would surely be a poor and difficult target. But the boy and the girl ... He reasoned them into nothing again: the young man asking after him being a fluke, someone wanting information; Eva Hirsch really searching for a pilot for a friend; the youths, no more than a pair of desperate, hungry children hanging around in the street, just to be out of the cramped, wretched rooms they lived in. And yet he felt very sad and his eyes stung unexpectedly, tears threatening to well up at their edges. He shifted forward on the seat and coughed hard.

Very close to his ear, so close that he could smell the vodka on his breath, and feel the damp of it on his cheek, a young man said, 'Herr Meier?' Kasper automatically touched his forehead with the tips of his fingers, covering his bad eye in the half-light.

'Hello,' said Kasper, avoiding confirming his name.

'I'm Peter Schwarzkopf.' The young man moved onto the sofa at right angles to Kasper's and wriggled forward in his seat, so that their knees were touching. 'So Frau Müller tells me you're a detective,' said the man, his confident tone a construct of the vodka, which was making him hiccup.

'I'm not a detective,' said Kasper. 'I just get things for people. Find things or source things.'

'Oh,' said Peter, the first in what Kasper was sure would be a chain of disappointments for the boy that evening. 'What sort of things?'

'Names. Addresses. Cigarettes. Sardines. Anything that people are missing.'

'That's a lot of things, in Berlin.'

Kasper laughed. 'Yes.'

'You earn a lot?'

41

'What kind of question is that?' said Kasper and Peter looked down at his lap embarrassed and a little put out – the expression of someone fresh out of school, who was used to being scolded by the teacher or the Hitler Youth leader. 'I'm sorry,' said Kasper and put his hand on the young man's leg. The boy looked down at the hand curiously, as if it were an animal that he was trying to recall the name of. Kasper was about to withdraw it, but the boy laid his own hand on top of his; the palm was soft, warm and damp. 'Do you have a place to go?' he said.

'We can find somewhere,' said Kasper.

'It can't be too cold,' said the young man, suddenly sounding his age. 'I can't get a cold or anything. I've got to work.'

'We'll find somewhere,' said Kasper.

As they walked out, Frau Müller called, 'Herr Meier!' He leant over to the bar and she whispered, 'I'll take that out of the cash too. And a couple of cigarettes if you have them.'

'He might just hit me over the head and run off with my money. I'll give you your cigarettes next week if I have a pleasant evening.'

'Herr Meier! He's virtually a friend of the family. No trouble. I could even take just one cigarette.'

Kasper took one out of his pocket and laid it on the upturned door. 'If it means I could win you over one day . . . '

Frau Müller laughed lavishly, taking the cigarette and dropping it into the now empty shell of her brassiere. 'And before you go,' she said, fishing around her bosoms again and drawing out a cigarette card with something scribbled on it, 'something from one of the customers.'

'What is it?'

'A woman.'

Kasper frowned at the short description. 'Who's it for?'

'I can't say. A customer. An American – he'll be here every day.

You can pop back in any time or just give me the note to pass on.'

'Why does he want to find her?'

'Scruples now, Herr Meier!' Frau Müller squealed.

Kasper smiled. 'Never, but it might be useful to know.'

'A matter of the heart, Herr Meier, that's all. Just another German floozy who's broken his heart.'

Kasper nodded. 'Do you trust him?'

'More than I trust myself.'

'That doesn't bode well.'

'Oh Herr Meier,' she said, pushing his shoulder and laughing again. 'If you can get him an address for her he's willing to give you money.'

'How much?'

'He wrote it on the back.'

Kasper turned it over. 'Huh,' he said. 'He'd better be trustworthy.' Kasper tucked the card into his inside pocket and put his hand on Peter Schwarzkopf's back, guiding him out of the room.

The street was black, but the rubble had been more or less cleared so that they were able to walk at a comfortable pace, though slowly, orienting themselves by the jagged silhouette of the broken buildings on either side. Despite the clean ruins around them, whose bricks had been chipped bare by the rubble women, the warmth of spring had begun, in places, to bring back the smell of buried death that had plagued the city the previous spring – a sweet rotten fragrance carried on the searching gusts of April wind.

'Do you live nearby?' said Peter.

'No,' lied Kasper, 'and we're not going back to mine.'

'Where are we going?' said the young man, sounding a little afraid, his worst fear perhaps about to be realised.

43

'Oh don't worry,' said Kasper, 'nowhere funny. There are some places I know. But we can't go back to mine. Obviously.'

The road lit up and they heard the sound of a car driving up behind them. They automatically moved away from the path of the oncoming vehicle drifting into a recess on what had been the pavement, between two large piles of dusty rubble, stripped bare of every last useful brick, or piece of metal or wood. As the car came nearer it became clear that it was a Jeep and they heard either British or American voices talking loudly – Kasper couldn't tell the difference. The light from the headlights crawled up the road and then up across their faces and Kasper turned to Peter just in time to realise that he was standing to his right and to notice him staring in brief horror at his dead eye.

The Jeep drove by fast and a spray of dust was kicked up in its wake causing them both to cough and Peter to rub at his face. The brakes on the Jeep screamed and the two Germans automatically pushed themselves back into the rubble as far as they could go, stumbling on stones and twisted metal until it felt too dangerous to push back any further.

Someone shouted, '*Ricky, Ricky!*' Another soldier laughed. Kasper's stomach tensed as he heard one of the men stumbling off the back of the vehicle onto the road, but then he heard a cough turn into a heave and it became clear that one of them was vomiting. The other soldiers kept laughing and one of them drunkenly said in English, '*Ricky, you old twat.*' Kasper sighed, but he could feel that Peter was still tense beside him, unable to fathom what they were saying, believing maybe that the vomiting was coming from a German that they'd picked up to beat or poison. Kasper put his hand on the boy's back, but he didn't relax until they heard the man climb back in and the Jeep tear off down the road.

'It's OK,' said Kasper and guided the boy back onto the street.

They walked in silence until the boy said again, 'Where are we going? Is it far? I can't be far from home – I've got to be back tonight and it's past curfew.'

'It's not far,' said Kasper, 'another five minutes maybe. It's on a road off this one.'

The young man put his hands in his pockets and looked up at Kasper's face, squinting in the dark, then back down at the road.

'Do you want to say something?' said Kasper.

'No,' said the boy, sounding like a grumpy teenager. He is a grumpy teenager, thought Kasper. The boy looked up again. 'What happened to your eye?'

Kasper sighed. 'It got injured.'

'You weren't born like that?'

'No,' said Kasper.

'How did it get injured?'

'Hindenburg did it with his Pickelhaube when I pulled his moustache.'

The boy fell silent again.

They turned off the main road into a side street that hadn't been properly cleared, just a channel cut through the middle for vehicles. They picked their way slowly, their eyes, now more accustomed to the blackness, able to see a burnt-out car and large lumps of debris. They kicked smaller stones and junk with their shoes, which tinkled and rattled as they rolled away from them.

'Here,' said Kasper and climbed over a small mound of dirt, disappearing into a black doorway. He looked up – the building was largely burnt out with nothing but the dark, dirty blue of the night sky to be seen through the windows on the top floors. Peter followed Kasper slowly and passed through the doorway where his hand was met by Kasper's. He led him up two flights of stairs in the front of the building and took him into an empty room that was still intact, the night palpable in the blue squares of its missing windows.

'Do you live here?' said the boy.

'No, of course not,' said Kasper, taking off his hat and jacket and putting them on the side of an iron oven that had been ripped from the wall and was now sitting in the middle of the room.

'It's cold,' said Peter.

'Well the Adlon's in ruins I'm afraid,' said Kasper, 'and, anyhow, I don't think they rent by the hour.'

Peter looked down at a pile of sheets by Kasper's foot that would serve as a makeshift bed. They heard the soft hush of dust and ash falling down the stairwell and then landing on the remaining steps.

'Someone's here,' said Peter.

Kasper turned and stared out of the open door, into the black rectangle. He listened – he heard nothing. 'No,' he said, putting his hands on his hips. 'There's no one.'

Peter didn't move for a few seconds, just looked around the room. Then he took off his own jacket and laid it on Kasper's, bit his lip and stood dumbly staring at the raggedy pile of material. Kasper held out his hand and the young man moved forward and took it; it was still warm from his pocket. Kasper pulled him towards him and kissed him on the lips. He had a little scratchy blond stubble and Kasper could smell the fresh sweat, like grass, coming from beneath the young man's shirt. Peter pulled back. 'What are we going to do?'

Kasper took the young man's hand and led him over to the pile of sheets. He lay down and pulled the boy down with him. Kasper kissed him again opening his mouth and the boy opened his and they kissed heavily for a few seconds. His mouth tasted of vodka and cigarettes, but there was something sweet and unadulterated beneath it. Kasper could see the young man's arms moving slowly around as if he was falling from a building and then he reached forward and put his hands on the small of Kasper's back. He pictured his fingers – large and plump, with bitten fingernails. Peter gripped him tighter and Kasper heard a sound he had always found beautiful – of fabric brushing across fabric in an otherwise silent room.

Kasper turned around and lay on his side, pushed back into the boy and pulled his arm around him, up towards his face, so that he was gripping him tightly, so that he could smell the smoke on his fingers. Kasper used his other hand to pull the boy's leg over his, so that he could feel the great, live weight of it. Kasper closed his eyes and emptied his head, he thought of nothing and tried to feel nothing except for the human pressure at his back, on his legs, across his side.

'Herr Meier?' whispered Peter, pushing himself up on his elbow.

'What?' said Kasper.

'What do we do now?'

'This.'

Something rattled softly outside the room – wind teasing a flap of torn-off wallpaper or an animal scuttling across broken plaster.

'Frau Müller said you wanted me for an hour.'

'That's right.'

The boy didn't move for a second, then lay back down and rested his head on the sheets. He kissed the back of Kasper's neck and left his lips there. His thumb began to rub the palm of Kasper's hand and he felt the boy drifting off, felt him breathing lightly, making the hair at the back of his head damp. He brushed the boy's fingers across his lips and tried to let go of Berlin, of his father, of his memories. Try and pretend that he was half asleep or half awake, that the city, his life was drifting away like waves retreating with the tide. And trying desperately to ignore the cold, the damp and the stinging in his eyes, he was briefly very happy.

A PIPE WITH AN IVORY STEM

Kasper sat in Dr Hoffmann's stuffy box room staring at the wall. It was bare of furniture except for two chairs and a Biedermeier wardrobe that had been pushed towards the back of the room, blocking the view out of the window. The light shone out from behind it, blue on the white walls. He could hear Dr Hoffmann muttering somewhere else in the small apartment and then the scraping of wooden drawers.

Kasper had one hand in his pocket, touching the soft torn edge of another piece of yellow paper that he had found pinned on his door when he had returned home the previous evening. It said, '*Your father will be first to go. First he'll die of shame, then he'll die. Everyone you love dead.*' Kasper had been struck rather by the truth of the sentence, than the cruelty of it. The fact that Fräulein Hirsch could write something so horrible seemed to him strange, but plausible, but that she could be so right? So right to see that his father would die, and then – *everyone he loved dead.*

But in Dr Hoffmann's box room, Kasper had stopped thinking about the note, though he had been stroking its edge habitually, like a totem. Instead he was tracing the stems of the

49

wild rose on the ugly wallpaper, trying to find the repeat. His face was slumped and inactive and he was thinking about whether he should try and locate Heinrich Neustadt. He would have to – he would have to find a way of keeping his mouth shut. It would be simple enough – a bribe, a little of the right information. But the abject lack of emotional attention that Kasper had given him meant that he knew almost nothing about the man. His presence in his bar before the war was formless and indistinct, and since they had met again at Frau Müller's, they had only seen each other there and in the apartment in Sybelstraße. Kasper was struggling to isolate any details about Heinrich's personal life; he had a vague recollection that he didn't even live in the Sybelstraße apartment.

He became glum and ashamed about their relationship, his sense of rage subsiding as he remembered Heinrich's excited grin and tender fingers on his chest – gestures that Kasper had purposefully not returned. He had been distracting for a few months, but Kasper hadn't come close to loving him. He thought about his high laugh, the thick black hairs on his toes and his constant joke telling, his curiously well-fed body and fine clothes, and felt no particular misery at the prospect of not seeing him again. But he felt stupid and culpable for the position he found himself in.

Kasper had thought of Heinrich as dumb and grateful, but he knew it was a disservice. Heinrich had offered himself to Kasper as fully as he was able and Kasper had ignored it. If they fell asleep after sex, Kasper would wake up to find that Heinrich's arm had found its way across his body, or that he had curled up and pushed himself back into Kasper, so that they woke up in each other's arms. And Kasper had responded by finding reasons to leave Heinrich: anonymous appointments that never existed, feigned problems with the apartment, with his father, with his clients. But recently he had even dispensed with these small acts of grace and had just left, sometimes when Heinrich was out of the room. Kasper had refused to act on it, but he had known that Heinrich was dangerous when he stopped lingering at the door as Kasper left, trying fruitlessly to get Kasper to kiss him goodbye. When Kasper had lost his temper with him and he had shrunk away into the shadows, Kasper knew he was a loose thread that he hadn't tied up.

'Herr Meier?'

Kasper looked up. The wizened doctor was standing in the doorway – his bald head was covered in dark brown liver spots, the same colour as his stained woollen waistcoat. 'Daydreaming?'

'Dr Hoffmann,' said Kasper and shook the man's hand. The grip was strong and the fingers so bony that Kasper's hand ached after he'd let go. 'I'm sorry – a busy day.' Kasper gestured to the other chair in the room, on which he'd laid out a half bottle of vodka, two syringes and two packs of dried beef broth. 'Your list.'

'What about the morphine?'

'Almost impossible – it would cost a lot more than you've got.'

The doctor nodded and picked up the items one by one. Once he had run his fingers over the last packet of broth he put it down and handed Kasper two packs of American cigarettes. On one of the packets he'd written a name and an address of a woman who was holding a box of penicillin to be collected on Kantstraße.

Kasper read the shaky handwriting and said, 'Does Frau Hannover know that someone will be coming for it?'

'Yes,' said the doctor. 'Will it be you?'

'No,' Kasper said. 'A woman – she'll call herself Marta. She won't use her surname. And Frau Hannover doesn't have any morphine?'

'Very little. I can't afford it there either. How much penicillin is your friend going to get off her, do you think?'

'I don't know – why?'

51

'I can't afford a whole bottle, and Frau Hannover won't split anything. But if there was a half-used one – one that your friend didn't need. It would be a boon to have some fresh. All I've been getting from the nurses here is the rubbish they get from boiling off the patients' urine.'

'I'll see what I can do,' said Kasper, slipping the cigarettes into the inside pocket of his jacket.

Kasper left the doctor's apartment block and made his way towards the café that Eva Hirsch had indicated on her little card. He took it out of his pocket briefly and checked the house number – a twenty-two written in broad, curling numbers. He knew the street, but didn't remember a café; though when the first tentative rays of warm sun began to melt the thick layer of ice that covered the city, cafés had bloomed out of empty houses as fast and numerous as the purple shoots of lilac – just a few chairs and mismatched tables and an elderly waitress selling grain coffee with powdered milk.

Kasper tucked the card back into his pocket. He wanted to show Eva Hirsch what he was made of, make it clear to her that she had blackmailed the wrong person, and yet, when he imagined her frown, it made him want to say something comforting to her, something paternal. He wanted to say, 'You seem like a nice girl, who's got mixed up in something.' If he was able to hold his temper, perhaps he might win her over. Herr Jung who sold watches at Bahnhof Zoo had a girl, it was his daughter, and she helped him sell things. She had a way with the women, got in on the gossip and knew what they wanted. She could get things Herr Jung couldn't. Kasper laughed to himself out loud – making plans to adopt his blackmailer. He shook his head and smiled at his foolishness and when he squinted up to look for the turning he caught sight of a young man lingering in a nearby doorway staring at him. Kasper stopped. The girl appeared beside him. Their eyes met his for a second, the girl frowning with her mouth open, the boy pushing his lips together tightly.

'Oi!' shouted Kasper.

They disappeared around the corner behind a stack of cleaned bricks.

'You!' Kasper shouted again and began to run, but before he had taken two steps he felt something hard beneath his shoe and heard the popping of its leather sole. He shouted out and hopped forwards, tripping and landing on the dirt of the road. He looked up. The dust settled, but they were gone.

'Bugger!' cried Kasper and slapped the ground. A woman at the other side of the street carrying a baby looked up briefly, then pushed her head down and walked on past him.

Turning up his sole, he saw the stumpy nail buried in its side, near the toe. He pulled off the shoe carefully and removed his tattered sock – the nail had only grazed the outside edge of his foot, taking off a little skin. Kasper spat on his thumb and rubbed the scratch.

'You'll want to see the doctor,' said a shrunken voice.

He looked up and saw an old lady sitting on a pile of bricks a few feet away. She had a red scarf around her head and was holding a stick, which seemed to be the only thing stopping her from rolling off her seat. She had the loose contented smile of a madwoman.

'I've just been to the doctor, as it happens,' said Kasper pulling the nail out of the shoe and inspecting the damage it had done.

'You need to go and get that fixed up – get that looked at. It'll get infected.'

'I need to get my bloody shoe fixed,' he said, briefly losing his temper and hitting it on the ground.

'You shouldn't curse, Phillip,' said the old lady. 'Shame on you.'

The name made him feel sick and afraid. He pulled his shoe and sock back on.

'Don't be cross with me for telling you off. Don't be such a baby, Phillip.'

'Stop saying "Phillip"!' said Kasper. The woman jumped. 'Sorry,' he said, 'I'm afraid you're a little confused.'

'What's your name then, little one?' she said, apparently unperturbed.

He smiled. 'Kasper.'

'Confused, says Kasper,' she said and clucked. 'Kasper says I'm confused.'

As Kasper stood and brushed the dust off his trousers she began to sing a tuneless song with nonsense words:

'Kasper and Phillip where are you?
Why are you alone, how do you do?
Kasper, Kasper where is Phillip,
Gone in the street and gone in the ...'

Kasper's eyes widened in brief horror and he said, 'Who are you?'

The woman stopped singing and looked up at him confused, her mouth open.

'Are you part of Fräulein Hirsch's little posse?'

The woman said nothing. A man shouted from the other side of the street and Kasper looked up. The man repeated himself: 'You there! Do you know her?'

'Mind your own business,' Kasper shouted back.

The man crossed the road towards him. 'You can't go around shouting at old ladies in the street.'

The woman began to sing her song again, but the names had changed:

'Hermann and Sasha in a tree,
You like him and he likes me ...'

The woman didn't seem to notice him anymore. The good Samaritan had paused briefly to wait for a military truck to go by, and Kasper slipped away quickly with a slight limp, the words of the woman's new song mixing with the consoling voice of the passerby.

It was warm enough outside that Kasper was sweating beneath his jacket when the café came in view, and yet he felt suddenly shivery and wondered if he'd caught a cold. He had had a permanently bitter taste on the back of his tongue since that morning and had a vague headache above his eyebrows. It might be a fever, he thought, his stomach turning over, worried that he might be incapacitated for any length of time. He wanted to laugh at himself for getting angry with a madwoman, but the names had disturbed him. He saw of course that he had offered her his own name and he tried to calm himself, but then the girl and the boy – it was no longer coincidental.

He saw from some distance that Eva Hirsch was sitting outside the café with her back to the window. She was in almost exactly the same position she'd been in on Kasper's crate: elbow on knee and two fingers to her mouth, except that now instead of a cigarette she was holding a slim red book, with familiar beige letters. Kasper smiled in recognition, recalling a young poet at his bar in the twenties, bursting with socialist fervour, angrily denouncing Kasper's apparent political passivity. But the smile faded when he recalled the same boy, his hair parted neatly at the side, stamping Kasper's employment book and pretending not to recognise him, his 'Heil Hitler!' weakened in apparent embarrassment. Eva was frowning at the book in fixed, angry concentration. When she saw Kasper crossing the street she stuffed it into an inside pocket and smiled at him awkwardly and supportively, standing and brushing down her coat. He arrived at her side but didn't look at her – he stared instead through the glazed door into the bare little café already full of people.

'Fräulein Hirsch.'

'Herr Meier,' she said, looking up at him and smiling.

'I didn't take you for a fan of left-wing drama.'

'I beg your pardon?' she said.

'Ernst Toller – the play you just tried to hide.'

'Oh that,' she said. 'I wasn't hiding it. There's a book exchange on our street. I just saw it was a play. I didn't really understand it, to be honest.'

'Well . . .' he said.

'I . . . can I get you something to drink?'

'I think it would be better if we were inside, don't you?'

'Really?' she said. 'Why?'

'It's noisier. Harder to listen. That sort of thing.'

'Oh,' she said, standing up and picking up her handbag. 'Well, you're the expert.'

Kasper let her go ahead. She had evidently dressed up for the evening, perhaps to impress whoever it was she was going to see after him. Her hair had been fought down with pins and a little oil or petroleum jelly to take out the frizz. The curls had become pretty waves that tumbled away from her side parting, forming themselves into a curling bob below her ears. She carried a long woollen winter coat over her arm and the green dress she wore was made of thin cotton with a printed pattern of small flowers. It seemed to have been sewn together from some other garment, because the two panels of fabric that met at the back were slightly different shades, the right side more faded than the left. Probably used to the freedom of the shirt and trousers that she wore on the rubble group, she walked uncomfortably in the heeled shoes and the dress, pulling at its waist, running her free hand nervously across the hem of the collar. She appeared to be wearing stockings, but there was a smudge in the line of the

56

seam that ran down the back of her legs, where it had been rest-ing against the chair outside. Her black leather shoes seemed newer than her dress, but she walked in a way that suggested that they were too big for her and that she'd stuffed the toes with paper.

Kasper could not fail to note those things that she had and those things that she might want; everybody was a potential customer. He could tell that she was proud of the dress and ignored its defects, but the shoes were too shiny and he sus-pected that she had borrowed them. It was shoes he might be able to tempt her with. And of course stockings, but everybody coveted stockings and there were others who would give him more for them.

The room was hot and full of voices. There were only two sol-diers – a pair of Frenchmen who could speak some German. They were sitting at a small table with four girls pressed in around them, laughing and touching the top of their bosoms breathlessly, lighting Gauloises off those of the soldiers. The sol-diers laughed too and the cigarettes poured abundantly out of their pockets and into the women's mouths.

Kasper gestured to a table in the corner of the room sand-wiched between a group of women who'd pushed back their chairs in order to scan the patrons for potential suitors as they came through the door, and three older men, who were drink-ing beer and talking to each other in low, sad voices.

'Going out somewhere nice, are we?' said Kasper.

'No,' said Eva, catching his eye nervously as she pulled out her chair. 'Just you.'

'Oh,' he said.

Eva held her chair by its top cross-strut and pushed it back and forward. 'What's wrong?' said Kasper.

'The joints are loose,' she said, lifting it into the air and hitting it down onto the table. Kasper jumped and Eva, not noticing his shock, hit the two back struts hard once each with a closed fist, spun the chair back off the table again and stood it gently on the ground. The café fell briefly silent. 'There,' said Eva, sitting down and laying her coat across the back. 'All fixed.' She looked about her, apparently surprised at the hush, which was broken by a few sniggers then a few words and within seconds the crowd had mumbled back to full pitch.

Kasper sat down, took off his hat and dropped it softly onto the table.

'What?' said Eva.

'Nothing,' he said.

A tired-looking waitress with a cold sore on her lip pushed through the crowd and appeared by their table. A curling tuft of red hair escaped out of a metal hairclip on the side of her head.

'A coffee,' said Eva.

'It's half grain, half fennel,' said the woman.

'Of course,' said Eva, 'That's fine.'

'Beer,' said Kasper, 'if you have it.' The waitress nodded without noting down the order and disappeared again.

He looked over at Eva – she was nervous now and uncomfortable, but when she looked up at him she gave him a comforting smile. 'I never actually come to cafés,' she said. 'Bit of a treat. But then I suppose there's no one to come with, really. I see so many girls with family, with friends, out in the city.'

'Really? Where?'

'Oh, all over the place,' Eva said. 'But then ... Well, perhaps it's like when you haven't eaten meat for a week and all you see is people carrying tins of ham; it's all you smell: frying corned beef and meat stock boiling up in some kitchen. Do you know what I mean?'

Kasper nodded. 'Yes,' he said.

Eva smiled and her face relaxed at his assent. 'It helps to be on your own,' she said, 'no friends or family or anyone else to look

58

after. It makes things easier at the moment, in a funny way. Makes things simpler, I suppose. I thought you were the same, but then you're not on your own at all.'

'Look, is this a social date?' said Kasper, suddenly feeling as if he was being manipulated.

She frowned and shook her head. 'Of course not, but . . . ' She found a crumb of something on the table and dabbed it onto her finger, investigated it then pressed it onto her tongue. 'I just mean, I didn't know you were looking after anyone.'

Kasper was prepared for this new attack. 'The man at the flat – it's a coincidence. And you can't prove otherwise.'

'That's not what I mean.'

'Then what do you mean? You are blackmailing me, aren't you? Or did I misunderstand? I thought . . . ' Kasper fell silent as the beer and the coffee arrived at their table, the beer impressively in a beer glass, though the glass was chipped and the beer was warm. Eva said thank you cheerfully, picked up her spoon and stirred the drink automatically, although there was no milk or sugar to go into it. The burnt scent of the ersatz coffee licked up past her hands and she tried another smile. Kasper looked away.

'You were meant to be alone. Living alone, that is.'

'What do you mean, "meant to be"?'

'Unattached. But you're not – there's your father.'

'He's not my father.'

'Huh,' Eva said, sitting back in her chair and blowing out a puff of air. 'He looks just like you.'

Kasper traced the brim of his grey hat on the table with his middle finger. 'Have you got a cigarette?' he said.

She took out a beaten-up cigarette case, made of cheap, thin metal, and handed him the longer one of two cigarettes inside. The second one had been cut in half at the middle, probably having been traded as part-payment for something small –

perhaps the last of the eye-pencil that she had used to draw on the line of her pseudo-stockings. She closed the lid of the case and tucked it back into her coat pocket in a rather clumsy, teenage gesture. She sighed. 'It was meant to be different. I thought I was going to see a criminal who didn't have any connections – any emotional ones.'

'Well, that's true.'

She nibbled at the cuticle of her index finger and then rubbed it with her thumb. 'You seem nice enough, though.'

'It really is a social date!'

'God, you're sarcastic,' she said, throwing her hand back down to the table.

Kasper laughed, despite himself. He took a packet of matches out of his pocket and lit the cigarette, blowing the flame out on the match immediately, licking his fingers and squeezing the blackened end, before putting the rest of the matchwood back in the box. He took a large extravagant drag, letting the smoke fall out of his mouth as he slowly breathed out.

'So what's this mean?' said Kasper. 'Does this change anything now? Am I nice enough for you to drop all this?'

'Maybe. Sort of,' she said. 'Can you still find the pilot for me?'

Kasper leant back in his chair and bit his lip to try and stifle a smile.

'Are you laughing at me?' said Eva.

'No it's nothing,' he said.

'What?'

'It's just . . . I mean you're hardly putting the thumbscrews on me, are you? I'm sensing that you're rather new to this blackmail business.'

Eva crossed her arms and frowned at her cup. 'I don't much like being laughed at.' She looked up at him. 'You know, I thought I'd enjoy it almost – catching someone out, but it's miserable. I'm sorry I started on it.'

'You have my heartfelt apologies,' he said.

'I don't know if I can just stop it. I mean, I can, but . . .'

'Who put you up to all this?'

She lit the shorter of her cigarettes and took a drag. 'You don't have to worry. It's not to do with you in particular.'

'It was someone who'd gone to the trouble of finding out who I was, who I lived with – whether they got it wrong or not.'

'No, it's not to do with you in particular – they promised.'

'Like they promised I was a lonely criminal?'

Eva shook her head slowly. 'What a business,' she said quietly.

'So you'll drop it?' he said again.

'Of course,' said Eva in a whisper, staring down at her bitten fingers. 'You're not who you were meant to be – not what I'd been promised, at any rate. I suppose it was easier to believe when they told me about you; you don't imagine your lot having people to look after, people that love them.'

'I beg your pardon?' said Kasper.

'I'm sorry,' said Eva immediately, throwing herself forward, rubbing her face, working her ring finger into the corner of her eye. 'That sounded horrible. I didn't mean it like that. Just . . . I didn't think. I didn't think about any of this – or didn't understand it. I don't know why I thought it was going to be so simple. I've just been stupid. And cruel.' Her fingers moved softly to her lips and she picked at the dry skin there. 'I'm not either of those things,' she said, avoiding his gaze, 'Certainly not cruel. I don't think I am.'

They sat in silence. Eva seemed to have forgotten her coffee. Kasper sipped at his beer and looked at Eva's knitted brow. He sighed. 'Look, you may as well tell me about your pilot – I'm not going to pass up a free drink. I'll tell you what I can before the glass is empty.'

'Oh! Well, thanks,' she said, brightening. A drunk French soldier passed by close to Kasper and knocked the leg of their table.

He bit his lower lip apologetically and Eva shot him a pretend smile, until he averted his eyes, knocking into the table behind them. She laughed a little, leant forward and whispered, 'Doesn't he look just like that chap in that film – *M*? The one with the googly eyes.'

'Who?' said Kasper, confused. He turned and looked at him.

'Peter Lorre – look at his eyes.'

Kasper squinted at the soldier and then pictured the actor suddenly, staring through the window of a shop. He let out a loud guffaw and the drunken soldier turned. Kasper spun back around and held his hand protectively onto the top of his head. The soldier shouted something out in aggressive French. Eva stared past him at the road and said loudly, 'Yes, it is a rather funny one isn't it, but it's gone now.'

The French soldier, barely placated by her cover, grumbled boisterously and one of his friends called out something offensive. But then their chatter rose and they began to laugh and talk among one another again.

'Smoothly done,' Kasper said and sat up straight.

Eva smiled and pretended to curtsey. She took a sip of her coffee and said, 'About the pilot – he's not mine, by the way. Really. He's my friend's.'

'Shall we dispense with that now?' said Kasper.

'It really is for my friend.'

'OK,' he said. 'What kind is he?'

'British.'

Kasper flicked some ash away from his sleeve. 'Name?'

'He called himself George, but said it wasn't his real name – so that he didn't get in trouble with the authorities.'

'So no family name?'

'He never said.'

'It must have been love. Where did she meet him?'

'In Willy's. It's a bar.'

'I know it's a bar,' said Kasper. Willy's was a narrow, grubby bar frequented by British soldiers and pilots on the top floor of an old library, where they served spirits from the check-out desk and clambered up the empty shelves when drunk. They didn't like male German company and Kasper avoided going except when he needed to secure something special. He knew a German woman who worked as a translator with the Americans – she had married a now-dead Briton before the war and would exchange small, waterproofed American K-ration packs for tins of tea.

'How many times did they see each other?' said Kasper.

'They met up, I don't know, a few times afterwards.'

'How many's "a few"?'

'I don't know. Seven, eight, nine times maybe.'

'And then?'

'He said that he wasn't allowed to see her anymore. He said someone at his base had found out and that it was illegal for him to "fraternise" with her, but that he'd send for her the moment he could.'

'And what makes you think he's still in Berlin?'

'She saw him.'

'When?'

'A week ago. He was manning a checkpoint. She tried to talk to him, but he pretended he didn't know what she was saying.'

'Can he speak German?'

'I don't know,' said Eva.

'And what makes you think it wasn't an excuse – him getting into trouble at the base? And don't say, because he loved her.'

Eva smiled and sat forward in her chair, her arms on the table. 'I suppose that could be true,' she said, 'But she's got her baby now. Well, his baby.'

Kasper looked down at his hat – at some ash that had fallen onto the felt. 'Unless you've hit upon some wonder of human nature, it strikes me that this soldier doesn't want her. The base thing sounds like an excuse. If he really wanted to go on "fraternising" with her, he could probably do it. And the baby will make it worse, not better.'

'Yes, I'm not stupid. I understand all of that, but this is important for her. She needs a bit of hope. Or doesn't that make any sense to you?' she said, taking another drag of her cigarette and flicking the ash onto the table. 'If it was me, well, I'd have just got it sorted out.'

'Would you now?' said Kasper.

She stroked the paper of her cigarette with her thumb. 'Of course. Don't you think I would?'

Kasper's eyes narrowed. 'I don't really care what you'd do,' he said.

She shrugged, apparently hurt, and put her fingers up to her lips.

'Stop biting at your nails,' he said, slapping away her hand.

Eva tucked her free hand under her armpit. 'Sorry, "Papa"!' she said.

Kasper shook his head, sucked the last out of his cigarette and stubbed it out on the table. 'And if you find him, when you have an address in your hand, what happens then to your friend's hope? What'll she do when she gets hold of him and he accuses her of being a slut and getting knocked up by a Russian and tells her never to come back?'

'That's for us to worry about.'

'It certainly is,' he said, leaning back and taking a couple of large gulps from the beer. 'What's he look like?'

'Tall – not as tall as you; maybe an inch or two shorter – ginger hair; curly ginger hair. A moustache, but not a very good one – you couldn't really see it from a distance. He has a big gap between his front teeth and she said he talked funny. I mean, when he was speaking English.'

'Sounds like a treat.'

Eva really laughed now; a deep laugh, loud, warm and joyful. 'Well,' she said eventually, 'there's no accounting for taste.'

'Do you know what rank he was?'

'No. No idea what he was, other than a pilot.'

'So he'll be at Gatow. RAF Gatow. Isn't that enough? There can't be a British pilot in Berlin who's not there.'

'Yes,' she said, 'but we need something in town. We can hardly drive up to the base. We need a hangout, somewhere he socialises, that kind of thing. We need him somewhere we can speak to him.'

Kasper nodded. 'That would require a bit more investigation. You'll need to blackmail someone else for that.' He dabbed his finger in the ash on the table and made a black print next to his extinguished cigarette. He looked up at her with his good eye. 'Am I really off the hook now?'

'Yes,' she said, putting out her own cigarette, beside his. 'I'll make sure.'

'What about your ... colleagues?'

'I'll talk to them.'

Kasper nodded.

'Oh I have this for you,' she said, taking a pipe out of the pocket of the jacket that hung across the chair and pushing it across the table.

'What am I going to do with this?'

'I thought you could exchange it for something. That bit's ivory,' she said, touching the stem. 'You don't have to take it. Do what you like, but ... you know, for the trouble.'

'OK. Thank you.' Kasper took it and slipped it into his pocket. 'So that's it?'

Eva nodded.

'No more notes.'

Eva frowned. 'What notes?' she said.

Kasper laughed. 'Right,' he said. '"What notes."' He picked up his hat and stood up. He looked down at her, at her pretty pinned-up curls, at the red corner of her book, poking out of the jacket on her chair. 'You sure you have enough money for this?'

She nodded. 'I'm sorry,' she said again. 'I really am. I do feel bad, if it's any consolation.'

Kasper put his hat on and buttoned up his jacket. 'Look, I don't know what you've got yourself into, but you shouldn't go visiting lonely criminals on a whim. There are some very bad people on the markets. Really bad.'

Eva smiled. 'I would have got out of there pretty quick if I thought you were trouble.'

'It's no good relying on intuition, my girl. You'll get yourself killed or . . . or worse.'

She nodded and held onto her cup. 'Sorry again,' she said. 'For everything. I hope your father gets better. He looked unwell.'

'He is unwell,' said Kasper. 'Thank you.' He smiled awkwardly, tipped his hat and made his way through the café. He looked back as he walked past the window. Eva sat, still holding her cup, slumped down in her chair like a teenager. The room was animated with light, noise and sound, but she was silent in the middle of it all, her face sad, if there was any expression on it at all, her fingers back at her mouth, worrying the skin on her lips.

KAZIMIR NIKITIN

Kazimir Nikitin woke up lying on his front. He felt around beside him for Sara, but the bed was empty. He pushed himself up onto his elbows and farted loudly. 'Sara!' he called.

'I'm just in the bathroom,' she shouted back.

Kazimir rolled over onto his back then reached down to pick up his pillow from the floor. He stuffed it behind him as he pushed himself up against the headboard. 'What you do?' he said in broken German.

'I'm in the bathroom,' she shouted back.

Kazimir reached under the covers to scratch his leg and sung a verse of 'The Song of the Volga Boatmen' at the top of his voice in rough, ungainly Russian:

> *Now we fell the stout birch tree,*
> *Now we pull hard: one, two, three.*
> *Ay-da, da, ay-da!*
> *Ay-da, da, ay-da!*
> *Now we fell the stout birch tree.'*

He had heard it being sung in English by Americans that morning and it had made him laugh to hear their strange, nasal voices intoning the boatmen's toil. Sara came into the room dressed in a brown woollen skirt and a jacket made of the same material that was worn and frayed at the elbows. She sat on the edge of the bed.

'Where you go?' said Kazimir.

'To get water from the pump.'

'I have drink,' he said pointing to a bottle of brandy on the table. 'You stay.' And he laughed in what he hoped was a friendly way. His laugh had made Svetlana, his university girlfriend, happy. When he had first seen Sara in the queue for bread he thought she looked like Svetlana when she was still a young undergraduate. He had ordered Sara out of the line and she had followed him falteringly and alarmed, looking back at the other people who were waiting, all of whom turned and stared earnestly at the road. 'No worry,' he had said, then, 'you no worry.' He had taken her into a side street and offered to bring her three times as much bread if she'd let him visit her. She knew what he meant, but she was so relieved not to be raped on the spot that she'd agreed and found him at her door that evening, with a loaf in each hand.

Sara smiled sadly at the Russian officer's joke and slipped some shoes on. 'Do you think I need a coat?' she said, looking out of the window onto the street.

'You want coat?' said Kazimir.

'No,' said Sara, pulling on her own coat, 'I was just asking if I needed one today. And I think I do.'

Kazimir shrugged and made a sad face. 'I cannot understand.'

'It doesn't matter,' said Sara and went to leave.

'Kiss me,' said Kazimir. Sara hesitated then went back to him, bent down and kissed him on his bald head, cradling his chin.

'I won't be long,' she said.

Kazimir listened to the door close and her footsteps on the stairs. He wondered if he would ever be loved again and felt miserable that he wanted to be loved by a German who accepted bread and tinned meat in exchange for having sex with him and pretending to enjoy it. After the first few months he had convinced himself that she was becoming fond of him and that she looked forward to his visits and enjoyed the sex they had, but increasingly he woke up in the night to find her gone and lay in bed with his eyes closed, listening to her crying in her little bathroom. When she came back to bed he lay still and pretended to be asleep. And when she was lying on her side, he waited a while and then rolled over, feigning an involuntary, unconscious movement so that he could put an arm around her to comfort her. The times that she let him leave it there, when she reached up and held his forearm, those were the times that he was happiest.

He heard the door being opened and smiled and called out, 'You coming back!' There was no answer and he sat forward and said, 'Sara?' But a different woman appeared in the doorway. She was middle-aged and skinny, with small round eyes and a crooked nose with a bony node where it bent, and she was wearing a long leather Wehrmacht jacket that had been adapted to look like a woman's coat. Her dark appearance and the empty look in her face of numb determination made her appear ghostly – as if she existed in another world and was only momentarily visible. '*Who the fuck are you?*' said Kazimir in Russian. The woman didn't answer. 'Who you?' Kazimir tried in German. And then, as her face tightened he thought he did recognise her. He squinted and wondered if she was a madwoman who lived in the building – perhaps he had passed her on the landing. But no, he had seen her somewhere else, somewhere outside of this building, outside of this part of town. And as it dawned on him he saw that she was holding a gun. And just before she shot, he said '*I didn't want to do it. Stop! I didn't mean to,*' in Russian and then '*No, don't.*'

A MOTHER-OF-PEARL HAIRCLIP

Kasper sat on a low wall, once part of the façade of a large Charlottenburg house, perhaps belonging to a dentist if the large reclining chair that had been stripped of its leather and now lay on its side in the field of rubble was anything to go by. Across the street a trail of women snaked up a small hill of brick, dust and stone, a set of misshapen metal buckets full of debris being passed up and down the line to the women on the street. They sorted the fragments into piles, while other women chipped the old concrete off the usable bricks and made neat little stacks with them, square and tall like chimney pots and garden walls.

The sun was warmer again, so there was a pile of dirty over-coats and torn pullovers draped over a large refrigerator that was lying on its side, near the road. The sun shone impressively onto the street, through the building behind him – precise shafts in the golden dust that hung in the air above the ruins. And the air was also filled with the sound of children screaming excitedly, their heads appearing periodically above the rubble piles, then disappearing again, like dirty mongooses.

Kasper picked at the bare mortar on the top of the low wall.

He was thinking about Eva Hirsch. He thought about the boy and the girl he had seen at his apartment, all of Eva's 'we's'. After leaving the café his fear had been replaced by a lightness and a sadness, seeing her biting at her fingers, alone. But slowly this lightness had, in turn, been replaced by an oppressive unease that he had become involved in something much larger than he could understand. It felt to him like a cancer. Fräulein Hirsch, the first, everyday symptoms, easily written off but nevertheless strange, unnerving; the girl and the boy, a second worrying, but persistent pain, a sign that something was deeply wrong. He still clung to the chance that Eva was nothing but a strange but benign anomaly, cut off and gone, the children an uneasy, but explicable coincidence; but deep down he was terrified that the cancer had already spread everywhere without him knowing, that it would be in every organ, at a stage far too late to be removed. Something just to be briefly kept at bay as it swiftly killed him.

Perhaps he really would never see her again. His memory of her, from two meetings, was filled with images of her anxious smile, her large eyes, so exposed that they heightened the vul-nerability in her nervous fingers. And yet she had a confidence, a comfort with her own being that Kasper was jealous of. She seemed to bite at her fingers, not out of worry, but because she didn't care for them; she picked at her lip because she was bored, because her mouth, her fingers were hers. It all amounted to a sort of scruffy awkward charm. She laughed, she listened to him as he spoke, she asked him things. Her presence in his thoughts was light, real and human in comparison to his usual reflections: a dark series of dull beats, some terrifying, some depressing, few happy: food, rations, tins and bottles, his father, his flat, all lead-ing back to Phillip. Phillip's voice. Phillip's lips at his neck. Phillip lifting up his bloodied head.

Kasper lit one of his thin cigarettes. He bit his lip and thought of the Märchenbrunnen, of Phillip waiting for him in the snow, he waited at the bottom of the steps, put his hand on a cold balustrade, but didn't come any closer. Phillip lifted his hand, pink against the white snow.

After a minute the cigarette had the desired effect: a nine-year-old boy, wearing a grubby white shirt and shorts held up by braces, climbed over the rubble to where Kasper was sitting and said '*Guten Tag, Herr Meier.*'

'Christian,' said Kasper, tipping his hat. 'How are things?'

'Oh, you know,' said the boy, wiping his nose on the back of his hand, making his face even dirtier than it already was, 'as well as can be expected.'

'Got anything for me?' said Kasper.

'Yeah, this woman you were looking for from Wedding – there are three women like you described who live round there and one of them even went to that bar you said, but then she's shacked up with a husband.'

'Could still be her – Frau Müller's customer's a soldier, an American, so she might just be playing him for some cigarettes.'

'Yeah, but they were in a state, you know, and if she could get anything from this guy I reckon she'd still be getting it. Anyway, there's this other one that seemed possible, but I never got a good look at her, only when she was on her balcony and she was on the fourth floor, so hard to tell, and then when she came out, it turns out she's got a wonky eye, and no offence, Herr Meier, but I think you'd mention something like that about a person if you were giving another person instructions, you know.'

'Maybe he's vain,' said Kasper, 'or proud.'

'Yeah, maybe,' said the boy, picking his nose and pulling out a long string of solidified snot, which he began to investigate, rolling it between his fingers

'For God's sake, Christian,' said Kasper. The boy put his hands in his pockets, but his fist continued to work the bogey

73

beneath the fabric. 'So anyways,' said the boy, 'last, but not least, so to speak, I think your girl's at Goethestraße 39 under the name of Frau Winkelmann.'

'Married?'

'Well, she's not called Frau Winkelmann. Frau Winkelmann is her employer, if you catch my drift. Whore.'

'Don't say "whore" Christian. You'll never get a wife with a mouth like that.'

The boy laughed.

'And the other girl?'

'Fräulein Hirsch – I found her. Works on one of the rubble groups here in Charlottenburg just like you said. They were on Düsseldorfer Straße, but they're moving tomorrow. Lives with some other girls on Sybelstraße.'

'Sybelstraße?' said Kasper.

'Mean anything to you?'

'A friend lives there.' He thought of his days with Heinrich Neustadt and wondered whether Eva had simply seen him leaving the apartment in Sybelstraße one day and followed him home. 'Who else lives there?'

'Other girls on her rubble group. Some woman owns the place – Frau Beckmann.'

'Beckmann? What's she do?'

'Works on the rubble group too. Can't find anything else on her either.'

'What about some juice, something I could use?'

'Nothing as of yet, Herr Meier.'

'What else did she do? She must have met someone. I just need something to scare her with. Just in case.'

'She goes to work with the other girls every day,' said Christian, 'Then comes back home. That's all she does.'

'She's not done anything else? Not one thing? Not even on the weekend?'

'Stayed in last Saturday. Sunday she did some trading.'

'Anything funny? Something odd?'

'There was something.'

'Well?'

'Books.'

'What sort of books?' said Kasper.

'Plays. Some French ones I think. Translated.'

'An illicit taste for French literature? I've hardly got her over a barrel there.'

Christian shrugged. 'She been causing you problems?'

'They may be already solved – we'll see. Well,' said Kasper, fishing ten undivided cigarettes out of his top pocket, 'another fine job.'

'Ten cigarettes?' said Christian, 'give us fifteen, at least.'

Kasper clapped the boy around the back of the head as he stood up. 'Learn to be grateful with what you've got.'

'That all?'

'Yes . . .' said Kasper standing, 'except . . .'

'I'm your man, Herr Meier. If there's something else.'

'Just keep an ear to the ground and let me know if anyone's asking after me.'

'After you? What would anyone want to find you for?'

Kasper laughed. 'To be honest, I have no idea.'

'Was it the war?' said Christian. 'Did you do something bad?'

'I didn't fight, Christian. I've got one eye.'

'Did you do it to yourself? The eye? Were you some sort of resistance? Everyone's saying they were resistance now – every-one you ask.'

'No,' said Kasper. 'I was nothing.'

Christian squinted and said, 'My dad was in the resistance. That's why he couldn't come home.'

'Yes,' said Kasper.

There was another clamour of high-pitched children's

screams, not enough to deserve a second look, except that it was followed by the short, shocked cry of a woman and a thick waft of death. The concentrated stench caused Kasper to pull out a handkerchief and hold it up to his mouth and Christian to pull his shirt out of his shorts over his nose, exposing his distended belly. They looked around them at the rubble and then over at the rubble women, who had all backed away, some holding children to their stomachs and legs, creating a large circle around the fridge. The door had been pulled open by one of the children, revealing the rotten body of a mother clutching onto something.

'It's a child! It's a child!' said one of the women, who were all so hardened to digging up bodies and body parts, that the discovery of one rarely caused more than a solemn backing away until someone arrived to haul it off. But the mother clutching the child had been grotesquely preserved, the clothes as good as new and the sun catching the rings on her fingers and the watch on the woman's decomposed wrist.

The eldest in the group, a short, stringy old woman, shouted up the street with a thick Berlin accent, appealing for someone to come and take the bodies. The other women eyed the dead woman jealously, noticing perhaps the mother-of-pearl clip in her hair. They swayed together for a moment and Kasper saw one of the women to the left of the group saying something to the little girl standing by her, who darted towards the open fridge door, causing two other children to break the circle. A grotesque scrap ensued as the women moved in to try and drag the children away. A little girl ran from the group over the rubble heap that the women had been clearing, clutching her fists tight, and then a boy fired out between their legs running down the street, despite a slight limp, the hairclip clear in his hands, a few strands of hair still attached to it.

The women moved away from the fridge again, revealing the

bodies, the mother on her back, her blackened arms out-stretched, stripped bare of accessories, and the child, still curled up, lying on his face. They also moved away from the mother whose little girl had run first. She sat near the fridge crying, while her co-workers shook their heads and began to slowly climb the rubble heap again. One of the younger women in the group retched briefly at the bottom of the slope, her arm held by one of her older co-workers. She wiped her mouth on her sleeve, before ascending to the sound of an approaching wooden cart that would carry away the bodies, pushed towards them by an old man with a crooked back.

'Jesus,' said Christian, looking up at Kasper.

Kasper put his hand on the boy's shoulder. Christian was silent for a few seconds then turned, without saying goodbye, and ran across the rubble, with his shirt still over his mouth, and joined a pack of running children, who swept him away into a side street.

Kasper stood and watched the old man for a few seconds longer; watched him looking down at the bodies, his hand on his hip, then touching the brim of his cap, before lowering him-self down to get his arms beneath the mother's corpse.

Kasper paid a visit to Frau Müller on his way home. In the day-time the door to her courtyard was unguarded and Kasper walked straight through, past the pyre of furniture, and knocked on her door. 'Who is it?' she barked from the other side.

'Kasper Meier.'

She opened the door a little and smiled at him through the gap. With a little daylight shining into the stairwell from the open courtyard door, she looked like any other old woman, who might be resting before going and hauling rubble on the streets. 'Herr Meier,' she said, 'what a surprise. You're naturally a little early.'

'I just had a message,' he said, moving away from the door a little, the smell of smoke, alcohol and sex that drifted from the apartment around her wholly disturbing in the early spring air, 'I have the address you needed.' He fished a card out from his inside pocket. 'The woman from Wedding. For the American.'

'Oh,' she said, holding out her hand.

'I'll give it to him myself,' said Kasper.

'I can do it,' she said, eyeing up the slip of paper hungrily, 'and give you the money. Save you making the trip twice.'

'I think it's best if I do it. In case he has any questions.'

'Oh, but he was very direct,' said Frau Müller, wetting her thin lips.

'Nevertheless,' he said, tucking the card back into his jacket, 'will you make sure he stays around for me tonight?'

'I can't be sure he'll be here tonight,' she said, now looking at him wide-eyed.

'I'll take my chances,' said Kasper. 'Anything else new?'

'Not that I can think of off the top of my head,' she said.

Kasper took two boxes of matches out of his pocket: one box of British 'Victory Matches', the second box celebrating the 'Day of the German Police Force', with stylised top-heavy policemen marching across its colour-blocked sides.

'Well,' she said, 'I did hear something happening at the Chancellery.'

'Anything in the British Sector?'

'It might be worth the trip. Tomorrow around ten. It's Maslov.'

'What use is Igor to me?'

'If you've got anything technical, he pays out. He really pays out and he's been very generous with the iodine recently.'

'He pays out if you're a woman.'

'There's that, but this city's full of women – I'm sure you

78

could find someone to go with you, for a cut. You have anything to exchange – anything technical?'

Kasper mentally skipped through the items secreted in the cracks and corners of his apartment. 'I've got a camera,' he said. 'A Leica.'

'A Leica, he says! Well, there you go, Herr Meier. It's worth the trip. I'd even come with you, if you needed, for a small share in any profits of course. I won't lie, tomorrow will be an inconvenience of sorts, but I could make some room – for you, certainly.'

Kasper smiled. 'That's kind of you, but I'll sort something out.'

'Well, if you change your mind, just knock, Herr Meier. You just knock.'

Kasper handed over the matches, which Frau Müller snatched away from the gap in the door, poking both boxes open, sniffing them, and dropping them into a pocket.

'Did that boy come back?' said Kasper, 'The one that was looking for me? Or a girl, similar looking?'

'Which boy?'

'You said a boy had been looking for me, a teenager maybe. Big eyes.'

'Oh yes, he did have strange eyes. Queer sort.'

'That's him.'

'No, he's not been back. Not last night. Not that I saw.'

'You don't happen to remember what he asked for the first time?'

'Oh Herr Meier, I wasn't really taking much notice.'

'But anything. Anything you can recall.'

Frau Müller opened the door a little wider and leant her head against the doorframe. 'He just asked if you were there. I was surprised Joachim and Max had let him in to be honest. I said you weren't, then he gave me a card I think and asked me to call the number when you were next in.'

'Have you got the card?'

'Of course not, I just threw it away. And what would a boy of that age be doing with a telephone. I thought it was all a joke, or at least rather cheeky, to be honest with you. Is everything all right, Herr Meier?'

Kasper looked down at the doorstep, at the cracked terracotta tiles on the floor in front of it. He traced a small black diamond with the toe of his shoe. 'Yes, fine,' he said.

'What does he want?'

'I don't really know. Honestly.'

Frau Müller sighed and looked off into her flat, her brow wrinkled with concern. 'Well, I'm sure it will all come right in the end.'

'Perhaps,' said Kasper. 'And no sign of Heinrich Neustadt?'

'Oh, all these names, Herr Meier. No, no Herr Neustadt. Now, why don't you just give me that card, you naughty boy, and make an old woman happy.'

Kasper laughed and looked back down at his cracked shoes. He wondered when he might have last bought a pair and recalled distantly the feeling of stiff new leather rubbing at his ankle. He thought of Eva's feet in those large black heels. 'How old's your granddaughter, Frau Müller?'

'My Birgit? Why, she's just turned nineteen. She's only open to reputable offers, though, if you know what I mean.'

'I didn't mean that.'

'Then what?'

Kasper looked up at the woman, at the soft skin of her jowls and sagging neck. 'How are they at that age?'

'In what sense?'

'As company. Is she good to you? Helps you out?'

'Well, of course. Are you thinking of taking her off my hands, Herr Meier?'

Kasper laughed. 'No,' he said, 'It doesn't matter.' He turned and walked out into the courtyard, 'I'll come back tomorrow,' he called.

'You're very bad to your Frau Müller,' she shouted, coming out of the door into the courtyard as he left, revealing that she was wearing a moth-eaten silk dressing gown with an incongruous line of matted fur that had been stitched around the hem. 'You're very bad to her.' He waved without turning back and she watched him go, before tutting and returning to the dim squalor of her apartment.

A WATCH

It was getting dark as Kasper turned into Windscheidstraße. The stream of rubble rose up, the white-grey of ashes, having poured from the buildings onto the pavement, spilling over the lip to the street's broken cobbles – bricks covered in rough mortar and oblong stones that burst out of the dust and spilled down its sides. He found himself trying to imagine what life Eva might have led had there been no war, or if this was 1920 or 1930 and she was just a bright, friendly girl, fighting that curling mass of hair into a boyish bob instead of a headscarf; worrying about the softness of her hands, rather than chewing them away; buying things, learning things, reading books. Perhaps she would be just the same – a girl getting herself into trouble. Perhaps she'd still be under someone's thrall, running jobs for some faceless criminal.

His mind stumbled into other places: a woman he was briefly married to with long hair and skinny legs crying disappointedly; his hand held against a tight, warm belly; sitting on a hard, wooden chair and hearing the sudden cessation of screams – adult or infant; sitting in silence beside his father in the church he had been married in just a year earlier, too young to understand what was happening to him.

Klara.

He tried to bury her memory whenever it returned, and it barely ever troubled him consciously anymore. There were only two instances that it was unavoidable: the smell of lavender, the oil of which she touched onto her breasts and neck, and the song of robins, which he had heard at night deep into the winter when he lay awake next to his wife staring at her belly in the blue-grey moonlight.

He dropped his head and tried to stop thinking, to concentrate on the road in front of him. On the rubble stream that held twisted metal shapes, strange skeletons of rusted iron, churned to the surface. He could recognise some forms – the sprung lattice of a mattress, the cloth and stuffing burnt away; the bent frame of an old bicycle, too formless to save, its one remaining wheel burst open, the spokes spraying upwards like stamen. But mostly the shapes were abstract, distorted and ugly.

Behind this rubble the front walls of the buildings were blackened, toothy stumps, the colour of the original stone only revealed where a bullet had ripped a layer from its surface, exposing the white flesh beneath. Some of the doors and windows showed signs of having been boarded up – a few on the ground floor had had heavy metal grilles affixed to them, to protect them from an enemy slipping in at the front, but that now covered blackened gaping mouths, their throats stuffed with debris.

Human traces were hard to find, but they began to emerge: a plaster garland above a door; a piece of white cloth caught on a nail; an extant window framing the void in which someone had once stood listening to the comforting tick-tock of the clock in their parlour, the idea of its non-existence impossible to comprehend. And while rejecting it, he felt the lives populating the traces and their absence ached in his belly.

In the buildings that had collapsed rather than burnt down, Kasper could see a mirror still nailed to a wall covered in chintz wallpaper; a sink hanging three floors up, with no floor beneath it, its toothbrush cup still attached to a modish chrome holder; part of a floor with the head of an iron bedstead still visible above it, as if someone might still be asleep, unaware that the street had dissolved around them.

On one building, high up, there was a picture of a man still attached to the wall. The close crop of the picture, and its military air, had made the local children decide it was a picture of Hitler. But since it was two floors up it could just as well have been the father of the household in his uniform, now either dead or in a prison five-hundred miles east, unaware that his family lay buried under layers and layers of dust and rubble. Unaware that his likeness was still in its place above the dining room dresser, except that now the glass was smashed and it sat in the middle of a constellation of white marks – holes in the plaster where for months the children had been trying to knock down the picture with stones.

As the sky darkened, the rough castellations at the tops of the buildings became silhouettes and, if the destruction below them wasn't so total, they might have appeared like melancholy ruins in the haze of a Casper David Friedrich painting. But the sickness in Kasper's stomach, which he was normally so good at repressing, was beyond melancholy, beyond the sublime.

As he neared his own building, Kasper passed the empty façades of blocks gutted by fires that had crept over from those that had been completely destroyed. In the twilight, they appeared to be inhabited still, but he knew that the light from the windows was the dying sun, so that the buildings looked like empty cardboard cut-outs, the large plastered frontages of fake buildings on a Babelsberg film set. The black tongues of soot that licked up from every window were the only trace of the life that had once existed inside; the routine, the arguments, the love-making, the child rearing, the crying, the book reading, the radio listening, the pride, the shame, the laughter, the hatred, the confusion, the misery, the relief and the fear, burnt up and belched out of the windows, into the Berlin sky, a few ashes catching on the brickwork as it all went.

Finally Kasper passed the two ruined tanks that lay slumped in the street, particularly popular with the local children, who clambered in and out of them, hanging off the long guns like monkeys. Beyond the tanks, even the rubble petered out and the pavement in front of Kasper's own lucky building was relatively clear, except for a small pile of chalky stone that the children had used to draw a grid for playing *Himmel-und-Hölle*. Kasper stood on the misspelt 'heaven' and 'hell' and looked back down the street, before entering his block.

Distracted, Kasper walked through the front building heavy footed, his forehead fixed in a frown. He entered the courtyard and was relieved to pick up the fragrance of freshly turned soil, rather than brick dust or mud; it was a light sweet smell, and he stopped in the fading blue light and looked at the neat rows of emerging asparagus stalks and the rhubarb that had begun to sprout four weeks earlier under the melting snow. His eye travelled over the black shapes of the vegetables to a thin slit of orange light from a downstairs window broken by the shadow of Frau Sauer, her chair pushed up to the window to keep watch on the shared patch of ground. There was a beauty in the walled space, he thought, and he closed his eyes and drew in a long breath and pretended that when he opened them there would be flowers in the beds, food in his belly, the smell of bread baking and coal in ovens.

And then he heard something: cloth touching cloth, perhaps a whisper, perhaps paper or dust falling to the ground. He opened his eyes. He listened, but nothing. It had come from above him and he looked up at the various unglazed windows of the lower floor of the back building. And then his eyes travelled to the single missing pane of glass in the stairwell window outside his own apartment. But behind it he could see only blackness.

As he moved past the vegetable patch he saw that the smell of earth, so strong in the still air, emanated from a small hole in the soil where someone had reached over the elaborate set of stringed-up cans that Frau Sauer had constructed to warn her of intruders, and pulled out a potato. A trace of black soil was on the concrete of the courtyard. He looked towards Frau Sauer's window then reached down and shook the string a little, causing the cans to rattle together. The shadow didn't move – craning his head, he saw the crown of her head pointing towards the window. She was asleep.

He entered the stairwell, black save for a little grey light that entered through the windows at each half landing. He paused again. There was no whisper, rather a tension, and it was impossible to say if it was real or imagined. He moved slowly to the staircase and began to climb, keeping away from the banister, where the steps creaked less. But the steps were so silent that his breath and the worn leather of his shoes on the ancient lino were clearly audible in the soundless space. A scent of kerosene was traceable through the door of the apartment below his and when he reached it his eye had become accustomed enough to the dark that he could make out the shapes there from the little light still afforded by the windows. But the landings outside each set of doors were full of metal, glass and Bakelite objects – the shells of telephones, clocks and radios, irreparable bedsteads, broken vases; those rare objects that were neither useful nor flammable – and Kasper found it impossible to clearly make out any human forms in the clutter. He paused at each landing and searched the shadows for movement, but found nothing.

The landing in front of his own door was bare and he approached it slowly. He looked into the empty corners, at the boarded-up door of the flat opposite his and at his own door, which was shut tight, a comforting line of yellow light coming from beneath it. He heard his father coughing. He smiled at himself, leant against the wall and rubbed his good eye.

But then, two short breaths. Two short breaths, high and girlish, like a child crying, or like a snigger. Holding onto the banister, he looked up the stairs into the final windowless landing that led up to the attic. He squinted. It was black, but there was something there, and as he stared, four eyes emerged, their whites just perceivable around their black irises, staring down at him.

'Who are you?' said Kasper. He tried to hit the right pitch, but in the silence his voice cracked and jumped.

The two short breaths came again – the girl was laughing.

Kasper put his foot on the first step and said, 'What are you doing here?'

The boy said something – barely a mutter.

'What did you say?' said Kasper.

The boy moved forward – the girl with him, holding his arm, smiling. The boy's head was large at the top, but tapered down towards his small, angry mouth. 'I said, "you're dead queer".'

'You little shit!' shouted Kasper. 'Come down here!'

The girl shrieked with laughter. Kasper thought that she was holding something in her hand. He steadied himself, ready to dodge a missile. 'You come down here now!' he cried again.

'Herr Meier?' The voice now came from below him. He looked down to see Eva Hirsch standing on the landing below his, the shape of her large woollen coat silhouetted against the window behind her, her eyes wide and worried in the dark. He opened his mouth and felt the gloom in the stairwell begin to contract.

'You said you'd leave me alone.'

'Who are you shouting at?' she said and turned her head to try and look up into the darkness.

Kasper heard a bang and a screech and something hit him above his bad eye, struck the bone. He was pushed back into the wall, something sharp held against his throat. He saw the boy's straight hair, whites of eyes, a shoulder, heard a scream – 'Get off him!' There was a thundering of feet on stairs. He steadied himself and lashed out with an arm, which was knocked back, turning him round. As he spun, he saw the girl's face suddenly, very close, the freckles on her nose, her sweet stale breath, her small sharp teeth, the boy's arm, the bulge of a potato in a pocket, Eva Hirsch's determined frown, her hands coming up, grasping someone, her shoving someone. 'What are you doing here?' she said. 'You're not meant to be here. Oi!' He grabbed again as the children pushed at him and he saw the girl twist as he pulled at her coat. The boy looked back as he passed Eva, now beside Kasper and then the boy was shoving Eva away, was already on the landing below. The girl slipped and her coat pulled out of Kasper's hand. He saw her mouth open and her knee come down hard against the edge of the step and then watched as she rolled down the stairs in a noisy tumble of limbs, stopping at the boy's feet.

There was no movement. Everyone was still. The stairwell was silent. Eva grabbed the sleeve of Kasper's jacket. He heard her breathing hard. The boy had frozen on the landing below, his hand on the banister, his head twisted backwards. The girl's hair was sprayed out around her head, which lay heavily on the floor. Kasper went cold. The boy bent down to touch the girl, but she rose up suddenly with a horrific scream and ran past her brother, moving awkwardly, dragging him away into the blackness of the stairwell with her. Kasper made for the stairs, but beneath the retreating rattle of the fleeing children he heard his father in the apartment, moving down the corridor, towards the door.

Kasper turned and knocked, pushing the door open in tiny jolts. 'It's me,' said Kasper. 'Open the door now. Open it.'

'Just a moment,' said his father.

Kasper stood back and after a chorus of clattering wood and metal, the door moved open a little and Kasper was able to push inside.

'Where is it?' said Kasper, squinting in the glare from the electric light.

'Where's what?' said the old man.

'The note, the note.'

'What's wrong with your face, Kasper? Who's that woman?'

Kasper dropped to his knees and felt around the floor for the piece of paper. 'There was a note here.'

'There,' said the old man pointing at his feet.

Kasper grabbed the little yellow slip.

Queers die. Everything they touch dies. Your days are numbered.

'Did you read this?'

'No,' said the old man. 'What is it? Kasper, your face. What was all that noise? What's going on? Who's this woman?'

'It's nothing,' said Kasper. 'You shouldn't get out of bed. You shouldn't come near the door.'

'I didn't. Only when I heard you. I thought you were in trouble. What's the note say?'

'Don't answer the door,' said Kasper going into the kitchen and throwing the note into the oven.

'Kasper, the paper.'

'Don't open the door!' shouted Kasper.

Eva was standing in the doorway to the kitchen now. She was crying.

'And you! Bugger off!'

'Kasper!' said his father.

'Off,' he said. 'And you.'

The old man huffed and left and suddenly the only noise in the room was Eva's gentle snivelling, muffled by her hands, which she was holding over her face. She mumbled something.

'I can't hear you.'

She took her hands away from her face and wiped her eyes with the sleeve of her coat. The skin around them was red and her mouth was drawn into a long quaking bow. 'I said, I'm sorry.'

Kasper went to the window and opened his cigarette tin. He sat down and tried to roll a cigarette, but his hands were trembling. He saw his father reading the note, his face twisting in disgust, he saw the girl's lifeless body at the bottom of the steps, he saw himself spinning, a breathless kick before he made contact with the steps, he saw the children cackling at the sight of Kasper's desperation. 'Damn it!' he said and threw the newspaper and tobacco back down onto the sill.

Eva moved towards him and lowered herself into the seat opposite. She picked up the newspaper strip and filled it with a few shreds of tobacco, licked the edge and rolled it shut. She lit a match, took a drag of the cigarette herself and handed it to Kasper.

'Who are they?' he said.

'I . . .'

He broke into an injured shout. 'Tell me!' Kasper looked down at his knees, embarrassed, and then up at Eva's face. His one eye met her two and he said quietly, 'Who are they?'

Eva put her hand up to unbutton her coat. Her fingers played around the edges of the top button, but then fluttered up to her eyes again and wiped away a final tear that had pooled in the light tips of her eyelashes. 'Hans and Lena Beckmann. They're siblings. Twins.'

91

'And they write the notes?'

'What notes?'

Kasper opened his mouth to shout again, but she cried out over him, 'I don't know what you're talking about! I don't know anything about any notes!'

'The notes under the door. The threats.'

'I don't know anything about that.'

'Well maybe you should find more trusting accomplices.'

'They're not my accomplices. I didn't know . . . I didn't write any notes. I thought it was only me doing this.'

'Doing what?' said Kasper.

'This. The . . .'

'Blackmail.'

'Yes,' said Eva. Her fingers moved up to the top of her coat again and she undid the first two buttons and sat back in the chair.

'But you know them?'

'Yes,' she said. She reached over to the windowsill. The cigarette case that she'd brought with her on her first visit was still sitting there. She touched its edge and pushed it so that it spun on its curved back. 'They're Frau Beckmann's children.'

'Frau Beckmann?'

'I live in her apartment. She's sort of the head of the rubble group. She's . . .' she stopped turning the cigarette case, but let the tips of her fingers remain on the sill. 'She looks after us . . . after me. I'd be dead if she hadn't . . .'

'Is she running this?'

'Not running it. It's not like a conspiracy. Not like that. It's . . .'

'Fräulein Hirsch,' said Kasper. 'It seems you're very deep into something you can't control, that you barely comprehend. You've now got me involved and if you don't start being honest with me, we're both going down in flames, do you understand?'

'It's not a conspiracy! She just needs to find this pilot.'

'So not your pregnant friend.'

'No, not exactly.'

'How, "not exactly"?'

Eva closed her eyes and reached up, touching her cheek gently with her fingers. She sniffed and breathed out in little bursts, like an animal. It seemed to still her. 'Frau Beckmann needs to know about the pilot. Where he is, where he goes. I'm finding out for her.'

'Why?' said Kasper.

Eva opened her eyes, and looked over at Kasper.

'You can't tell me?' he said.

She shook her head.

She reached over to touch the cigarette case again, but Kasper snatched it up and threw it across the room. It clattered onto the planks and spun around, disappearing beneath a narrow chest of drawers in the opposite corner of the room.

'Do you know why she's looking for him?'

'Yes.'

'Is it to do with me?'

'No,' said Eva, 'it's nothing to do with you. Not personally. This is just how Frau Beckmann does things.'

'What things? What is she?'

'She's just another rubble woman. But ...'

'Fräulein Hirsch – if you're being honest ...'

'I am!'

'If you're being honest with me,' Kasper said more quietly, 'then her children are following me around Berlin, they're writing me notes that are threatening me, my family – she sent you here to blackmail me to find information that you could just as well search for yourself. She's threatening my life and if you don't realise it already – and to be honest, I'm starting to worry that you don't – I think you've got yourself into a very, very dangerous situation.'

93

'She's not trying to. It's the children – I'll talk to her about them.'

'You told me this was over.'

'I thought I could just find someone else to search. Someone different without connections, just like she promised. But then ...' She touched the skin on her bottom lip, where her incessant picking had opened up a thin bloody line. 'She said I can't change anything. That the job's just got to get done.' Kasper felt the tired inevitability of it all in his shoulders, in his back, in the pin-point impression still on his throat. 'Her children aren't well,' said Eva. 'Hans was in the fighting in April, when the Russians came. The Youth. They made them kill people – deserters. Terrible things. And Lena ... well, they're not right. They're just children. Frau Beckmann just needs this information. If you find it, it'll be over. I've seen it before – that's how it goes. I can't tell you anymore. Not about why she wants to know. I want to, but I can't.'

'You've got to give me something.'

'I can't. I'm not even supposed to say her name. And you don't need to know. It doesn't matter.'

'Well, why did you come here tonight? You can answer me that, can't you?'

'To convince you that you had to keep looking for the information – to tell you I was sorry. That I can't get you out of it.'

'Looks like you were beaten to it.'

She reached up to the sill again, where the cigarette case had been. Her fingers climbed the window frame and stroked the line where the glass joined the painted wood. 'I suppose. Frau Beckmann was angry I tried to change things. Very angry.'

'And why doesn't she just send you out to find the information?'

'Because I work with her. There's a connection. She gets us girls – the other rubble women on her group – to get other people to find things out or do things. It's all about separation. But the people are never used more than once – you don't have to worry. It's all just randomly done. It means nothing can be traced back.'

'So this is some sort of operation? There are others?'

'Operation makes it sound official – it's not like that. She's helping us. She's helping us girls out.'

Kasper sighed. 'Well, what else is she trying to find out? What's she need all this information for?'

'Does it matter?'

'Yes.'

'Why?'

Kasper was unable to answer. 'What if I find this information and the pilot gets killed? Then I'll be the one hanging.'

'No, it's just the opposite. She wants to keep him alive, that's all. She knows things – has connections. And someone's killing military people.'

'That's very insightful of her.'

'No, ones who've been with German women. They're being killed. All the girls on the rubble groups know about it.'

'Have you been with this pilot?'

'No, of course not. Stop making me talk about this. I'm not meant to be talking about it – I promised.'

'Who's killing them?'

'What?'

'Who's killing the soldiers or pilots?'

Eva sighed. 'Germans. It's been going round the rubble groups for ages. Women who've been with soldiers – their soldiers get killed.'

'And Frau Beckmann's saving them?'

'No – just this one. That's not what she's doing, I . . . That's not important. She trades things, sorts things out for people – just like you do – it's no different. It's nothing worse than that.

95

I've told you too much about it, and it's really not important, Herr Meier. Just ... Please just get this information. And quickly – and then it's over.'

Kasper touched the skin above his bad eye with his fingertips. The flesh was tender – not bleeding but damp with the blood that was sitting just beneath the surface.

'And the demonic twins?'

'Hans and Lena? They keep an eye on things for Frau Beckmann.'

'What does she need to keep an eye on?'

'I've already said more than I should.'

Kasper went to stand up, but his muscles contracted, and a sharp pain clamped around his lower back like a corset. He only hovered over his seat for a few seconds before sitting down again.

'I wish you hadn't got me involved in this,' he said. 'I wish you'd never come here.'

Eva looked down at her lap and nodded. He noticed, only now, that she had pinned up her hair into smart waves, that she was wearing a little kohl around her eyelids. 'I didn't think it would turn out like this,' she said. 'I didn't realise that Hans and Lena were involved. I'm sorry. I thought it would be quick – that you could just get the information off one of your contacts and it would be over. You seem like a nice man.'

Kasper looked up at her. 'I'm not a nice man.' She returned his stare, the blue of her eyes a dark indigo in the dim electric light. 'I think you should leave now,' he said.

'But you'll get the information? About the pilot?'

'I don't think I have a choice.'

'It wasn't planned like that. Not by me. I didn't know. I'm sorry. And I'll talk to Frau Beckmann. The children shouldn't be involved.'

Kasper held onto the back of his chair and this time managed to get to his feet. 'Get out of my apartment.'

Eva stood up as well. 'I really am sorry . . . '

'You've said sorry enough times. It doesn't change anything,' said Kasper. 'Now, get out.'

Eva nodded and walked out of the door, but was only gone for a few seconds. She returned with something in her hand. 'Take this,' she said. She lay a watch down on the counter top. 'It was Frau Beckmann's idea. The cigarette case and the pipe as well. The watch is Swiss, she says. She wants me to bring you things when I come. So you're remunerated.'

Kasper turned away from her. He listened to her leaving, struggling with the door and descending the stairs.

Kasper kept his eyes shut and pushed his elbows towards each other so that his ears were completely covered. He took in three long breaths, then dropped his arms to his side, opened his eyes and looked up at the light bulb that hung down from the ceiling, the light drawing a black-blue line in the vision of his healthy eye.

'Herr Meier?' said the old voice from the other room, followed by a crackling cough.

'You don't have to call me that. There's no one here. And you forgot it pretty quickly the moment it was necessary.'

'What's going on, Kasper? Who have you brought home?'

'No one. It's nothing.'

'Is everything all right?'

'Yes.'

'Are . . . '

'Just leave it!'

The old man was silent.

Kasper went and picked up the watch that Eva had brought and sat back on his chair. He looked down at the face: thick Art Deco numbers, a brass surround. A Russian would pay well enough for it. He threw it down onto the windowsill where the ugly cigarette case had lain, that he would never be able to shift, except maybe to a child for a few cigarettes or some information.

He breathed heavily, and then reached up and touched the cheap wooden board covering up the hole from the broken window frame. He stroked the rough grain and swallowed to fight off a rising contraction in his throat. He could feel things coming apart, cracks in the carapace that were allowing emotions in; emotions that were making his stomach sour and his heart ache like the strained muscle in the small of his back. He was afraid for his father, but it was more than that. It wasn't Hans and Lena Beckmann – that sort of pain didn't scare him anymore. It was something older. He was frightened of the girl. Because she had that terrible brightness that Phillip had had. That optimism and ridiculous trust. And Phillip would have said, 'trust her, you grumpy fool. Win her over.' 'It would be just as easy to break her,' Kasper would answer. 'No,' Phillip would say. 'She's a good one in a bad situation. You're blind,' he would say. 'Half blind,' Kasper would reply. And when Kasper closed his eyes to force out the thought, to get back to the snow-covered steps in the Volkspark, he only saw his eyes, wet with tears, red with blood. His love for Kasper, for the world, undiminished.

SHEETS

Kasper woke at seven. The pale morning light was streaming through the curtainless windows of the kitchen, creating a luminous pink field of colour beneath his eyelids. He turned to the wall. He was thinking about floating on his back in the Tegeler See before the war, his eyes closed and his ears under the water so that he could only hear the deep hush of the lake. Soon the silence was disturbed by the splash of a wooden paddle and then the deep rush of a body diving into the water. He could feel his own body being tossed up on the wake of the waves, shaped by the man who was swimming over to him. He could hear his muffled laugh above the water and feel his fingers on his skin. Then he could see things that he can't have seen, and heard things he couldn't have heard – the image of their submerged bodies; the freshness of the bubbles escaping from their extremities as they thrashed in the clear water; the sound of his own laughter.

Kasper gasped, rolled onto his back and opened his eyes. He blinked and stared at the long crack that ran up the wall from behind the sink, across the ceiling and down to the doorframe.

He thought about the lakes around Berlin as thin watery cracks in the land and he closed his eyes again and tried to imagine the water seeping under the city until it broke free and shot up with a rush, floating on top of the water then drifting away to the sea.

The bell of a church rang distantly and he became aware of the remarkable silence in the apartment – aware that he hadn't heard his father coughing, that he hadn't heard a sound from his father. He turned his head on the pillow – the thin feathers crackled loudly beneath his ear. The church bell echoed. His forehead tightened and his lips opened. An empty sickness pulled at his stomach and then he was overcome with a terrible lightness, a strange, frightening freedom.

He moved to get up, then heard a sudden, spluttering cough coming from his father's room. The sickness dissipated and was replaced by a familiar relief mixed with a weight of responsibility, dragged back on like a coat. Kasper pulled himself round on his single mattress, pushing aside the blanket, and rubbed his stinging eyes. He held his head for a second, sniffed and listened again, and now heard the old man's mattress creaking as he turned over in bed.

Kasper stood up and undid the buttons on the one-piece he had worn to bed, urinated in the sink and then splashed some water onto his face from the bucket on the floor. Kasper became very aware of the certainty of the moment when his father wouldn't cough, when Kasper would make the slow walk down the corridor and put his hand against the man's cheek and find it cold as metal. Before, this thought had led to a vague picture of the grey, ruined city, covered in snow. But now he felt something new – a fragile link to life beyond the ruins. It was a feeling beneath his heart. It was preparing the apartment for someone; caring that the sheets were as clean as he could make them with soap, a bucket and his sink; an image of himself in a field, raising his head as someone called for him; outside a station or on a platform waiting for someone to come home.

Kasper lit one of three thin cigarettes already lined up on the windowsill. He thought about the teenagers and looked over at the dark windows in the top-floor flat opposite his. He tried to recall when he had last seen a face there or a light and shivered at the thought of Hans and Lena Beckmann, standing in the silent dark of the room at that very moment, watching him.

Kasper washed carefully in front of the sink, taking a chipped saucer and lathering an amber slither of transparent soap from a block bought from a British nurse in exchange for a genuine piece of Hitler's bunker. He took a thin slice from the bar with a knife, like a curl of butter, and mixed it with a little water. As he washed, he caught the falling foam in a white, enamelled cup and shaved with the greying suds and an ancient cutthroat razor.

Kasper dressed and left the cup of suds for his father's wash. He called to him: 'Papa?'

'Yes.'

Kasper went to his door. The old man was awake, a bound copy of *Der grüne Heinrich* open on his lap. His finger marked a spot on the page, but he was staring down at the corner of the room, his silver-framed glasses held delicately between his thumb and forefinger. He looked up at Kasper and smiled. 'You off?'

'Yes. I'll be back in the middle of the day probably, but then out again after that.'

'Yes, yes,' said the old man. 'As you wish.' He put his glasses back on and looked down at his book.

Kasper put on his winter coat, the remains of the silk lining hanging down from the wool in long threads, like hair, and again he heard a cough, but lighter and shorter than his father's. He stopped and stared at the front door. Buttoning up his coat he moved closer and looked through the spy hole, but saw nothing. He put his ear to the door and heard breathing, reverberating through the wood.

Kasper took up a poker, resting against the side of the doorframe. He quietly removed the planks holding the door shut and lifted the handle of the door. He took a breath, pulled the door open and yelled, waving the iron poker above his head.

Eva screamed awake and scrambled across the hallway floor into the doorway opposite, like a scolded dog. She blinked and looked up at him, trembling, taking in heavy, shaking breaths. Kasper frowned. 'What the bloody hell . . . ?' he said. 'What the bloody hell . . . ?'

'It was past the curfew,' she said, her teeth chattering. 'I couldn't have gone back on my own, not in the dark. Not on my own.'

She tried to stand up, but fell back down again. Kasper put the poker down and moved forward to help her, but she said, 'No, no, don't worry,' and began to feverishly rub her arms. 'It's just my legs have gone dead. I just need to warm up again. I hadn't realised it was morning. I was going to sneak off, I promise.'

The old man appeared at Kasper's side. 'Who's this?'

'What are you doing out of bed?' said Kasper.

'I need to pee. Who's this girl? Wasn't she here last night?'

'Fräulein Hirsch.'

'Are you going to just leave her out here to freeze?'

'I was considering it,' said Kasper.

'Ridiculous boy,' said the old man and staggered past the girl. Kasper held his cigarette between his lips and dragged Eva to her feet.

'Oh no,' she said, 'Please.'

He walked her to his mattress where he helped her take her coat off and then laid her down and covered her with his blankets and the old rug that concealed his tins, bottles and cartons during the day. She shivered beneath the sheets, burying her head like a bird sleeping beneath its puffed-up feathers.

'Just until you're warm enough to get down the stairs without breaking your neck,' he said.

He saw the top of her head moving in a nod.

Kasper looked at his watch, wound it and then sat down by the window. Silly child, he thought. He searched about for something to do and landed on a shirt of his father's that he'd been mending. He picked it up, the bent needle hanging from the open hem beneath the armpit. He began to sew, tilting his head and bringing the white cotton up to his good eye, turning it to the pallid morning light. Eva stopped shivering and began to breathe deeply and slowly. He lowered the handiwork down to his lap and looked over at her. She rolled onto her back and pushed at the top of the sheets, letting her hand fall backwards to lie palm up on the pillow. It tightened into a fist as she kicked one of her legs and then ceased to move, the hand unclenching, the fingers opening out gently, like petals. He noticed something black on the side of her hand, with a bloody end: a large splinter that had gone deep into her skin. He wondered whether he might be able to remove it while she was sleeping, without waking her. Then his eye wandered – below the bitten skin around her fingernails, and above the grey bruises of her slim white wrists, she had a scar, still pink, the shape of a skewed star. Slightly puckered in the centre, its arms reached out, one almost white where it reached the edge of her palm.

Kasper heard his father's cough echoing up the stairwell and then listened to the gentle see-saw of Eva's breathing, her pink healthy lungs bringing the air in and pushing it out. He pictured this woman, this Frau Beckmann, both promising her and threatening her; all she would have needed was the irresistible allure of a meal and a dry room with a lock on the door. He found himself hoping that the outcome for the girl would be upset and disappointment, perhaps a few days without food or shelter, and not something more terrible, not something that would ruin her, or worse.

'Kasper?'

He looked up. His father was at the door. 'I'm fixing your shirt,' said Kasper, holding it up. 'I'll let her sleep and be out in an hour or so.'

'Fine, fine,' said the old man. 'So who is the girl?'

Kasper looked down at her. Her mouth was ajar, her ring and middle fingers twitched. 'Someone I'm helping out with something.'

'She's pretty.'

'She's a child.'

The old man squinted. 'Twenty?'

'Or younger.'

'What a start in life. At least we had some good times, eh?'

'She'll have some good times,' said Kasper.

The old man smiled. 'That's it, my boy. A bit of optimism.'

'Enjoy it – that's your lot for the year.'

The old man laughed. 'She's not a hooker, is she?' he said, suddenly concerned.

'No, of course not,' Kasper said. 'I hope not.'

The old man scratched his beard and leant heavily on the doorframe. 'But she's in your line of business?'

'Sort of. She's caught up in something.'

'Can you get her out of it?'

'That's not my job.'

'You could do with a woman around here. We both could.'

'She tried to blackmail me. She's twenty years younger than me. Thirty years maybe.'

'Pickings are slim, Kasper,' said the old man. 'You've got all your limbs – you're a catch in this town.' Kasper started laughing and set his father off. His mouth opened wide as he started to cackle, but it caught at his lungs and he started to cough, bending over and gripping the doorframe. He stilled it, hitting his chest with his fist. Kasper put the shirt down and stood up, but the old man waved him away.

'Come and smoke with me,' said Kasper, 'It might do your lungs some good.'

'No, no,' said the old man, pushing himself back up and off the doorframe. 'I've got my pipe and a few threads of tobacco if I need it. I'm going to have a lie down. You look after your new charge.'

'She doesn't need looking after – certainly not by me.'

The old man nodded and disappeared down the corridor.

When Eva woke, Kasper was sitting in one of the kitchen chairs, with the second cigarette in his hand, unlit. He passed it absently to his lips every now and again to suck at it.

He looked down at Eva on the floor. 'You have a splinter,' he said. 'I could get it out with a pin.'

'From sleeping on those floorboards,' she said and Kasper squinted as she casually bit into her hand, then delicately removed the splinter of dark wood from between her small teeth.

'I'm sorry about this morning,' Eva said, putting her hand in her mouth and sucking at the cut the splinter had left behind. 'I thought I'd be awake before you.'

'It's fine,' said Kasper. 'You can repay me.'

'I can't repay you,' said Eva. 'I don't have anything.'

'You can help me out,' said Kasper, standing and pulling his coat back on. 'Come on, get up.'

'Help you out with what?'

'I need a woman – to trade something. You'll get a cut – a small one.'

Eva shrugged her assent and pushed the sheets aside. She slowly pulled the bed straight behind her, far neater than Kasper had ever kept it. 'Have you got a mirror?' she said.

'At the sink.'

'Oh yes,' said Eva. She stood in front of the small square of mirrored glass, hung by a pretty ornamental chain on a rusty nail hammered into the wall. She sighed and began to fight down a frizzy layer of hair on the side of her head that had become almost horizontal as she slept. 'It's like a bush,' she said. 'The one thing my mother gave me that the Russians didn't get.' She turned her head and frowned. 'One day I'm going to have a dressing room full of irons and creams and all sorts and I'll be able to make it into something resembling hair.'

'You've got plenty of it,' said Kasper.

'There is that,' she said smiling at him in the reflection of the mirror. She finished clipping and pressed the edges down with the palm of her hand. She took a last look in the mirror, biting at the skin on her thumb. 'That'll have to do,' she said. She turned and caught sight of the back of her head. 'Oh,' she said frowning. 'Could you . . . ?'

'What?' said Kasper.

She turned her back to him and offered up two clips that she recovered from the nest of her fringe. 'Could you just clip up this bit?' she said, touching a messy patch of curls at the back of her head.

Kasper came forward and took the clips off her. 'I don't really know what I'm doing,' he said.

'Just get it off my neck – I assume we're not going to the opera.'

Kasper laughed and pushed up a tuft of hair and put his other hand on her neck to steady himself. Eva pulled away with a shocked intake of breath.

'Are you all right!' said Kasper. 'Did I hurt you?'

'No, no, I . . .' she half laughed. 'I'm sorry. I just can't bear people touching my skin, I suppose.'

'Oh,' said Kasper, 'I'm sorry. I can . . .' and he pushed up a tuft of hair and clipped it in without touching her. 'Like that?' he said.

She pressed it, trying to look at it in the tiny grubby surface of the mirror. 'Great,' she said. 'Yes, that's fine.'

Kasper picked up the glass bottle standing by the leg of his chair and took a swig, swallowed, breathed out, then took another.

'What's that?' said Eva.

He hit his chest as the alcohol went down. 'Aspirin,' he said.

Eva held out her hand. 'Go on, then,' she said.

Kasper kept hold of the bottle and licked the brandy, still clinging to his lips. 'It's for grown-ups.'

'I'm helping you out, aren't I?' she said. She kept her hand held out, her eyes wide open.

'I don't have a glass.'

'Come on,' she said.

He gave her the bottle and she knocked back the last half-inch of liquid. She hit the bottle down on the counter top and coughed, putting the back of her hand to her mouth. 'Jesus,' she said. 'Quality stuff.'

'I keep it for special occasions,' said Kasper, and pushed her towards the door.

As they left the apartment Kasper paused, and looked up the attic stairs, to where Hans and Lena Beckmann had stood the morning before.

'They're not there now,' said Eva.

'How dangerous are they?'

'They're children.'

Kasper nodded and made his way down the stairs ahead of her and exited the building fast. Eva took a few quick steps to catch up with him. 'Where are we going? Is it about the pilot? Because I can't meet him myself. That's the point.'

'It's nothing to do with that.'

'Why not?'

Kasper stopped. 'Listen, I'll find your pilot in good time, but this morning I've got to make a living and I need your help, understand?'

He walked on and Eva followed him in silence, her hard shoes rattling against the broken pavement. As they came closer to the park the towers of the Kaiser Wilhelm Memorial Church, almost beautiful in the sunshine, rose up like the ruins of a fairy-tale castle.

'Will you tell me where we're going?' she said eventually, as Windscheidstraße turned into Kantstraße.

'We're going to see a man named Igor about a camera.'

'To the Russian sector?'

'Yes – why, is that a problem? Broken a few hearts over that way?'

'No,' she said. 'Why would you say something like that?'

'It was a joke.'

'Well, it wasn't very funny.' She pushed her hands into the deep pockets of her coat. 'Is he a soldier?'

'Of course he is.'

'And he's going to sell you a camera?'

'No, he's going to sell me something in return for a camera. He sees himself as a collector.'

'What does he give you in return?'

'I don't know – he's never sold me anything before.'

'Why not?'

'He doesn't sell to men.'

'Why?'

'Oh, you know, he's a pervert or something. But he's very generous with medical supplies when you've got a camera. And a girl.'

'What else does he want in return?'

'Don't worry about anything like that. I'm not going to leave you with him.'

They approached the Tiergarten, and skimmed the edge of the great park, now empty of trees. The roads here had been fully cleared and the walls of the ruined diplomats' houses seemed scrubbed and purposeful. The sun behind them cast strange shadows across the wide street – great dark shapes punctured with the bright rectangles of missing windows. And through the mountainscape drove a few cars, the grinding roar of their motors accompanied by the propellers of planes coming into land in the airports of the occupying powers.

'You know you could make a safer living doing this sort of thing,' said Kasper.

'Cameras?'

'Well, anything,' he said. 'Trading. You could get a roof over your head, some food, without having to rely on this, Frau ...'

'Beckmann.'

'Yes,' said Kasper. 'The soldiers trust women – they can get anywhere.'

'It's not being trusted by the soldiers that I'm worried about,' said Eva.

'Yes,' said Kasper. 'There is that, I suppose.'

Kasper watched the sparse spread of people walking along the street towards them. With Eva beside him he had a strange sense of belonging to these people, of being involved in some sort of social relationship that they might recognise, might comprehend. What other history might they be imagining for this man and his supposed daughter?

'Why don't all the women do it then?'

'Do what?' said Kasper.

'Make a proper living off the black market – if it's that easy, I mean.'

'You need to build up a network. Not be too moral about it all.'

'How?'

'Someone could show you.'

'Like you?' she said.

He turned to her. She was looking up at him seriously. 'I'm just saying, if what you've got yourself into is just about food and shelter, there are other ways. That's all I'm saying.'

She turned away from him and looked over the great muddy mass of thawing vegetable patches and the shimmering spine of powder-white ruins in Moabit on the other side of the park.

Kasper spotted a rusted twist of metal protruding onto the pavement and pulled her towards him. She crossed her arms over her chest as he released her and a gust of cold wind blew at them, pulling at the tails of their long coats. Kasper looked down at her as she lowered the crown of her head into the wind. 'So you live with this Beckmann, then?' he said.

'Frau Beckmann rents a room in her building to me and five other girls,' she said, 'Bit of a squeeze, but we're working mostly, so . . .'

'Sounds like she has her fingers in a lot of pies.'

Eva laughed. 'Yes, you could say that.'

Kasper slipped his hands into his pockets. 'Are the other girls friends? Is that why you're not living with your parents?'

'No,' Eva said. 'They're not friends. And my parents are dead.'

'I'm sorry about that – your parents,' he said. 'But what about living with friends?'

She shook her head, confused. 'I don't have any "friend" friends, I suppose.'

'What about from before the war? There can't be no one.'

'Well, don't make me feel bad about it,' she said. 'I used to get sent to a lot of Girls' League things, but all that haymaking and gymnastics – I just hated all that and I was bad at it. Anything that involves rhythm or obedience, you know? And then I got sent off to Brandenburg to farm, and I wasn't so bad at that bit – that was just work. I didn't make friends there either, I suppose.' She squinted thoughtfully. 'It's just, the girls were only interested in sitting round and dreaming about their beaux coming home and starting up a family. I didn't have a beau and it's not that I never thought about having a family, but I was hoping for more than just that. And then by the end of the war I thought, well they're all dead or damaged beyond recognition – the men I mean. Who didn't know what was coming, by then? But if you said it, well, it didn't make me very popular.'

'And since then?'

'Since the war ended?' Eva said. 'Well, that's just survival, isn't it?'

A passing British Jeep kicked up some dust and Eva and Kasper briefly closed their eyes as it settled around them. Kasper licked his thumb and rubbed it along the rim of the lid beneath his milky eye.

'Does it hurt,' said Eva, 'your eye?'

'No.'

'What happened to it?'

'It was pecked out by an ostrich.'

'Ha. Ha. Ha.' said Eva in a slow staccato. She patted her pockets and said, 'Do you want a cigarette?' Kasper shrugged and they stopped walking. Eva took two out of her cigarette case. 'Help with the match, will you,' she said. 'It's windy.' Kasper undid his coat and held it around her. The shelter of the coat created a strange, brief intimacy and he could smell her breath, stale from bed. Some strands of hair blew up from her fringe and tickled his chin and his nose. She put both cigarettes between her chapped lips and lit both tips with the same flame.

'You shouldn't pick at your mouth like that.'

'Nervous habit,' she said out of the corner of her mouth,

111

throwing the match to the floor. 'And I don't do a lot of kissing.'

'Don't waste it,' said Kasper, letting go of the lapels of his jacket as the wind swept away the warmth and quiet of the space between them. He bent down and picked up the smoking matchstick from the pavement, spat on the end and slipped it into his jacket pocket.

'Sorry,' she said and handed him one of the cigarettes. He sucked on it and a stray thread of paper flamed briefly, then curled slowly into the glowing tip, where it blackened and disintegrated. He looked away from her, at the smoking end of his cigarette. He breathed in to extinguish a pressure that was building up beneath his chest. He could pretend he was faint, he thought, if he needed to vomit.

'Excuse me?' A man on crutches, addressing himself to Kasper, had appeared at their side. The wind flapped the worn cloth of his demob suit trousers, around the thin, poker-straight columns of his metal legs. 'Is your daughter exchanging cigarettes?'

'No,' said Kasper automatically.

Eva laughed.

'Something funny?' said the man.

'No,' said Kasper. The man's hollow eyes searched his face for a response. Kasper smiled and said, 'She's a little disturbed this one.'

'They've become brassy, these girls,' said the man. 'Lack of discipline while we were away. You can't stand for it, I tell you. You need to nip it in the bud.'

'Oh no, Papa's very hard on me,' said Eva, 'Honest he is.'

Kasper laughed and the man let out a knowing 'Huh!' He looked over at Eva and twisted his face, squinting his eyes. 'How old are you?' he said.

'Me?' said Eva, 'What's it to you?'

'You're pretty enough,' he said. 'I've got a big room in the British Sector, flushing toilet.' He looked up at Kasper. 'Good

112

contacts with the French, if a sweetener was needed. Could be advantageous on all sides, if you see what I mean.'

A gust of wind threw up a smattering of grit that crackled on the metal of the man's crutches. 'Are you bloody kidding me!' shouted Kasper, making Eva jump. He pushed his face in close to the man's, so that he was knocked off balance. 'Bugger off, you filthy letch. Get out of here.'

'Jesus!' cried the man, almost falling as he scrabbled away down the street, leaning onto his crutches like a crab. 'That was an offer you had there,' he shouted back at them, 'a good offer.'

Kasper looked down at Eva; she looked back at him, almost smiling, shrugging away what the man had said.

'Unbelievable,' said Kasper.

'Not so unusual,' said Eva. 'At least he asked.'

Kasper shook his head slowly, his eyes wide. 'Get moving!' he shouted again at the man's back, though he was already some distance off, his head down, the a-rhythmic clatter-clatt of his metal legs and crutches already being swallowed up by the wind.

Eva put a hand on Kasper's arm. 'Come on,' she said. 'It's fine. I'm a big girl.' She pulled him back into step and they walked on in silence. 'It happens all the time.'

Kasper looked around him at the men on the street leaning on the ruins, standing in doorless porticoes, the soldiers passing in their Jeeps, directing traffic, striding in laughing, confident groups. With Eva beside him, the men transformed into a menacing group of new possibilities; a new danger that had never troubled him before, quite different from the threat of violence, from the threat of death he was used to. He noticed eyes turning briefly to Eva, narrowing, sizing her up, then him, and then flitting away. He moved in closer so that the cloth of their jackets swished where they rubbed past each other. 'Are you OK?' said Eva.

'Fine,' said Kasper. 'Yes, fine.'

They passed the last of the remains of the zoo. Across the park they could see the Russian war memorial, its giant metal soldier with its back to them, erected within months of the victory. Kasper saw Eva's door being kicked in by a soldier's boot, recalled Phillip's curious eyes meeting his at the sound of an unexpected knock at the door, a calm, perfunctory rap. The wind elicited a thin tear from his dead eye. He stared down at the road and tried to concentrate on the broken concrete, following the lines that parted and intersected like rivers on a map.

'Herr Meier.' They had reached the border into the Russian sector and were approached by a group of soldiers almost immediately who asked to see their IDs. As Kasper's papers were being checked, Eva said, 'It's open again, you know, the zoo. Frieda wanted to go, but I just thought it was a bit silly, to go and stare at a couple of animals that survived the bombing. Poor things. I wonder what they thought was happening.'

A Russian soldier signalled for her to be quiet and she fell silent.

They arrived at the back of the Reich Chancellery and stopped on the corner of Voßstraße. Standing side by side they looked across the barren grounds that had once been the Chancellery's garden. Surrounded by thin barbed wire in a meagre effort to deter souvenir hunters, it was now a strange landscape of charred trees, scrap metal and fallen stone. The concrete masses of the exploded bunker, with their intensely black shadows, appeared like a geometric puzzle – an upturned cube, a cylinder, a cone. Behind it, the Chancellery itself had retained only a few solid buildings, lone rooms amid rows of ruined walls, like broken teeth.

'You can still see some of the red marble,' said Eva pointing to a distant window.

'It's paint,' said Kasper. 'Graffiti.'

'Really?' said Eva, pushing herself up onto her toes to get a better look.

Kasper looked around and spotted a large Russian Army vehicle on An der Kolonnade, and beside it, with his back against a graffitied concrete wall, Igor basking like a seal, his jacket open so that the sun fell on the black hair of his chest.

'It wasn't marble anyway,' Kasper said absently, 'it was granite.'

Igor's eyes were closed and his foot was up on a stack of crates in front of him. Droplets of sweat were gathered on his lips and chin.

'What's wrong with his foot?' Eva said.

'He's just keeping an eye on whatever he's trading.'

'But his boot's unlaced.'

Kasper squinted – this was true. 'Oh yes,' he said. 'He always has his leg up like that – you'll have an easier of job of running away if there's something wrong with it.'

'Why will I have to run away?'

'You won't,' Kasper said. 'It was a joke. Don't take this so seriously – nothing's going to happen.'

Kasper looked down at Eva, who was shading her eyes and staring towards Igor with solemn intent. He saw her as a girl with another life, not a grown woman scrambling about in the ruins of a dead city. He saw her standing beside her father on some grassy Bavarian mountainside, on a bone-white cliff on Rügen, looking out over the green sea, with gulls swirling in the sky and cormorants diving into the water. She would be worrying about nothing more than the tenderness in her legs from walking, or the hunger in her stomach – a joyful hunger that she knew would be sated within hours. Her heart would only be aching for some local boy, some crush, some lost love or minor incident that she would one day look back on and laugh about. 'Maybe you should just wait here after all,' he said.

She looked up at him, her hand still at her brow, creating a grey-blue band of shadow across her narrow eyes. 'I thought you said he'll only see women. I've come all this way now.'

He looked up at Igor again and then back at her face. 'Maybe it is dangerous. I don't know.'

'Well, I owe you don't I? Tell me what to do.'

Kasper sighed. He took the camera from his pocket, feeling the cold weight of it through the paper. He handed it to Eva and ran his finger down the seam that ran along the side of his coat, by the buttons. He flicked out a tiny sliver of silver metal, which he pulled on, unzipping a hidden pocket, from which he took another package covered in grease-proof paper.

'What's that?'

'Money.'

'No, the zip.'

'In case I get searched or robbed, of course.'

Eva laughed.

'What?'

'No, it's just so small – unbelievable. It just seems a bit . . . well it's a bit paranoid isn't it? Going to all that trouble.'

'You think the authorities don't confiscate ration coupons or notes? That people aren't going to get them off you if they can?'

'I know that sort of thing happens, sometimes, but if you're searched they'll find it anyway and if you keep your coat closed and do up your pockets and, well, be careful . . . I don't know.'

Kasper pulled her coat open. 'You keep yours here?' he said pointing to an inside pocket.

'No actually,' said Eva. 'You see – not so obvious.' Kasper lifted her lapel and she grabbed his wrist. 'Ow!' he shouted, as her fingers clamped around it and forced his arm away from her. 'There's nothing up there,' she said, letting go.

'No,' said Kasper, rubbing his wrist against his leg and holding out some coupons and a key in front of her face with the other. 'But it's not that hard to find, if you know how to get at it.'

She stared at the key hanging from his outstretched fingers on a grubby string and the perforated sheets of paper. 'Hey, give me that,' she said, snatching them off him. 'I . . . When did you do that?'

'Just now, when you were trying to break my wrist.'

'Sorry,' she said and stuffed the items back into an inside pocket on the other side of her jacket and pulled her coat closed, folding her arms in front of her and frowning. 'Point nicely made.'

'Don't get cross with me!' said Kasper. 'I don't want your coupons – I just wanted to show you how easy it was to take things.'

'Well done,' she said.

Kasper laughed and held out the packet of cash. Eva looked at the floor and her hand jumped up to her arm, then the top button of her coat and then her fingers began to worry the skin on her lips.

'Come on,' said Kasper. 'Cheer up.'

She shook her head, reached out and took the money.

'OK?' he said.

'OK,' she replied. 'What do I do?'

'Just tell him you have something to sell – tell him it's a camera, that it's a Leica. Actually, tell him it's a Leica first, then it sounds like you know what you're talking about – like you have more, you know?'

She nodded.

'He'll try and haggle with you, but stay disinterested – don't look desperate or you'll get bugger all. You want medical supplies. If it's penicillin, it comes in glass vials as powder, and you'll want about thirty vials. If it's just powder in anything with a lid, refuse it – it'll be boiled down from piss and there's no way of checking what it is. Then just get dressings or iodine.'

'How many of those?'

117

'If it's dressings – actually don't get dressings, just iodine. Or morphine – that comes in little metal tubes with glass stoppers and about thirty would be perfect. He probably won't give you morphine – there are people addicted to the stuff who'll give him their house keys for it.'

'OK.'

'Be confident, but don't flirt.'

'I'm not crazy.'

'No, of course not. I didn't mean . . . I just mean, make it clear that he can't refuse, but also make it clear that you're in control.'

'He's got a gun.'

'Pretend you've got a gun. Pretend you hold the power – otherwise you've had it. You'll get nothing back.'

'OK,' she said.

'He wants the camera – it'll be enough, but just in case,' he said, pointing at the small packet he'd removed from his jacket, 'there's five dollars in one dollar bills in here, understand? If he won't budge, be friendly and walk away. He'll try and stop you. If you can't budge him, or if there's something else that will sweeten the deal, you can use the money. Tell him how much money is in the packet, but don't let him see it, it's too risky in the open. There's a hole in the corner,' he said, pointing it out to her, 'he can look at the side of the notes, but he can't open it.'

'What if . . . what if he just takes it?'

'Make sure he doesn't. Say "we" the whole time – then it sounds like other people are involved or waiting for you. Be confident and if it looks bad, run for it.'

'He'll shoot me.'

'I doubt he'll shoot you.'

'You doubt it?'

'He won't shoot you,' said Kasper.

Eva looked down at the packets in her hands. 'What if he grabs me?'

'Scream for me. I'll come.'

'You promise. You don't owe me anything.'

'I'll come,' Kasper said.

Eva nodded. The wind dropped away and for a second there was almost no sound except the crinkle of paper beneath Eva's fingers. And then a bird sang – a blackbird. A pretty, high whistle that echoed off the skewed concrete surfaces around them. 'I wish you'd found me before Frau Beckmann did.'

'What do you mean, "found you"?'

The wind picked up, moving the loose strands of Eva's hair, tugging at Kasper's hat. 'It doesn't matter,' she said and slipped the packages into her pocket.

She made her way down the street towards the van. Kasper followed her for a few metres until he reached a spike of brickwork, the corner of a room, which he slipped into so as not to be standing alone in the empty street. When a vehicle drove by he pretended to be searching for something on the ground, looking up intermittently to check Eva's progress.

She performed the task perfectly, her walk becoming more confident the further away from him she went. Igor looked up at her and she appeared not to notice, stopping by him as if she had just caught something he had said.

Kasper felt the imprint of her fingers still on his wrist. He was struck again by the idea that he might be able to extricate her from the blackmail. She was a good one, wasn't she? Yes, he could feel it. She just needed a little firm guidance, someone to look out for her. But what did he have to offer? A bed in the corridor, a slice of his slim pickings, which were barely enough to keep him and his father alive?

Another Russian truck drove by and he dropped his head. When he looked up again Igor was standing talking to her. He saw her face turn to him briefly, as she was led away, behind the van, the Russian limping as he went.

119

'Herr Meier?'

Kasper's stomach cramped at his name. He looked down. A girl of about six was standing next to him holding up a folded scrap of newspaper.

'How do you know my name?' said Kasper.

'The woman told me.'

'Which woman?' said Kasper.

'She was there,' said the girl, pointing to the corner of the Reich Chancellery. Kasper looked up – an empty patch of muddy grass, a bent metal rod with a fluttering scrap of cloth caught too high up to snatch. He took the piece of paper off her and unfolded it.

Your priority is your search, Herr Meier. Line your own
pockets when your work is done. Do not use our
resources – they are expendable, as are you.

He stared down in horror at the words, written in brown ink over the newsprint. 'What did this woman look like?' said Kasper.

'She had a big funny nose,' said the girl and took off, disappearing into the rubble.

'Hey,' shouted Kasper. He went to go after her, but heard a man scream out in Russian and a bang. Kasper shoved the paper into his pocket and ran down the road towards the van. 'Oh God,' he muttered. Sweat broke out across his face and back, his feet slapping the ground loudly. He was assaulted by appalling images of Eva being dragged away, a thick hand around her thin wrists. He saw her being pushed down into a basement, somewhere terrible and black, the dark mass of a Russian shoulder looming over her.

He ran to the van and found, behind it, Igor writhing around on the ground clutching his foot. He had pulled off the shoe and

Kasper saw that blood was seeping into his thick, green sock. Igor screamed out in Russian and made a grab for his gun. Kasper turned and ran from the van, away from the Reich Chancellery and back to the border.

FRANÇOIS WENGER

François sat on the edge of the bed looking down at Hilda. She looked up at him, one arm stretched out across the pillow that he had been lying on, the other holding a cigarette above her head. François reached over and touched the soft skin of her underarm, then traced it down to her armpit, to the dark hair there, and then down to her bare breast, half covered with the bed sheet.

'American women shave their armpits,' he said in German, heavy with an Alsace accent.

'What for?' said Hilda.

François shrugged.

'Like children,' said Hilda. She glanced out of the window at the white blue sky. François looked at her face, her small nose, the blackness of her eyelashes, her strangely cropped hair. He touched the soft strands of it at her ear. 'Did you ever have it long?' he said. 'You would look pretty with long hair.'

She looked at him, her eyes wide. He couldn't read her expression.

'I had it long – I'll have it long again.'

'Why did you cut it?'

She looked out of the window again and took a drag of her cigarette. 'I didn't have a choice,' she said eventually.

'What do you mean?'

She shrugged. 'Nothing,' she said and adjusted the pillow behind her. 'I suppose it will look strange when we go to France. I suppose they'll think it's strange.'

'Who?' said François, getting up off the bed and walking over to the window.

Hilda laughed and reached over to grab at his bare behind. 'Come away from there!' she cried. 'Come away! Someone will see you.'

François jumped away from her flailing hand. 'You are being made love to by a handsome officer of the French Army. You must not be ashamed.'

Hilda cackled and rolled back onto the bed. 'You ridiculous little man.'

François put his cigarette in his mouth and began to dance in front of the window naked, adopting balletic poses and leaping about, accompanied by Hilda's laughter and disbelieving shrieks and protests. 'Come away! Good God, come away!'

François came towards her and bounced onto the bed, causing the base to bow and the two iron bed-ends to briefly lean, bowing to one another. Hilda put out her own cigarette and pulled François' from his lips. She lay back and pulled up the sheets to cover herself and took a long, serious drag.

'Hey!' said François, lying next to her and playing with the fronds of hair that fell down over her forehead. 'Why so sombre? Shall I dance again?'

'No,' she said, forcing a smile. 'You stay where you are.'

'What is it?'

She looked at him and frowned.

'So serious!' he cried and covered her neck in rapid little kisses, causing her to squirm and push him away. 'So serious.'

'Stop that.'

'What is it? Hilda?'

He pulled himself onto his elbows and she looked up at him, moving her cigarette into her left hand so that she could touch his cheek, and then the lobe of his ear. 'What will your family think of me? If we go back to France.'

'What do you mean?'

'You know what I mean.'

'We'll say you're from Alsace, on the border,' he said. 'We can say you were in the Resistance.'

'Oh for God's sake,' she said and pushed him away.

'Well, you resisted didn't you?'

'Resistance?' she said. 'I was late to the munitions factory one day, because I'd got drunk the night before. My father didn't report one of his employees at the bank for being half Jewish, so he disappeared four weeks later than he would've done when my cousin got scared and reported him. It's hardly de Gaulle.'

'No one knew where they were going.'

Hilda huffed. 'We knew they weren't going on holiday.'

'You did your best,' he said, reaching out to her.

'No I didn't,' she said, pushing him away again. 'No one did their best.'

He fell onto his back and put his hand on his chest. He imagined bringing Hilda into the kitchen of his parents' farmhouse. He saw his mother holding out her hand and then hearing the woman's accent and pulling it away from her as if burnt, staggering back until she was stopped by the wall and could get away no further. He saw Hilda running from the farmhouse, down the track that led to the village, surrounded by vineyards, the leaves dead and brown.

'They will love you. Who could not love you?'

There was a knock at the door.

'Who's that?' said François.

'I don't know,' Hilda said, 'I'm not expecting anyone.'

'Don't answer it.'

They waited, but the knock came again. Hilda got out of bed and pulled on the dress that lay in a crumpled pile on the floor by her shoes. She walked barefoot to the front door, which led straight off the bedroom-cum-living-room-cum-kitchen and looked through the peephole.

'Who is it?' said François, whispering.

'It's just children. Cover yourself up – like you're ill.'

François got under the covers, pulling them up to his neck and making his face into a ridiculous pastiche of someone in poor health. Hilda smiled at him sadly as she came back to the bed to slip on her shoes.

François turned away from Hilda to face the large mirror propped up against the opposite wall and watched her return to the front door and open it. In reflection he saw a girl and a boy standing side-by-side, their large eyes blinking up at Hilda, who was a little taller than both of them.

'Can you help us?' said the girl.

'Help you with what, little one?' said Hilda. 'Do you need food? Because we hardly have anything ourselves. And my husband's poorly,' she said, gesturing towards the bed.

The boy looked over at François and then shifted his gaze, so that their eyes met in the mirror. François made his mock sick face again and when the boy's cruel little mouth failed to break into a smile François crossed his eyes and stuck out his tongue. When he uncrossed them, the boy was looking up at Hilda again.

'We don't need food,' he said, 'it's our mother. She's fallen down in the street. No one else was in. Can you come and help?'

François rolled over and said, 'Just a moment. I will put on some clothes. Hilda – close the door.'

'No!' said the boy.

Hilda and François both looked at him.

'It's . . . women's troubles,' said the girl abruptly.

Hilda nodded and turned to François. 'You stay here. I'll be two minutes.' He smiled at her and she tried to smile back, but she looked as if she was about to cry. She seemed to force herself to turn away from him, pull on a coat and leave with the two children.

He got out of bed and pulled on some underpants and then his trousers. He lit another cigarette and looked out of the window, down onto the street below. He couldn't see anyone on the opposite side, and was too high up to see the pavement by their own building, so opened the window and leant out. The children's mother wasn't there either – perhaps she had collapsed in the courtyard of the building. He could only see the bare head of an old man sitting on the steps up to the front door, and five women in a line, that turned the corner and led down the adjacent street for half a kilometre, to the working water pump.

'*Ah! Mon beau château! Ma tant', tire, lire, lire,*' he sang, '*Ah! Mon beau château! Ma tant', tire, lire, lo.*'

He felt something press against his ankle and thought for a second that he had backed into something, but no, it encircled it and then the other and, before he could turn, his legs lifted painfully into the air, his knees bending to kneel, but finding no surface, because they were already out of the window, his hands reaching out, grabbing, grabbing, wheeling, trying to find something to give him a purchase, and a terrible noise, colours, the sun, the sun, windows upside down, a scream, at first smooth like a flute, then breaking into a horrible vibrato.

PAPERS

Kasper sat in his chair in the kitchen, staring at the dark window of the flat opposite. His mind jumped between images of Eva, robbed, raped, afraid, got rid of. He saw faceless Russian soldiers, her stubby fingernails clawing at someone's arms, her tears – he couldn't bear to imagine her tears.

He tried to fathom what might happen without her, who might come to his apartment to force him to finish the job. He saw the twins in his room, standing over him, he saw an imagined Frau Beckmann, a tall big-boned woman, giant and terrifying. He saw Phillip, slowly lifting his head, his nose misshapen, broken, his eyes glittering.

There was a light crack on the staircase. Kasper's eye darted downwards, into the courtyard, which was of course empty. He went to the kitchen door. 'Who is it?'

'Herr Meier,' came the voice. 'It's me. Eva Hirsch.'

Kasper removed the planks that held the door shut in such a rush that the bottom one slipped from his fingers, scraping a thin layer of skin off his thumb, gathering it up in a stinging ruche by his nail. He kicked the plank aside and pulled the door open. 'Fräulein Hirsch,' he said.

Eva was standing in front of him, dressed in the clothes she had slept in on that very spot the night before, but now there was a dirty white dressing on her forehead, peeling and grey at the corners, and a trickle of dry blood running down the side of her face, pooling in a small crusty patch just beneath her cheek.

'What happened?' said Kasper.

'He took me behind the van,' she said. 'He didn't have any penicillin, but he gave me the iodine. But then he said he wanted something else. I showed him the money, but that wasn't what he meant and he grabbed my wrist.'

'Did he hit you?'

'No – not really. He shoved me into the van and I cracked my head on something. But then I remembered his foot, so I stamped on it.'

Kasper laughed.

'What? What is it?'

'Oh God, you should've seen his foot – he'd pulled off his boot by the time I got to him. I don't know what was wrong with it, but it was a mess. Blood I mean.'

She smiled, but didn't laugh. 'You came for me.'

'Of course – I said I would, didn't I?'

'I know you did.' She smiled, but just with her mouth, and went past him into the kitchen. 'I didn't even think to scream.' She lifted up the handbag and said, 'He only had iodine, just thirty bottles.'

'He let you have thirty bottles of iodine?' said Kasper, following her in.

'Yes.'

'Did he give you that bag?'

She paused. 'Yes,' she said. She put it down on the floor and unpacked ten small bottles of brown liquid, which she'd wrapped in a headscarf. Kasper took one off her, turned on the light and held the bottle up to the bare bulb.

'Was ten not enough?' said Eva.

'No,' said Kasper, 'Too many.' He took the orange rubber stopper off the little bottle and sniffed it. 'It's not iodine.'

'What is it?' said Eva.

'God knows. Sugar water, maybe. Sewage.'

'Oh God, I'm sorry,' she said. 'He seemed very genuine at that point. I'll pay you back. I can get something else for you.'

'No, no – it's fine,' said Kasper distracted, staring at her head again. 'I should've explained better. I shouldn't have taken you.' He frowned and took her gently by the shoulders and pulled her into the centre of the room. She let him take her and tipped her head back automatically as he inspected the dressing. 'I have some clean Band-Aids.'

'Clean whats?'

'American *Hansaplasts*.'

'Are they better?'

'Better than the one you've got now. Who did this for you?'

'One of the girls.'

Kasper looked down at her hands, fidgeting in front of her. He took hold of them and brought them up to her face. 'Your knuckles are red! One of them's cut!'

She pulled her hands away and put them behind her back. 'That wasn't to do with the deal – it was something else.'

'Fine,' said Kasper and shook his head. 'I don't want to know.'

Kasper sighed and peeled back the dressing, which came off easily, its adhesive barely attached. The inside of the little square dressing was black in the centre, where her blood had wet the weak stain from another wound, half rinsed away. The cut beneath was a crooked bruised line, still oozing, surrounded by an aureole of raised red skin. He pulled the two chairs into the

131

middle of the room, beneath the cone of light that radiated down from the light bulb. 'Sit,' he said. She paused at first, but then let herself be led.

Kasper lifted up the rug in the corner of the room and picked up a battered metal tin, the size of a shoe box. He pulled over the bucket of water that lived by the sink and sat in front of her, the box on his lap. The water lapped against the bucket's metal sides and the bottles, cartons and tubes in the box exuded a light, but comforting medicinal smell. He took a cloth from the bucket and wiped the dry blood that had trickled down her face. 'You shouldn't reuse dirty dressings,' he said, dabbing at the blood around the cut. 'It'll get infected.'

'It's all I had.'

'Then better to leave it undressed.'

She nodded.

'I got a note,' said Kasper, 'after you disappeared. It said I was expendable, that you were expendable. That I should be looking for the pilot. I thought they'd done something to you.'

'Frau Beckmann,' said Eva.

'What is this?' he said, pausing in his work, but keeping his left hand on Eva's shoulder. 'What have you got us into?'

'I told you, I can't say,' she said, almost in a whisper. 'Nothing's changed. You just have to find the pilot, then it's over. I promise you. I really do promise.'

'Where did you find my name? It wasn't Neustadt, was it?' She didn't answer.

'You didn't, did you? Someone got it for you.'

'I can't . . . ' she said, then 'there's no point.'

'You think you're in control of this?'

She shook her head, no. 'But I've seen how it works before.'

'And you can't get out of it? For you, I mean.'

'I need to work, to eat.'

'What if there was another option?'

132

'Like what?'

'I don't know. You could help me.'

'Like today, you mean?' she said and smiled properly for the first time.

'You could learn.'

She shook her head. 'We shouldn't be talking – I shouldn't have gone to the Russian Sector with you. It was stupid of me – I knew she would know.'

'You can deal with these things – I've done it before. With the right information you can get rid of anyone. Maybe you could come here. I could use an extra pair of hands – someone healthy to help out. It's not much – it's nothing. But it's better than this,' he said, nodding at the cut.

She looked up at him, her eyes wet and wide. 'You wouldn't want me. I'm trouble.'

Kasper frowned. 'I don't mean ... I mean, I can't want you like that. You know that ... but we could help each other out. Stay safe.'

She put her hand up to his, where it lay on her shoulder, and held it. 'I know – that's why it's such a wonderful thought. But I can't leave Frau Beckmann. It was the right choice at the time. I'm fed and I've got work – it's better than most.'

Kasper nodded and looked down at the box in his lap. He let go of her shoulder and took out a small brown bottle with a thin layer of liquid at the bottom. 'This is real iodine,' he said, taking the stopper out. He rinsed his hand in the bucket, dried it then tipped a little onto his index finger, which he dabbed onto the cut, staining it yellow. Eva didn't flinch, but a tear welled up in her eye, and escaped down the side of her face. Kasper wiped it away with his thumb. 'We're almost done,' he said.

They sat at the window smoking, the chairs back in their places. Eva's cut was covered by an oblong fabric plaster.

'I have to go home,' said Eva.

'Why don't you really go home? I mean to your family.'

'I told you – my parents are dead. There's no one else.'

'Yes,' he said, 'you did say.' Kasper flicked the end of his cigarette and a smut of ash skipped away from the tip. 'I'll get this pilot – I'll find him. It won't take long.'

'Yes,' said Eva. 'Then we're done.'

'Yes. I'll come and find you within the next few days – tomorrow even, once I know something. Where do you live?'

'I can't tell you that,' she said.

'Then where do you work?'

'You can't visit me.'

'Come on,' he said.

She chewed her lip and then said, 'Near Pariser Straße. I don't know what the exact name of the street is. But don't come. And we might have moved to a new site by next week.'

He put his cigarette out on the windowsill. 'There's a note there.' He indicated a folded piece of paper on the shelf, by his rations. 'Pin it to the information board on Karl-August-Platz.'

'Why?'

'There are some British soldiers that help me out with a few things – they might have some information about this.'

She looked down at the note and frowned. 'It doesn't make any sense.'

'It's not meant to. But they'll know what it means.'

'And then they'll just give you a name?'

'I doubt it. Not for nothing, and even then they're unlikely just to give it up, but I'll also try Marta.'

'Who's she?'

'A friend. But she knows a lot of soldiers and pilots and things. Intimately.'

'She's a prostitute?'

'If you like,' said Kasper.

'OK,' she said, put the note in the pocket of her jacket and stood up to leave. She went to the door, where she hovered for a few seconds. 'Is it dangerous, what you have to do?'

'No, not particularly,' Kasper said. 'Not more dangerous than anything else these days. You're the dangerous one – you and the twins.'

'I'm not dangerous – not to you. I promise.'

'And the twins?'

'You won't do anything to them, will you?'

Kasper laughed. 'Don't worry about those two – they can look after themselves. I don't think you or anyone else has any control over them though, so I will be seeing if I can get some information on them, just to make sure that they're – what's the word? – neutralised,' he said. 'I'm sorry, that's just the way these things go. No one's going to get hurt, but if you're being blackmailed you can't leave it open. Otherwise it never stops.'

'Are you going to do that for me? Get information. Neutralise me.'

'No one's going to get hurt,' Kasper said. 'Not because of me.'

'OK,' she said and peered mournfully out into the hall, to the front door, then looked back at Kasper's face. 'Can I ask you something?'

'OK.'

'What was it really? Your eye I mean.'

'Goodbye Fräulein Hirsch,' he said.

She sighed. 'Yes, goodbye.'

He watched her leave again, then he closed his eyes and put his hands in his lap. She was only gone a few seconds when Kasper heard a little shriek. He turned to the doorway and watched her run back in, followed by a tall, very thin man, wearing a black suit beneath a large, heavy coat. He had a long white scar, which pulled his lip up on one side, revealing a few teeth, like a growling dog, and carried a large, grey leather Gladstone bag, fixed with thick black cotton threads in one corner, where the lip of the leather met the large silver clasp.

Kasper scrabbled up onto his feet and moved forward to the kitchen counter top, to the razor secured below it.

'I think you're expecting me,' said the man awkwardly, stooping as he came through the door, into the kitchen.

Kasper looked over at Eva, who looked back at him, her eyes round with worry.

'That depends who you're looking for,' said Kasper.

'Schwalbe,' said the man.

Kasper nodded slowly, realising that it was a contact of his now deceased downstairs neighbour. He saw a row of fine kerosene cans lined up along his wall. He briefly weighed up the possibility that lying might put him in danger, but decided to say, 'You're not the same man as last time.'

The man shifted and said 'Herr Reichmann never sends the same man twice. But you know that. You are ...?' The man looked at Kasper suspiciously now and then over at Eva. 'Tell me who you are,' he said to her.

'She's ...'

The man held his hand up to shut Kasper up.

'His daughter of course,' Eva said without hesitating.

'What's your name?'

'Papa,' she said turning to Kasper, without pausing, 'I thought you said it was all sorted. Do we have to go back to Reichmann again? I won't be questioned like this.'

'Margareta!' said Kasper, putting a finger to his lips. 'Let the man do his job.'

'I'm sorry,' said the man. 'You just hear stories about set ups. Things like that.'

'Of course,' said Kasper, 'she's had a hard week. It's a year since her mother ...'

'Of course,' said the man. He looked up at Eva briefly, then produced a crumpled envelope from his pocket, which he lay on the counter top, near where Eva was standing. 'These are the papers,' he said.

Kasper and Eva moved closer. The man scratched his cheek and looked again at Eva and then Kasper. Without returning the man's gaze, Kasper felt her lean into him and then her hand curling around his, their fingers interlocking. She placed her head on his shoulder. Kasper paused for a second and then kissed the crown of her head, the hair surprisingly soft beneath his chapped lips. The smell of a girl's head, of hair and soap was both disconcerting and comforting. And for a few seconds the sense of her, this person, this counterfeit daughter, grounded him in the room, in the world – paired him up and made him briefly human.

The man seemed happy with this mime of affection, and from the Gladstone bag he produced a black box made of thick, battered card, peeling into its constituent sheets of paper at its corners and edges, tied together with frayed, yellowing string. 'This is the punching machine,' he said, 'and the ink stamp – you only get one go at the punch, so you need to be careful. You need to use fresh photographs – you can't use your old one from your German ID. There's also a model ID in there, to get the stamps right, otherwise all the information's already in there.'

'Of course,' said Kasper.

The man nodded and said, 'There's an address on the back – it's a pawn shop. Once you're done you take it there and pawn the machine, but you won't get any money – don't try it. Then it will be returned to Herr Reichmann. If you get caught with the equipment, he'll deny any knowledge.'

'Right.'

'And the ticket's in the envelope,' said the man. 'If you missed the train, you would have trouble using the IDs again. They're not bad, but you're on a list for this journey and the tickets will appear as if they were booked by the Americans, so it's your best bet. The Russians are in Czechoslovakia now, of course, so Czech IDs like this aren't much use without a proper connection. And if one of you doesn't manage it, for any reason, the tickets are also void – it's one ticket, for two travelling, and the tickets are named, so you can only use them with the ID.'

Kasper stared down at the envelope, its unglued mouth slightly open. He could just see the corner of a small stack of cards and papers. He felt a strange sort of sickness, high and hollow. 'Thank you,' said Kasper. 'Can I give you anything?'

'No, no – Herr Reichmann doesn't allow that.'

'I see,' said Kasper.

'Thank you,' said Eva.

The man dipped in an awkward little bow and backed out into the hallway and then out of the front door.

Kasper and Eva turned again to the envelope and the strange box. They heard the man's heavy footsteps echoing back up the staircase, until they became distant, sharp clicks on the courtyard floor.

'They're identification papers.'

'Yes,' said Kasper.

'Who's Herr Schwalbe?'

'My downstairs neighbour. He lived with his daughter, but they died a few weeks back – kerosene poisoning.'

Eva reached up and shook out the envelope. Three green folded cards dropped out, impressively aged at the corners, and a long, beige ticket.

'Could I . . .' said Eva, smiling at Kasper. He realised he was still holding her hand and that she was tugging it away.

'Sorry,' he said, letting go.

'It's fine,' she said smiling, 'I just needed it.'

She reached forward and picked up the ticket. 'They're steamer tickets from Hamburg,' said Eva, almost whispering.

'They're for a ship. For two weeks tomorrow.' She opened one of the two blank ID cards. 'Anyone could put a picture in here,' she said, 'Just about anyone.'

They heard Kasper's father coughing in the other room and Kasper quickly put the tickets and cards back into the envelope and placed it on top of the box. He picked it up and looked around his kitchen.

'What are you going to do with it?'

'Hide it.'

'Then what?'

'I don't know. Probably sell it.'

Eva grasped his arm. 'Or use it. We could use it. It's perfect. Beckmann wouldn't mean anything if we get out – get right out. A father and daughter. It's like—'

'It's not fate,' said Kasper. 'This isn't your ticket out, Fräulein Hirsch. I'm sorry. You'll have other chances.'

'Other chances?'

'I'm sorry.'

Eva bit down on her lip. 'Please, Herr Meier, just think about . . .'

'I said no. Do you know what I could get for this? I have other things to worry about outside of myself and you.' He moved closer and whispered, 'I can't leave my father.'

Eva turned away from the tickets with apparent effort. 'Of course you can't. I'm being selfish.' She closed her eyes. 'I suppose I'll be off then.'

'Yes, I suppose,' said Kasper.

She nodded and left the room.

Kasper stood for a while holding the envelope and the little box. He saw himself and Eva standing at the front of a great Atlantic liner, her holding a hat onto her head, his old torn winter coat snapping behind him in the wind. He smelt salt water, tasted it on his lips and felt it stinging his face, heard gulls screeching. And then he saw towers, dark buildings, clustered together, looming out of the fog.

'She gone?' His father was at the door.

'What does it look like?'

'Can I eat some of your ham?'

'No, I need to save it in case I need it.'

'Seems silly just to leave it there when there are hungry people around. Hungry sick people. You were always terrible at sharing. I suppose that's my fault for not getting married again and having more children.'

'Hide this in your mattress, will you,' said Kasper.

'The box as well?'

'It's important. You're not a princess.'

'It's already like a shop in there.'

Kasper handed him the box and picked his coat up off the back of the other chair.

'Where are you going?' said the old man.

'I'm going out for a walk.'

'I know your walks. You won't be back till the middle of the night and you'll wake me up stumbling in drunk.'

'You should be more grateful,' said Kasper pushing past him. 'And don't eat any of that ham,' he said, dragging the door shut behind him.

On the street, Kasper held his head up and took in a deep lungful of the cool evening air, spiked with plaster and brick dust. Desperate to clear his mind of the tickets, of Eva, he ran through what he might usefully do now, right this minute, but each time it came back to her. And then, from some dark corner, came the image of Heinrich Neustadt. He had barely tried to find him, to silence him, and it could be done in an evening. Yes, he could fix something now, could do something. He pushed on, towards Frau Müller's, feeling purposeful, and began to pick over his relationship with Heinrich. Berating himself, his thoughts softened as he recalled the feeling of walking to the apartment in Sybelstraße to find Heinrich, of knowing that he was being waited for. He remembered the feeling of Heinrich embracing him and that pleasant guilty feeling, like smoking a last cigarette or having a last drink that you knew you didn't need – that mix of pleasurable guilt and inevitable disappointment. Tonight, though, Heinrich would have to pay for what he had done and in that moment, as he hopped from the pavement over a gaping crack in the road, Kasper was almost sorry about it.

A PAIR OF GREEN SHOES

Rolling in a half-sleep to try and ease the pain throbbing above his eyes, Kasper became aware of the forgotten sensation of turning his head in a plump, down-filled pillow and for a second his face came to rest in the cool cotton.

He jolted up onto his elbows, held his breath and stared at the strange pillow, then turned slowly to the empty space beside him. The sun shone blindingly onto the white sheets and the chipped paint of a narrow iron bed. Naked, confused and, he realised, horribly hungover, he was aware of the remnants of a nightmare: a church and a bride, Eva in the congregation, but younger – a child of eight or ten, Kasper searching the gathered celebrants, trying to guess which was Frau Beckmann, then seeing with horror that it was the veiled woman standing at his side.

He turned to take in the room: a medium-sized kitchen containing the bed he was in, a threadbare armchair, a small chair with a typewriter on it, an oven and a badly repaired occasional table, in front of which a naked man was standing running a plate under the tap and putting it on the side of the sink. The man was thickset with thinning hair, flecked with white, but black where it sat wiry at the base of his spine and down his legs.

Heinrich turned, his face beaming. Kasper was overcome with a weary sense of shame, of failure.

He looked back down at the beautiful pillow. He touched one of the bed's cool metal struts, a smooth brown patch where the paint had worn away. Beneath the pain in his head, the terrible taste in his mouth, the hungry ache in his stomach, he felt terribly sad. Sad for himself, for the vague memory of his drunken self, angry and determined, lingering near the door of Frau Müller's, then outside the apartment in Sybelstraße that they used to meet in, until he finally found Heinrich coming out of a bar he had often mentioned, near the edge of the Grunewald. Kasper had grabbed him from behind in the dark, pushed him up against the remains of a wall when he screamed and told him he was going to kill him; that he was going to kill him if he even mentioned Kasper's name again. If he ever ... But Heinrich had held onto him and Kasper collapsed beneath those arms that were so desperate to hold him, shaking and drunkenly crying until he felt the strange, beautifully familiar comfort of Heinrich's wet mouth on his neck.

But he also felt sad for Heinrich, for that ridiculous grin, for an indistinct memory of his wide grateful eyes in the dark, for his terrible, 'You've come back to me,' whispered in his ear, as Kasper pulled off his coat in the dark of the stairwell, as Kasper leant on him until he fell onto the bed.

'Where are we?' Kasper croaked.

'My place.'

'What about Sybelstraße?'

Heinrich paused. 'That's my sister's – do you remember?'

Kasper didn't. 'Yes, of course.' He rolled over onto his back and tried to rub some of the aching weight from his eyes. 'Isn't someone going to see us?' he said, gesturing at the curtainless windows.

'No, the building opposite's completely destroyed. Aren't any floors, so you couldn't even sneak in for a peek. Look,' Heinrich said, 'running water. Started yesterday.'

Kasper covered his eyes with his forearm. He heard Heinrich put the plate down and come over to the bed. The springs creaked as he sat down on the edge and put his thick, damp fingers on Kasper's naked belly. 'You all right? You look a bit peaky.'

'I'm fine,' said Kasper, 'just a little confused.'

'You were quite drunk, when you found me,' said Heinrich. 'Do you need to be sick?'

'No. I hope not.' Kasper swung himself out of bed, trying to extricate himself from Heinrich's touch, but the cast-off hand moved up his back and perched on his shoulder. Heinrich leant, reached across to kiss him, pursing his chapped lips, but Kasper stood, steadying himself on the bedpost before the lips reached his skin.

'Everything OK?'

'Fine,' said Kasper. 'I just need to get back home. My father,' he added, when Heinrich's gaze dropped to the floor and his hand began to nervously paw at his head, his fingers undulating along his thinning hairline.

'Can't you stay a bit?'

'No, I'm sorry,' he said, searching for his underwear and trousers, which he found had been cast off together and were sitting in the middle of the floor as if he'd been lifted out of them in one go.

'Why do you have to leave so quickly?'

'I think you know why,' Kasper snapped.

Heinrich looked down at the thin rug on the floor. Beneath it came the sound of a woman shouting at her children and a

145

baby's sharp wail. 'You weren't so unforgiving last night,' he said.

'I was drunk last night,' said Kasper, feeling wretched. 'I'm sorry – it was very wrong of me to come here.'

'I thought you'd forgiven me.'

'Well,' Kasper said. 'You've got me into a lot of trouble.'

Beneath them the door slammed and they heard little feet thundering on the staircase, down to the hallway and then onto the street. Heinrich touched the sheets and rubbed them gently with his middle finger. 'I thought you might eat something before you went.'

'Did you?' Kasper said.

'I've got some knackwurst.'

Kasper slowed as he was pulling on his vest. 'Sausages?'

'Yes, I know the butcher – he tipped me off.'

Kasper turned away from him and searched the kitchen counter. 'Where?' His stomach emitted a loud, audible squirt.

Heinrich took a paper packet from under his bed and opened it out, exposing two large knackwursts, not even dry; plump and red and spotted with fat. Kasper's mouth started watering. He looked up at Heinrich who was smiling at him tenderly. 'No,' said Kasper, 'They're yours.'

'Please,' Heinrich said. 'Stay. We don't need to talk about what happened. We can just eat.'

Kasper met his large cow eyes, the irises so dark that they bled into the blackness of his pupils. Heinrich blinked, and what appeared to be a hint of a tear widened the thin reflection of white light at the rim of his eyelids. Kasper nodded, yes. A loose smile fluttered across Heinrich's face. 'It's good,' he said, with undisguised relief. 'The sausages are really good.'

Kasper smiled tightly and finished dressing while Heinrich cut up the meat and sliced a small black loaf of rye bread.

'Are you going to put some clothes on?' Kasper said.

146

Heinrich laughed and said, 'Yes, I suppose I should,' and stopped what he was doing to pull on an all-in-one and then some trousers.

'Do you mind if I . . . ?' said Kasper pointing at the tap.

'I'm not sure if it's drinkable,' Heinrich said. 'I boiled some water. It's in that saucepan.' Kasper went to the stove and poked his finger in the water. It was only lukewarm, so he picked it up by the handle and gulped down the whole pan.

They sat down in silence and began to eat. The sausage tasted as good as it looked – skin that popped as he bit into it, soft smoky meat, even a smooth mustard seed that he left in his mouth for a while, rolling it around on his tongue.

'You don't seem to be doing badly for yourself,' said Kasper.

'What do you mean?'

'Good meat, those pillows.'

Heinrich shrugged. 'Just things I've exchanged.'

'Well, it's . . . it's impressive.'

Heinrich smiled and took a bite of bread. 'You're the expert.'

'Hardly,' said Kasper, pleased with the compliment.

Heinrich shifted in his seat. He pushed his plate forward a little with his thumb. 'It's funny,' he said, 'I saw that old accordion player, the other day.' He looked up, smiling.

Kasper shook his head slightly. 'I don't . . . '

'Do you remember? He used to play at the corner of Sybelstraße and he would always play "Die Gedanken sind frei", except when he thought you were a soldier and then he would play the national anthem of that country.'

Kasper feigned a vague recollection.

'You remember!' said Heinrich. 'But he always got it wrong. And he used to play the "Marseillaise" whenever he saw us.'

Kasper could suddenly see the man's face, twisted in song. 'Yes,' he said, laughing, 'He wasn't that old though.'

'No, he was probably thirty or forty, wasn't he. And he always did that little dance when he played the "Marseillaise", as if he thought that made it especially French.' And Heinrich mimicked the silly little jumping dance in his chair, pumping his hands back and forth. Kasper laughed, he laughed hard – it was exactly right, it was exactly how the funny little man had danced.

'Yes,' he said, 'God, that's good. Yes.'

Their laughter faded away, but they kept smiling.

Heinrich took another bite of his bread. Kasper looked down at Heinrich's hand holding a centimetre of black crust. His fingers were short and covered with curling black hairs, but his fingernails were short and smooth, the beds tidy and clean. Heinrich dropped the bread and brought his hand up to his face. 'Are they ugly?'

'No,' said Kasper. Heinrich looked up at him so wounded, that Kasper said, 'No, you have nice hands.'

Heinrich's mouth opened slightly revealing the bottom curves of his front teeth. He smiled and picked up the bread again, looking down at it between his fingers in wonder as if it was a sentimental treasure, just unearthed. 'You remember,' he said, almost in a whisper.

Kasper smiled supportively and took another slice of sausage. 'Remember what?' he said.

'Was it nineteen-twenty-nine?' he said, and then, laughing at himself, 'I know it was twenty-nine. I'd been coming to your bar for months.'

Kasper's smile weakened and he fixed his eyes back on his plate.

'Others – some of those awful old queens – they were always harping away about your Phillip, but, you know, from the moment I went down those steps and I saw you ... it was always you.'

'Heinrich,' said Kasper, but Heinrich held up his hand to stop him.

'Just a moment – because one day Phillip wasn't there—'

'Heinrich,' said Kasper again.

'No, let me finish … He was away for a whole week. And on the first day he was gone, and in the first hour you passed my table and you looked down at my hands and you said, "you have nice hands". Just as you did then – that exact tone of voice. And I thought, he's noticed me. He's noticed me. He's always …'

'Heinrich, don't!' said Kasper.

Heinrich looked up at him, stung. Then he nodded his head, slowly, but firmly. 'I know,' he said, 'I didn't know if you would be able to forgive me, but I thought you'd left me – you have to understand. I didn't believe for a second you were coming back. I was angry, just very angry. And Beckmann paid me and she just asked if I knew anyone like me – like us – who might be able to help them find information and might be … vulnerable – if they refused to help. I was angry Kasper and I gave her your name and I regretted it straight away and if I can do anything to help you now I would. You know I would.'

'Do you have any idea how much trouble you've got me into?'

'They just needed some more information – I thought you'd accept the deal.'

'They're blackmailing me. And not that poor girl, who's just some pawn – this Frau Beckmann. And her children, for God's sake – they're terrorising me.'

'What do you mean?' Heinrich said, his face falling.

'They're leaving notes – vicious notes – that anyone could find, they attacked me in my apartment, they're following me – I can't work. I can't do any trading without having some warning shoved into my hand.'

Heinrich shook his head desperately, his mouth hanging open like a fish. 'I didn't know,' he said. 'I've been working for her –

getting information for her – and it's been fine. I haven't had any trouble, otherwise I'd never have given them your name.'

'You said they needed someone vulnerable, someone like you. You just said that.'

'Yes, I know,' Heinrich said, 'I know. But that was just protection, I thought – so that you wouldn't want to go to any authorities. I didn't think that they were going to come to your apartment. Or the notes. I didn't know she was going to send the twins.'

'Oh, so you know the twins.'

Heinrich nodded. 'And they're terrible,' he said quietly. 'But I didn't think they'd be involved in this.'

Heinrich stared miserably at the table. He had turned pale and Kasper was afraid he was going to start crying. 'I'm so sorry,' he whispered. 'I was angry, but I didn't think this would happen. Not like this.'

He reached over to touch Kasper's hand, but he pulled it away. Heinrich snatched his hands up to his mouth as if they'd been burnt. 'I can help you,' he cried.

Kasper's knee hit the bottom of the table in shock causing the plates and the cutlery to jump in a clattering jangle. 'For God's sake, Heinrich!' he said, wanting desperately to stop talking and to be gone. 'It doesn't matter now. It's done now.'

'If I'd known what this Beckmann wanted, I wouldn't have said anything, no matter what they were offering. I misunderstood. And I was frightened. Her children . . . I hear things about them – awful things.'

'I don't want to know. I don't want to know anything about it.'

'I can help you.'

'I don't need any help.' Kasper finished his sausage quickly, determined not to incite any more emotion from the man, just to be pleasant and reassuring, to finish his food and then to leave.

He swallowed the dry bread too fast and it dragged down his oesophagus in a dry, painful lump. He put his fist to his mouth.

'Do you want some more water?' said Heinrich.

Kasper shook his head.

Heinrich looked at him sadly and hopefully.

Kasper searched around for a subject, something that might distract Heinrich and briefly imply interest. 'You don't have to share with anyone here then? Not even family?'

'No, they all shipped out. My siblings, my sister and her children. I told you that. You know all this.' Heinrich was frowning.

'Yes, of course,' said Kasper, but couldn't recall any of it. 'Did you tell me they'd shipped out?' he said.

Heinrich nodded and took a bite of his rye bread, a few crumbs escaping, falling down onto his chin, dropping and finally nesting in the chest hair at the open neck of his all-in-one. 'To Brazil – we have family over there, in the South.'

Kasper nodded. 'Was that easy to organise?' he said. 'I mean, how did they manage it?'

Heinrich put his bread down and crossed his arms. 'You're not ... You're not planning to go are you? To leave Berlin, or anything? Because of what I've done?'

'No, not at all,' said Kasper. 'It's a friend. Someone I know who might be able to get hold of some tickets – or at least that's what he's been told. They sort of fell into his lap, but he's not sure how flexible it all is.'

'A friend?'

'That's right. Not close.'

Heinrich unfolded his arms and took a bite out of his sausage. 'What do you mean by flexible?'

'I don't know,' said Kasper, pleased that Heinrich was engaging with a line of conversation that didn't involve the two of them, 'Whether you've heard of people not being allowed on

151

board, problems being German, getting into other countries.'

'They're pretty keen on young people and people with skills.'

'What about someone older – would they not let someone in who was old and sick? If he was someone's father?'

Heinrich shrugged. 'To be honest, I don't know in that much detail. Where's this friend thinking of going?'

Kasper licked his finger and wiped up the last crumbs on the plate. 'It was nothing planned, I think. Just something he was considering.'

Heinrich finished his bread and picked up a serrated knife. 'Do you want another slice?'

'No, I've got to go,' said Kasper. 'You've been generous enough.'

'I see,' said Heinrich, not hiding his disappointment.

Kasper nodded and smiled, then got up to leave.

Heinrich searched Kasper's face, then the room, his mouth opening, desperate for something to say. 'Look,' he said standing, 'I'm going to help you. I have to help you.'

'Heinrich – it's done now. I will deal with it.'

'But I can help. I've met Frau Beckmann. She's not a monster and you could make a deal with her – I know you could. Perhaps her children have got above their station – she probably knows nothing about it. You could stop this if you could talk to her, I know you could.'

'Eva doesn't seem to think so.'

'Who's Eva?'

'The rubble girl she sent to blackmail me.'

'Well, I'm sure the girl can't. She's hard on those girls.'

Kasper crossed his arms and said, 'You really think Frau Beckmann would stop these twins?'

'If you still gave her the information. I'm sure of it. She's not unreasonable, but you need some protection from those children, if they've got you in their sights. I've heard things.'

'I don't want to know.'

Heinrich went to the drawer by the sink and found a pencil and a torn Russian pamphlet in a coat hanging on the back of the door. He sat back down, tore off a strip and wrote some notes. 'Here,' he said, handing it to Kasper.

'What's this?'

'The top bit is Frau Beckmann's address in Sybelstraße.'

'Where your sister's apartment is?'

'That's right. I'm sure that's where she saw me and you together – why she singled us out. If she was there, maybe you could reason with her. At least get the twins off your back. I'm sure she thinks they're helping you find whatever you need to find. If she knew the truth . . . '

'I thought she worked on the rubble?'

'She does, but she's back and forth. Worth trying the apartment. I've met her there during the day before. And I don't know where her rubble group works.'

Kasper pictured her and Eva chipping away at bricks on Pariser Straße, but said, 'A shame – they could be anywhere.'

Heinrich nodded. 'It's worth a try at least. There's always a deal to be made.'

'Maybe,' said Kasper.

'Will you go there today? For me?'

'Maybe,' Kasper said.

'You can stay here until then,' Heinrich said. 'It's closer than your place – I have a little brandy and the wireless works. I fixed it.'

'No, but thank you,' Kasper said. 'It's a trading day.' He looked at Heinrich's slim, curling handwriting on the paper strip, at the second name and address. 'Is that Spielmann as in Otto Spielmann?' Kasper said.

'Yes – he came back.'

Kasper smirked, recalling Spielmann leaning on his bar, stroking the arms of some new boy who had wandered in unexpectedly.

And at some point he would whisper into the boy's ear and if the boy smiled they would leave together without finishing their drinks. 'I thought he was killed in Russia,' Kasper said.

'He was a POW, but he was demobbed a few months ago.'

'Who was that meat-headed thug who was always following him around?'

Heinrich laughed. 'Linden! He's still around.'

'No!' said Kasper. 'How did those two survive the Eastern front?'

'Snuggling up to keep warm?'

Kasper laughed. 'Weren't you there?'

'No,' Heinrich said, put out again at Kasper's misremembering, 'I was in France.'

'Yes, of course,' Kasper said. 'Of course, I remember now.' He looked back down at the note. 'What would I need to see Spielmann for?'

'What did anyone need to see Spielmann for?'

Kasper's heart sank. He shook his head. 'I don't need a gun.'

'What about the twins? What they say about those twins. If I'd known, when they came to see me . . .'

'What am I going to do – shoot them?'

'No. Just so you can scare them.'

Kasper shook his head and put the paper in his pocket.

'At least go and see Beckmann – you could go now. I'm sure you can sort this out between you. All she cares about is the information and she's got a network, Kasper – what a network. If you can get her on side, show her how useful you are, it might be a good thing, what's happened. You might look back on this and think, God, after all that, what Heinrich did was a good thing in the end.'

Kasper pictured the twins following him there, holding the door shut as Beckmann pushed him up against the wall, a gun to his throat. 'Not straight away,' Kasper said, 'I need to sort a few things out first.' Heinrich looked as if he was about to cry again. 'But I'll go this afternoon,' said Kasper. 'Once I've secured a few things, OK? I'll be fine.'

Heinrich smiled, comforted.

'Look,' Kasper said, 'If I'm going to get to Berlin Zoo and trade, run these errands and get to Beckmann I'll have to go now. I can't stay all day.'

'Yes,' Heinrich said, seeming to believe that his advice was being taken. 'You used to call me Heinchen, do you remember?' he said, smiling.

'Really?' Kasper said. 'I don't remember that.'

Heinrich's smile faded. He touched the tip of the pencil in his hand, then put it down on the table beside the plate he had been eating off. 'It's petty holding a grudge, Kasper. I'll say it again: I didn't know what Beckmann was going to do. I thought you'd left me. I thought you weren't coming back. I know I've got a temper, but ...'

'It's not about Beckmann.'

'I know what you think about me.'

'I don't think anything,' Kasper said.

'You think I'm stupid, or ... You think I'm small-time, you think I'm provincial.'

'Small-time?' said Kasper, 'What are you talking about?' He frowned in angry feigned confusion, because that's exactly how he felt about him. He was a sad small-time man – tedious and pedestrian. Even in Kasper's most affectionate moments, when he had held him tightly and drunkenly, he had only taken pleasure in Heinrich's pleasure, in holding someone who was so desperate to be held.

'Why did you even come looking for me last night?'

'I thought we'd just ... you know, have a nice evening, and ... I was drunk, and ...'

'That's nice.'

155

'I don't mean that . . . '

Heinrich looked up at him, his mouth stretched wide, trying desperately to hold back tears that were already falling from his eyes in big wet drops. 'You can't just use me when you feel sorry for yourself. I don't want you pitying me.'

Kasper, angry at having his feelings dictated back to him so accurately snapped back, 'No, Heinrich, I don't pity you. I don't feel anything. I don't feel anything for you.'

The muscles in Heinrich's face relaxed and his eyes lost focus. His hand went limp and dropped to the table.

Kasper felt pathetic and cruel, but didn't it have to be said? Wasn't this his last chance? 'And if you think it's a great idea to go running to Fräulein Hirsch, or Beckmann, or whoever it might be, because of all this, you'll be in trouble. Things are going to get pretty rough for you, understand?'

Heinrich looked up, his eyes thin black slits beneath his lowering brow. His limp mouth closed and his lips thinned. 'The way you treat me, even when I help you . . . Whatever I do . . .' he whispered and dropped his gaze to the plate again. 'You'll be sorry one day – you'll look back and be sorry about the way you treated me.'

Kasper shook his head. 'Heinrich,' he said, 'Look, I'm sorry now, but you can't . . . ' Heinrich didn't look up again. He sat back down at the table and seemed to stare through it into the apartment below. Kasper did want to make amends, but the draw of leaving, going through the door and leaving, was far stronger than any desire to alleviate Heinrich's pain. It had been cruel to find him, to treat him the way he had, but, God, just to be outside. He turned towards the door, paused, but decided not to look over his shoulder at Heinrich. He turned the handle, exited and pulled the door softly shut behind him. He slipped away, down the stairs and out of the house.

*

Kasper came out into the sunny street, blinking, tired and terribly sorry. But as he descended the short row of steps in front of the block, a ripple of pain folded over his eye, knocking away the shame in his stomach. It was just the schnapps, he thought, but then: perhaps a stroke. He imagined a shocking wave of pain and a sudden blackness; being drawn, cool and dark, into unconsciousness, beneath the ground. He didn't believe in anything beyond death, how could he, but he would be the same as his Phillip. Seeing his eyes, perhaps a final touch, his morning stubble against Kasper's cheek, briefly conscious of the smell of his body, before the eyes would finally close.

There was a bang – a crack like a shot from a gun. He looked up and realised that he was standing still. A little boy stood alone on the street, one strap of his dungarees missing. He was holding a cobblestone with a white edge where he had just struck it against a piece of fallen plaster; a section of a frieze with the end of a spear and the head of a lion. He looked up at Kasper, his shadow dark purple on the dusty street. When Kasper didn't say anything, he looked away and struck the plaster again, sending shards flying from the lion's head and echoes ricocheting off the walls of the surrounding apartment blocks.

A plaster ear spun across the ground and came to rest in front of Kasper's toe, over a white chalked line. He followed the line and saw that it was part of a larger picture. He looked back up at the windows of Heinrich's flat above him, then down at the lines again.

'Did you draw this?' said Kasper.

The boy turned to him and shook his head.

Kasper stepped backwards, back towards the house, to the shade of the building and saw that the lines made up a large crudely drawn eye, with stubby eyelashes. The iris was coloured in white and inside the pupil Kasper could make out two stickmen holding hands. They had nooses around their necks. At first he thought that the men had been given vaginas, but what he had understood as guns, he now saw were depictions of two dismembered penises, the mess at the men's crotches, the wounds where the genitals had been sliced off.

Kasper felt dizzy, his lips wet. 'Who drew this?' he said.

The boy stopped again and turned to him, squinting. 'It was there already.'

'Was it here yesterday?'

'No,' said the boy. 'It was there this morning.'

Kasper looked up and down the road. The main part of the street had been cleared of rubble. It had been pushed into great piles, sitting between the entrances of those buildings that were still standing. He looked up at some of the intact windows, but either the sun or the shade was too strong for him to see anything behind them. He searched the doorways, the piles of rubble, the remains of a ruined car, but there were too many places to hide for two young teenagers. He pulled at his collar – it felt tight and was scratching at his neck – his heart was beating hard.

He turned and walked quickly onto the adjoining street, which was long and wide and had been fully cleared. There were three remaining trees on the road and their budding green leaves seemed incongruously fresh in comparison to their surroundings. In one direction he could see a woman talking to two soldiers sitting in a Jeep and in the other a group of people waiting by a temporary bus sign. A teenage boy with black hair was sitting on an old toilet that had been dragged onto the pavement.

Kasper walked up the street and joined the group of people at the bus stop.

'Excuse me, but where does this bus go?' he asked a thin old woman in a camel-coloured coat.

She looked up at him and stared for a second at his dead eye. 'Zoo,' she said.

Kasper nodded. 'Perfect.' He lit up a thin cigarette, his hands shaking again. Of course he could do a deal with Beckmann, he thought. Her twins were surely idiots and she probably had no idea how violent they had become. All of the other fools she had dealt with were likely too afraid to deal with them properly and too stupid to get an address for Beckmann and use it. But then what sort of mother would send her children out to hunt down contacts for her? A large, brutish figure formed in his head, giant and powerful, her children clutching at her legs, staring out at him angry and spiteful. Perhaps a visit to Spielmann on the way to Sybelstraße wasn't such a terrible idea, he thought, and he shook out his arms to try and rid them of their trembling.

The old woman who'd given him directions looked up at Kasper's cigarette and then at Kasper and said, 'Are you selling anything?'

Kasper took a drag and said, 'I'm always selling everything. What have you got to exchange?'

She shrugged. 'Depends what you want.'

Kasper bit his lip. He looked at the woman's wrinkled, frowning face and felt miserable and angry. 'Well, this is a fun game,' he said. 'Let's say I'll potentially take anything you've got if I can use it.'

The woman looked at him suspiciously, then looked down into a well-used brown paper bag that she was holding. She lifted it up and held it against her waist and reached in, slowly pulling out a battered tin.

'What is it?' said Kasper.

'Shoe polish.'

There was another crack, like gunshot. Kasper started and stared in the direction he'd come from.

'You're jumpy,' said the woman. 'You all right?'

'Of course,' said Kasper. He turned back to her. 'How much

159

is in there?' She opened the lid to reveal a little dry, cracked lump sitting at the bottom. 'Not on your life. What else?'

'It's very good polish. It's from London.'

'And I'm from Leningrad. What else?'

The woman huffed and put the lid back on the tin protectively, dropped it back into the bag and pulled out a wool tie and two almost complete candles, to which he shook his head. 'Well,' she said.

'Well what?' said Kasper. 'Are you keeping something from me? The good stuff you're going to trade at Zoo?'

She tilted her head and then drew something out, wrapped in a soft rag, which she opened up to reveal a pair of green, leather women's shoes, with a medium heel and almost no damage, just a few scratches on the black soles.

'Now,' said Kasper, putting the cigarette between his lips and holding out his hands, to take the shoes, which were given up reluctantly. 'Yes,' he said, turning them over and inspecting them gently like a pair of prize racing pigeons. 'I'll give you twenty cigarettes.'

'Twenty!' said the woman, grabbing them back off him. 'Ridiculous. These are my daughter's. She's dead. She only wore them once, just round the house to try and break them in, but she never got to wear them out. She was killed. She was a dancer.'

'Big feet for a dancer,' he said, 'I'll give you twenty-five cigarettes, final offer.' The woman huffed and turned her back to him, rewrapping the shoes delicately and placing them in the bag, before walking round to the other side of the temporary sign. The boy that was sitting on the old toilet looked up at him, his grubby face squinting. 'What?' said Kasper, 'Have you got something to sell?'

The boy shook his head, but kept staring at Kasper's face. 'What?' said Kasper.

'What happened to your eye?'

'Your mum scratched it out when I was fucking her.'

The boy turned away from him; the shoe woman and the other man at the bus stop grumbled to themselves and moved another two paces further down the road. Kasper turned away from them, embarrassed, and rubbed his eyes. He opened his mouth to say something to the boy, to make amends, but it was useless – he just sneered and the boy turned away, afraid.

After twenty minutes the bus came and was already full. Kasper squeezed on, staying on the lower deck, making him briefly nostalgic for the smell and sound of an empty bus. He scoured the crowd, but it was only made up of women and two old men. The shoe woman was pressed against his chest, but was trying hard to pretend she didn't know he was there. He was aware that he still stank of alcohol and the taste of it was leaking back into his mouth, overtaking the pleasant taste of real sausage. And yet he felt a confidence growing in him as he considered the day ahead, a lightness, a clarity. Snatches of his evening and morning with Heinrich made him briefly miserable.

He looked down at the back of the woman's head. Her hair was thin and greasy, but it looked like she'd tried to make it fashionable, by putting it into curlers that morning – though the curls had now all but fallen out – and by clipping the side with what may have once been something made out of ivory, but which was now so broken that it looked as if she had a splinter of bone in her hair. As the bus slowed down Kasper fished something out of his pocket and leant down, his hand appearing in front of the woman's face holding the mother-of-pearl hairclip that he'd bought two days earlier from a child out-of-breath from running – a bargain for just five cigarettes that he'd already shortened by emptying a little of the tobacco out of each one, after he convinced the little boy that the clip was made of plastic. The shoe woman's eyes widened as Kasper turned it in his fingers, the small amount of light in the dim downstairs of the bus still catching the iridescent blues, greens and purples, like peacock feathers.

'I'll give you this hairclip and fifty cigarettes for everything in your bag,' he said. 'You can get off at the next stop and you're still close enough to walk home – a trip saved.'

He pushed the clip into her hair and, with his other hand coming up under her arm, he wrapped her fingers around fifty cigarettes as his other hand left the clip and made its way down to the thick roll of paper at the top of the bag. He tugged at it gently until the woman's grip loosened and he was able to pluck it from her. She reached up and touched the clip on her head, and keeping her hand there, she moved forward as the bus slowed to a stop and jumped off the step into the street, fingering the clip protectively as she walked away.

THE HEEL OF A SHOE

Kasper leant against the railings with his back to the Spree, facing the Lustgarten. In the middle of the great open expanse – flanked by the antique ruins of the Schloßpalast, the Berliner Dom and the Neues Museum – an attractive woman was talking to a pair of Russian troops. She was short, perhaps five-foot-four, and her thick hair had been set into a glossy brown coiffure that radiated away from her forehead and reached the base of her neck. She could have been twenty-five, though she was actually ten years older. The skin on her well-fed face had already turned a nutty brown colour in the little sun afforded by the middling beginning of Berlin's spring. She exuded an air of health that was rare in the city and caused passing groups of women to eye her disdainfully, because they could guess how she got the food to fatten up her cheeks. She was leaning up against a large placard, cemented into the dusty white of the ground, with a picture of Stalin on it and to the right of her stood an identically sturdy placard that read:

The Red Army is free from feelings of racial hatred. It is free from such a debased feeling, because it has been raised on the equality of races and regard for the rights of other peoples.

Kasper had stood at the same vantage point on a sunny May Day in 1937. He saw the square that day, dressed in a disturbing recreation of Imperial Rome, surrounded by row upon row of soldiers holding the crowd into a neat pattern, long red flags flanking both sides of the gardens, their swastikas perfectly aligned. A giant Maypole had been erected in the centre, which, like the church behind it, the Nazis had claimed for themselves, decking out the topmost point with more thin red flags, strung up on thick rope, flapping in the spring breeze like bodies hung from a tree. Kasper had come with Phillip to gawp at the crowd and laugh at the pomposity of it. Phillip. Phillip Vögt. The pain came like a brain haemorrhage, spreading down through his body, and he turned away from the square dizzily and looked down into the brown water of the Spree.

They had laughed. They had sat on the railing, then intact, Phillip with his legs wide open, so that one knee touched Kasper's. Kasper did an impression of one of the officers leading the parade that was now making its way down from Alexanderplatz, marching ridiculously slowly, his mouth set in a rictus grimace. A group of women had shot glances at them and a boy dressed up in his Hitler Youth garb spat on the floor in front of them. Phillip had laughed so hard that he fell backwards off the railing and was only saved from falling into the filthy water when Kasper grabbed his arm and dragged him back over the railing, onto his feet, where they collapsed into backslapping giggles.

Kasper smiled a resigned thin smile at the thought of Phillip's deep, ridiculous laugh. And for an agonising second he was overwhelmed by the memory of Phillip's stale breath in the morning and the sweat in his shirt at the end of the day, the feel of his belly beneath Kasper's hand, the sound of him in the kitchen making coffee in the morning, the fleck of brown in his blue eyes, the patches of light hair at his temples that were fading from blond, to ash blond, to grey, the mole on his lip, the chewed fingernails, the down on his earlobes, the crooked tooth in his bottom set, the white scar on his buttock from sitting on a broken bottle in a Mainz beer garden by the Rhine when he was twelve.

Kasper pushed himself away from the railing and took a few deep breaths, his hand on his chest. He thought about the snow. He bit into his lip and slowly he was able to look back at the woman who had been talking to the Russian soldiers. They were now sloping away from her and she was pulling out a cigarette from a small metal case that she slipped into her skirt once the cigarette was lit.

Kasper started moving towards her disinterestedly as if he was just trying to cross the great clearing in the rubble to get to the other side. He passed her and then, as if noticing the smell of smoke from her cigarette, he turned back and asked her if she had a light.

She feigned confusion and said, 'Pardon?'

'A light,' said Kasper taking out a cigarette. 'Have you got a light?'

'Oh,' she said, 'yes,' and held her cigarette in her mouth and took out a Red Army issue lighter.

Except for the distant sound of a heavy vehicle somewhere behind him, the square was almost silent; he could hear the crackling of the tobacco as the cigarette lit and the amber line of embers moved towards his lips.

They started walking across the Lustgarten up towards Unter den Linden.

'What are you doing up here? I thought you were meeting me at Frau Müller's this afternoon.'

'I've got an appointment with someone now,' Kasper said, 'and I'm not sure when I'm going to be done. I've sorted out your penicillin, so I thought I'd just come and find you – didn't take me long.'

'Oh you are a darling, Kasper. Where is it?' said the woman.

'Charlottenburg.'

'Can you get it nearer?'

'I don't want to lose it. If I get stopped I'll be less likely to get away.'

'And why is that?' she said.

'You're more charming, Marta.'

She laughed. 'Is it anywhere near the border?'

'Five minutes away, maybe ten.'

Marta shrugged. 'OK. I'll pick it up tonight. Who do I talk to?'

'Frau Hannover,' said Kasper. 'The address is 102 Schillerstraße.'

'Hardly a side street.'

'You didn't ask for a side street.'

Kasper heard the crackle of splintering wood and looked up into the burnt-out windows in the high, monumental walls around them, but saw no one. Falling timber and masonry rattled down as the broken building settled. 'What do you need that much penicillin for, anyway?' he said.

'You get a bomb for it from my girls and the other madams – there's not a thing you can catch that it can't cure. Except babies, I suppose.'

'No cure for that.'

'Certainly nothing one can speak of in polite society,' she said.

'If there's anything left or any opened vials, I can sell them back to Dr Hoffmann,' Kasper said.

'There won't be anything left. What's in your horrid little sack?'

'None of your business,' Kasper said, hugging the brown paper bag to his chest.

Marta raised her eyebrows. She pointed to a left-hand turning up ahead. 'Let's end up at Gendarmenmarkt. I'm not catching much here.'

'You make it sound like fishing.'

'It's not dissimilar,' she said, 'The bait, the waiting, the grim ending.'

'Can't you give this up, now that you've got yourself a harem of your own?'

'The cut I get from that lot for a week doesn't pay as well as one drunk soldier will. I try to do as little as possible, but who's getting so much these days that they can forgo anything?'

'I suppose,' Kasper said.

'I'll leave your cigarettes with Frau Müller tonight.'

'If you don't mind I'd rather have some information,' said Kasper.

'Really? From me? For all that penicillin? Who on earth do I have to fuck?'

Kasper smiled. 'Any RAF in your British boys?'

'Of course darling. They're the handsome ones – pay well and not too much weird stuff.'

'You're sounding very cheerful today.'

'It's the sunshine, Kasper darling. And spring. You can feel the city coming back to life. Starting to breathe again.' She inhaled deeply and pushed her hand dramatically against her breasts.

'You can smell it coming back to life,' said Kasper.

A Jeep drove past, followed by a truck full of Russian soldiers. One of the soldiers in the back jeered something and Marta turned and threw up her hand enthusiastically as if she was waving off a warship at the docks. The soldiers shouted and whistled. She fell back into step with Kasper and laughed. 'Those Russians.'

'Most of those Russians won't pay for it.'

'They will if it's good enough; if it's what the general's getting. There's the most wonderful rumour among them at the moment that some ghostly woman is going around doing them all in. Some Frenchman flew out of a window over near Savignyplatz.'

'Strong woman! And I haven't noticed the numbers going down.'

'No,' said Marta, 'Quite. I mean they're all quietly shooting each other the whole time – I'm sure it's all a big cover up, but some of them have this idea that the ghosts of their rapees are coming back to kill them or some Amazonian group of women vigilantes are going round getting their revenge. It's all rather gothic. Anyway, I stopped you. British boys?'

'Yes. I need to find an RAF man. He'll be at Gatow, but I need to have a few other locations for him – where someone could reach him. By the sound of it, he doesn't want to be found, so it might require a bit of coaxing, if you know what I mean.'

'All too well. What do you know about him?'

'He's ginger . . .'

'Oh, I'll have to get one of the girls involved. They're very discreet. I just can't bear the ginger bushes. Oh, but you had a ginger, didn't you? That little Rhineland Communist.'

'That was Spielmann's boy.'

'Oh,' said Marta, 'I saw Spielmann. I couldn't believe it – I thought he was six feet under in Pomerania. And that ghastly Linden. Freshly demobbed – he didn't starve out there, more's the pity.'

'I'd heard he was back.'

'Who told you?'

'Heinrich Neustadt.'

Marta put the back of one hand up to her mouth as if she was going to be sick and slapped him across the shoulder with the other. 'Oh God, Kasper, you're not sniffing around that again, are you? Is that why he's suddenly all shiny shoes and double chins?'

'No,' Kasper said. 'We ... I ... well, I bumped into him. But you're right, he does seem to be doing well for himself.'

'Oh, you know what it is? It's that Beckmann. Fattening him up like Hansel.'

'You know Frau Beckmann?'

'Of course,' Marta said. 'Everyone knows Beckmann.'

'I didn't until last week.'

'Don't tell me you're trading for her now? Everyone's trading for her. God help us if she moves into the prostitution racket.'

'No, not trading for her. Well, not on purpose. She's black-mailing me.'

'The little bitch.'

'I know,' Kasper said. 'Is she just black market, then? Is this all that this is about?'

'I don't know exactly,' said Marta, 'because she doesn't work directly. I've never met her, it's just that people are always doing things for her, or for people who work for her. She works through other people. That nosey little boy you use ...'

'Christian?'

'Yes, him – grubby little bugger – he came to me a few weeks ago trying to pay me off with some very dodgy looking Reichmarks and a hairdryer.'

'Did you give it to him?'

'The information? Of course. I haggled that poor boy to death, but I got cigarettes – packets of them – tinned meat and chocolate, for God's sake. They weren't coming from him, and I'm sure he didn't get them from you. This was quality stuff – very good. And I never saw him again – the soldier, I mean. Stepan, I think. No, Sergei. Sweet boy, as well.'

'Was he British?'

'With a name like Sergei? No, he was Russian. Young lad.'

'So Christian's working with Beckmann?'

'No,' said Marta, 'that's the thing. He was getting the information for some widow that worked on a rubble group with Beckmann.'

'Wasn't military was it?'

'I honestly can't remember now, darling. And then Linden came to see me last week – that's why I saw Spielmann. That knuckle-head came and found me at the cinema and I refused to speak to him. And then Spielmann arrives, who you never see alone out of the house, and asks me if I still know anyone from the bar, just casually, like that, as if I didn't know that Linden had been snooping around. I pushed him and pushed him until he eventually said that some short-haired woman who buys guns off him – guns in the plural – wanted the information. She works with Beckmann directly, but she didn't come to see me – she sent Spielmann.'

Kasper felt breathless and his palms began to sweat. 'Why did she want names of people from the bar? Did he say?'

'Well, by the sound of it, to blackmail them. I'm sure it's got nothing to do with you, just that it was the sort of bar it was. They'd have probably tried to blackmail me if there was anyone left to care about what I was doing. Then again, they all seem to be doing all right out of it – Spielmann, and certainly Heinrich if he's involved too. You seem to be getting the thin end of the wedge, though.'

'Jesus Christ,' Kasper said.

'I wish I could tell you how to get to her, Kasper, but I've never even met the woman, nor anyone that works with her directly.'

'Oh, I know a few,' Kasper said. 'And I've got an address for her.'

'Really?' Marta said, she bit her cheek. 'Be careful, if you're going to go for her. She's everywhere. Shit!' She stopped suddenly and held onto Kasper's arm as she lifted her leg behind her to inspect the sole of her shoe. 'I've ruined the heel.' She peeled the thick leather from the bottom of it and slipped it into her pocket. As they walked on her feet made a strange double click, as the metal in the broken heel cracked onto the ground.

'So this information you need me to get about the pilot's for Beckmann?'

'That's right.'

'Well, if you need me to get it for you, darling, I'll do it. You know I will.'

'Eva Hirsch, this girl she sent to get the information. She told me something about Germans killing soldiers who've been with German women.'

'There have been these rumours about the women, like I said, but I'm sure they're bunkum. And I haven't heard anything about German men killing soldiers. All sounds far too honourable for Berlin.'

'And a bit too neat,' said Kasper.

'I'm sure it's far more sordid than that. The women who work for Beckmann – they're around for a while, but then you don't see them again – they go missing. You warn this girl of yours – it's all rather fishy.'

'She's not my girl,' Kasper said. 'She can look after herself.' He pictured some faceless woman dropping Eva's body into the Spree. 'Missing in what way?'

'Not dead, I don't think. You just don't see them again. Tell me about this pilot then? Am I going to get anything more than ginger?'

'Oh, yes. Gap in his front teeth, a couple of centimetres shorter than me. He has a moustache and hangs out at Willy's bar.'

'What a dive!' Marta tripped slightly on an upended paving slab. 'And that's it?' she said.

'That's all I've got. Oh, except that my friend thinks he has some sort of regional accent.'

They were now on the Gendarmenmarkt. The buildings here were also grand and imperial, but smaller and more intact than those surrounding the Lustgarten. When they reached the corner of the square she stopped walking and turned to him. 'The RAF is probably full of ginger pilots with bad teeth.'

'Probably,' said Kasper. 'But do your best. Maybe see if there's a Beckmann connection.'

Marta took his hand. 'And then Beckmann's going to leave you alone?'

'That's what this rubble girl says.'

'Well, I'd get some security on that if I were you,' Marta said.

Kasper smiled at her. 'I've got something in mind.'

The breeze carried ash and dust across the stone slabs and they both squinted as a gust threw it up into their faces.

'Well, it doesn't sound like much of a stretch,' Marta said. 'Do you want me to dig out a queer one for you?'

'No thank you.'

Marta looked down at his hand sadly. 'You know, I passed the bar in Kopenhagener Straße the other day.'

'Really?' said Kasper. 'Is it still there?'

'No – it's a wreck. You haven't been past? Just to see if it was still standing?'

'No.'

'You don't like talking about old times, do you?'

Kasper let go of her and put his hands in his pockets. 'I try not to.'

'Oh,' said Marta, 'but we had fun didn't we? I was so happy. I don't think I'll ever be as happy. Sometimes, especially through the last winter or when some Russian's sweating away on top of me, I close my eyes and I think of your bar.' She shut her eyes and breathed in, then shook her head smiling. 'I think about the smell of the smoke and the music. I think about the chatter. I think about Phillip at the bar, you behind it and the taste of champagne.' She opened her eyes. Kasper was staring blankly away from her at the ground.

'You never . . .' He was going to make a joke, but he shrugged it off, shrugged off the gaze and began to walk backwards away from her. Turning, he said, 'Thanks Marta. See how you do with that ginger pilot.'

She smiled and waved him off and he listened to the double click of her shoes making their way across the square to the group of Russian soldiers standing by the statue of Schiller.

IGOR MASLOV

The surgeon stood over Igor grimacing, scratching at a small patch of psoriasis on his face. He swept the flakes of skin off his tunic unselfconsciously and said, 'What was your stool like this morning?'

'It was normal,' said Igor.

'And you have no temperature?' said Dr Yablonski.

'No. No temperature.'

The doctor nodded sagely. 'The stool is nature's thermometer,' he read the name off his ward notes, 'Maslov. There is almost nothing I couldn't diagnose if I was able to see everyone's stool.' His request to do so had been denied.

Igor had in fact not had a bowel movement that morning, but the former schoolteacher with ulcers down his leg, who was in the bed next to him, had told him it was best to lie to avoid censure. He had said that a sniper from his unit had not produced a stool for a week and Dr Yablonski had wheeled him back into the operating theatre behind the canvas curtain. He died two days later from blood poisoning.

'Yes,' said Yablonski to the nurse at the other side of the bed, who was holding the dressing around Igor's foot open as if offering up the contents as a gift, 'all looks in order with the toe.' He was paying scant attention to it. 'Re-dress it and then I think he can go.' He turned to Igor and said, 'Keep it dry if you can, but you can walk on it now. The nail will fall off no doubt, but it should stop oozing in a week or so.'

Igor sat down outside the medical tent and smoked a cigarette. It was already early evening and it looked as if it was about to rain. A chubby Mongolian soldier was grooming two horses in front of him. He had taken off his padded jacket, which lay on the ground, and his shirt was unbuttoned to the middle of his chest. He was apparently completely hairless. Igor would make a joke about him later in the mess, saying that he looked like an enormous baby with a gun.

'Where are you from?' called Igor.

The soldier didn't look up at first, but hearing no reply from anyone else, he looked around him and then over at Igor. 'Me?' he said.

'Yes,' said Igor.

'Ulan-Ude.'

'In Russia?'

'Yes,' said the soldier, 'Of course.'

Igor nodded.

The horse flicked its black tail. The soldier was silent. As he began to brush the animal again he could see Igor in his peripheral vision looking up at him expectantly. As he finished off the flanks on her left side and moved around to her right, he said, 'You?'

'Pereslavl-Zalessky.' The words had been waiting at his lips and they tumbled out quickly.

'Oh,' said the Mongolian soldier and nodded.

'You have many horses in Ulan-Ude?'

'Yes,' said the soldier.

'You heard of Lake Pleshcheyevo?' said Igor. The soldier shook his head. 'The funny flotilla? Peter the Great?' The soldier shook his head again. Igor shrugged. 'It's the most beautiful lake in the world. Beautiful. You can't live anywhere better. The lake really is beautiful. You swim every day in the summer. The city's amazing. Not too far from Moscow if you needed something special, but, you know, until the war started I never had to go to Moscow – there was still nothing I needed that I didn't have there.' Igor lit a new cigarette from the old one and threw the butt onto the ground at his feet. 'You have a family?'

'Four children,' said the soldier.

'Four? I have two. Young – the war came and interrupted my flow.' He winked at the soldier, but didn't get a response. 'We'll have more when I get back and then Rada and Matvei will be old enough to help their mother, so maybe it's not such a bad thing.'

Igor thought about his children and then his wife. He recalled holding her in the lake one summer when they were courting. They had been either swimming or lying in the sun all day and the skin on their faces was hot and tight. The sun had made Igor feel sick, but he didn't want to leave Anna's side – he felt for the first time that a woman he adored felt the same about him. Not like the farmer's daughter or the frigid teacher from Rostov. As the sun came down they ran into the water again and swam until they were far enough out that their toes barely touched the bed of the lake. Anna bobbed down into the water and when she came up she threw her hair back and Igor saw that her shoulders were bare. She took Igor's hands under the water and guided them up to her breasts – she had slipped down the top half of her costume under the water. He had never touched more than a woman's arm before and he shuddered as he touched her flesh, firm with goosebumps from the cold water.

'What happened to your foot?' the soldier said.

Igor looked down at it and shivered, recalling the infected toe-
nail that had been plaguing him for months and the shuddering
pain, the pop as the skinny blonde rubble girl stamped on it.
'Got into a fight with some old fascists – down on Helmholtz-
platz.' Since he had started dealing with Frau Beckmann and her
girls he had nothing but angry German women plaguing him.
Ah, but that Leica. He recalled the cold weight of it in his hand,
like a gun.

'Well, goodbye,' said the soldier, taking the horse by the reins
and leading it away behind the tent.

'Yes, goodbye comrade,' said Igor. He stood up and walked
slowly away from the hospital. His toe felt huge in his boot, but
at least it no longer hurt.

His father had moved in to help look after Anna and the children when Igor was told he'd been conscripted. Late one night,
after he had spent the evening getting drunk with his father, they
wandered out of the house and walked along the lakeshore. They
were trying to wait for the sun to come up, but while it was still
black his father had gripped him round the neck, his large beard
crackling on Igor's cheek, the sour smell of vodka on his breath,
and said, 'If those fucking Germans get to Moscow I'll take
Anna and the kids to the lake and then I'll lag behind to pick
something up – pretend I'm picking something up – then,' he
said aiming his fingers like a gun, 'crack, crack, crack. Don't you
worry. No German's going to touch them.' Igor was appalled by
this idea, but hadn't said anything. He had just stared into the
inky water, watching the small waves stroke the silty shore.

Igor looked up and found a wall of rubble in front of him and
realised that he'd taken the wrong road back to his base. The sky
was darkening – there were rain clouds hovering in the west. He
tried to climb over the rubble, but when he pushed himself up
on tiptoes to try and peer over it, his toe throbbed and he

thought better of it. When he turned back on himself he found his route back blocked by a short woman in a thick woollen overcoat with straight mousey hair and incongruously thick black eyebrows. He looked around the street to see if she was with anyone else, but she seemed to be alone, so he said in Russian, *'You lost too?'* He didn't know the German word for lost, so he tried to mime the look of lostness: a shrug of the shoulders and a searching look.

The woman looked behind her and then back at Igor and when she turned he saw that she had a large port wine stain birthmark – a scarlet pool that curved down from her eye, around her cheek and ran dry at her throat. He stopped in front of her and took one hand out of his pocket to touch a limp brown lock that was escaping from beneath her headscarf. *'It's Frieda, isn't it?'* he said in Russian. *'You've come back for another go, then.'* He stroked her hair gently and looked down at her – she was shaking and staring at the chest of his green, padded jacket. He took his hand away and moved it to his groin, which he squeezed.

He felt something pushed against his stomach and looked down in time to see the gun barrel against it. There was a bang and the girl screamed and a hot pain burst out across Igor's abdomen. *'Ah shit!'* he said, *'Daughter of a whore!'* and fell backwards grappling at his side, warm blood seeping through his fingers. The girl had dropped the gun and covered her face. She looked through her fingers now and cried out when she saw that he wasn't dead. *'You crazy bitch,'* he said. *'You crazy fucking bitch.'*

He scrambled up and kicked away the gun before she could get to it again. He went for his own gun, but as he scrabbled around at his side he remembered it being removed from him when he was admitted to the hospital. He lurched towards her but she sprang backwards, and he doubled over as the pain in his stomach rippled up through him. He heard her sobbing and her

179

feet moving away from him, crunching on the brick dust on the ground. He dropped to his knees and bent over. '*I've just been in fucking hospital, you German whore,*' he said.

He curled up trying to gather up the strength to stand and stumble back to the hospital. He breathed deeply and decided he would have to call for help. When he raised his head to cry out though, he saw the girl running towards him again. She was holding a lump of concrete above her head, supported precariously by her thin wrists and as Igor tried to scramble up to stop her, she brought it down on his head. The first thump didn't hit him directly – instead it cut a large gash out of his forehead down to his eyelid. Igor screamed and his arms flailed about wildly above him, trying to grab at her. The second hit was more accurate though and hit his skull with an ugly, dull thud, spraying blood up into the girl's face. She hit Igor again though and then again and then hit him and hit him until he had stopped twitching.

She searched the little leather bag strapped to his front and took out cigarettes, a lighter, and a little hand-carved whistle and finally took the watch off his wrist before she ran away down the street.

A BROKEN GUN

Kasper stopped at the door of a boarded-up cobblers in Hildegardstraße. The door was guarded by a large man dressed in a grey woollen suit, wearing a black bowler hat that almost completely covered his short, Neanderthal-like forehead. At his feet, sitting on the step that led up to the door, sat a young boy, perhaps ten, his red hair and the deep auburn freckles that peppered his face causing him to look even more pale and malnourished than he might have otherwise done.

'Herr Linden,' said Kasper to the taller man.

The man's eyes switched momentarily beneath their shadowy ridge. 'What do you want?'

'A hero returns!'

'Take your shit elsewhere, queer.'

'We've all been terribly worried about you, Linden – everyone's delighted that you've come back in one piece. You have come back in one piece, haven't you?'

'You think you're clever with all this bullshit, but you're actually just a fucking cunt and an ugly cunt at that.'

'Enough of the pleasantries, Linden, I need to talk to Spielmann.'

'What do you want with Spielmann?'

'What does anyone want with Spielmann?'

'That ain't your game.'

'What's it to you, if I can pay?'

'He won't want to see you.'

'Tell him I'm here.'

Linden stood silently, pushing his jaw forward, taking little sniffs like a bulldog. He coughed hard and spat onto the floor near Kasper's feet. 'Ernst!' The boy scrambled to his feet. He looked up at Kasper in bored disgust and opened the corner of his tight jacket, to reveal a tiny gun, sewn roughly onto the torn lining with a strip of grubby elastic.

Linden stood reluctantly to one side and the boy passed, pushed the door open and slipped in. Kasper heard a single brief ring, like a bicycle bell, then nothing for some time until the boy stuck his head out of the door and said, 'Come in then.'

Kasper followed the boy into a small dark room, the former shop, lit only by the meagre light from the window at the top of the door. The room smelt strongly of leather and chemicals, because, although trading had ceased years ago, the walls behind the high counter were still full of shelves, from which hung the tools of the former shoe shop, as well as piles of leather, tins of polish, tubes of glue, soft rags. Further down the wall were small wooden drawers with pretty brass handles holding a glut of nails. The boy reached up and hit the bell on the counter, then stilled its ringing with his slim index finger.

Kasper heard Linden coughing outside, but no sound from the blackness of the open door that led out from the shop into the rooms beyond. Kasper looked jealously at the array of wares behind the counter and then down at his own ruined shoes.

When he looked up Spielmann was standing in the doorway, leaning against the frame. His hair had turned white and was brushed into a neat side parting and greased down with a strong-smelling pomade. He was dressed smartly, but the collar of his white shirt was missing, as if he had been preparing to go to the opera when the bell rang.

'Kasper Meier. Well I never.'

'Herr Spielmann.'

'To what do we owe this pleasure?'

'I heard you were back.'

'That's right,' Spielmann said.

'Must be a relief.'

'Oh yes,' said Spielmann. 'Wonderful to be back home in Berlin. What you've all done with the place since I left – well, it's quite remarkable.'

'Yes,' said Kasper, 'Though the inspiration was all yours, after the job you and the boys did in the East.'

Spielmann laughed grimly. 'There are a few differences, thankfully.'

Kasper watched Spielmann's hand touch his scrawny neck and then the ragged bags beneath his eyes as if he was checking whether he was still there. He recalled that Spielmann had disappeared from the bar and that a year later Phillip had seen him on stage in Spandau, the sun shining off his high boots as he whispered a joke to his commander.

'I heard you've been asking after me,' Kasper said.

'We're old friends, aren't we?'

Kasper smiled. 'Apparently, you were asking after people who used to come to the bar.'

Spielmann shrugged. 'It was one person – not you. And it wasn't for me, it was for one of my clients.'

'Frau Beckmann?'

Spielmann frowned. 'Well,' he said, 'I never name names.'

'What did she want this information for?' Spielmann didn't answer. 'How about bending a little for an old friend?'

Spielmann moved into the shop and brushed some dust from the counter. 'My client – not Beckmann, but an acquaintance of hers.'

'A girl?'

'That's right.'

'Blonde, young?'

'Young, but not blonde. Very scrawny, with her hair chopped short, as if she'd had lice.'

'And what did she want this information for?'

'She didn't say. But she made me a good offer.'

'She blackmailed you?'

'Yes, and no. Some friends of hers – children – made it clear that I couldn't refuse the offer, but there was an offer no less. And a good one. And since then this girl's been a good customer. Their connections are good – very good.'

Kasper nodded.

Spielmann folded his arms. 'Are *you* in the market to buy something?'

Kasper looked down at the counter and felt afraid. 'Perhaps,' he said.

'Well, my product range is small Herr Meier, as well you know. Nothing that doesn't fit inside a pocket. I can offer you a Luger – something you're used to. Nagants are cheap – those Ivans just can't keep hold of their pistols. If you're looking for something special . . . well, I could give you an address, but then you're getting into even murkier waters than these.'

'I just need some protection. Something small and cheap.'

'Well, the Browning's small, but expensive, the Nagant's bigger, but cheaper.'

'What's he got?' said Kasper, pointing at the boy.

'It's a toy.'

Kasper frowned. 'I suppose I'll take the Russian then. I can give you dollars,' said Kasper. He reached into his coat pocket and laid a small bundle of green notes on the counter top. Spielmann smiled and splayed them out, then held one up and rubbed it slowly between his thumb and forefinger.

'Dollars, eh?' he said. 'Seems like everyone from your bar's come out the other side all right.'

'Not everyone,' Kasper said.

'Hmm,' Spielmann said a little ruefully, inclining his head in thought. He picked up the pile of notes, tapped them on the desk and disappeared backwards through the darkened doorway.

Kasper's gaze returned to the shelves of wares behind the counter. He mentally totted up the amount of goods he could exchange for all of those items. After a few minutes had passed the red-haired boy, who was standing behind Kasper, with his back to the door, said, 'He ain't coming back,' and laughed a high little laugh.

'Oh, he's coming back,' said Kasper, not turning around, but looking at the black doorway.

'You've been stiffed. He's gone off with your Ami money.'

Kasper smiled. 'No, no. Your Herr Spielmann and I have too much history.'

'I hope you're not talking about the past, Herr Meier.' The voice came from the dark doorway, followed by the figure of Spielmann himself.

'Not at all, Herr Spielmann.'

'As it should be.'

Spielmann put an object wrapped up in a soft cloth on the counter top. Kasper picked it up, felt the cold weight of it, and slipped it into an inside pocket in his jacket.

'It's loaded. There are a pack of bullets in there too – on the house. Favour for an old friend.'

'You know if you wanted to do a favour for an old friend, I could shift all this tat for you,' said Kasper nodding at the shelves behind Spielmann.

'How could I possibly run my shoe shop then?' said Spielmann.

Kasper laughed and nodded.

'I bumped into an old friend of yours the other day,' said Spielmann.

Kasper frowned. 'Oh yes.'

'Do you remember a Heinrich Neustadt. He was always at your bar?'

Kasper shrugged, surprised at how predictable the information appeared to him. He said, 'Yes, Neustadt. All these old names, coming back together.' He looked down at the red-haired boy. 'Say,' he said, 'How much for his gun?'

'Like he said, it don't work,' said the boy, looking suddenly nervous. 'Keep your hands off it.'

'Five dollars,' said Kasper.

'Give him the gun, Ernst,' said Spielmann.

The boy stared at Herr Spielmann imploringly, but when the man didn't return his gaze, he handed it over to Kasper, dropping it as if by mistake when Kasper tried to take it. Kasper smiled, picked it up and put it in a side pocket.

He tipped the brim of his hat. 'Always a pleasure. Do send my greetings to Frau Spielmann.'

'I certainly will,' said Spielmann. 'Ernst – show Herr Meier out.'

The boy pulled the door open just enough to let Kasper slip through, and followed him outside. Kasper squinted as he came out and stood for a second in front of Linden and the boy, looking either way down the street.

'Herr Linden?'

'Bugger off.'

Kasper took five cigarettes out of his pocket and held them up in the air, without looking round. 'Anyone been down the street since I've been inside?'

'Can't say I was paying attention.'

Kasper fished out five more and held up ten.

He heard Linden sigh. 'Three old women, one man, couple of kids.'

'The kids.'

Linden lifed his arm, but Kasper snatched the cigarettes away. 'Who were the kids?'

'Five-year-old.'

'Any others?'

'Girl and a boy.'

'Go on.'

'Maybe twelve, maybe older. Fourteen at the most.'

Kasper swallowed, his throat tightened. 'Did they look like twins? Big eyes.'

'Could've been. Yeah probably.'

'Which way did they go out of the street?'

'Down towards Berlin Zoo.'

Kasper held out the cigarettes and Linden took them. Kasper heard him spit onto the pavement as he walked away.

Kasper walked towards Berlin Zoo, along the cold, shaded side of the street, where the air seemed fresher. The fallen walls of the buildings allowed the sun to hit him at irregular intervals, filling the vision in his good eye, blinding him with golden, watery light. When the cool shade washed over him again, his eye darted about, searching the dark corners of the ruins. The Russian gun in his inside pocket knocked against the bones of his chest as he walked, pulling down his loose jacket on one side. Its presence made him feel nauseous. But the twins, he knew, were round some corner, hiding in some doorway, and if he was going to get to Sybelstraße and find Frau Beckmann, it would have to be without them. He wouldn't touch the gun, simply lose them in the crush of traders at Berlin Zoo, but it would be there if there was a confrontation, if he was backed into a corner. He imagined their shocked faces, them turning and fleeing, as he fired into the ground at their feet. Then he imagined the same faces, stone cold, them both taking guns from their own pockets and raising them up, pointing them at his head.

As Kasper approached the zoo the large flak tower loomed solid and grey from the ruins around it, like a besieged castle, with its pockmarked walls and strange, shuttered windows. Kasper remembered it being a monstrosity when it was first built and hugged the vast Tiergarten park, whose great trees reached up as if trying to hide it from view. But what had once been the great lung of the city was now dead and brown. The park was a colossal vegetable field, the dark spring soil scattered with the classical sculptures that had once nestled in groves and gardens and marked the ends of bridges. They stood bare and random, graffitied and lost, like lonely overseers, watching imperiously over the bent backs of the surviving Berliners tilling the soil.

In the shadows of the stained concrete flak tower, crowds swarmed, shouting and jostling, sifting through bags, frowning and calling to friends. A few women stood against the tower walls, exchanging sex for cigarettes, shoes, dresses, tinned ham, coffee and canned vegetables. They stood tall and paced slowly and purposefully behind the mob. One woman had her back against the tower, her leg cocked backwards so that the sole of her shoe was pressed against the wall, provocatively exposing her knee, which was marked with a series of small white scars. She had fallen briefly asleep, her head bobbing lower and lower and her fingers keeping only a light grip on her handbag. Held in such tired, loose fingers, it was a far more tempting prospect to the black market crowd than her bare knee.

Kasper stopped in front of an emaciated cobbler. He saw flashes of pale skin, dark hair, staring eyes, but the twins were nowhere to be found. The cobbler, sitting on the ground on a square white rag, started to make disparaging remarks about the state of Kasper's shoes and pointed out the array of tools he had to fix them, and the quality of the American tyre-rubber that he offered to stitch onto the bottom to replace his broken sole. At first Kasper pretended not to hear, but catching himself, he turned to the man and said, 'I've got polish.'

'What kind?'

'Black.'

'Let me see it.'

Kasper opened the brown paper bag and took out the little tin. He stepped a little closer, putting the toe of his shoe on the edge of the rag, to avoid any possibility of the man flicking the tools up in it and escaping. He had once found a missing wife for a husband returning from the Eastern Front and had even got him a key to her apartment, only to have the man knock him out in the courtyard of a ruined house near Savignyplatz. He woke missing the key, all his cigarettes and a chunk of his tongue.

The cobbler opened the tin and looked inside with a sneer. He shook it a little and the dry polish rattled around inside. Kasper put his free hand in his trouser pocket and looked around him again. He stared between the frayed coats, bent hats, shabby headscarves, chatter and shouts. Perhaps they were behind the flak tower, perhaps among the crowd of women swarming around the laughing soldier with seven blue-and-white tins of dried milk in the crook of his arm.

'I'll polish those up for you,' said the cobbler, looking down at Kasper's shoes, 'and fix the toe. But there's not much in here and it'll need softening up, which means I've got to find some oil from somewhere.' Kasper put his hand out to take the polish back. 'Those shoes look pretty bad to me. They must take in water when you walk.' This was true: even before he had trodden on the nail there had been a hole in the bottom layer of leather that had created a sort of valve – it was particularly adept at sucking water in and keeping it there, so that he would often have to take it off and tip the water out of it, before he climbed the stairs to his flat.

'I can survive wet feet,' said Kasper.

'You could get pneumonia,' said the old man. 'My nephew died of pneumonia this winter. Christmas Eve. Never got to see 1946.'

'He didn't miss much,' said Kasper. The man huffed and put the lid on the tin, offering it back up to Kasper. 'What about your watch?'

'A watch for a tin of dry boot polish? You're crazy. You must be bloody crazy, or something. Take your bloody polish.'

'It's a cheap watch.'

'Take it.' The man seemed agitated now and wanted Kasper to leave. Kasper's heart was beating hard – he was about to win. He felt ashamed, but elated.

'Ten cigarettes,' said Kasper, 'for the watch. Look I'll even throw in a lighter.' He took out the ugly Russian lighter that Eva had brought him and threw it down on the cloth in front of him.

'Ten cigarettes?' said the man. 'You must be . . .' he shook his head. 'Two packs.'

'Fine,' said Kasper, 'but I'm keeping some of this polish.' Kasper took out a handkerchief and pocketed a nugget. The old man unclipped the watch and handed it to Kasper, who put it to his ear briefly to check it was running.

'It works,' said the man. Kasper shrugged and handed the man the packets of cigarettes from his top pocket.

'A pleasure,' said Kasper.

'Lunatic!'

There was a snap and Kasper looked up to see a soldier with a small box camera. 'What are you doing?' Kasper said.

The camera clicked again and the man looked up. 'Don't worry, don't worry. For magazine,' the man said with a British or American accent, 'For magazine.'

'What do you mean? Don't take pictures of me.'

'He's always round here,' the old cobbler said. 'He works for one of those illustrated magazines.'

Kasper looked down at the cobbler long enough for the cameraman to disappear into the crowd. He saw the man's hands poking out above their heads, pointing elsewhere and the camera being fired again: snap, snap, snap. Kasper followed him, but the hands dropped down beneath the teeming traders and, for a moment, he thought he saw two pairs of large, angry eyes. He pushed into the crowd until he found his way to the emptier space around the flak tower. He went up on tiptoes, but recognised no one. The sky had begun to cloud over and he thought he felt some spits of rain on his face. One of the prostitutes sidling along the side of the tower seemed to have the same thought and squinted up at the now white sky, her eyes so green and the surfaces so wet-looking, that it seemed as if she was about to cry. She looked away, over at Kasper, sized him up, then turned so that she was walking backwards, facing him. 'On your way somewhere?' she said.

'Something like that.'

'Want some company?'

'No thanks. One of life's loners.'

'Sounds lonely.'

'Well, that's rather the point.'

The hooker turned round, so that she was walking alongside him. 'You a clever dick, then?'

Kasper laughed. 'A clever loner.'

'Doesn't sound so clever to me.'

He turned now and faced her briefly, 'I suppose not,' he said.

They had reached the far corner of the tower and the woman slowed and stopped, as if she had been tasked to stay within its boundaries; as if it was so soaked in destruction and misery that it acted as a huge, grey magnet for sin, pulling the residents of West Berlin towards it, the stronger its attraction, the lower the Berliner had fallen. The woman shrugged and turned and made her way back along the wall to the crowds at the other side.

Kasper looked at his watch and back at the woman and then behind her. He saw two British soldiers walking up through the crowd of people, who folded their goods away into sheets and stuffed them into coats and pockets as the soldiers passed by. And as a group of women moved swiftly away, disappearing behind the flak tower, he caught sight of a large, piercing eye, and a flash of dark hair and freckled skin, a small angry mouth.

'Hey!' said Kasper, calling the woman back.

The woman turned smiling and leant against the dirty concrete wall. 'Changed your mind?'

'Not really, but you might do me a favour.'

'A favour, he says!' She pushed herself up, her hand now resting flat against the wall.

Kasper smiled. 'A paid-for favour.'

'Are you one of those weirdos?' she said. 'I don't do anything funny.'

'This isn't funny,' said Kasper. 'Not in the way you're thinking.'

Kasper walked fast, almost breaking into a run, making a circuit of the flak tower. He kept one hand on the loaded gun in his inside pocket, to stop it drumming against his ribs. The cloud had brought with it a certain mugginess and a line of sweat formed at his hairline. The tips of a clump of his white hair caught on his forehead, tickled his skin, and he brushed it away with his little finger, the scratch of his fingernail remaining, a stinging line above his eye.

As he came round the corner, completing his circle of the tower, he saw the two soldiers walking towards the woman he had just left. Kasper stopped and placed a hand against the cold, smooth concrete surface, his ring finger finding a sharp-edged hole, an ancient air-bubble. The tip of his finger traced its circumference and he watched as the prostitute walked backwards, trying to talk to Hans and Lena Beckmann, who were trying to pass her, trying to follow Kasper around the side of the tower. She jostled them, pinched their cheeks, and laughed loudly as the twins pushed her away, staring at her angrily with their wide eyes and shouting at her with their small, cruel mouths. Turning as if to strike her, Hans Beckmann made eye contact with Kasper, not noticing the woman's hand come round his side and place something into his pocket, gently, as if she was returning a bird to its nest. Hans said something to his sister, but was too far off for Kasper to make it out, and then the girl turned too, her eyes widening and her mouth shrinking.

The noise of the crowd dissipated. Kasper pushed himself away from the wall and stood up straight, trying to stand as tall as he could, his chest pushed out like a child soldier, standing to attention. Hans and Lena continued to stare. He tried desperately not to look away – because he felt their terrible gaze physically, a nauseous heat behind his ears, in his neck, at the back of his legs.

The woman followed their gaze and when her eyes met Kasper's he lifted his hand, as if in a wave. She turned instantly and looked at the soldiers, now only a few feet away from her, and cried 'A gun! My God, they've got a gun!'

The soldiers were on them immediately and as the twins

screamed Ernst's replica gun was produced triumphantly from Hans Beckmann's pocket.

'He planted it! He planted it!' Kasper heard Hans' voice now, high and shrill in the still air, but Kasper was already walking swiftly along another side of the tower, sweating, shaking, but smiling, his fingers still tracing the concrete, keeping him upright, as he made his way to Sybelstraße.

A SHEET OF PAPER

As Kasper arrived in Sybelstraße, and tried to slow down to a more natural pace, his calves ached, and the skin on his legs was flooded with a hot, burning itch. His brief sense of triumph at detaining the twins had already been swallowed up by his anxiety about finally confronting Frau Beckmann. The woman herself loomed large, a tall faceless shape at an open door; but more frightening still was a sense that he might be about to understand exactly what Eva was involved in, to finally bring together the twins, Frau Beckmann, the pilot and Eva into a comprehensible whole. The tension of a discovery might have been thrilling if he wasn't also sure that the explanation could only appal him.

He found Beckmann's apartment and her name on the nameplate, one of only two that hadn't been struck through, their fates or new addresses chalked and painted below to direct husbands and sons who had not yet returned or, more likely, would never return. The muscles in his legs stopped aching and began to shudder lightly, to shiver. He knew the door, he knew the building – it was, as Heinrich had said, adjacent to the apartment block he had visited him in for weeks. He rang the bell. It elicited no response. Kasper leant on the main door – it was locked.

He pretended to inspect something on the step, waiting for an opportunity to get inside, and pictured Frau Beckmann seeing Heinrich and him come and go. He imagined her older now, stretching her scrawny neck like a turkey, squinting her eyes in the sun, as Heinrich left the building behind Kasper, not conforming to their agreed ten-minute gap. He saw a smile playing at the edge of her lips, her grip tightening around her handbag. How stupid he had been, how ridiculous to believe he could hide anything in a city with a population trained to search out filth, trained to know how much power knowing the right, or the wrong, information endowed.

He gained entry behind a child who was barely able to reach the keyhole of the door with the key that was tied around her neck on a string. He walked into the front of the building and was relieved to find a strip of ancient carpet running up the middle of the staircase. He crept up, keeping his feet on its edges, where the pile was thicker. He looked for Frau Beckmann's name as he passed the doorways and found it on the third floor.

He put his ear against the painted wood of Beckmann's door and listened. He heard nothing, except for a soft hush, like the sea. Without moving, he rang the bell briefly. He heard it ring inside. An ache in his chest throbbed in anticipation of both finding her there and of not finding her there. He rang the doorbell again and closed his eyes. The apartment was empty.

He turned, pretended to read the nameplate again, and walked on as if going up the final flight of stairs to the fourth floor, but instead turned with his back to the wall. He took his handkerchief out of his pocket, from which he extracted the small piece of boot polish he had saved from the tin that morning. He rubbed it between his fingers, protected by the handkerchief, and then smeared the softened black blob across the spy hole on the door across from Frau Beckmann's.

He wondered whether he should go straight to the rubble groups' site to find her there. He believed, momentarily, that she would be a sensible, reasonable woman – a trader like him who would understand immediately all the ins and outs of their misunderstanding and make a deal – a simple deal – and this whole business would be done with, without suspicion, without pain. But as these thoughts comforted him, he was aware that he had already removed an ancient nail file with a yellowed, ivory handle, lined with grey cracks, and slipped it beneath the latch, then brought out a small metal pick, with a curved end, which he inserted into the keyhole and began to work the catches. The lock popped quickly and, when he put his weight against it, he felt it give way easily beneath him – no one had latched it from the inside.

He pushed the door shut behind him and stood for a minute in the corridor of the apartment. It was windowless and quite dark and all three doors were shut. He listened – still no sound. He had a sense that he was about to find something that would explain everything, but when he tried to form this object, this person, into something concrete, it morphed and dissipated into a frightened nothingness. And yet he felt sure he was close, he felt sure it could be here.

He opened the first door – a bright, white light flooded into the hallway and shone diffusely off the scratched parquet floor. It was a bathroom with the rare luxury of a toilet in the flat itself. The white light poured into the dry air of the narrow room from a tall window at its end, but failed to illuminate the porcelain and the metal of the various taps, all of which had long since lost their sheen.

He heard a dull thud and a grunt, muffled and close. He froze, his hand still on the door handle. But then there was a brief, happy screech and footsteps, sounding through the floor of the flat above.

He pulled the door of the bathroom to, darkness descending again on the little hallway. He inhaled – the air smelt cold, of dust and old polish.

There were only two other doors in the corridor, both double doors, one leading left, the other right. He first opened those on the left.

The light here flooded grey through long net curtains onto a cool and empty reception room. It looked as though it had been decorated by Frau Beckmann as a young bride just before the first war: it contained rather cheap-looking veneered furniture, a worn, sprung sofa upholstered in a threadbare green fabric and a faded rug almost covering the whole of the parquet, that dampened the sound of his shoes, of his breathing, making everything seem a little more close, a little more intimate. The sun briefly broke from behind the clouds and a warm yellow lit the carpet, revealing a shimmer of floating dust and a long hanging cobweb, arching down from the ceiling almost to head height, slowly bowing out, then turning in the imperceptible eddies in the still air. The sunlight was cut off again and the room became dull and cold.

There were a few photographs sitting on a small table inlaid with a chess board that stood by the sofa. There was a picture of a woman that must have been Frau Beckmann on her wedding day. She looked unlike her children – big and broad, her husband thin, with a large waxed moustache, dressed in military uniform. The twins themselves were in another picture, much younger, but their wide, ruthless eyes were unmistakable. They were sitting on two heavy wooden chairs in a photographer's studio, their legs not touching the floor, staring angrily into the camera like a pair of medieval monarchs who had come to power long before their majority.

There was a roll-top bureau, unlocked, which was only unusual in that it contained nothing except for a glass inkwell, with a dark slick of desiccated ink in its cup. There were no letters, no postcards, no papers. Kasper tapped around at it, but couldn't locate any hollow parts, draws or switches. Standing and looking around the room – a room that appeared to be unchanged since the war had begun – the emptiness of the flat, the dry museum-like quality of it, began to unnerve him. No books to speak of, no chest of drawers, no piles of paper. And the room had the cold unheated atmosphere of a civic hall. He felt a familiar nauseous pressure at the back of his head, in his stomach.

He left the drawing room and crossed the hall to open the second set of doors. It opened onto another reception room that itself led to another door. Its only furnishings were a large, black chest with faux-gothic carvings, and three narrow beds made of metal tubing, painted white, spotted with rusty flecks. The bedding on each of them was neatly stacked into a square of blankets, with a thin pillow sitting on top. He looked into the chest, which was empty, and then crouched down and looked under the beds – each one had a green military duffel bag beneath it. He pulled one out. It contained women's clothes – some smarter than others – and two pairs of shoes, but no other personal effects. He lifted a light, cotton shirt to his face and finally detected the smell of a living person, a trace of antiseptic soap and water, mixed with sweat. He went down the row of beds checking each bag – each one contained a similar array of items with little to identify the owner.

He turned his head and looked over to the corridor. There was no sound in the apartment – he heard his heart beating, felt the pressure of the heavy gun in his inside pocket. Distantly he heard the high squeal of an accelerating truck.

Past the second door he found a bedroom with two more

narrow beds in, with a third wood-and-canvas camp bed folded up and pushed into the corner of the room. Again, each bed had a similar bag beneath it. The first of these contained a patterned dress that Kasper recognised. Kneeling in front of the bed, he held the garment up and traced the small floral pattern with his thumb – it was the dress Eva had worn to the café. He folded it up again and gently tucked it back into the hold-all from which it had come. There were three books in the bag: a battered book of fairy-tales and two books of plays. One contained three translated works by Molière, the other was an ancient, peeling volume called *New German Drama*. He flicked through the pages, thick and irregular, and on the final page found a beautiful pencil drawing; a consciously naive sketch of a great ship between two continents, the sea and clouds made of delicate swirling lines.

He slipped the books back but stayed on his knees in front of the bag. Despite the beds of other girls, he imagined Eva awake and alone, her eyes bright in the darkness of the bare little room, cold and unsure; he imagined her sick and hungry with no one to tell, no one to lay a hand on her head, to say it would be fine; he imagined her waking from a nightmare, sitting up, her heart still beating in her ears, remembering where she was, remembering where she wasn't. Desperate to do something with his sadness, he felt around his jacket and landed upon the secret pocket in the lining of his coat. He unzipped it and tore a row of three ration coupons – two for butter and one for sugar. He carefully searched through the clothes in the bag and decided upon a cardigan, slipping the coupons into one of the two pockets, embroidered with daffodils, where she might have slipped them and forgotten about them; where she might find them with a rush of pleasure and surprise.

Someone slammed a door elsewhere in the building. Kasper quickly packed the clothes back up and pushed the bag beneath the bed. He stood and listened. Silence.

There was a second door in the room. He pushed it open and found a bare kitchen behind it. He touched the range – it was cold and there was no fuel in it. An enamelled basin stood on a sideboard with a film of water at the bottom of it, but the kettle on the stove top was dry.

He closed the door and stood staring at the bed that Eva must sleep in. There was no bed for Frau Beckmann, or the children, unless they slept on the floor of that cold dusty living room. There was surely no family life here.

He looked about him. There was one other piece of furniture in the room – an odd washstand with a marble top, sitting squat on the floor, as if its legs had been chopped off. He bent down and opened the door – there was a basin in it, but when he slipped it out cautiously, he saw that it was dry, filled with one or two desiccated insects. He put the basin back and tried to look behind the washstand, but it was pushed flush against the wall. Levering it forward, with his knees against the marble top, he saw that there was a sheet of thin white paper, slipped behind it. He reached down and pulled it out. The paper was old, faded on two sides where part of it had been sitting exposed to the sun for some years, but the ink on it was fresh and a quite startling lavender blue.

The paper was titled 'Group 5: HV, FS, SP, EH, MN' and contained lists of initials, with dates and locations organised into sections. The first section of dates was labelled 'HV — TN — SI(R)'. Beneath were a list of either specific dates or general times, such as 'Mon. 8–9 a.m.', and by these dates were specific locations: 'F. Schornstein', 'Leibnitz, 23 Sch. Allee', 'Mauerprk, Nrth.', 'hosp. P.Berg'. All of the dates in this first section and the two following had passed and the respective sections had been completely crossed out.

There were six sets of initials in all, each beginning with three initials. The first set of initials corresponded to those at the top of the paper – Kasper presumed they were the names of the members of the group, probably the girls that were sleeping in these beds – and the initials in brackets were either R, F, A or B, which almost certainly denoted Russian, French, American and British, so the final set of initials were presumably those of soldiers or pilots.

The middle set of initials would have perhaps been harder for Kasper to fathom, but were easily solved, when, with a tired inevitability, he scanned down the list until he found 'EH — KM — ?(B)' second from the bottom, heading a section not yet containing any found information, and recognised his own place between Eva and the man she was searching for, his initials not yet confirmed. Kasper looked up at the other middle initials in the sections above, and saw that he was just one of a number of middle men and women, helping these girls connect with their soldiers. But then a brief, cold sweat washed over his body, when he saw that it was only his initials that had been underlined.

'Excuse me?'

Kasper froze

'Sorry, do you live here?'

Kasper turned slowly. Standing in the doorway was a man wearing an ill-fitting suit. Around the arm of the jacket he wore an armband that read 'Police', but was otherwise un-uniformed and unarmed. He was very young, clearly newly recruited, and appeared to be as shocked as Kasper.

'Yes,' said Kasper. 'I live here.'

'Sorry,' said the policeman, 'I didn't mean to surprise you. Someone reported a disturbance in the building and I saw that the door was ajar.'

The policeman looked down at the paper in Kasper's hands.

'Just doing a bit of tidying up,' said Kasper. 'Four daughters.' He dropped the paper back behind the washstand and righted it. 'Looks like you've found my little hiding place ... for our papers,' he said, brushing down his trousers. 'You can never be too careful.'

'It's pretty tight by us too, space wise,' said the policeman. 'But you have the living room.'

'We sleep there – my wife and I.'

The policeman nodded.

Kasper recovered himself and said, 'Well, I've got to be off myself. Shall I walk out with you?' He led the policeman away from the door and back through the first bedroom, into the hallway.

'I'll need to see your identification card,' said the policeman.

'My identification card?' said Kasper. 'What was the disturbance?'

'I'm sorry.'

'The disturbance. What was it? You said someone had reported a disturbance.'

'Yes, that's right.'

'Was it anything to do with me? With this apartment?'

'No,' said the policeman. 'But the door was ajar.'

'I must have forgotten to close it, but I'm sure no one reported that.'

'No, but I need to check all possibilities.'

'What did they say it was exactly – this disturbance?'

'They said . . . well, I'm not at liberty to say, of course.'

Kasper had now led the policeman into the stairwell. He pulled the door shut, which locked with a heavy click. The policeman looked at the shut door a little desperately, then back at Kasper.

'Sorry sir, could you tell me your name?'

'Beckmann.'

'Herr Beckmann?'

'Yes.'

'And could you show me your ID card.'

'It's in the apartment,' said Kasper beginning to descend the staircase. Being questioned by a now unarmed policeman was a strange novelty and Kasper felt sorry for the young man who had done so badly at staking his authority.

'In the apartment?' said the policeman. 'You're still required to carry your ID at all times.'

Kasper, already a few steps down the staircase, looked up at him. 'Yes,' he said. 'You know, I think I heard something actually – something like a disturbance.'

'Oh yes?'

'Top floor,' said Kasper descending away from him. 'Try up there.'

Kasper came out of the door, his pulse audible in his ears, and walked briskly down Sybelstraße away from the apartment. The appearance of the policeman still lingered in the tight feeling around his heart, but his mind was occupied with the list of names, the two thick lines beneath his own initials. It was also occupied with Frau Beckmann's strange home, empty of personal goods except for that odd, stage-set living room and the rows of beds, like a sanatorium. It was an apartment that could be left immediately, within minutes, seconds even, leaving no trace of the former occupants. He saw Eva there again, cold beneath the thin blankets, with girls snoring lightly around her. What had become of those other soldiers and girls and middle men? Those whose names had been struck through with a dark, heavy line.

A PACKET OF CIGARETTES

Kasper squinted, his head aching, trying to pick out Beckmann. He stood behind what had once been someone's bathroom wall; some of the thick green tiles were still in place. He watched the rubble women from a distance and stroked the rough grout between the tiles with his thumb, still stained black from the mildew that had once flourished in the warm damp of the room.

A rough wooden tray the size of a coffin was stood upright in front of him: a makeshift stretcher used to carry away the dead, uncovered by the clearing work. One had already emerged since he'd been standing there, blackened, dry and mummy-like after a year beneath the ruins.

There were three groups of rubble women at that end of Pariser Straße. Their hair, skin and clothes, as well as their shapeless gloves, were covered with so much dust that they seemed to be painted from the same pallete of beiges and browns as the ruined landscape they worked in, like the daubed under-painting of a half-finished picture. They were strung together by a temporary railway that ran down the centre of the street on which wooden

205

and metal carts sat, pulled away again sometimes by horses, more often by women or old men.

Eva's group was working the final corner of the street. She was sitting with one of the women, perhaps in her mid-forties, the both of them with wooden stands between their legs, on which they balanced their bricks, hacking cement off with rough hammers. Holding her chisel and mallet, Eva was the picture of industriousness plastered across the Soviet propaganda leaking across the east of the city. She looked up at her companion, muttered something to her and the two of them burst into laughter, her teeth small and her mouth wide beneath those indigo eyes. Kasper had been lost in thought, picturing futures for her, trying her out at a desk in an office, as a teacher at the front of a class, as a mother, two small children at her side. She would be a good mother, he thought. He realised that he was smiling. And then a flicker of a memory caused his lips to relax, to drop – he thought of Klara again, pregnant, lying in bed, sleeping but frowning, her long brown hair spread out across a large square pillow which was as white as her face.

The sound of the metal on the masonry rang down the ruined street, sharp and repetitive. Eva's companion stopped to take off the scarf tied around her head and he saw that her dark hair was cut short, like a boy's. This was not how he'd imagined Frau Beckmann and she seemed barely old enough to have twins. She shook the scarf out and wiped the sweat off her face with her bare forearm, then held it up to the sunlight briefly, with her eyes closed. In this position, her small, pretty features were subsumed in white sunlight, except for the short dark shadow cast by her nose, like the stylus of a sundial. No, thought Kasper, surely not Beckmann. Her eyes flickered and she lifted her hammer again, bringing it down hard on the brick below it.

Another woman in the group, strong and square, was working her way through the rubble above them. She threw bricks into the bent buckets next to them, only one still with its handle, and other objects that she dug up into a small pile on the street, near to where Eva was sitting. Her stoutness also didn't fit his conception of Beckmann, nor the picture from her apartment of her as a young woman, but he couldn't see her face from this distance.

There was a fourth woman who had descended the slope and was talking to a short man wearing a smart, black hat, with his back to Kasper. The woman was tall, with long thin hair bunched up and tucked into her scarf. She was rather plain, with small round eyes and a long nose with a bony nodule where it bent in the middle. She was familiar to him, he thought, but he couldn't place her. She held her gloves in one hand and had the other hand on her hip, her head bent towards the man, listening with a sad, concentrated frown. This must be her, he thought, and shuddered.

Kasper approached them. The sun had baked the mud on the street dry and had brought up the corporeal whiteness of the mortar dust that enveloped everything. The fine powder and the sloping, broken buildings made Kasper feel as if he was walking down the bed of a long-since dried up river, with traces of a dead empire littering the banks. But there were signs of a resilient nature where plants had taken root in any damp patches they could find, including lilac, which had burst up in the courtyard garden of a collapsed building, firing its lurid stems out like rockets, causing butterflies to jump dizzily across the street to feed off the bush, its branches weighed down by the burden of its flowers.

Eva caught sight of him mid-sentence, as he was passing the man with the black hat. Kasper smiled at her. She was tracing the passage of an aeroplane with her chisel. She stopped talking and let the chisel travel slowly back down to the bench, without taking her eyes off him.

'Hello!' said Kasper.

'Kasper Meier!' said Eva, her voice exaggeratedly loud.

The other woman's eyes darted past him.

Kasper turned to see that the man in the black hat was quickly making his way down the road, from where Kasper had come, his hands in his pockets and his head down. 'Who's that?' said Kasper.

'Who?' said Eva.

Kasper squinted and studied the sloping shoulders, and the nervous, paddling gait, a hat, trousers, shoes that he had seen just hours earlier on a bare wooden floor. 'Jesus Christ!' said Kasper. 'Neustadt!' he shouted. Heinrich now broke into a run, grabbing at his hat as it came off his head, revealing his balding pate. Kasper went after him, but Heinrich had made too much progress and disappeared into a side street before Kasper had taken more than a few steps.

'I'm going to break your nose!' shouted Kasper, his voice echoing off the bare ruins. He turned back to Eva, marching towards her, sweat stinging his armpits. 'Unbelievable! What the bloody hell was he saying now?' he said. 'This is ludicrous!'

Eva stood up, threw down her gloves and pulled Kasper away from the group, over to one of the red-painted tool wagons. She stepped briefly inside and said 'Marie!' A filthy girl with a cut cheek exited the wagon, down the narrow wooden steps and returned to the group working the rubble. Eva came back out holding a large bucket of water in one hand, the tendons down her bare forearms standing proud, her long muscles rising and falling as she put the bucket down on the steps in front of him. She splashed the water onto her face and rubbed it behind her ears and on her neck. 'Pass me a cup, will you?' she said, pointing at a row of chipped metal mugs hanging from nails along the open door of the wagon. Kasper paused, but then put his brown paper bag on the floor and gave her a mug. She dipped the cup into the water and gulped it down, revealing the large sweat patches at the armpits of her shirt. She threw the cup into the wagon, where it clattered against metal and wood. 'Well?' she said.

'Well what?'

'I told you not to come.'

'Lucky I did. What the hell was Heinrich Neustadt doing here? What was he telling you now? Because if you two think you're going to do me over as part of some pathetic revenge plan of his and some idiotic goose-chase for you, then you're both fooling yourselves. You're idiots.'

Eva sighed and pulled off the red, cotton scarf around her head. Her hair fell out in curling, sweaty clumps. 'Well, luckily for you your friend has a little more respect for you than you have for him.'

'Oh, is that right?' said Kasper, wide-eyed, shaking his head in disbelief. 'Respect, is it? Is that what this is? Is that why he's back whispering in your ear two hours after I . . . '

'After you what?'

Kasper put his hands on his hips – his fingers shook on the bony edges of his pelvis. 'What was he telling you?'

'Nothing about you.'

'Huh!'

'You don't have to believe me – I don't care. But he didn't say anything about you, or . . . whatever you've been up to. He's like you – he's getting information for Silke. Silke from the group. And you know what, it's better for you to know as little of this as possible – I'm telling you. Everything you know just makes you more vulnerable.'

'He's a piece of work. Jesus Christ,' said Kasper, kicking a lump of broken plaster into the wheel of the tool wagon, creating a star of white dust on the toe of his shoe. 'You used him to blackmail me and then you blackmailed him? That's nice. That's charming. So you're rooting out all the queers, are you? Nice and systematic. That's beautiful.'

'No. Not me. Frau Beckmann. And Silke's not blackmailing him – he's getting paid. He accepted being paid.'

'You didn't even try to pay me – you didn't even haggle.'

'You refused.'

'Why did you need to blackmail me?'

'The job just needs doing.'

'I am doing it. I've just been doing it, but I don't see why I'm being followed by these twins, being harassed, being black-mailed. Or is that just part of the fun?'

'No, of course not. It's Frau Beckmann. I suppose your job's important. It will be over though when you've done it.'

'I know you think you can't tell me about what's really going on, but this? Neustadt now?' Kasper shook his head. 'I've been worried about you, I trusted you – can you believe it? The girl who's blackmailing me. What an idiot.' He grabbed his head. 'Jesus, what's wrong with me?'

Eva looked down at the red headscarf. 'You can trust me.'

'Really? About what? Tell me one thing you've told me that's true.'

She rubbed the fabric between her thumb and forefinger and tried to look up at him, but failed. 'I can't explain.'

'It's fine,' said Kasper. 'I didn't come here for you anyway.'

'You didn't?' she said, confused.

'No, I came for Beckmann – I've been searching for her all over the place, but she's a slippery one.'

'You don't need to see Beckmann – don't see Beckmann.'

'Listen,' he said, trying to sound more reassuring. 'I think maybe this has all been blown out of proportion a little. Let me just speak to Beckmann and I know we'll be able to come to some arrangement. For you too; to make sure you're safe.'

'That won't work.'

'Let me try. I'll make it work. Just tell me which one's Beckmann. We'll have a quiet word, I know I have things that she'll want – she doesn't understand that yet. I'm not like Heinrich Neustadt – I'm useful. Show me. Which one is she?'

'She's not here,' Eva said.

Kasper felt the anger rise again; it was in his throat, in his heart, pushing against the heavy Russian gun. 'I know she's here,' he said quietly. 'She's always here – she's your rubble group leader.'

'She's not here today.'

'Where is she then?'

'Back at her apartment I suppose.'

'Fuck you,' shouted Kasper. 'And fuck her too.'

Eva looked up at him, appalled. She stood and retied the scarf around her head. 'You don't understand,' she said.

'Too right I don't understand.'

She came close to him, grabbed his hand and lowered her voice, 'I don't want to do this. I don't want you involved any-more, but I can't change it. They said . . . You've just got to find the pilot and quickly. But you're running out of time. And then it's done. Then you won't see me again. But you've got to go. You're making too much of a fuss about this and people are talk-ing. I'll say you had a lead, that you had to come and talk to me. But you've got to go – you can't come here.'

Kasper pulled away from her. He turned to go, but then came back and leant in close to her face. 'Listen. I've been around a long time – a lot longer than you, and I'm telling you this is bad. What you're involved with is bad. I've been talking . . . '

'Don't talk to anyone.'

'Just listen to me,' he said, gripping her wrist, 'she's up to her neck in everyone's business – people are talking about soldiers being killed and . . . '

211

'You don't know what you're talking about. You don't know her.'

'I don't think you do either. This is fishy – it stinks. There is no reason this woman needs to go to this much trouble to find some information on a pilot.'

'It's about separation – I told you.'

'The trouble she's going to – this has got to be bad. I'll get your information, but I've been looking into what's around the edges of this, because I need a little insurance – for you and for me.'

'Insurance? What are you talking about?'

'There's some leverage to be got with your Frau Beckmann and her twins. Trust me. You don't just let blackmailers get away with it – you close it down.'

'Oh God!' said Eva. 'Maybe I could stop it all. Maybe I could talk to Frau Beckmann again.' She was looking up at him, wide-eyed and desperate. 'It's all . . . I didn't know it was going to be like this. Not you . . . not other people. Just . . . I could just stop it all. I'm sure I could.'

'Really? Could you really?'

She looked away from him. One of the rubble women called out and waved to a friend on the street below. A nearby horse, tethered to a rusty curl of metal, scraped at the ground with its hoof. 'No,' said Eva eventually. 'No.'

'I'll get you this information, and soon, but I need to know that we can control the situation if it goes any further. If I have some information about Beckmann, we're back in control, what-ever happens.'

'What do you mean "we"?'

'If I could get you out of this . . .'

'You can't.'

'But if I could, would you leave her rubble group? You don't have to come and help me, but I could point you in the right direction. I'm telling you, I've dealt with worse.'

'A second ago you said you couldn't trust me.'

'I don't trust anything you've told me – that's not the same.'

'And what would I do when you've got your leverage? When you've rescued me? Once I've been thrown out on the street, without a job? Help you trade tins of ham?' Kasper let her wrist go and the white hand print on her skin turned blood red.

'You can do anything you like,' he said. 'I don't care.'

Eva rubbed her wrist. 'I'm sorry,' she said. 'I didn't mean ... I just don't need rescuing.' Kasper picked up his brown paper bag and hugged it to his chest. 'I'm sorry, Herr Meier. You have to go now. They'll start gossiping.'

'I'll sort this out.' She looked up at him imploringly. 'You can trust me,' he said and turned away from her.

As he passed the rubble pile he looked up the slope at the women working through the debris. The two women now on the slope stopped and turned to look at him. 'I don't suppose you girls have any cigarettes to sell? I have stockings,' he said, holding up the brown paper bag, which contained none. The stout woman that had been on the rubble when he arrived shielded her eyes and he saw that she had a large port-wine stain, that ran scarlet down her cheek, into the neck of her filthy shirt. The tall woman with the long, crooked nose, who had been speaking to Heinrich, squinted and said, 'We don't have any need for stockings. What would we do with stockings here?'

He stared up at her, at her eyes that were like black pinpricks on her flat face. 'Have we met before?' Kasper said.

She shrugged. 'If we have, it can't have been very memorable.'

Kasper laughed. Then he noticed the sleeves of the stout girl with the birthmark, which were flecked with red blood. 'You all right?' he said.

'Why?' said the girl.

'Your shirt.'

213

She looked down at herself and then found the marks. 'Oh,' she said. 'It's not mine.'

'It's mine,' the tall woman said. 'I cut my leg – we're always cutting ourselves out on the rubble.'

Kasper nodded. 'You need penicillin? Or dressings?'

'We don't need anything from you,' the tall woman said and put her arm around the other girl's shoulder.

'Yes,' Kasper said, 'I see.'

He moved away, past where Eva had been sitting with the short-haired girl, but the girl was gone. Eva was returning to the rubble pile and stared up at him angrily.

'Where's your friend gone?' Kasper said, 'The girl with the cropped hair.'

Eva opened her mouth to answer, but behind him the tall woman called out, 'She's done for the day.'

Kasper turned. 'It's barely lunchtime.'

'What do you know about working the rubble?' the woman said.

Kasper looked at Eva and gave her as comforting a smile as he could. She stared down at the floor.

He strode on, his head up and listened to the burst of exasperated muttering once he was out of earshot. He hoped that Eva might be standing, her gloves hanging loose in her hands, watching how confidently he was walking, watching how stubborn and exacting his dealing of this situation would be, so that she would trust him to extricate himself and her from this, so that she would know that he could do it, that he would do it. That he could rescue her.

MATTHEW LOPEZ

'He going to be much longer?' said Lopez.

The Lieutenant's secretary stopped typing and shrugged. 'I don't know,' she looked at her watch, then shrugged again and said, 'You know I really don't know.' She smiled at Lopez supportively until he looked down at the cap in his hand nodding and she started typing again.

Lopez tucked his feet up underneath the chair and looked at the hat, then at the shining green linoleum on the floor and then around the office. Although it had been freshly painted, there was some brown damp creeping through from a seam at the edge of the ceiling. A clock from the original German office was attached to the wall high up, but had stopped running.

'You from Texas?' said Lopez looking up.

The secretary didn't stop typing this time and said, 'Me? No I'm not from Texas.'

Lopez nodded. 'I'm from New York,' he said and then laughed. 'But you probably already got that from the accent and all.' The secretary's eyes flicked up towards him and she smiled, but didn't stop typing. 'You sound like you got a Texas accent,' said Lopez.

The secretary stopped and leant on the desk frowning. 'Really?' she said.

'Sounds like that to me. You ain't from Texas?'

'No,' she said.

'Where you from?'

'Missouri.'

'Missouri!' said Lopez, 'Huh. I would'na guessed Missouri. Whereabouts in Missouri?'

'You know Missouri?'

'Not so well, but I might'a heard of it – where yer from, that is.'

'Well, you ever heard of Viburnum, Missouri, Private?'

'Matty,' he said getting up off his chair and holding his hand out towards her. She took it briefly then went straight back to typing. 'I ain't never heard of it,' he said, 'Virbinum.'

'Viburnum,' she said.

'Yeah,' he said, 'I ain't never heard of it. Sounds nice.' The secretary stopped typing and referred to some notes on the desk beside her. She scribbled something on the piece of paper then began typing again.

Lopez looked out of the window behind her, at the barely sprouted leaves that were waving there at the top of the tall tree. 'You got an oak there,' he said. The secretary didn't answer. 'Me, I'm good with trees. Don't have many where I'm from, but I know'm. I got sick once, when I was a kid, and I was in bed for a month. I learnt all fifty states and their capitals, then I learnt about the countries in the world and then I learnt about trees. So I'm good with trees.' The secretary was now staring iron-faced at her work. 'You like trees?' he said.

She burst out laughing and fell back into her chair.

'What?' said Lopez, smiling too. 'What did I say?'

'Oh God,' said the secretary smiling, 'do you ever stop?'

Lopez shrugged in a goofy way. 'I was just askin' questions.'

'"Do I like trees?"'

'What? It's a question.'

She shook her head smiling. 'You're persistent,' she said, 'I'll give you that.'

'That's what they tell me,' he said.

The door opened and the Lieutenant looked out. He was a short Irishman from Union County, New Jersey, with black hair and a red face. 'What the hell's going on out here? Mary?'

The secretary sat up straight at her desk and said, 'I'm sorry Lieutenant Keating, I was just . . .'

'It's like a madhouse out here,' he grumbled. 'Who the hell is this?'

'This is Private Lopez, sir.'

'For God's sakes man. Get into my office.'

Twenty minutes later, as Private Lopez edged out of Lieutenant Keating's office, Mary was putting on her coat. She tried to get around her desk and out of the door, but couldn't find her cap.

'You off home?' said Lopez, his voice boyish and a little weaker after his meeting with the Lieutenant.

'Um,' said Mary, kneeling down. 'Yeah, I . . .' Her cap had fallen off the desk – she picked it up off the floor. 'Got it,' she said, picking it up and squaring it on her head. She pretended she hadn't heard what he'd said.

'I said, are you walking back now?'

'Oh,' she said, 'Well, I don't walk back – I mean, it's too far. There's a truck that takes all the girls back to base.'

'I got my own Jeep!' said Lopez brightening. 'I mean it's not my Jeep, but I got it to use this afternoon. I'll give you a lift back.'

'I don't know,' said Mary, walking towards the door. 'I don't want to put you to any trouble.'

'It's no trouble,' said Lopez, throwing his arms into the air and almost shouting. 'Come on, will ya!'

'Oh, all right,' said Mary shrugging. 'But no funny business,' she said frowning.

He followed her down the steps of the building, which was still ridden with bullet holes like acne scars. 'You're a real ball breaker, you know. Anyone ever tell you that?'

'You keep your mouth shut,' she said smiling and he laughed.

As the Jeep pulled up to the checkpoint at the front entrance, one of the privates on guard leant in grinning and said, 'Hey Mary, this one causing you any trouble?'

Lopez looked round her and said, 'Hey, why is everyone bustin' my balls?'

Mary and the guard laughed and Mary said, 'You think I need to watch out for him, Charlie?'

'I don't know Mary,' said the guard, feigning consideration. 'These Italians.'

'I ain't Italian. Lopez! That sound Italian to you?'

'Sounds pretty Italian to me,' said the guard.

'Then you ain't got no culture,' said Lopez leaning back in his seat. The guard smiled and slapped the side of the Jeep twice, before lifting the barrier.

'He's in Europe and he don't know nothing about Europeens!' said Lopez miserably under his breath.

'Oh, Charlie's not so bad,' said Mary, looking out of the side of the Jeep at the woods around Dahlem. She was glad to have been posted on the edge of Berlin where she could stare into the forest and pretend that she was somewhere beautiful. She had been a romantic teenager who had opted to take extra French in high school and had begun eating up European novels: Flaubert, Stendhal, Zola; then Tolstoy and Chekhov's short stories; then Goethe and Schiller. She'd pored over the landscapes of the Romantics at the library and drawn castles and boulevards on

218

her copybook during history lessons. And on many humid nights she would fall asleep in the room she shared with her sister, listening to the leaves on the cottonwood tree stirring, and dreaming of the life she would lead once she escaped to Europe: drinking coffee, slipping cigarettes from the silver case that she'd been given by her French, Italian or Spanish lover, waking to the sound of the city alive beneath her apartment window and the sun streaming through the closed shutters onto her naked body and her disarrayed sheets.

When she first arrived at Hamburg, she'd delayed getting into the truck by fussing with the buttons on her jacket, so that she could sit at the back and watch the continent streaming away behind her, but all that she saw was rubble; and the few beautiful buildings that were still standing, and the pockmarked monuments, only served to compress her misery even more until she pushed through the other girls to sit at the front of the truck, her heart broken.

Mary looked over at Lopez. He undid his top button and ran his finger beneath his loose collar. There was something attractive about him, she thought. Something about all that pomade in his hair, his smooth brown skin, the St. Christopher's medallion that he'd just revealed around his neck as he loosened his tie, which reminded her of the boys back home. 'What were you seeing Keating about?' she said. 'Seemed pretty rankled.'

'Aw, nothing really. He's just het up about some black market stuff.'

'Black market? You into that?'

'Me? Na. No way. Some of the boys though – nothing serious.' Mary seemed disappointed. 'There's a name that's been coming up. A Kraut. It's kinda funny. Frau Beckmann – that's what she's called. She's got something going on, I don't know what it is. Nothing big.'

'Why is it funny?'

'Most of her stuff's with Russians. And Coco – he's just a driver really – but he knows some Russkis and she's got a reputation – this Beckmann. People go missing if they work with her. Then this guy Bobby, he's doing some deal with this Frau Beckmann, and Coco's like, this Frau Beckmann – people who do deals with her go missing. And Bobby's kind of a soft guy, you know. Kind of a pansy. And he's all freaked, and suddenly it's all, "Oh God, Frau Beckmann's after me, she's got me watched, she's got her kids coming after me". It's kind of stupid. It's funny. If you knew him, that is – then you'd find it funny.'

'I suppose,' said Mary. 'But you're not involved.'

'Ah, no,' said Lopez. 'Not me. I don't get involved in that stuff. You stick with me – I'm honest me.'

Mary laughed. 'Are you really Spanish?' she said.

'Sure,' said Lopez. 'Spanish American.'

'Were your parents from Spain?'

'My pop's old man.'

'You speak Spanish?'

'*Hable Espanol?*' said Lopez in his thick New York accent, turning to her and smiling. She tried to smile back, but he could feel her disappointment. 'Na, not really. My pa don't neither.'

Mary nodded. They were in sight of the main road when something hit the windscreen of the Jeep causing it to crack. Lopez slammed on the breaks and said, 'What the fuck!'

'Drive,' said Mary, 'shouldn't we keep driving?'

'It'll be ... goddamn kids,' he muttered to himself and got out of the Jeep. 'Sorry for cursing.'

'Take your gun,' said Mary. He wandered round the vehicle so that he was standing at her side, staring into the wood. A breeze moved the trees – they leant away from them and then they were still. 'Hey! Come out here. Hey!' The only sound came from the engine of the Jeep ticking over. Mary crouched down in her seat and stared into the forest.

'Let's just drive,' said Mary. 'Come on Lopez.'

He waved away her comment and shouted. 'Hey.' There was silence again. Lopez shrugged. 'These kids. We save their lives and all they can do is . . .' a shot rang out – Mary thought Lopez had fired his gun and that the force had pushed him back causing the Jeep to rock. She felt somehow as if Lopez had hit her with his elbow, but then the pain came, running down her arm from her shoulder. She looked down at the little hole in her jacket and at the brown-red stain beginning to form. She was breathless for a second and looked up Lopez who had turned to her. 'They shot me,' said Mary. 'Someone shot me.' As she said it the front of Lopez's head burst across the driver's seat of the Jeep and she was covered in blood and the heat of it covered her face and she screamed. She screamed and she cried 'Oh God! Oh God! They're shooting us!' She wiped the blood from her eyes and when she flicked her hands she heard it hit the window screen like rain water. She gagged and tried to scramble forward to find Lopez, but his body was already lying on the ground at the side of the Jeep. As she slipped out of the side door she wondered whether she should have tried to drive the Jeep back, but she was already running, running and screaming down the forest road back to the offices.

CIGARETTES

Kasper squatted, out of breath, with his back against a boarded-up tobacconist opposite Berlin Zoo station. An American or British medic was talking loudly to a female colleague, then their voices were drowned out by the clunking roll of a tram and then of a train, its brakes eliciting a long, steady scream. Kasper stood up and rubbed his chest with a balled fist. His appointment with the British soldiers had arrived and gone, but they hadn't appeared – perhaps they had moved or been demobbed. Perhaps they had found a new trading partner, perhaps Beckmann, he thought and smiled at the irony of it. Beckmann who, like God, was nowhere and everywhere. If his British contacts were lost it could take days to find the pilot, which wouldn't have mattered, he supposed, if something wasn't so deeply wrong, the emblem, those rows of metal beds, that cold, unused living room, the spider-web thread moving in the imperceptible currents of the room, towards him, the tall woman on top of the rubble, her small eyes fixed on him.

With a breathless relief, Kasper saw two British soldiers appear on the corner of Budapester Straße, opposite the jagged fang of the Kaiser Wilhelm Memorial Church. He picked up his brown paper bag, his hand shaking, and dipped into a doorway to loosen one of his shoelaces. He walked towards them confidently enough to have the shoelace flapping loose by the time he had reached them. He slowed down until he was within earshot and bent down to tie it up. They were talking English with strong accents of some kind – he couldn't understand what they were saying. He stood up and brushed something from his knee and then pretended to notice them, smiled, walked past them and then stopped as if remembering something. 'Excuse me,' he said in German, and then in English, '*need tsigarette,*' and he mimed the action of smoking, then pointed to himself. '*Know where?*'

The shorter soldier, barely eighteen, turned to him and said, '*You been writing notes?*' He took out the note that Kasper had given Eva to pin to the board at Savignyplatz. Kasper nodded.

'*You got money?*' said the soldier, and rubbed his fingers together. 'Geld,' he said in German, without attempting the accent.

'*Yes,*' said Kasper and patted his top pocket.

'*Show me,*' said the soldier.

Kasper shook his head. '*Not here. Other place.*' The soldier turned to his friend, a tall, blond man, who moved towards them, turning, putting his arm over his friend's arm and pulling Kasper in until he was one edge of a tight circle, shielded from view. The little soldier said, '*Show me. Zeigen. Show me. You have to prove it.*' He punched at Kasper's top pocket with his finger.

'*Other place,*' said Kasper again.

'*No one can see, mate,*' said the soldier. '*Come on,*' and moved in closer. Kasper sighed, opened his jacket and showed him the tops of the dog-eared Marks he had in his top pocket. The soldiers loosened, the circle went slack and fell apart. The short one said, '*Come with me my friend. Lots of cigarettes.*' And he mimed smoking. '*Lots of cigarettes.*'

'*Informations,*' said Kasper.

'*What information?*' said the little soldier.

Kasper pointed at the soldier's pocket, where he had put the note. '*Also informations. Not bad. Just informations.*'

The little soldier said something to his friend and he laughed. Kasper hadn't understood. But the soldier patted Kasper boisterously on the back and signalled for him to follow him. The other soldier followed too, the deep laughter erupting again, bubbling over the sound of a pneumatic machine, up high where the train tracks were, firing rivets into iron.

They walked down Kurfürstendamm, the tall blond soldier behind, the shorter soldier by his side, and turned off into Joachimstaler Straße. The sky was thickening as the clouds built up above them. The weight of the air made Kasper tired, and following the soldier, being led and, briefly, not thinking about his destination, about the twins or his next turning, his lips parted and he became dreamy. He barely noticed the direction of the next turn, or the one after that. And as the clouds blackened, and the light implied evening, he thought he could hear a record being played – a low German woman's voice. But no, it was something mechanical. A spinning wheel in a machine. And there was something else – laughter again.

Kasper wiped at the sweat forming on his brow and noticed that they were in a relatively intact street and at moments, if he ignored the uniformed Briton, it could have been 1926, a residual taste of red wine in his mouth, the certainty of being in love. He thought he picked up the smell of fried potatoes with onions. Frying in a black, cast-iron pan, the fat bubbling up around them. He saw a hand gripping the wooden handle of the pan – Phillip's hand. He saw him at the stove wearing Kasper's long-johns, which were too big for him – his bare back and the constellation of three dark moles at his shoulder, the final one with a thin white aureole. Phillip turned to Kasper who was sitting at the kitchen table – he held a cigarette in his mouth and

225

smiled. No, he was laughing; he laughed and he turned the pan up and Kasper saw that he'd burnt the onions. Kasper was angry and stood up to march out of the kitchen – he knew he was being ridiculous. But Phillip caught him and wrapped his arms around him from behind. He took his cigarette out and put it between Kasper's lips and kissed Kasper's neck.

'*Oi, Jerry,*' said the short soldier. '*You still with us?*'

Kasper looked up. He realised they had slowed down. Kasper smiled and nodded. He no longer knew where they were and had lost his sense of which direction they'd walked in.

They approached a block of flats with cracked, but otherwise intact, plaster on the outside, painted white and yellow, in the form of bouquets of flowers over the windows on the first and second floor and over the doorway. The soldier knocked on the door and said, '*It's Coleman.*'

'*Coleman's Mustard?*' came the reply and the soldier said, '*No, Coleman Hawkins.*' The soldier smiled at Kasper, who smiled back, assuming that there was some sort of joke contained therein, which he was supposed to have understood. The door opened to reveal another soldier with an indent around his slick pomaded hair, where he'd recently been wearing a cap. The two men talked briefly and laughed and there was some hand-shaking and back-slapping and then Kasper was introduced. He recognised the words 'cigarette', 'Kraut' and 'cash' before he was ushered in. The tall blond soldier stayed outside, turning and kicking a lump of plaster into the street.

The hall of the building was dark and damp and smelt of mud, potatoes and vegetable water. The Art Deco tiles that ran up to shoulder height had been covered over with brown paint, the colour of faeces, above which the rest of the walls and the ceiling were painted in an oppressive claret red, so thick that the shapes in the plaster work around the ceiling were unrecognisable.

They went through a door into the ground-floor flat, into a

room even darker than the hall. The windows had been boarded up almost to the top, leaving just a foot of unencumbered glass to light the room. It was empty of furniture except for a round, scratched mahogany table in the centre and a few chairs. Three British soldiers sat around the table, one with his jacket hanging on the back of his chair, and his sleeves rolled up. They were smoking and playing cards and there was a small stack of dirty plates, one with an ugly picture of a boy playing a pipe in a pink surround. The room smelt of smoke, tinned meat and cheap brandy, undercut with men's sweat and the scent of the brown transparent soap that he often picked up from British soldiers in exchange for schnapps.

The soldier with rolled-up shirtsleeves said something in English and the short soldier replied and Kasper heard 'cigarettes' again. The soldier at the table motioned Kasper forward and said something directly to him, hitting his finger on the table. Kasper turned to the short soldier, who said, 'Geld. Zeigen.' Kasper opened his jacket and rippled his finger across the edges of the paper.

'*How much?*' said the soldier.

Kasper said, '*Not for cigarette.*'

'*What are you talking about? What's he talking about, Frank?*'

The soldier who had led him in shrugged. '*On the note, it said cigarettes.*'

'*Yes,*' said Kasper, struggling with the English, '*But now, informations.*'

The soldier sitting opposite him sat back in his chair and frowned. '*I don't much like the sound of that. What kind of information?*'

Kasper said, '*RAF. To find. Red hair.*' The soldier frowned and Kasper shrugged his shoulders. '*Not bad.*'

'*I think you've come to the wrong place my friend. We're not about to sell out our boys, you understand?*'

227

'*No,*' said Kasper struggling, sweating, '*Not bads. To explain.*'
Kasper took some more notes out of his pocket.

The soldier shouted and after a few seconds a man came in wearing civilian trousers and a torn, green British Army shirt. He was young and fit looking, except for his right arm which ended at the elbow in a messy, red scar. The soldier said something to him in rapid English, and the man turned to Kasper and said, 'What information do you need?' He was German.

'I'm looking for someone. I need to speak to them. Someone in the RAF. A German woman wants to get in touch with him. She's aware of the difficulties, but the woman's daughter had a child. She thinks it's this pilot's.'

The German smiled comfortingly. He translated and the soldier laughed and replied. The young man with half an arm said, 'The British armed forces don't fraternise with German women.'

Kasper nodded, 'Yes, of course,' he said, took the notes he had counted out and stood up to leave.

The British soldier said something and the German man held out his hand to stop Kasper. 'But if this person has responsibilities, then he should honour them. As long as nothing's going to happen to him – that it's just about a child.'

'Yes,' Kasper said. 'The woman doesn't want anything from him. It's just about the child.'

The German translated for him and asked Kasper to describe who he was looking for. The British soldier nodded as the German interpreted the rough description and scant facts, but shook his head.

'A red-haired pilot isn't really enough to go on, and these guys are army, so they only know people they see around in Berlin. If he keeps to Gatow, they won't know him. They don't really know many pilots.'

'Me neither,' Kasper said, 'but I'm sure he doesn't keep to

Gatow. I'm sure he's around. Aren't there any British people, red-haired British people, that are trading as well, that he or one of the soldiers might know?'

The German passed on the question, but again, the answer was, 'There are plenty of red-haired British people. If he's about in Berlin, is there nothing else you can think of, where he might go, who he might know.'

'Beckmann, perhaps,' Kasper said.

The soldier's eyes narrowed. The German repeated the question in English and he answered curtly.

'Yes, there are few people that deal with Beckmann,' the interpreter said, 'and he would be happy to give you any information you want about them.'

'Red-haired pilots or even soldiers – perhaps she was mistaken about him being a pilot.'

The British soldier looked Kasper in the eye and said, '*Gareth Edwards, James or Jim McGovern, Malcolm Butler and David Penn-Wallace.*' He then took a piece of paper and wrote down their initials against a few bars and areas of the city. He handed it to Kasper, said something in quick hard staccato to the interpreter and left the room.

'What did he say?' Kasper said.

'He said that you didn't get this information from him, but he wouldn't be sorry to hear that any of these men had been dealt with. He says he knows others involved with that woman and that you would be welcome to come back for information again, if he could be of help.'

Kasper nodded. 'OK,' he said. 'Thank you.'

The German man looked concerned. 'You know, you really should be careful. You can't go round trying to blackmail them, if that's your plan.'

'No, of course not,' said Kasper. He took the piece of paper and pushed the notes towards the interpreter, trying not to tot

229

up the amount of money, time, goods Eva had cost him since she'd barged into his flat.

'And this Beckmann . . .'

'Yes,' said Kasper, 'One hears about her.'

The German nodded. He looked sad.

'How old are you?' Kasper said.

'Twenty,' the young man said.

'They treat you all right here?'

'Yes,' he said, 'They're all right.'

'Good,' said Kasper, picking up his brown paper bag. 'That's important,' he said. The small soldier who had brought him to the apartment block took him out again, leading him to the front steps of the building where he stood laughing and waving with his blond colleague until Kasper had turned the corner.

INFORMATION

Kasper reached a nameless side street near Schloßstraße. He tried to keep up a rapid pace, but his exhaustion, his wandering thoughts, slowed him down. He kept finding himself standing still, his fingers lightly touching the skin beside his blind eye while a series of interconnected thoughts and images ran together, like a snake eating its own tail: the soldiers, Eva alone in the flat, the figure of Frau Beckmann, the twins at the attic door, Eva in the dark of a stairwell, soldiers. When he became conscious of his immobility he would look up and around him into the darkening sky, would walk on then slip into a doorway, around a corner, behind one of the rubble women's locked up wagons, and listen.

He was tired. His mouth was dry, the balls of his feet ached, his back was stiff; he was infused with a heavy weariness, a feeling that pervaded his limbs, his face; made him want to find any soft dark corner and lie down, fall asleep. He felt like he'd been on the move for days, for years, ever since the bar had been closed and he had sat with Phillip in that empty room, snow showering through the smashed windows, settling dry on the freezing floorboards at their feet, like volcanic ash. Resting at his apartment seemed a brief fitful pause in what had become constant, never-ending movement. Like a shark, he had often thought, stopping would mean the death of him, but oblivion would also mean peace, silence. He dreamed of enforced rest, being stuck on a ship; God, even in prison. A life in which he would be fed and no more would be expected of him than to lie on a bed and sleep. Perhaps he really was alone. Perhaps he could rest.

The city was almost silent here except for a gathering wind that blustered gently down the streets, a precursor to an oncoming storm that was accompanying the approaching dusk. It was cool and strong enough to flick off the dead leaves that had remained attached to trees throughout the winter, their dry edges clicking along the broken concrete of the road at his feet. And strong enough to pick at loose plaster, letting it smash on the ground, whip up a little dry dust, flap a loose piece of raggedy material, mimicking the sound of two children creeping along behind him in the half-light. But hadn't he heard a voice, a muttering whisper, a giggle?

As he turned onto Seelingstraße, a large v-shaped cleft opened up in the wall in front of him, the rubble leading up to it low and trodden down. He picked his way over to it, disappeared through the gap and found himself in a house, empty of floors – a square tower, with tall thin walls, peppered on one side with empty windows. Everything had been cleared and in the grey light he saw that the ground beneath his feet was smooth, flattened earth. He moved into a dark corner and waited. He felt sick and feverish again, trying to focus on the destroyed building, and not on the brief snatches of images in his head, those rows of empty beds, the thick inky line beneath his name, the strange coldness of that living room.

Some plaster dust fell somewhere outside the walls. Stones knocked against one another. He imagined Hans and Lena

232

circling the building, he saw them entering the ruined tower, approaching him, holding sticks, holding guns. He saw him lifting up his own gun, children dead at his feet.

His head ached. He heard rubble moving beneath feet. A short gasp as someone almost lost their balance, then the sound of shoes treading on soft earth.

He squinted. A woman entered the square. 'Kasper?' said a voice in a whisper. It was Marta.

They stood leaning against the gatepost of the Schloß Charlottenburg sharing a cigarette. Above them the two gladiators still stood with their shields held above their heads, their swords outstretched. The entrance to the palace was blocked by three sad iron rods, bent and rusted, with a sad thread of rope drooping down between them.

The smoke from their cigarettes mixed with a rich, thick scent that curled up from beneath the cloth of Marta's thin dress.

'Why aren't you over at Alex?' said Kasper.

'Oh, boring squabbles. Everyone's so horribly territorial these days.' She looked at him and smiled. 'I followed you from Gierkeplatz – I was going to shout out, but you were being so shifty and walking so bloody fast. What's going on? Should I be worried?'

'It's nothing.'

'I've been looking for you all day – you were so odd last time we spoke I thought something terrible had happened. Something awful.'

'Sorry,' said Kasper. He looked up – there was an American photographer in uniform taking pictures of the front of the palace in the dying light, his face scrunched up behind the little black box in front of his face. Kasper thought for a second that it was the same man that had taken a picture of him at Berlin Zoo that morning, but he hadn't been wearing uniform.

'Is something up?' Marta said.

'Do you think this soldier's taking photos of us?'

'What for?' Marta said.

The man looked down at his camera and then squinted up at the palace behind them. Kasper shrugged. 'Nothing, I suppose.'

'Well, there is something up,' she said, 'You haven't commented at all on this ghastly perfume I'm wearing. Isn't it horrible?' she said offering up her wrist.

'I can smell it from here,' said Kasper.

'Some Ivan gave it to me last night – he said he had cash. They're all the same. I only put it on this morning to make my landlady jealous. She wasn't even up – lazy old cow. It really is putrid isn't it? Smells like church incense.'

'It probably is church incense.'

'Hmm,' she said dismally sniffing her wrist again. 'You look horribly glum, Kasper. Worse than usual.'

'Just more misery, you know.'

'Never seems to end, does it?' she said.

They heard the whir of the photographer winding in his film. 'Why were you looking for me?' said Kasper.

'Well, a thank you for the penicillin,' she did a little faux curtsey. 'Secondly a rather promising start on your pilot, I think,' she said, pulling a small, worn envelope out of her handbag. The back of it was covered in neat pencilled handwriting.

'What's this?'

'These are all British soldiers or pilots who I could find who either hang out in the bars that they can meet German women or do some sort of "trade" with German women full stop. Including the biblical kind. It's a long list, but he's got to be on there somewhere.'

He took it and stared down at it. The paper was soft, Marta's writing hurried and messy. 'These are bars?' Kasper said.

'Yes, and addresses of the places they always hang out.'

'And the German names?'

'Connections of these pilots – there's also a soldier or two.'

Kasper took out the piece of paper he had been given by the British soldiers.

'What's that?'

'Something I got from another contact.'

He compared the two lists and found two names that were on both.

'Helpful?'

'Yes,' said Kasper. 'A shortlist of two.'

'Oh, well that's done it then. That's surely enough. What's he called then, this pilot that's been giving you so much trouble?'

Kasper squinted, and said quietly, 'James McGovern or Malcolm Butler.'

'They don't sound that horrific at all.'

Kasper looked at the two sets of initials. Small insignificant letters. It was done. It was over. A door was closed, a terrifying miasma of possibilities blown away to reveal his grey life, lying there behind it the whole time. He had a profound sense that he had lost something. And now just this piece of paper, now just this hand, now just this emptiness.

'My pleasure,' said Marta.

'Sorry,' said Kasper. 'That's incredible. Thank you. That's wonderful. Really.'

'Well, I'm a fast worker,' said Marta, 'And luckily for you I was passing Willy's last night and met the most charming little English man – hairy as Esau, but a fighter pilot no less.'

Kasper continued to stare at the pieces of paper.

'He had the most amazing hairy bottom,' said Marta, lighting another cigarette. 'It was like fur. Like animal fur.'

'Maybe they're all like that,' said Kasper absently.

'What the British? Oh no, not at all. Especially not the ginger ones – your friend's lucky. Gosh, Kasper,' she said. 'Is everything really all right?'

'Yes,' he said. 'Just this girl. I'm worried about her.'

'You haven't fallen for her, have you? You're not turning?'

'No, no,' said Kasper, 'nothing like that.' He tried to imagine handing Eva this piece of paper, giving her the information that she had asked for, fulfilling the service he had been hired to do. The work of moments, of seconds, and yet it seemed unfathomable. But then what had he really seen or found out to make him think that Eva was in danger? The twins? The apartment? This list of names? They were all strange and unnerving, but what did it all really add up to? Perhaps just a lonely man looking for someone to save.

Marta sighed. 'It's been lovely seeing you a bit,' she said, suddenly sounding sad and rather serious.

'You too darling,' said Kasper.

'You know I feel it too – I do. Everyone does. Sometimes I don't know if I can keep doing it Kasper. All this.'

Kasper pushed himself upright off the gatepost and picked up the paper bag he had taken from the woman on the bus. He smiled and stroked her shoulders and said, 'You're doing fine. It'll change.'

She forced a smile and said, 'Yes, of course it will. Yes.' She shook herself. 'We should get moving – some of the girls have been having problems with the curfew – they're suddenly getting all serious about it again. I hope you're not going to be skulking around the streets all night.'

'No.'

Marta squeezed his arm. 'How's your father, by the way?'

'Fine. I mean he's still sick.'

'On his way out, you think?'

'Maybe. Yes.'

'He's, what, in his seventies now? Not bad going.'

'I suppose. Glad he didn't get to miss all this.'

Marta laughed a little. 'You need a plan, Kasper. You need something to do after this.'

Kasper pictured the tickets beneath his father's mattress, lying flat and silent in the dark. 'What like?'

'Like another bar.'

'What's the point? What kind of bar? Serving British soldiers, widowed women and children?'

'Doesn't have to be Berlin.'

'I don't know anyone outside of Berlin,' he shrugged and rubbed the side of his face. 'I mean, I barely know anyone in Berlin anymore.'

'Because it's gone – our Berlin. Why cling on to ruins?'

Kasper nodded. Imagined being packed into a queue of people at immigration, Eva pushed up against him, taking his hand. 'You're right, I suppose. What about you?'

'I'm saving up – I'm not doing all this for fun.'

'Saving up for what?'

'Daddy's vineyard in Ahrtal.'

'Back to Rhineland?'

'Why not? You can almost pretend the war never happened there at times. In the right light. It's a bit silly, isn't it?'

Kasper smiled. 'No, I can see it.'

Marta finished her cigarette and threw it onto the pavement. 'If you ever want a job.'

'Treading grapes?'

'Why not?'

A door slammed in a courtyard a few streets away. Someone coughed. A window closed. Marta brushed down her skirt. 'Well,' she said, 'once more into the breach dear friend, once more into the breach,' and she turned and trotted away across the square, disappearing into a side street.

*

Kasper made his way back to Windscheidstraße. The dusk was half eaten up by thick dirty clouds that promised rain. He would find Eva tomorrow, he thought, but tonight he would exchange some cigarettes for a bottle of schnapps on the way home and get drunk. He tried to imagine his life with no Eva, no notes, no Hans and Lena Beckmann. The colour was grey, his sleeping father becoming thinner, the creak of his mattress, sex among the rubble, watery brandy, potatoes, snow, broken floorboards, the wasteland of the city, stretching out hoary and dry, Eva alone in that living room, awake in that iron bed, surrounded by rows of strange women, the twins in the dark, their eyes open.

Kasper stopped again and looked around him – the street he was aiming for had changed, a wall of stacked bricks and a giant bomb crater blocked his way. Another street had been newly cleared though, and he made his way down it, then turned and turned again, trying to find his way back to a familiar street. But the street made a diagonal and he found himself on a road he didn't recognise, almost fully destroyed, except for two large blocks of flats, one of which had a candle burning in a top window, surrounded by a diffuse corona flickering in the dirty glass. This street hadn't yet been cleared, except for a strip down the middle, wide enough for a vehicle to drive down. He turned and looked back up the road he'd just come from, but he didn't recognise anything there either. He decided to try and aim in a westerly direction and keep walking straight, hoping to eventually meet a main road, with a bit of luck the Kurfürsten-damm.

And then he sensed that there was someone lingering behind him. He moved to get a better look, but in the failing light the rubble was full of dark shapes. He felt rain spitting on his face and decided to move on, pretending to look around him with interest rather than confusion, in the hope that anyone following him would not take him for lost. He pulled his paper bag closer to him, hugging it to try and keep it dry. He straightened up as he walked, so as to appear tall and confident, and listened out for footsteps, but he heard none, and soon the only sound was the rain beginning to crackle on the brim of his hat and on the rubble around him.

He had planned to take a left at the next crossroads, but the road there had also been destroyed, and was as yet untouched by the rubble women. It was impassable, littered with great heaps of detritus, including the thick round barrel of a Howitzer, that stuck up vertically on the debris, like a slender chimney.

He walked on, but the next left-hand turning was also blocked, so he pushed on again, hoping to meet another larger, connecting street. The rain was coming down harder and the smell of wet masonry filled the air. He tripped on a rusted twist of metal and, lifting his foot up to see if it had ripped his trouser leg, he noticed something behind him again and turned to see a piece of rubble roll inoffensively onto the street from one of the piles of debris. He felt his heart beating high up in his throat. The oncoming rain had brought an oppressive pressure and clammy warmth with it and he felt a trickle of sweat run from his armpit, down the side of his chest.

He passed yet another blocked road, he turned right and disappeared into the open doorway of a ruined building. The stairs were missing, so he slipped into the courtyard, turned left and pushed himself against a wall.

He strained to hear something. He heard only the loud hush of the rain and slapping wetness of water gushing from a broken gutter. He wondered whether it was the little soldier who was following, tasked to rough him up for asking too many questions.

The rain began to pour down in a noisy grey shower, falling freely into the roofless buildings, playing on surfaces it was not normally allowed to touch, soaking burnt carpets, swelling wood to splinter brick, making streams of mud from the debris and collapsing piles of rubble.

Kasper looked up at the sky, a dark, dirty brown, and water dripped from the brim of his hat onto his nose. He heard a shoe scuff on broken tiles and he fixed his eyes on the doorway to his right. He breathed slowly and quietly and tried to make himself as flat as possible. For a second he could imagine Phillip walking in, soaking wet, searching for him. But no – two skinny teenagers came through the door – Hans and Lena Beckmann. Thin, dark shapes, their hatless heads topped with glistening caps of wet hair. They walked past him, very slowly, perhaps believing that he had gone straight into the back building. He would not be afraid of them, he thought, and yet his stomach lurched and the saliva disappeared from his mouth. He felt a stinging in his eyes and a shaking, miserable anger.

He waited until they had gone far enough into the corridor that he might have a chance of outrunning them, then slipped as quietly as he could to the doorway and made a run for the street.

He passed through the hallway and into the relative brightness of the murky road. He turned the corner and seeing a great wall of debris rising up before him, peppered with the dark brown, pink and yellow of broken brick, he turned again, hoping to find a way out or even a whole building with a light or a candle. Beyond the terror that drove him he felt a strange exhilaration at the speed his legs were carrying him. He was stunned at how fast he was running and he felt suddenly as if he would be able to make it all the way to Windscheidstraße, bursting through the door, panting and running straight up the stairs. And the Beckmanns began to shrink away, become small, laughable, nothing.

He wouldn't have stopped at all, but something whistled through the air and hit his shoulder causing him to stumble and

240

then something hit his head and he was on the floor, the paper bag rolling away from him, the gun in his inside pocket thumping painfully against his chest.

He heard his breath close and tasted mud in his mouth and blood. There was water near his face. He saw Phillip on the floor of the apartment. He saw his bloodied eyes and his hand lifting up, shaking, falling back to the floor.

Kasper pushed himself up and got back on his feet and looked around dizzily. It was darker still, and now the muddy paths between the piles of earth and plaster barely glowed, except for the shiny off-white of the puddles. The rubble had grown around him, giant and black behind the curtain of rain, which continued to pummel the soft ground. He squatted down and found the paper bag, and wrapped his arms around it tightly. But he felt the paper begin to give beneath his fingers, beneath the watery onslaught.

'Where are you?' he shouted. The sound of his voice was swallowed up by the banks of earth around him and made it sound small, close and oddly domestic. But somewhere nearby Lena's laughter echoed, high up. He backed away and searched the tops of the rubble piles, but saw only the broken walls of the buildings behind them.

'Come out here, you little cowards,' he shouted.

The laughter came again, but closer. He turned and ran a few paces in the direction he thought he'd come, but there was a dead end, another bank of earth. He turned again. He felt that the knee of his trouser leg had ripped. The skin underneath stung, as did the skin beneath his arms, where his now-sodden shirt had begun to rub.

'Where's Eva's pilot?' said the boy. It seemed far away, down the street, but low, blocking Kasper's only route out. He squinted, but saw nothing, only the brown of the street turning blue as the blackness of the night took its final hold.

'Where is he?' said Lena, still high up, but closer to him than before.

'I've found him, you little fools,' shouted Kasper, desperately looking around him. 'And what the hell's it got to do with you?'

'What's our flat got to do with you?' said the boy, closer now, but his voice muffled, as if he was standing behind something. Kasper squinted. Beneath the black sky and with the rain in his good eye he could see nothing.

'I've had enough of this,' he said and ran forward, but a shower of rocks and stones caused him to fall painfully to his knees, and the bag to lurch forward. A great tear opened up in it and the green shoes fell out. Kasper scrabbled for them and managed to wrap the bag up around them and enclosed the whole thing in the wings of his jacket.

'You better not trick us again, Meier,' said the boy.

'Get away from me!' shouted Kasper. 'Or I'll sort you, you understand. I'll make it difficult for you.' A single, large rock landed hard in the mud in front of him, spraying water and dirt up into his face. 'Jesus!' he cried, 'You're going to kill me.'

Hans and Lena's laughter rattled off the walls of the buildings behind the piles of earth. Kasper scrambled to his feet, tripped and fell sideways into a soft wall of earth. Another rock flew down, but it landed where he'd just been kneeling. The children couldn't see him anymore. Something metal was sticking into his side, but he remained still. 'Why have you been poking around us, queer?' It was the girl's voice, near where he had been standing. 'What's it got to do with your little pilot?'

Kasper moved slowly along the bank of earth, away from the dead end.

'Tell us Meier. Or we *will* kill you,' said the boy, but their voices had converged on the point where he had been kneeling, already a few metres away. He kept moving in slow measured side steps. He heard one of them running up the earth bank again – it must have been the girl. High up, she shouted, 'You can't hide from us, queer!' The boy whooped like a Red Indian, running past Kasper, close enough that water splashed up from the ground, onto Kasper's trousers.

Kasper shuffled on until he reached the end of the pile. His next move would have to be into the open, where his steps might be heard. He listened for Lena and Hans. He could only hear the rain – it had come under brim of his hat and was running in rivulets down the neck of his shirt, running down his cheeks like tears and out of his mouth like spit. The paper bag was in pieces, but he continued to cradle it at his chest like a child. He felt a packet of cigarettes, still in the remains of the bag, mulch into a lump of pap and dribble away between his fingers. And then, so close that he could feel the heat of her breath on his ear, he heard 'I said you can't hide from us queer.'

Kasper flew from the bank into the road. He stayed on his feet and was briefly upright, unassailed. He looked up. He saw the shadow of Hans and, shoving the remains of the bag under one arm, he took the Russian gun out of his jacket pocket and held it up, his arm shaking. The shadow shifted – it seemed too tall to be one of the twins. It moved suddenly away. Kasper was winded by a kick planted in his lower back. He fell forward and hit the ground hard, the gun rolling away from him into the dark. 'I won't fight children. I won't fight you, you cowards.' He was aware of a sharp boot thudding against the base of his back repeatedly, one hitting his chin and someone stepping on his fingers, before he drew them in around the remains of his goods. They upturned him like a turtle and ripped them from him, along with the money in his jacket pocket.

Kasper lay with his hands over his ears. He listened to his shallow breath and felt the beat of his heart in his head and in the bruises that were blooming beneath his clothes.

243

Then the lips at his ear again. 'You leave us alone, queer,' said the girl, 'or they're coming for your father. He won't make it to prison alive.' Kasper felt a warm gobbet of spit hit his cheek and run down his chin, into his open mouth, and then heard the sound of the twins as they moved away, until the sound of their steps was swallowed up by the sound of the pounding rain.

Kasper lay where he was, not wishing to move, afraid of discovering that something was broken; but then the water began to pool beneath his face and so he rolled onto his back and managed to sit up. He was in pain, but so far it was only surface aches and the sting of broken skin. He could taste that his lip had split, but when he ran his tongue around his mouth he was relieved to find that all his teeth were still present. He turned and crawled forwards, into a kneel, and felt around him, finding at first only sodden scraps of paper. But then, half submerged in water, he found the heel of the green shoe and then he found its pair. The gun was gone.

He stood up and began to walk. He moved slowly. His muscles felt as if they'd been tightened and weakened – as if at any moment his tendons might snap. He felt a heavy twinge of pain by his kidneys. He stopped and leant forward. It came like a wave up through his back and then was gone and he was able to move again.

He stumbled, dropping the shoes. He put his head in his hands, just to be still for a moment, just to breathe. He saw Phillip again, standing over him while he lay sick in bed. The palm of his hand resting on his forehead. The bass vibrations of his voice running down his arm, vibrating on Kasper's skull. He heard the rain on waxed cloth, smelt the foul mud of those long trenches winding through the Belgian countryside, felt the earth, metal, bone showering up into his face, hitting his eye like a fist.

He gathered up the shoes and slowly buttoned them into his jacket with his aching fingers, his burning fingernail beds, then forced his head up, and pushed into the rain, searching again for an open left-hand turning.

AN ENAMELLED CUP

The rain came heavier still. Kasper rested against the building opposite his apartment block, in the spot where he had first seen Hans and Lena Beckmann. Perhaps they would be there now – Kasper was too exhausted to care. The pain that throbbed in large hot patches around and inside his body was accompanied by a cold sweat seeping out of his skin in the places that the rain couldn't wash clean.

He looked up at his door. There was a woman there – sitting on the steps. She pulled her knees up and rested her chin on them and watched the spray from the rain make droplets on the dark green wool of her coat. It was Eva. He was overcome by a wave of relief, cut off by a sickening wrench in the small of his back.

He heard someone running down the street; the dark figure of a woman, who suddenly stopped at the doorway. Eva jumped to her feet.

'Who are you?' said the stranger, her screeching voice carrying across the street to where Kasper leant against the wet plaster. She pulled a sodden scarf from her hair. 'What do you want?'

'I'm waiting for someone,' said Eva, her voice echoing off the street's barren walls.

'Who?'

'Herr Meier.'

The woman laughed, and pushed past Eva, letting the door swing back and crack loudly against the frame.

Kasper waited until he believed he could move without falling, and made his way across the street to the door of his building. His feet fell heavily and awkwardly into pot holes and puddles, splashing rain up his sodden trouser legs, muddy water hitting his face. Eva turned, her face contracting, toughening, her shoulders pushing back, but, recognising him, her mouth opened, her body loosened. Within a few steps he was by her and looked up at her and she saw the cuts and bruises on his face. Rainwater ran over his hat down a kink in the brim, dribbling away from him in a thin stream. She reached up – he felt her cold fingers on the skin of his cheek. She tried to say something, but her mouth opened and closed like a fish's, and Kasper looked up at her like an animal about to be slaughtered.

Unable to speak, to acknowledge her presence except with the tears that were hidden by the water that soaked them, he pushed on past her, through the door, into the black hall and then the half-light of the courtyard, where he stumbled to his knees and a green shoe fell out of his jacket and rolled across the courtyard floor. Eva ran and tried to pick him up by the shoulders.

'The shoe,' said Kasper. She fetched it and then pulled him to his feet with just one arm; he felt it around him, slender but unyielding. It held him tight, like a rope, and she levered him upright and walked him towards the backhouse staircase.

Kasper didn't remember climbing the stairs. He remembered not being able to get his face comfortable on the pillow and lying on his back. And he remembered struggling with the hands that were trying to remove his jacket and them pinning him down until he stopped moving and abandoned himself to their control.

He woke late in the night. He saw that Eva was asleep in one of the kitchen chairs, her arms crossed, her legs stretched out in front of her and her head bent backwards, leaning against the wall. The window had been propped open with a tin of British corned beef and cold air dribbled through it, across the floor towards him. He wanted to shut the window, but when he moved a wave of pain surged up from his hips and caused sweat to break out across his forehead. He could feel the cold air on his neck and eased his blanket up – although his arm ached – and managed to pull some of the rug over him. This was the last fully conscious memory he had for twenty-four hours.

The flash of spring had come to a temporary end and winter took its final grip on the city. Cold air from Russia descended on Berlin and crept through the streets, finding its old resting places among the ruins and the gloomy rooms of the residents.

As people turned sadly to furniture and half-empty book-shelves, selecting the few volumes they had hoped to retain and threw them into the ovens to burn, Kasper himself caught light and the stinging sweat of fever burst across his skin.

His blanket, the old rug, the sound of the window being closed, a woman and a man's voice, Phillip at the stove, all merged into one set of dark characters who huddled together and demanded that he search for the green shoes and make the pair, and whenever the left shoe was in his hand, the right shoe was gone, and when he had the right shoe the left was gone and sometimes he would fall deeper into the blackness and then would return to the surface, pulled up by his dry tongue, to dis-cover that both shoes were gone and that he must find the brown bag, collect the mother-of-pearl clip from the old lady's hair, and exchange the lot with the naked man in the forest, who was also Phillip, but wasn't Phillip, because Phillip was also sitting in the corner of Heinrich's room staring jealously at Kasper in bed, his face streaked with tears, and the whole time the edge of the rug scratched at his neck, so irritating that it teased bile up from his stomach, so that suddenly he erupted into consciousness, pushed himself up, his back and arms aching, and threw up, but not on the floor, because a basin appeared in Eva's hand and his father stood at the doorway and Kasper was briefly incredulous before he slipped back down, under the blanket and the rug, back into the brown darkness, where the figures surrounded him and ordered him to search for the shoes, for the green leather shoes and the paper bag.

Someone said, 'Kasper. Kasper.' Fingers touched his face, then the cold back of someone's hand.

The ringing of a metal handle against a metal bucket. The bored tap of fingers on the windowsill.

A woman was singing.

'Want to go to my little kitchen, Want to cook my little soup,
A little hunchbacked man's there, He's broken my little pot.'

The boarded-up windowpane.

He woke late at night and was aware of someone snoring, but was too tired to lift his head. He was thirsty too, but too tired to lift his hand and too tired to feel around for a cup.

Children screamed in the courtyard below them. Their feet squeaked on the snow.

*

Kasper's father was at the door. Young again.

'When they ask: Who has to die? And they'll hear me say: All of them! And when their heads roll I'll say: Hooray!'

He was falling helplessly and terrified into a deep sleep, dark and solid, like death.

And he awoke to laughter.

His head was heavy and ached and he couldn't open his eyes. He lay on his front now, gripping the thin pillow. He felt a strange hot tingling around his back and down his legs. Again, a girl laughing in the room.

'His shorts were actually frozen,' said the old man, laughing as he told the end of his story. 'We took them off him and his mother stood them up – I'm not joking, you could actually stand them up.'

The laughter – of the girl and the man – rose again and then petered out.

'He's a good lad really, you know. You must ignore his moods. He's had some knocks.' The leg of a chair creaked. 'But you mustn't keep coming if you have other things to do – he won't tell you he's grateful. He will be, but he won't tell you.'

'I don't mind coming,' said the girl. 'I like coming.'

'He likes you.'

The girl laughed.

'Honest to God, I can tell. You'd know if he didn't.'

'Maybe you're right,' said the girl.

'But what you get from coming, I don't know.'

'He's actually quite charming when he wants to be,' she said. 'And he's funny. And there's, I don't know, a . . .'

'Sympathy,' said the man.

'Yes,' she said, laughing. 'In the eyes.'

251

'In the eye.'

Kasper heard the wind throwing a light handful of hard snow at the window, sounding dry as dust.

'And he doesn't want anything from me,' said the girl.

'Yes,' said the old man. 'That sounds right.' The man stood up, groaning as he went. He yawned. 'He'd have done well giving me some grandchildren, but . . . It wasn't to be.'

The girl didn't answer at first. Then offered, 'Never met the right woman.'

'No, he was married,' said the old man.

'Pardon?' she said.

'Oh yes – very briefly. Many years ago now. He was very young. She died, poor thing. Blood pressure. They'd barely been married nine months.'

'Blood pressure?'

'She was pregnant – same thing happened to Kasper's mother.'

The girl was silent. Kasper tried to swallow, tried to work up enough energy to call out, to stop them talking. 'Does Herr Meier have a child then?' the girl said eventually.

'No, no,' said the old man. 'The little girl died with her mother. He'd have been a good father. I was a bad father.'

'I'm sure you weren't,' the girl said quietly, politely.

'No one tells you how to do it. This one would have been good at it. If he'd just . . . well, hell would freeze over before he took any of my advice.'

The man crossed the room. Kasper tried to make a sound. He loosened his grip on the pillow, but wave after wave of fatigue washed over him, pulled him back down, the conversation breaking up, mixing with visions of the sheets he was sleeping on. Tossing him up and around in endless spinning eddies.

He woke again as the sky was beginning to darken. He was unsure whether he was hungry or sick. He moved and his muscles shook in a dull, tight pain and he was wet with sweat. He turned in bed and opened his eyes. The room was blue-grey, unlit in the twilight. He pushed the sheets away and enjoyed the coolness that came from letting himself dry, like a butterfly, wet from the chrysalis.

'Hello?' he croaked, but there was no reply.

After half an hour he managed to turn onto his side for a moment and saw that the corner of the kitchen had been turned into a sort of nest: a chair pushed against the wall with a blanket over the back, a small brass bowl on the neighbouring crate filled with cigarette butts and ash, an empty plate, one of his own books open, lying face down. He rolled onto his back again and heard his father stir in the other room.

'Kasper?' The old man's mattress creaked and he shuffled down the corridor and appeared at the door. 'You awake, boy?'

Kasper tried to say, 'Yes,' but the word caught at the back of his throat and he began to cough, the shock of it throbbing in flashes of pain at his ribs; a crackling cough that pulled up a day's worth of sour, rattling phlegm. He leant over to spit it out and the coughing made him retch until he was exhausted and fell back onto the mattress.

The old man brought him water from the bucket in an enamelled, metal cup with rusty chips around the rim. He crouched down slowly, his bones and joints cracking, and Kasper managed to sip from it, dribbling a little onto his chin and onto the sheets. The old man refilled the cup and put it down by Kasper's side, on the floor, and went and sat in the chair by the window. He put his hands on his knees and coughed himself, almost as deep and sharp as Kasper's own. Stilling it eventually with his mouth buried in the crook of his arm, he sighed and said, 'It's snowing again. Wet snow. I wonder if winter will ever end this year. Perhaps this is it.'

Kasper bent his head back enough to see the heavy clumps

falling on the other side of the windowpane, but stretching his neck caused him to start coughing again.

'I thought Fräulein Hirsch had been here,' Kasper managed to say in a whisper.

'She has!' said the old man. 'Lovely girl. She's been here two nights nursing you. I told her not to stay – I couldn't imagine you'd be grateful, but she said she had nothing better to do.'

'Will she be back?'

'Probably. She's been coming early evenings.'

'I suppose I shouldn't send her away.' Kasper tried to smile. 'Probably not going to get much nursing from you.'

His father laughed, then frowned and looked down at his son. 'I don't suppose you're going to tell me what the bloody hell happened.'

'Disappointed customer.'

His father sighed and pulled himself to his feet. 'It's not a joke, Kasper. You'll get yourself killed.'

Kasper pushed himself forward so that he was sitting up on his mattress. He licked the hard edge of the dried cut in his lip and felt phlegm and inflamed flesh irritating the top of his lungs, plucking at his throat. 'I've got to get back out.'

'You've got to rest,' said the old man.

'Someone's got to get water, pick up rations.' His back twinged. 'Shit,' he said, squeezing his eyes tight shut. He tried to breathe deeply, slowly. He opened his eyes again – they were watering. 'We can't eat up all my stock, otherwise I'll have nothing to exchange. Then we're really done.'

'How long have we got? Without you getting anything?'

'Less than a day or two will be OK.'

'You can't get back out tomorrow, Kasper.'

'I'll have to try.'

'What about the girl? You two are close now, aren't you?'

'No,' said Kasper.

'Well, she's been cleaning up your sick – I'm sure she wouldn't mind picking up a bucket of water.'

'We shouldn't be relying on anyone else. And if she's here she's using up our rations, our food.'

'Yes,' said his father, turning away from him and leaving the room. 'We wouldn't want her getting a share of our little pleasure palace.'

'You've got very sarcastic in your old age,' Kasper tried to shout after him, his raised voice catching at his dry throat, causing him to cough again.

He sat on his mattress, sick and anxious, listening out for footsteps on the stairs, for Eva. He looked over at his jacket, which had been hung from a nail on the kitchen wall. He thought about the slip of paper in there. He felt a pain in his stomach, in his bowels. It was just the last of the fever, he thought. This nervousness, this feeling of being exposed. As he gained his strength these feelings would dissipate. They would ebb away, would almost be gone when he was up and about, back on the streets, moving again.

AN ALL-IN-ONE

Kasper had tried to make it down to the lavatory on the second-floor landing. Going down had been possible, but as he closed the door and sat on the toilet with his head in his hands, he knew he wouldn't be able to get back up again. He managed half a flight before he collapsed onto a step, his hand still on the banister in the hope that he might be able to haul himself up again.

The thin claret lino on the floor was as cold as stone and there was a heavy draft through a crack in one of the windows that reached the back of his neck, where his hair was damp. Eventually his hand slipped down to the stair rods and he rested his head on the embossed wallpaper beneath the dado rail and closed his eyes.

He saw Phillip again. He tried to go back to the Volkspark, waiting at the bottom of the steps in the snow, but it was impossible. He tried to think about something else; to think about nothing, but he was too exhausted to fight it. Phillip came to him in waves. He saw him at his office window on the second floor of the bank. He saw him at the other side of the road in the sunshine, squinting left and right, looking out for trams. He saw him running towards him and felt his warm body beneath the cotton of his shirt as Kasper's hand dived beneath his jacket when they embraced. He heard his voice, he heard him singing a ridiculous carnival song when Kasper was trying to read and he saw him sulking on the sofa after they had argued. He saw his naked body misty beneath the dirty water of the bathtub and he smelt the comforting human smell behind his ears, when he clung onto him in the morning, waiting for him to wake up.

He heard footsteps on the stairs and pushed himself into the wall and covered his face with his hands. If it was the twins, they could have him. He was too tired now. But no, it was Eva.

'What an earth are you doing?' she said. Her voice was calm, smoky, pleasing.

'Having a sit down.'

She stopped in front of him, her wiry health a terrible contrast to the weakness he felt through his dead limbs. She smiled. 'Still cracking jokes, eh?'

He shrugged.

'I was really worried about you. I thought we'd have to try and find a doctor.'

'They're thin on the ground round here.'

'That's true,' she said.

They heard Frau Langer shouting goodbye to one of her grandchildren, her voice echoing up the staircase.

'Thank you. For staying.'

'It's all right,' she said, 'I didn't have anything else to do.'

He nodded.

'And I wanted to.'

Kasper looked up at her, feeling like a child in his pyjamas, sitting on the stairs on Christmas night. Frau Langer's door slammed. 'Can you stand?' Eva said.

'I can try.'

She pulled him up by his arm. He gritted his teeth to stop himself crying out when her fingers encircled his bruised flesh as she pulled his arm over her back. His head flopped onto her thick jacket, which was wet with snow and smelt of damp wool.

'Just a few steps,' she said. She led him back into the flat, onto his mattress.

He rolled onto his back. 'Look,' he said. 'You don't have to do this, you know. I'll live. If you leave me. I'll finish the job. I just need a day or two.'

'For God's sake,' she said, 'Don't be such a martyr.'

She removed her coat and threw it onto one of the chairs, suddenly comfortable in the room, as if she were undressing in her own apartment.

'I got some sugar,' she said, 'I'll put it in some milk later, if you can hold it down. I found some ration coupons I'd forgotten about.' She picked up the coat and ran her finger down the seam. She flicked out a little sliver of metal and pulled at it, unzipping part of the lining. From the little pocket she removed a small piece of folded paper, bulging with sugar. 'What?' she said, feigning surprise, 'You can't be too careful with pockets.'

'Nice trick,' said Kasper.

Eva shrugged. She filled a pan from the bucket by the sink and put it on the stove top. 'Who did this to you?' she said, quietly, filling the stove with a few scraps of wood that she produced from the pockets of her thick woollen skirt.

'Hans and Lena Beckmann.'

She lit the fuel, blew it gently until it began to flame and then closed the stove door. She stood up and her eyes remained fixed on the pan. 'I wondered ... I thought maybe, it was, but ...' She found a sliver of soap and put it by Kasper's side and then filled a basin with two thirds of the hot water. 'Well, it'll be all over quite quickly now, I'm sure. You'll have to have some luck with getting that information soon won't you? One of your sources must come in.' She turned to Kasper, holding the basin in both hands.

He pictured that slip of paper in his jacket pocket, a secret nestled in the ragged silk. 'Yes,' he said. 'You'd think so.' His mind wandered, seeing Eva hand over her piece of information, hearing a shot, seeing a flash, seeing her floating face down in the Spree, in the Landwehrkanal, rubbish and dead leaves gathering in her crooked arms. And then something more pleasant, more comforting: of Eva standing in his kitchen with him, counting out rations, counting out coupons; of them reading in silence; of her teasing him, getting angry about his mess, about his temper; of him smiling, with meat on his bones, listening to her talking about some boy, some man; of him in some church with Eva on his arm, not marrying her, but handing her over to someone, sitting stiff-lipped on a pew, concerned about her choice.

'Herr Meier?' she said. 'Are you OK?'

'Hmm?' said Kasper. 'Oh. I was wondering what you were going to do with the rest of that water.'

'There's still some fuel, so I'll let it boil. For tea or something. Or maybe your father wants some for something.' She put the basin down by the soap, which rang like a Tibetan bell when it struck the floor, the lapping water distorting the sound into a long undulating vibrato. 'I'll come back in fifteen minutes,' she said, 'and I'll knock, so you can shout if you're still naked.'

She left the room and pulled the door to.

He listened to her shuffling feet in the corridor. His head throbbed. He saw himself descending the stairs, with his father limping along beside him. He saw the twins waiting for him. He saw a stone, a piece of rubble, hitting his father in the head. A weak dribble of blood, surprisingly red, unbleached by age. He saw them huddled in a doorway. Him returning to the empty apartment alone. His father's anonymous body, prised rigid from the ground. He saw his father, young, lifting him terrified onto the high step of a carriage, cologne and talcum powder and the sharp smell of the sweating horses.

Kasper turned and looked at the bowl of steaming water. He reached over and held his hand over it and felt the steam dampening his palm. The room stunk of burning paper and probably his sick body, but he had already become too used to it to smell it. He sat up and unbuttoned the front of his all-in-one and glimpsed something that had attached itself to his skin. He unbuttoned faster and discovered the red top of a large bruise. As he unbuttoned down to his groin and began to pull his arms out – a movement that made his back tremble with pain – he discovered that the bruise stretched from the side of his stomach around to his back. It was shaped like a giant eye, a deep, necrotic purple in the centre, red on the outside, with a light flurry of yellow forming at the side. As he traced his finger along the stinging edge, it reminded him of pictures of the sun eclipsed, with solar flares escaping around the edges of the moon.

Peeling the bottoms of the all-in-one away, his lower-back muscles shuddering, he found that his legs had been turned into two thin maypoles, banded with blue and red, and that three of his toenails had turned black.

He moved himself naked onto the floorboards, so that the water wouldn't make the mattress wet and, feeling the cold, dry wood beneath his buttocks, he felt childish and alone and for a few seconds sat with his head on his knees and thought about crying.

He dipped a cloth in the water, squeezed it out and held it up to his face, breathing the damp air through it. He wetted it again, rubbed it with soap and began to clean himself, the hot water on his skin briefly releasing the stink of him before he could get the cloth back into the water to wash it away. He found more bruises, though he couldn't turn around far enough to see his back, where he felt most of them lay. And although his eye was drawn to the heavy bruising on his side and on his legs, the rest of his skin, especially that on his arms and torso, was decorated with light, chromatic hues, the colour of oil spilled on water.

Finally he soaped his hair and rinsed it over the bowl by cupping the water in his hands. The water splashed out onto the floor and onto his legs and he could smell the earthy wood of the wet boards. When he was finished he dried himself with a rag and then pulled himself up, the cracking of his joints a percussion to the pain in his muscles, and stood in front of the black metal stove shaking, feeling the back of his legs begin to warm up.

When Eva knocked at the door he didn't answer.

'Are you still naked?' she pushed it open gently. 'Herr Meier?' she said.

The bowl sat by the bed and the wood on the floor around it was dark with water. The all-in-one was soaking in the bowl, the sliver of soap sitting on top of it. Kasper sat on the chair by the window, a thin, lit cigarette in his hand, wearing nothing but a pair of trousers. 'Gosh,' she said, 'your tattoos—' But then she stopped.

He looked down at the remarkable, inky colours of the bruises across his body. She walked over to him. He turned to the window and the white light felt pleasant as it streamed into the blue of his eye. She put her hand forwards to touch him, but stopped before she reached his skin – he felt her hand hovering above the heat coming from his back.

'You'll get sick again if you sit around in your trousers. There's still snow on the ground.' He dragged on his cigarette and blew the smoke out slowly, coughing in hoarse, staccato puffs as he did so. She rested her fingers on the back of his chair. 'I went ice-skating on the Krumme Lanke the winter the war started – I went a lot. I was a terrible skater. I broke my arm twice when I was ten. God, I was always breaking things, falling out of trees, that sort of thing. I don't know how I survived, really. I always got so hot skating, so this time I left my jacket hung from a tree. It got stolen and my aunt made me walk back home without it. I got so sick – flu I suppose. I was in bed for two weeks.' He felt her eyes on him, looking down at the bruises that ran from his elbow to his wrist. His arm shook when he tried to hold his cigarette up to his lips. 'She fussed so much, my aunt. And she got bombed of course. They all did. Makes you think of all the silly things you could've done, doesn't it? Things that wouldn't have mattered. I sometimes think that, when we're all waiting for the bus or queuing for our milk. Still just following the rules. I sometimes want to just run into the street screaming until people act like something terrible's just happened to them. Like something terrible's still happening. To make them feel it.'

Kasper sucked the last out of his cigarette and dropped the tip onto the floor. 'Oh they feel it,' he said. 'But being normal's the wonderful luxury. They won't stop pretending to feel normal.'

He rested his arms on his knees and hung his hands between his legs. Eva touched a small red bruise on one of his shoulders. She traced her finger along a thin white scar that ran through to the middle of it, like an arrow in a target.

'Where's this from?' she said.

'A broken bottle.'

'Was it bad?'

'It didn't go in very deep.'

'When?'

'A long time ago. A drunk in a bar. I ran a bar.'

'You ran a bar?' she said.

He nodded. She took her hand away. There was another scar lower down, below the large bruise on his lower back. It was newer, pink and straight. 'This one?' said Eva, letting her fingers touch either end of it gently.

'A knife.'

'When?'

'When they closed down the bar.'

'How awful.'

'Others died.'

'Was it a queer bar?' she said.

Kasper laughed a little. 'You could say that.'

'I'd never met anyone who was queer.'

'Oh, I'm sure you have. We're everywhere. We're just hard to find. Well . . . harder to find.'

'Your father . . . '

'Yes?' said Kasper.

'He said something about a wife.'

'Did he?' Kasper saw Klara, a quiet violin teacher, sipping water from a glass he was holding, him feeling nothing but numb fear as he sat watching her sleeping, holding her pregnant belly. He saw himself in the same chair, the bed simply empty, the woman and unborn child gone, felt that first stunned shock as one possible future disappeared completely. 'It was all rather quick,' he said. 'I was barely twenty, just back from the first war. I was drinking a lot, trying to work things out for myself, trying out a . . . normal life. I got a local girl pregnant. On my first try, so to speak. She was sweet, but . . . well, I married her. I became a husband, a father and a widower all in one year.'

'Did she have a name?'

'My wife?'

'The child.'

Kasper shook his head. 'She was never even born.'

'How old would your daughter be now?'

264

'I don't know. Older than you, I suppose,' he said. 'One can't think like that, though.' He looked out of the window, at the dirty layer of snow on the sill.

'And you talked about Phillip a lot – with the fever. Was that ... was he ... ?'

'Phillip ... ' Kasper's mouth dried up. He turned away from the window, looked over at his jacket on the nail on the wall. He felt as if he was stepping off a plank, that terrible rush of falling. 'He worked in a bank.' The words conjured up Phillip's face, laughing, his wonky front tooth and his curling blond hair; Kasper's first glimpse of him standing open-mouthed near the door of the bar in a long woollen coat with snow in his hair; the sound of his voice, the softness of his Frankfurter 'ish', the way he said *'net'* instead of *'nicht'* – *'geh net arbeiten; Ish liebe dish'*. He remembered lying in bed in the afternoon – the smell of smoke and spirits still on his skin, Phillip asleep on his back, his hand on Kasper's thigh. He stroked his finger in a circle around the back of Phillip's hand, which was rough and dry and he touched the wart that Phillip had on the side of his middle finger, which made it uncomfortable for him to write. He remembered the weight of Phillip's body and how much he liked to wake up with some limb of his own trapped under Phillip's leg or arm or under his neck.

'Where is he now?' said Eva.

'Dead,' said Kasper. 'I saw him die.'

He stared at the gap in the floor, in the corner of the room, where one of the floorboards didn't quite meet the wall.

'We were naive – or we didn't want to see what was happening. We had lived together for ten years when they started closing things down and people started disappearing. The bar had to close and I had to get work as a waiter, which I hated. But we never thought about one of us moving out.

'A friend, Marta, told us about someone she knew who'd been

deported – we knew others in prison. We made up a spare room, so that we could pretend Phillip and I had separate rooms. It didn't make much sense, because everyone knew in the block, I'm sure – people know even if they pretend they don't. We seemed to exist in a bubble of luck. We seemed invincible, but I suppose that's what anyone in . . . '

Kasper closed his eyes. Tears escaped from the edges, ran hot down to his chin. He put his head in his hands and felt his voice vibrating through the bones in his arms, into his legs. 'They kicked in our door – we weren't even in bed. I was reading and Phillip was in the kitchen. They beat me up and then held me by the arms while they beat up Phillip – they took him away, but I knew he was already dead. I don't know where they took him. I don't know where he is. I've tried to find out, but it seems to be the only thing I can't find.' He saw Phillip looking up at him from the floor of their apartment – blood pouring from his nose and mouth. He kept eye contact with Kasper for as long as he could and they sparkled, even when his eyebrow had been split. 'I don't know why they left me, why they didn't put me in prison,' he said. 'Maybe they weren't meant to kill him. I don't know.' He found two of Phillip's teeth on the floor after they'd left. He covered them with his hand and they stayed under his palm until his father came by the next day when Kasper had missed their lunch appointment.

'I don't know what to . . . ' Eva's voice was hushed and broken. She said, perhaps to herself: 'What can I say?'

'There's nothing to say,' said Kasper, sniffing and rubbing at his eyes. 'What could you say?'

Kasper tried to turn towards her, but twisting his torso caused a tight ache to splinter up his sides and he let out a strained gurgling sound, bowed his head and clenched his teeth. 'Damn it!' he said. 'Damn it!'

Eva took a few steps back and walked over to the stove as if she urgently needed to do something there. She touched the handrail, put her hand on the counter, turned, then turned again to face the door and wipe at her eyes.

'I tried to put a shirt on, but I couldn't. I tried to wash the all-in-one, but ... Well, my ... '

'Yes, of course,' she said, sniffling. 'Can I find something in here?' She pointed to a crate at the other end of the room. He nodded. She fished out a vest and a white shirt that was missing its collar. She wiped her eyes on her sleeve. Her shoulders heaved. She crossed her arms, the clothes still in her hands, and put her hand up to her eyes. She stood like that for a minute or so, an audible sob escaping every now and again. Kasper waited, saying nothing, his own tears beginning to dry.

Eventually she turned around and came towards him with feigned cheerfulness, her face red and her mouth switching involuntarily back and forth between a smile and a grimace.

'Can you put your arms up?' she said, standing behind him with the vest.

'I don't think so.'

She rolled the vest into a ring, which she slipped over one arm, over his head and then the other arm.

'This one ... ' she said, nodding at a pale scar on his chest. But she stopped herself, bit her lip and pulled the vest down below his nipples.

'Shrapnel. In the first war,' said Kasper.

She touched his back gently to make him sit forward enough for her to pull it down. She walked around to the front of the chair and tugged it down over his stomach. 'Not so bad, eh?' she said.

He looked up at her. His eyes were watering and hers were wet and trembling. 'It's the shirt I'm scared about,' he said. She laughed a little and then he laughed too, before putting his head down again and holding out a shaking arm as high as he could to receive the first sleeve. 'Why don't you go home?' said Kasper.

'Who has a home these days?' she said.

She reached up and touched a tiny scar on his forehead. 'And that one?'

'Falling out of a tree. I was eight.'

She stood up and smiled, then shook out his shirt. 'I fell off a rock at the Baltic Coast once. It was my fault – my cousin flicked a jellyfish tentacle onto my arm and I pretended to drown him. Sounds awful when you say it out loud, doesn't it? I was running away from my aunt and I slipped and sliced my leg open on a razor clam shell on the way down. It bled enough that I wasn't in trouble anymore and . . . ' He closed his eyes and listened to her voice washing over him. It was surprisingly low and warm and there was a power behind it, rarely called upon, but latent and vehement. He tried to think of nothing, just picture her story and take on her memories and try and replace his own with them, just for a while, just for a few minutes.

A SMALL PACKET OF HORSE MEAT

Kasper woke up aching, but less weak. He stood up like a newly born fawn, his feet far apart, shaking as he got his balance. He went to his door, rested briefly against the frame and stepped out into the corridor to make his way down to his father's room. But his father was already awake, standing in the corridor with his hands in the pockets of his trousers, his braces loose, his feet bare, his head angled up to the ceiling. From his face emanated a ray of silvery light, filled with sparkling smuts of dust.

'Papa?' said Kasper.

'There's a hole in the roof,' said his father, not turning away.

'Big?'

'Big enough.'

The old man looked at his son. 'You feeling any better?'

'A little. Less sick.'

The old man nodded. 'Fräulein Hirsch due?'

'So she said.'

A gentle wind ran across the hole, hidden from Kasper's view; a low whistle, like someone blowing across the top of an empty wine bottle. 'Weren't you meant to be getting something for her? Doing a job for her?'

'I was. I am. Information.'

'That hard to come by?'

Kasper scratched at the two-day old white stubble on his neck. 'Not really.' The old man's eyes narrowed. 'I have it,' Kasper said.

'I see,' said the old man, looking back at the hole.

'I know what you're thinking.'

'You do, do you?'

'That I'm not giving it to her so she'll keep coming back. So she'll nurse me – something like that anyway.'

His father took in as deep a breath as he could, the air crackling in, crackling out. 'Once you can get up a ladder you should at least block up the ceiling. No good waiting until it rains.'

'It's not what you think. I'm getting more information for her – to protect her. She's in a situation.'

'What kind of situation?'

'I don't quite know. Not yet. But if I hold back ... I suppose I might just give her the information. Maybe I should. I might today. I don't know.'

The old man looked back at his son. 'Well, you know best my boy,' he said.

Kasper attempted his most withering smirk. The old man smiled knowingly. They heard Eva's footsteps on the staircase. Kasper turned to the door and lifted away the planks lying up against it, dropping them to the floor as his arms gave way. 'Don't strain yourself!' came Eva's muffled voice through the wood. He pulled the door open and she swept past carrying a bucket – he could hear something sloshing inside it as she went through into the kitchen and swung it up onto the counter. 'Where's your father?'

'He was here moaning a second ago. Now he's magically disappeared.'

She smiled at him. Her coat was open and she was wearing a dress he hadn't seen before – it was red, but gathered up strangely beneath her armpits where she had tried to make it fit her flat bust.

'Why aren't you shifting rubble again?' said Kasper.

'It's Sunday.'

'What's that?' came a voice from the other room. 'Is it Sunday?'

'Yes, Herr Meier!' cried Eva. 'Don't you boys keep the Holy Sabbath?'

'We don't keep the holy anything,' said Kasper.

'Well, it's a beautiful day, the sun is shining, barely a smattering of snow this morning, we have heavy-worker milk rations, courtesy of me,' she said, patting the side of the bucket.

'What's that on your face?' said Kasper.

'Where?' she said.

'Come here.'

He licked his thumb and rubbed away some brown spots. 'It's blood.'

She frowned and then, said, 'Oh, it's from the meat, of course.'

'Meat?' said Kasper.

'Yes,' she said, taking a small, bloody packet of newspaper out of her coat pocket and putting it down on the counter. 'Fresh meat!'

'What kind of meat?'

'Horse,' she said. 'There was a skinny one that had died near Savignyplatz – it was still attached to the cart. I heard people shouting as it went over and ran towards the shouting. They were on this animal like hyenas. It was bestial.' She opened up the packet and the silvery smell of blood drifted from the small pile of dark flesh to where Kasper stood.

271

'Do you keep a knife in your pocket?'

'No, but I know the butcher that works round the corner and he sliced a bit off for me.'

'What did he want in return?'

'Not everyone wants something in return.'

'Everyone wants something in return.'

Eva shook her head. 'Well, anyway, we were chatting afterwards . . .'

'I bet you were.'

'Oh, do be quiet. We were chatting afterwards, for maybe five minutes at the most and by the time I went to leave, the whole horse was gone. I mean completely gone – not a speck of anything on him, except his bowels, which were hanging off the bare rib cage like a bag of . . . well, I don't know what. It was unbelievable. And then some awful little runt shoved a stick in it and it started stinking of, well, you know, poo.'

Kasper laughed at the childish word.

'It was horrible,' said Eva. 'Don't laugh at me!'

Kasper's laughter petered out and he sighed. 'Thank you for the meat.'

'That's OK,' she said.

'Will you help me onto the chair?' he said moving in front of it. 'I'm not bending very well – I get half way and then just drop.'

'Just a moment, I've got bloody fingers.' She wiped them on a rag and then wrapped her arm around Kasper's back. He put his arm over her shoulder and they knelt together. Kasper twisted and Eva moved around to hold him up and suddenly they were embracing. Kasper tried to move away, embarrassed, but she held onto him for a second, her face pressed against his chest. 'Are you going to be alright?' she said.

'I'm fine once I'm down,' he said.

She let him go slowly until he was sitting and then stood and looked away awkwardly.

'You don't have to bring us your milk rations,' he said.

Eva lifted the bucket of milk onto the counter and took a deep breath. 'Are you always this ungrateful about everything?'

'I wasn't being ungrateful, I just meant . . .'

'I can do what I like with my rations.'

He looked up at her. She had turned and had her hand on her hip, frowning, waiting.

'God, I want to get out of this bloody house,' said Kasper.

'You need some fresh air. It's so musty in here.'

'I'm not sure I'm ready to tackle stairs.'

'It's a shame you don't have a balcony.'

'Oh, we have a balcony of sorts,' said Kasper. 'Give me a blanket.'

Eva took the brown woollen one from his bed and he wrapped it around himself. He lit one of two pre-rolled cigarettes that sat on the windowsill – the glowing tip trembled as he took his first drag. He pulled himself to his feet and stepped into the corridor; he walked past his father's room, to the door at the end of the corridor. 'Come on,' he said.

'I thought that didn't lead anywhere.'

'It doesn't,' said Kasper.

He pulled away the rags that were stuffed under the door and felt a breeze running over his feet. 'Give it a shove,' he said.

Eva turned the handle and shoved the door twice. She shoved it again, harder, and burst forwards into the void beyond. Dust fell down onto her head, followed by a waft of cool, clean air. She spluttered and shook the dust off her hair, brushed it away from her face and opened her eyes. They were in a room – the roof and back and side wall were open to the sky, but the floor was still intact, a rug still sitting in the centre of the parquet floor, bent and weathered and peppered with burnt wood, ash and a light sprinkling of snow, like icing sugar. The front wall

273

was still partially standing and was covered with the remains of a striped wallpaper.

'My God,' said Eva. A great tit fluttered down onto the top of the large, tiled oven that had once heated the room. It bounced a few times, jumped down to the floor near her feet and cocked its head.

Kasper gestured for Eva to follow him. 'Shut the door,' he said. 'Don't want to kill the old man.'

He sat on a fallen rafter which was supported, bench-like, by a second at one end and the remains of a sink at the other. She sat by him and stared out across the devastation below, the strange sea of vertical walls, like ancient ruins.

'This is unbelievable,' she said.

'It's quite warm in the sun,' he said, blinking.

'Look at the sky,' said Eva.

Kasper looked up. It was blue and cloudless. There was bird-song, though Kasper couldn't see any birds, and a light crisp breeze was blowing snow crystals into the air that refracted the light into rainbow colours as they spun. Eva put her hand out and twisted it around, then turned to Kasper and laughed like a child. 'Oh, it's so beautiful. Let's eat out here – are you warm enough? The fresh air will be good for you.'

Kasper shrugged. 'I'm sitting now,' he said and took a drag of his cigarette.

'How wonderful,' she said. 'How wonderful.'

Kasper looked at her, her eyes reflecting the blue of the sky, the fine white hairs on her face lit up, longer above her thin open lips. He noticed a few brown spots, near her ear. 'You've still got blood on your face,' he said.

She licked her fingers and rubbed at her temple self-consciously. 'There,' she said. 'Is it gone?'

He nodded and turned away from her. 'What will you do?' he said. 'When all this is over? Back to normal.'

'Me?' she said. 'Why are you asking me that now?'

He shrugged. She turned and smiled at him and then looked back down over all the ruins. 'Back to normal? I was five when the Nazis took over. And I was eleven when the war started. What would be normal?'

'I thought you were twenty.'

'Almost twenty,' she said.

'When?' said Kasper.

'The seventh. That's Tuesday, I suppose. I hadn't really thought about it.'

They watched a plane coming in to land from the east, the sound of its purring propellers echoing in the still air.

'What's your plan then?' said Kasper. 'Your great plan of escape?'

'Why should it be an escape plan?' said Eva.

'Everyone wants to escape Berlin.'

Eva placed her head on Kasper's shoulder. He looked down at her. 'Mmm,' she said in distant agreement, 'I suppose. What's your plan?'

'Mine? Ha! I'm the only one not trying to escape.'

'Why not?'

'Responsibilities.'

'Your father? He looks just like you,' she said. 'I can't believe no one guessed before.'

'No one cared to,' said Kasper.

They were silent. Eva pulled a bit of her hair forward and stared at the tips, searching for split ends. She looked up and brushed the end of the lock against the tip of her nose. 'I do have a plan actually, but you'll only laugh at it.'

'Go on,' said Kasper.

'You promise you won't laugh?'

'I promise,' he said, 'go on.'

She moved her head. Kasper's shoulder was beginning to ache under the weight of it. 'I want to be an actress.'

'Ha!' said Kasper.

'I knew you'd be like that. I don't know why I ...'

'Sorry,' he said. 'I'll keep my mouth shut.'

She concentrated on the tips of her hair again. 'I don't want to be a Hollywood actress or anything. I mean I wouldn't mind that of course. If someone offered, you know ... I just want to be a normal, theatre sort of actress. Maybe some German films one day, if we start making films again. It doesn't have to be Hollywood. That's not so bad, is it? I know it's the sort of thing stupid, proud girls wish for.'

Kasper rubbed his face. 'No, it's not stupid,' he said. 'What sort of plays?'

'I don't know,' said Eva and then after a pause, 'I've never seen one.'

'You've never seen a play!'

'I've read lots – anything I can find. But I've never seen one,' she brushed her hair across her lips. 'I found a copy of *Maria Magdalena* at a book exchange near the station and there were some stills inside. Some production shots. Looked very strange, but when I read them, I imagine being there in the dark. I imagine it's quite magical. It'll probably be a terrible disappointment if I ever manage to see anything.'

'Your parents weren't culture lovers?'

'No, not really. Not that kind of culture. And I wasn't really old enough to go. Have you been to the theatre?'

Kasper laughed. 'Yes, I've been to the theatre.'

'Did you like it?'

'Yes, I did,' he said.

'What's it like?'

'What do you mean?'

'What's it like? The experience.'

'Well,' said Kasper, 'You go in. Everyone's milling about at the front.' Eva closed her eyes. 'Everything's carpeted red, very thick

276

carpet. You have a drink – used to be Sekt, sometimes even champagne. Then you go into the stalls downstairs or onto the balcony.'

'Were you ever in a box?'

'I ran a bar.'

Eva smiled and nodded, her eyes still shut. 'Go on.'

'Well, then you go and sit down, and the seats fold down – they're sprung. Quite comfy at first, but they can get a bit itchy – it gets hot with all the people in summer. And it smells like – I don't know. Bodies, perfume, wine. And then the play starts.'

'And is it wonderful?'

'It can be,' said Kasper.

'And what do you wear?' she said.

'You wear something smart – black tie.'

'I bet you looked very distinguished in black tie.'

Kasper laughed. 'Like a schoolboy – I always borrowed Phillip's and the sleeves were too short. He never came, he hated it.'

'He hated the theatre?'

'Yes. I don't know why. If he did come he fidgeted through it, then either got drunk during the interval or left. He couldn't concentrate for more than about ten minutes. Barely ever got through a whole book.'

'What was he like?'

'Phillip?' Kasper shook his head. 'Lovely.' He was smiling, running into the lake, calling him. 'I . . .' He was laughing, asleep on his shoulder, on a train holding Kasper's hand beneath the coat on his lap. 'How do you sum someone up?' He was lecturing Kasper on inflation, looking bored in a bookshop, weaving drunkenly down the road, dressed as Struwwelpeter. 'We were very happy,' said Kasper. 'Very happy for a long time. I find it hard to talk about.'

'That's all right,' said Eva. She sat up, took a cigarette out of her case and lit it. 'You want another?'

'No.' There was an acidic sickness in his stomach, and his lungs ached.

'Talking of plans . . .' said Eva.

'Yes.'

'I . . .' She took another long drag and blew a thin stream of smoke out into the clear air.

'Spit it out.'

'I wondered if you'd sold those tickets and papers.'

'Not yet,' said Kasper.

'Are you going to?'

'I know what you're asking,' said Kasper. 'But my father . . .' He looked over at Eva, who was staring blankly ahead. He imagined himself sitting in a theatre in one of those big sounding cities – New York, Chicago, Los Angeles. He imagined cars, planes overhead, millions of people, tightly packed buildings, plates full of food and men laughing and drinking. He saw Eva on a stage, lights so bright you could feel the heat from them, her skin matt with powder, her lips rouged, someone, a man, pressing his leg against his. Then he saw his father alone in the empty apartment, struggling and then falling down the staircase. Powdery snow gathering in the angles of his body from the broken window. 'If something changes – God what a thing to say. I can't now. It's no good.'

'It's fine,' she said quietly. 'I don't think I'd even leave. I can't speak English – not really. Barely a word.' She inspected her broken thumbnail, then put it in her mouth.

Having given a few lumps of blackened horseflesh to the old man, who stumbled back to his room with it, Eva put a second plate containing the remainder on the rafter between her and Kasper.

'Are you not cold?'

'It's good to be outdoors,' said Kasper. He looked down at the horsemeat. 'Did you just fry it?' he said, picking up a piece.

'What else?'

Kasper turned it, then sniffed it. It looked like coal and smelt like burnt beef. 'Did you put anything on it?'

'What like?' she said, frowning. 'You were out of saffron. Just eat it will you.' She put a whole lump of it in her mouth and chewed with grim determination. Kasper bit his piece in half and ground it slowly between his teeth. It was very tough, still tasted bloody and had a strange sweet aftertaste.

'Which bit did you cut it off?'

'I didn't cut it off. The butcher did it.'

Kasper managed to swallow the first half. 'I think he kept the good bits for himself,' he said. There was a hint of a smile at the edge of his lips. Eva laughed and Kasper began to laugh too. He took another bite, but had become giggly and had trouble swallowing.

Eva tried to shake the laughter out of herself, through her arms and her legs, so that she could swallow her chunk of horse, but she began to quiver and when she tried to swallow she choked on the meat and became red faced as she coughed it up, laughing simultaneously. She jumped up and waved her hand at her face as she walked over to the edge of the room, as Kasper wiped tears from his eyes.

'You enjoyed it,' she said, using her inside arm to wipe her tears away, because her fingers were still greasy.

'Yes,' said Kasper, 'it was delicious.'

'I don't like to boast.' She did a little bow. 'You should try my donkey,' she said, and they began to laugh again. He imagined her coming into his bar, before the war. He would have spotted her, taken her under his wing then. She would have become part of the group. He saw her on a rug, by the side of the lakes. Marta outstretched, Phillip swimming, Eva laughing.

Something caught Eva's eye and she looked down, over the edge of the floor, down the side of the building. She picked up a large lump of fallen masonry and flung it away from her with frightening ease. It hit the ground with a thud that shook the beams that Kasper was sitting on. She moved closer to the edge. 'There's a proper bomb crater back here,' she said, rubbing the dust off her hands. 'Makes it go down so much farther.'

'You should get away from there,' said Kasper.

She shuffled a little closer and looked back at him. 'Would you try and save me, if I said I was going to jump?'

'Fräulein Hirsch, don't be silly.'

'I hardly think Frau Beckmann would miss me, nor the girls.'

'Eva – the floor's not secure. You'll lose your balance.'

'We're on first name terms now,' she said, and looked up at him and smiled. 'I've had as good a day as any,' she said. 'A good day to go,' and she hopped, a little meaningless jump and dropped off the edge of the roof.

'Eva!' screamed Kasper, running forward, his sheet coming loose, his weak limbs shaking with pain.

'Kasper! Kasper!' she cried. She was only a foot lower than she had been. 'There's a little ledge here. It was a joke. It was a joke of course.'

'You little idiot,' he cried. 'Get off there.'

She stepped back onto the floor gingerly. 'Get back inside,' he said. He tried to push her forward, but a sharp pain rippled up his arm. 'Damn it!' he cried. He followed her through the door, pulling it shut behind him, and down to the kitchen.

'For God's sake. For God's sake. You can't do this to me. You need to go now. Go home,' said Kasper. He went for his jacket and pulled out the creased slip of paper that he had transferred the two pilot names onto. He held it out to her. The blanket slipped from his shoulders, falling into a heap around his feet.

'What's this?' she said.

'The information. About the pilot. There are two names, but it's one of them. I assume that's enough.'

She stared at it. 'How long have you had that?'

'Just before Hans and Lena . . . Just before you found me in the street.'

'Why didn't you say anything?'

Kasper's arm was beginning to shake. He lowered it. Eva went to his chair and sat in it, slumped down, with her arms on her lap, her hands hanging down between her legs.

'You're angry,' said Kasper. 'I'm sorry. I should have told you. But I didn't think you were ready.'

'Not ready?'

'If you can wait, I can still deal with the Beckmanns.'

'You can't . . . '

'I can and we can beat this. We don't need to get some ship – I can sort this out.'

She stared down at the corner of the room. 'You don't know what this is.'

'Because you won't tell me.'

Kasper sat down in the chair beside her, lowering himself slowly by holding onto the back. 'But you've got your information now,' said Kasper softly. 'It's done.'

'Yes,' she said distantly.

'Then is it over for you? Once you sort out this pilot thing?'

'In a sense,' she said.

'If you can't come here, can't you go home?'

'I told you, I don't have a home,' she said.

'Will Frau Beckmann look after you?'

Eva laughed. 'That's not home.'

'What about your family?'

'I don't have a family.'

'There must be someone – an aunt.'

'No one. There's no one.'

281

Kasper huffed. 'There can't be no one.'

'You want to know about my family?' she said, almost shouting now. 'Really? You ...' she broke off, and bent her head, supporting it on one hand, the other touching her temple, where he had wiped away the horse's blood. 'They were very keen on Hitler – that was my family. They did all the parades, sang the songs. Daddy worked for the Reich Main Security Office. He worked on logistics – on transportation, if you see what I mean. Troops, guns and bombs ... people.

'When we heard the Russian guns, Mama and Papa pretended they weren't close, so that I would sleep. But then I heard a bang and I knew that they were in the house. And then I heard my mother crying. I wanted to run to her, but they'd taught me to lie under my sheets and be very quiet if someone came in. Not make a sound, whatever I heard. So I lay as flat as I could. Then I heard someone coming up the stairs. I thought, well ... this is it. And I prayed – even though my parents didn't believe – I prayed to God that he would save Mummy and Daddy and that we would meet in heaven. It sounds stupid, doesn't it?' She smiled briefly and bit her lip as it faded.

'My door opened. I heard someone come in. I knew I wasn't meant to move, but I couldn't help it. I curled up into a ball, just automatically. But I didn't say anything,' Eva sniffed and swallowed hard. Her hand fell away and she looked up at Kasper, as if asking permission to go on. His good eye quivered. He nodded. 'I felt a hand on the sheets,' she said, 'Feeling its way up me until it found where my head was and then I felt a bang.

'I was very lucky really. The gun was very old and the bullet went through my hand – I'd wrapped them round my head. And it had only grazed my head and went into the mattress. It hurt – God it hurt – but I didn't move. And there was blood everywhere, in my hair, my ... in my mouth.

'And I just played dead. But then I heard my mother crying and I thought, they've brought her up here to see me shot. But I didn't move, because I thought they might leave it at that. But then there was another shot. I tried not to cry – I managed. I thought I was going to throw up. But no one left the room. And after a while my hand hurt so much and . . . Well, I pulled off the covers. And my mother was there – she had shot herself in the mouth, you see. After she'd shot me.

'And I went downstairs. And of course my father was dead too. His . . . his head was . . .

'The Russians arrived the next afternoon. They found me and they took me to a hospital. Isn't that a joke?'

She looked up at Kasper and smiled, then she tried to laugh, but it came out as a strange, strangled grunt.

'I don't cry about it – I really don't. I do have an uncle who's still alive. He used to tell us stories about the invasion of Poland. I remember one: about a hospital for children – crazy children, idiots, you know. And they went into the hospital and shot all the children one by one in their beds. They were all tied down, so it was very easy. So that's my family,' she said, 'I cry about the children in the hospital. I still do. I can see their faces, their eyes, like I was there. Like I know what they looked like. I cry about that sometimes. Oh and I cry about all sorts of other things really.'

Kasper reached out and took her hand.

She sniffed a few times. 'So you knew people? I mean people who were taken away?'

Kasper opened up her fingers and looked at the thick pink scar on the palm of her hand. 'Yes,' he said.

'Anyone here?'

'A family in the front of the building I think. Before my time.'

'All of them?'

'Yes,' said Kasper. 'All of them.'

283

'And friends?'

'Yes.'

'Queers?'

Kasper nodded. 'Yes. Of course,' he whispered.

'I didn't know they took . . . them,' she said. 'I thought they just went to prison.' They heard the gentle creak of the springs on the old man's mattress. 'Did they survive?'

'One survived that I know.'

She nodded. 'What's he doing now?'

'He's still in prison. They made him finish off his sentence in jail. As you said, everybody still hates queers.'

She lifted her arm up and covered her eyes again, then fell forward and put her head into her lap. Kasper stayed by her side and put his hand on her back as she shook. He turned his head and stared up at the crack in the ceiling, and imagined Phillip, in the snow, in the park.

'You can stay, if you want. You know you can stay if you need to.'

Eva sat up slowly and gave him a smile that died away as she wiped her chin with the back of her hand. 'Well,' she said, touching her pocket where she had secreted her precious piece of paper, 'I've got my information now. Got to get back with it.'

'To whom? Why? It's over. Why can't you tell me now? Why do you need to know about this pilot?'

'I already told you.'

'But really?'

'It's for Frau Beckmann, she . . . '

'None of it's true,' he said.

'I know this is all horrible – don't you think I know that. Of course I do. I'm so sorry about it all, but I've told you the truth, all you need to know.'

'What are you all doing? Really?'

'All?'

'All you girls. In that apartment. Frau Beckmann doesn't live in that block. Nor do you really, nor do those girls. You're all there temporarily. You're all up to something.'

'You ... How do you know about the apartment?'

'Because I checked up on it. Because it's crazy. I needed to know what was really going on,' said Kasper.

'You shouldn't have ...' Eva shook her head. She looked down at her thumbnail, half black where it had been hit with a hammer. She stroked it with her ring finger. 'Well, it's over now.'

'What if you're wrong?' said Kasper. 'I know you don't want to explain – that you think this is all done, but I believe ... I feel that this is deeper. That you want to believe it's OK, but you know it isn't. Because it doesn't make any sense. Why did you need me to do this? Why was Frau Beckmann so desperate that I do this, that I get this information? The apartment, Hans and Lena, you – it's too much. It's all wrong. And if you tell me what you're doing, I can help, don't you see? We can stop this. And maybe you could come here, maybe we could make something work with you here, if you've really got nowhere to go. I do well on the black market and with you helping ... I mean that's not so odd, is it? If we can't use those tickets, at least ... At least we could have each other. Friends, you know. Like people used to have friends.'

Eva came forward and took his hand. She was smiling. Her eyes sparkling. 'How wonderful. How wonderful that would be,' she said. 'Maybe. Let's say yes to that wonderful possibility.'

'Why isn't it possible? What's going to happen to you?' Kasper grabbed Eva's arms. 'What's going to happen to the pilot?'

She closed her eyes tightly, her face twisting suddenly. 'Nothing he doesn't deserve,' she said, tears escaping again from their red edges.

'Oh God,' he said. 'What is she making you do?'

She opened her eyes and fixed his own, 'She's not making me do anything. None of us. We want to do it.'

'Do what, for God's sake?'

She pulled away from him. 'Oh God,' she said. 'You'll be left alone now. Beckmann promised me. She always keeps her promises.' Eva grabbed her coat. She looked down at it in her hands.

'When are you coming back?' said Kasper.

'I don't know,' she said. 'Let's just pretend it'll be soon, OK?'

She took a silver St. Christopher medal from her coat pocket. They both looked down at it, the delicate silver chain catching in the light. 'I was going to give you this,' she said, her voice breaking.

'That's not yours, is it?' said Kasper.

'No,' said Eva. 'Frau Beckmann gave it to me. Maybe she feels guilty about it all.'

He took it out of her hand.

'Don't come for me,' she whispered, 'Whatever you do, don't come. I'll be gone.'

She turned and left the room. He heard her descending the steps. He tried to stay still. He closed his eyes and touched the windowpane, trying just to concentrate on the cold at his fingertips. But he saw a sunny living room, Eva frowning at a book, her walking beside him on some foreign hill, him explaining some idea, pointing out some bird, some flower, listening to her worried about some problem, some friend, some boy. He cried 'Eva, wait!' and limped to the door. He made his way down the steps after her. Halfway down, he could already hear her feet on the concrete of the courtyard. He was sweating and his lungs ached. He stopped at the bottom of the staircase to catch his breath then set off, squinting as he came through the courtyard, through the front building and into the sun of the street. It was cool and empty of people. He saw Eva about to enter a small park, near the end of the road. 'Eva!' he called out. She stopped and turned, beneath the only surviving horse chestnut in the street, its leaves almost wet looking in their green brightness, a tear in its bark, revealing its brilliant white flesh. He walked towards her as quickly as he could, his legs still weak from the fever, a sticky, cold sweat on his face. She looked at him shocked, but then happy, those astonishing eyes softening, her lips parting as she smiled, her hands drawing out of her pockets to receive him, to hold him, because it was simple – she needed him and he needed her.

As he reached her a gust of wind set the branches of the horse chestnut in motion, the rocket-like spikes of blooms lavishly shedding petals, falling over them like confetti.

'Look Eva,' he said. 'I've been thinking about those papers. You were right.'

'Was I?'

'I was thinking last night – we'll take my father with us. He's elderly. We can work on them – get their sympathy. And if it didn't work, we'd find a way out of Hamburg, I know we would. Maybe I could work out a way to get him some papers too, I don't know. It just seems – suddenly it just seems like a gift, like it's been dropped in our lap. It's perfect. Do you see? It's all finished now. You can sort out this thing with the pilot, put an end to that. Then come back to me. We have time. It seems impossible to have a chance like that and to ignore it.'

She took a sharp intake of breath and put her hand on her chest. She reached up and took his hand. She seemed to be on the verge of laughing, but she didn't laugh. 'How wonderful,' said Eva. 'Where would we go, do you think?'

'I don't know. New York at first. I don't know how it all works. But there must be so many theatres there for you, so many places.'

'Yes,' said Eva. 'Yes, it would be wonderful, wouldn't it?'

He took her by the arms. 'It's the right thing to do, isn't it?'

'Yes,' she said. 'Completely.'

'When do you think you'll be back?'

'Oh, but I can't come back. Not now.'

She wiped her eyes with her middle fingers.

'What do you mean?' said Kasper.

'Frau Beckmann. She wouldn't allow it. It's too late now. I'm so happy that you want that. I want it too. But she'd never allow it.'

'But she wouldn't know it. She wouldn't know anything about it. We've given those twins the slip enough times haven't we?' he said, smiling, laughing, 'It's easier than you think.'

'But Kasper,' said Eva, 'they're already here.'

Kasper's fingers loosened and dropped to his side. He turned and looked at the entrance to the park. Hans and Lena Beckmann sat on the empty concrete struts of a bench, the wooden slats of which had long been removed and burnt. Hans had his hands in his pockets, Lena was plaiting the ends of her thick hair. They were staring over at them, unsmiling.

'You don't have to do this Eva,' whispered Kasper desperately. 'I'll come and find you. We'll get away from all this.'

Eva smiled and took Kasper in her arms. She whispered into his ears, 'We can't change it now. But I'll think about us on the ship to America, you think about it too.'

She pulled away from him, turned and walked away, through the entrance to the park. Lena and Hans moved away too, following her at a distance, keeping their eyes briefly fixed on Kasper. Kasper stood on the path, squinting in the sunlight. The wind was in the tree again, it rustled angrily and the white petals began to cover the road at his feet, mixing with the last of the winter snow, beginning to melt on the warm broken concrete.

OTTO SPIELMANN

Spielmann looked up from his book; his wife sat by the window with her own open in her lap. Her fingers touched the paper as if she was marking her place, but the page had been open on that page since Spielmann had returned over a month ago.

She noticed him staring at her and smiled. 'You're back!' she said, as if still disbelieving.

'Yes,' said Spielmann.

Her smile faded and she pretended to read her book again, but her eyes kept switching upwards to check whether she was being watched.

Spielmann turned to his book, ashamed of himself for having no desire to ask her how she felt. What could he say to comfort her now?

He stared at his hand on the page, the joints wide on the thin fingers. All the things that these hands have done, he thought: lifting children; lifting up his own child; touching men; touching women; pulling pin after pin from grenade after grenade; the fingers searching the bloody pockets of a dead Pole for food or tobacco; squeezing the neck of one Russian – maybe others –

until their eyes bulged and their hands stopped slapping at his shoulders and arms; holding some Slavic village woman's hair in his fist in a tight clump as he raped her. And now, quite astonishingly, they were lying on a book in the apartment, the fingers thin, the nails marked with a grey line of gun oil, but quite decent apart from that, despite everything they had touched. Quite normal hands that would now do quite normal things, he supposed, except touch his child or his grandchildren – that was all gone now.

He closed his eyes and recalled seeing his son by chance at Anhalter Station, dressed in his uniform when he was dressed in his. His son, who was some way off, had stretched out his arm and saluted him. He wanted to run over and hold him, but instead he raised his hand in salute as well, believing that that was what he would have wanted. His son smiled, so perhaps it was the right thing to do after all, but that was a wonderful decade when there were people to tell you what was right and what was wrong.

A bell rang. His wife didn't move – she was staring out of the window, her irises a pale grey-green.

'The bell has rung,' Spielmann said.

'Yes,' she said, but didn't look away from the window this time.

Descending into the shop, Spielmann was shocked to find someone already inside – a tall woman with straight dark hair and an odd knot in the bridge of her nose; a bony nodule where it bent downwards.

'Ah!' she said, as he slowed down and stopped in the doorway.

'You know Linden?' Spielmann said.

The woman frowned, as if she hadn't caught what he had said.

'Did Herr Linden just let you in? He usually calls for me.'

'Oh,' the woman said, 'the man outside? Or the boy? I just explained what I was here for, who I was, and they just let me in.'

'Really,' Spielmann said.

'A trustworthy face,' said the woman and smiled, 'though I am here about a gun.'

'Yes,' said Spielmann. 'We didn't introduce ourselves properly, I don't think. I didn't catch your name?'

'Silke,' she said.

'I mean your last name, Frau . . .'

She dismissed further enquiry with a wave of her hand. 'That's not important. Just show me what you're selling.'

'What are you interested in?'

'Well, you only sell one thing.'

'In multiple variations.'

'A Luger then,' she said, 'Get me a Luger.'

Spielmann nodded and pushed himself upright off the door-frame. He moved with affected sluggishness and uncovered the cheapest Luger in the dark back room. The metal was chipped, there was a deep silver scratch in the barrel and its hammer was so stiff that it was almost impossible to fire, the trigger cutting into your finger as you pulled it back, stinging after you managed to fire it.

'There you are,' said Spielmann, laying the gun softly on the counter top. 'The best I have.' He moved forward, so that he was able to put one finger on the loop of cord that rang a bell by Linden's head and hold the trigger of a small, smooth pistol that lay on its side in the dark recess beneath the counter.

The woman picked up the Luger and weighed it in her hand. 'It's heavy, isn't it?' she said.

'There are heavier.'

The woman turned and wandered about the room like a bored visitor to an exhibition, looking at the shelves, the peeling images of shoes and soles, the flaking paint. 'Kasper Meier was here, I heard,' she said.

Ah yes, Spielmann thought, as the reason for her visit began to clarify.

'What did he want?' she said and poked at a few women's lathes that clattered together as she moved them with the point of the gun.

'He was wondering why people were going around asking after him.'

'And what did you tell him?'

'Nothing much – I just confirmed it. Said that Beckmann had sent a girl.'

The woman smiled. 'Well,' she said, 'Beckmann is always poking her nose in where it's not wanted.'

'Indeed,' Spielmann said.

The woman looked at the gun and said, 'Yes, this will do.'

'And what have you got to offer me for it?'

'For this?' she said, holding it up. 'Some advice, perhaps.'

'That must be some valuable advice.'

'It is,' she said. 'It's to forget everything you hear and every-one you meet.'

'The girl who visited me here said something similar.' He recalled the woman's sad eyes and the angry looking birthmark, like a great bleeding wound that ran down her face.

'But you ignored her.'

'I didn't see that it was very important.'

The woman pointed the gun at him. 'Oh, it was impor-tant.'

Spielmann pulled the string under the counter and squeezed the trigger of his gun, but the barrel clicked empty. He opened his mouth and stared at the door, at the still shadow where the sunlight usually shone through the crack, and saw a thin line of blood slowly seeping from underneath the door towards the woman's foot.

The woman squeezed the trigger, which creaked and stuck

and Spielmann threw himself against the door behind him. It gave, but only briefly – it was being held shut.

'Oh, that's a bit stiff,' the woman said, shaking it and lifting it again, her face straining, the trigger creaking, until it finally released with a painful crack.

JELLY

Kasper smoked a second cigarette with his feet up and then a third. He poked at the largest bruise on his side, testing where it hurt the most. He pushed the burnt stub against his chair leg and pulled himself to his feet, lit the stove and began to heat up some water. He took four small potatoes from his pocket and scrubbed as much dirt from them with his toothbrush as he could before dropping them into the water to boil. As he waited for them to cook through, he leant up against the counter and looked around the cramped little room.

He closed his eyes, pushed his four fingers against his forehead, his thumb anchored beneath his cheekbone, and swallowed hard. It's over, he thought. He had done what he was asked to do and now he would probably never see her again. He'd never hear what had happened to her. She had already become just another memory to be avoided, something to be pushed out. The thought made his stomach convulse again and his eyes sting.

He pushed his fingers harder against his forehead. He'd lost far worse than a brief friendship with a nineteen-year-old rubble girl. But he heard her laughing, saw the lilt of her head when she was embarrassed, her curling mass of hair, her nervous fingers at her lips, felt her powerful, enthusiastic arms around his shoulders.

The water foamed up and hit the hotplate, sizzling. Kasper turned and pulled the pan aside, fished the potatoes out onto a plate. She will be fine, he thought. Yes, she would be better off without him. She didn't need some old man's documents, because she had her youth, she would thrive. He poured the hot vegetable water over two mugs of ersatz coffee and carried them in one hand, the plate of potatoes and two forks in the other and a tin of ham tucked under his arm.

'You still alive?' he said.

'Just,' said his father, pushing himself up on the bed so that he was sitting upright. Kasper put the plate onto the mattress and the mugs of coffee on the floor. 'Ooh ham!'

'We're not having the whole tin.'

'Can I have the jelly end?'

'You'll have what you get.'

'You had all the jelly last time.'

Kasper opened the tin with a small knife that he took from his pocket, emptied it out beside the potatoes and cut off two large slices. He dropped the remainder back into the tin and put it on the floor out of the way of his father. He wiped the blade of the knife on his trousers and dropped it back into his pocket. They both speared a potato and began to eat. The old man sighed and put his head against the wall. 'Fräulein Hirsch again?'

'Yes,' said Kasper.

His father began to cough. Kasper watched as the old man hit his hollow chest with his fist. He swallowed hard and said, 'I think she's good for you.'

'Oh do you?'

The old man shrugged.

'You know,' said Kasper, 'her parents tried to kill her.'

'Really? When?'

'When the Russians were coming. They tried to shoot her. They did shoot her then they shot themselves.' He picked up his second potato. 'But she lived.'

'Terrible.'

While Kasper was staring at his plate his father slipped a jelly-covered chunk of ham into his mouth.

'Did she tell you this?'

'Yes.'

'Have you found her soldier?'

'Pilot. Yes. It's done now.' He weighed a piece of potato on the end of his fork. 'It's all over. No more Fräulein Hirsch.' Kasper ate the potato then his piece of ham in three bites without looking at it and washed it down with the coffee. He drank the last dregs with his teeth clamped to the rim to filter out the grains at the bottom, which he cleaned from beneath his lip with his tongue and spat back into the cup.

'Aren't you scared she's going to blab? About us not sharing our rooms?'

Kasper shook his head. 'No, not her.'

'Isn't that why you did it? Searching for the pilot?'

Kasper shrugged.

'I wonder if you even wanted to find him.'

'What are you talking about?'

'Well, the longer it took the longer she was hanging around here.'

'That's ridiculous.'

His father pushed himself up on his pillow again and took another sip of his coffee. 'You could have got in trouble poking around in military things. Are you sure you did it for the right reasons?'

297

'I don't know,' said Kasper, but it came out choked and strange.

'What's wrong, Kasper?'

He was crying. His father moved the plate of potatoes off the mattress and leant forward to put a hand on his son's back.

'Kasper?'

Kasper looked up at him – his good eye was bright with tears and his bottom lip shook miserably. He rubbed his hands across his face and said, 'I don't know. I can't stop thinking about before. And what's coming next. I can't keep it out since she's been around.'

'Is that bad?'

'Yes,' said Kasper. 'Yes, it's bad.'

'You were happy weren't you? I thought you were happy.'

'I was happy. That's what makes it bad.'

'The ending doesn't change what went before.'

Kasper shook his head. A tear ran down to his chin where he brushed it away with the back of his hand.

'Then be with her, Kasper,' said his father. 'You've got years left – who knows what the world will be like in ten, twenty, thirty years. Don't give up yet. Don't worry about me. Be with her and enjoy yourself.'

'It's not like that.'

'I don't care what it's like. But if it makes you happy being with her, then why not do something about it?'

'You don't understand. What are you going to do if something happens to me?'

'Oh for God's sake Kasper, what's wrong with you?'

'What would you do?'

'I'm almost eighty. I would wait around to die. I've been practising.' He put a potato in his mouth. 'And what's going to happen to you, for God's sake?'

'Anything can happen – what if you were left on your own?'

'I can get by.' The old man coughed and pushed himself further up the wall, adjusting the pillow behind his back to make himself comfortable. 'I could get by better if you'd let me have the rest of that ham.'

Kasper handed the tin over and his father shoved his fork in and ate the remaining lump of ham off it like a toffee apple. He dropped his hand down and laid it on the back of Kasper's. 'Did I do a bad job with you?'

'What's that supposed to mean?' said Kasper.

'I could have protected you more maybe.'

'You did fine,' said Kasper. He rested his head on his hand and looked up at the old man. 'You have ham in your beard.'

The old man found the bright pink flesh and popped it in his mouth, followed by the remainder of the tinned ham on his fork.

'I'm glad mama missed all this,' said Kasper.

His father looked about the room. 'She'd have done it better than you and me, my boy, I'll tell you that. We wouldn't be eating cold ham out of a tin for a start.' Kasper laughed. 'Even after all this,' said the old man nodding towards the wallpaper, 'I'd have rather had her here. If I could have done anything to keep her I would have.'

Kasper looked down at the dish; it was a small side plate with a scratched scene of a woman with a goatherd in the centre, surrounded by faded blue garlands. He wondered if his father had brought it with him – if it had been his mother's. But no, he thought, it had been here when he moved into the flat.

'Does it get easier?' said Kasper.

The old man looked down at the empty plate. 'No. Less frequent maybe. But then I have a lot of time to think.'

They stared at the plate for a little while. The woman was sitting on the goatherd's lap, laughing. He had a brief fantasy of his mother coming in and taking the plate away from them, of listening to her humming as she cleaned the dirty plate in the kitchen. Her face was vague, but he could feel her cold dry hands on his cheek, smell orange peel on her fingers, hear her tuneless, warbling voice singing nonsense songs as she worked. He looked up at his father. He had his eyes closed and he was breathing lightly and regularly. Kasper stood up and took the plate and fork and left his father alone in the room to sleep.

FROSTING

Kasper stood in front of Eva's building in Sybelstraße; in the pale blue-grey light it was stage-set still. He stared at the black-out blinds of the living room window, where Frau Beckmann might be sleeping. He imagined her giant, powerful, in a single large bed, her children nestled up against her side, Eva and the rubble group girls sleeping anxiously in their hospital-like cots.

He looked at the pair of green shoes in the broken handbag he was cradling, wrapped in brown paper, tied with rough, green gardening twine, which he had incongruously found while scavenging a bombed-out mental hospital. He had written Eva's name and address on it as formally as he could, then 'Contents: Repaired shoes for Fräulein Hirsch', and into the toe of the shoe he had pushed in a note saying, 'Remember: tickets. K.' Looking at the shoes now, he felt that the note was too concealed, the message too subtle, and was sure that he should try and see Eva now himself – that it was imperative that she continued to know he was waiting for her the moment she needed him.

He pushed the front door open – it had been left unlocked. He crept up the staircase – there was no sound – and placed the package gently at the bottom of the door. He felt a draught on his neck, wind pushed up the staircase from outside, causing the door of Eva's apartment to move, banging the lock against its housing. He froze frightened, but elated, at the thought that he might be found, that he might be thrown out or invited in and might see Eva for a brief second, know whether she was alive, miserable, happy, alone. But the draught died away to nothing, the building became silent. He tapped at the door three times, his heart beating hard. No one came.

Kasper left the building. By the time he was at the corner of the street he heard footsteps – the feet of two people scuttling behind him. He quickened his pace, chastising himself for coming, and slipped into the ruins of a house at the corner of Nehringstraße and Seelingstraße. He kept his shoulder to the wall and stared out of the square hole where a ground-floor window had once been, searching the doorways and side streets for a sign of Hans and Lena Beckmann. He wasn't sure how long he stood like this. But no one passed. They weren't waiting for him. No one was waiting for him now. His back ached around his kidneys where the children had kicked him. He sat down with his back to the wall and decided to wait until the pain made it too unbearable to stay still – then he would move.

He tried to concentrate on the hiding places around the street in front of him, but his mind wandered. He burst out of a downstairs bar, arm-in-arm with Eva. She was wearing a trench coat, camel-coloured, tied tightly around her waist. She leant into him as the wind rushed down the long avenue from the Hudson, or a lake or the Pacific Ocean. She shook her head, her hair shivered as it flew away from her face, her indigo eyes and her wide smile. She lifted her hand to a friend coming towards them, dark hair, silver at the edges. He greeted Kasper with a kiss on his cheek, the edges of their lips touching.

Kasper heard the scream of a baby, above the slow rumble of

wooden wheels on broken cobbles. The first of a column of evacuees from the East were walking past the window – a girl holding a crying baby, followed by three children and an older woman, hobbling behind them, her head wrapped in a scarf. One of the children, a boy, had a streak of dry blood beneath his nose, another, perhaps his sister, walked proudly beside him, her chin up, her face covered in the sores of malnourishment. They moved on, followed by more families, women, children and old men, their possessions lashed to their backs, or pulling wooden carts, wrapped in blankets, secured with rope. Their clothes were torn and dirty, but apart from three women in country dresses, the skirts, jackets, blouses and shirts of the women and smattering of men were finely cut, fashionable just four years earlier, beautifully tailored to fit bodies five sizes larger than those they now swathed. As the last of the directionless line passed, a boy shouted out with a light Danzig accent, and a curious smell, of dirt and a musky perfume, blew briefly through the empty window.

Kasper pushed himself to his feet – there was no one to hide from – and moved slowly to the black market at the end of Kurfürstendamm. He found a spot next to an advertising pillar, but forgot about the goods he had brought with him, and stood with his back against a wrinkled poster, watching the crowd swarming around him towards the broken spire of the Kaiser Wilhelm Memorial Church. Perhaps Eva was here, perhaps he'd bump into her somewhere – it wasn't impossible. If he hung around in the right places, he might see her, there might be time.

A woman in trousers, her hair gathered up in a grubby blue rag, was pasting a poster onto the pillar, the rolled sheets of paper and the battered pot of glue sitting in a white, wicker pram beside her. He stared at his feet, at the cracked leather, riddled with light beige lines, like a delta. He was suddenly very aware that the shoes were hide, that the cracks were the cracks in skin.

A spot of paste landed on the ruined toe.

'Excuse me,' said the woman.

'What?' said Kasper.

'I need to paste this up.'

'You've already done one.'

The woman put her free hand against her waist. He could smell the sharp sweat from the encrusted armpits of her shirt.

'Fine,' said Kasper and pushed himself forward.

'What's in there?' said the woman, pointing at the large woman's handbag that Kasper was holding beneath one arm. 'What are you selling?'

He looked down at the bag. 'Well, what've you got to sell?' he said. 'I don't need paste.'

'You first.'

'Jesus,' said Kasper. He pulled out a packet and showed it to her.

She read the label slowly: '*Jack Frosting*. What is it?'

Kasper turned the label to face him. 'It's American. It's like icing sugar. Like butter cream.'

The woman screwed up her face.

'You asked,' he said.

'Hey,' said the woman, turning back to her pram of posters, 'You should get down to Lehrter Bahnhof. It's full of refugee children – they'd go crazy for it. Those East Prussians haven't seen any sugar for years.'

'Thanks for the tip,' said Kasper miserably, moving away, letting the mass pull him along towards the ruined church. The crowds of people – a sea of women still in long, dark winter coats, with a peppering of skinny old men – opened and closed around him as he moved forward, as women clustered into groups, their hands darting in and out of pockets and bags, inspecting, turning, smelling and touching goods to exchange. The chatter was punctuated with consumptive coughs and crying babies, the women swarming around soldiers like bees, parting again as bikes and prams were pushed through. Kasper saw a woman looking around anxiously, hungrily. He dug his hand inside for the frosting, but the woman had moved on. He looked back into his bag to try and remind himself what else it contained, but stumbled off the pavement, his leg twisting. He half fell, his knee hitting the ground hard. A hand came down and pulled him up. 'You all right?' said the woman.

'Yes,' said Kasper. 'Yes, thank you.'

He got to his feet and pulled his bag up to his chest.

'What are you selling?' she said.

'I ...' said Kasper. He shook his head, felt hot and sick. 'My ... I have a headache.' The woman looked confused. 'Frosting,' he said suddenly. 'I've got frosting.'

'What's frosting?' said the woman.

'Like sugar.'

Someone in the crowd shouted 'Cornflour!' The woman turned. 'Oh, I need cornflour,' she said and was enveloped in the mass. His eyes followed her and caught sight of a face moving past in the crowd – it turned and briefly opened up in recognition and as the slight smile faded, and the man's head turned forward again, the eyebrows dropping, Kasper recognised Heinrich Neustadt's small, dark face.

'Wait!' said Kasper. Heinrich didn't turn around. The herring-bone fabric of his coat fluttered and then he was gone. Kasper moved forward, using his outstretched arm like a keel, parting the women who moved back and forth in front of him, turning, then turning again, like a school of fish. A child nearby shouted, 'Matches!' He heard a plane taking off from Gatow, but couldn't see it rise above the buildings around them. He heard the high song of wheels on rails from Berlin Zoo. He saw

Heinrich's hat – a hand went up to hold it onto his head, and Kasper surged forward, desperately – desperate to reach Heinrich, a connection to her. He grabbed forward, grabbed forward again, had his hand on his sleeve.

'Oi!' said Heinrich, 'Get off me.'

Kasper was suddenly close to his face, could see his red cheeks and a spot of hair on his neck, missed when shaving.

'I need to talk to you.'

'I don't have anything to say to you.'

'You, come with me,' said Kasper, holding onto his jacket as hard as he could, pushing him out of the crowd, into the ruined atrium of a café. Kasper shoved him back against the bare brick wall and threw the strapless handbag full of frosting on the floor.

'Get in here,' Kasper said and clapped him about the ear.

'Ow!' said Neustadt and made as if he was going to run, but Kasper took him by the collar and shoved him backwards onto a heap of bricks. 'Why are you being so rough? What's wrong with you?' said Heinrich.

'So rough,' said Kasper, 'you bloody shopped me in again – I saw you at Beckmann's rubble group. I've spent the last week or more being blackmailed and beaten up, because of you.'

'What are you talking about? I gave you Beckmann's address. I sorted you out – made sure you were safe.'

'You lied to me – you were already working with her, and pretending to warn me off her. What the hell do you think you're playing at?'

'I was trying to protect you and you threw it back in my face. And yes, I'm doing some work for her, but I don't see that it's any of your business anymore.'

'Right. And how's that worked out for you then, eh? You're in exactly the same position as me now. Not much fun is it?'

'They're paying me – they didn't need to blackmail me. I can get out whenever I want to. I deal with Beckmann directly.'

306

'You've met her?'

'Of course I've met her – I told you. But you never remember a word I've said to you, because you don't care. Even when I'm trying to help you, you don't care. I gave you her address, so that you could sort this out with her.'

Kasper's hands were gripping Heinrich's coat so tightly that they had begun to ache. He let him go and stepped backwards, rubbing his palms on his trousers. 'No, I didn't find her. I can't find her anywhere, and no one else I know's clapped eyes on her either. I've met her charming children though.'

'The twins?'

'They've been following me.'

Heinrich eyes searched around for them. 'Are they here now?'

Kasper looked at the open doorway and glassless windows then to the back of the shop, past the ruined counter to a door hanging off its top hinge, sagging awkwardly to one side. 'I haven't seen them for a while. I've been ill. And the job's finished.'

'Ill with what?'

'Doesn't matter,' said Kasper. 'How well do you know Frau Beckmann?'

'I don't see I should be telling you anything, for all the thanks I get when I do try and help.' Heinrich straightened the lapels on his coat. 'I don't know her well, but I've met her, as I said.'

'At Sybelstraße? Did she come and find you there?' said Kasper.

'No,' said Neustadt, 'My cousin lived with her for a while – that's how she found me.'

'Why?'

'Didn't the girl tell you why? Aren't you looking for a soldier?'

'A pilot. And I've found him. But none of it makes any sense.'

'It makes sense,' said Heinrich.

'Why?'

'Oh, I don't know why. I mean, if you don't know.'

Kasper pulled Heinrich up again and shoved him against the rubble. 'They blackmailed me, you little shit. They beat me up. This is serious. Now you tell me. You bloody tell me.'

'You're hurting me,' cried Heinrich.

Kasper pulled him round and shoved him to the ground. 'You bloody tell me.'

Heinrich cowered beneath him. He lifted his hand up to shield himself and whimpered. 'Don't hurt me, please Kasper.'

Kasper closed his eyes and crouched down. He felt sick. 'Why did they want me to find this pilot?' he said quietly.

'Don't hurt me again,' said Heinrich, 'but it's better if you don't know. Honestly. It's not bad in the way you think, but it's terrible if you know. If you like this girl, if you like her you won't want to know. I didn't want to know about my cousin, but then they told me. I said I didn't have any information, didn't know anyone. I didn't want to tell them about you, Kasper. I swear, but then they told me what it was really about – they told me about my cousin. And you know it, you suspect it, but not your family. You hope. And I tell you, if you like this girl, you'd be happier just getting on with your life, just for-getting about it.'

Kasper reached down and took Heinrich's hand. He held it firmly and said, 'Heinrich. Who's Frau Beckmann? What does she do? Who's she trading with?'

'She's not trading with anybody.'

'Heinrich.'

'It's true. She doesn't do anything herself. She just supports the girls who come to her. They want justice done and she can help. It's only information. They get the information about the sol-diers and then Frau Beckmann deals with it. She has contacts, that's all. She's well connected. And then they're dealt with – as it should be. It makes the girls feel better – because there's some justice. You can understand.'

'Justice for what?' said Kasper.

'Well, what do you think?' said Heinrich. 'When the soldiers came, well, there was nothing but girls, wasn't there. It's what happens, but it's not right. My cousin too – she was fourteen when the Russians came. Marie. Fourteen. Even when she was pregnant it didn't make any difference.'

Kasper's legs wobbled and then crumpled beneath him. He fell backwards, so that he was sitting on the ground beside Heinrich. Kasper was overwhelmed with a glut of images and sounds: Eva's hands flapping, her falling, a pilot grabbing at her breast, hitting her, the tearing of cloth, screaming. Repressed sobs and terrible, rhythmic grunts. The silence of a cellar, an empty hospital room, a ruined alleyway, a roofless bedroom, the rain coming through the open ceiling, soaking cloth, diluting tears and blood. He dry-heaved, putting the back of his hand to his mouth. His stomach convulsed, but he managed to hold it down. He leant forward and rested his head in one of his hands.

'It's no wonder they're all so secretive,' said Heinrich. 'They just want justice.' He moved closer to Kasper. 'Is she a good one?' he said. He put his hand on Kasper's back. 'Is she a good one, like my Marie?'

Kasper nodded.

'They just want some justice, Kasper. Let them have their justice.'

Heinrich stood up. Kasper heard him moving away tentatively, his feet crunching on the dust beneath his shoes. He stopped. 'You shouldn't have hurt me Kasper. Why couldn't you be good to me like you were to her? You'll see that you only make it worse for yourself in the end.'

Kasper didn't look up. Someone trod on broken glass. A child in the crowd on the street screamed. He heard Heinrich move on, his weak 'excuse me,' as he was swallowed up by the crowd. Eventually Kasper stood, shakily and looked around him, his body wincing. He pulled down the brim of his hat and moved on, out of the crowd and into the city until all he could hear was his own steps, his own breath, his own heart.

JAMES MCGOVERN

'Jim,' shouted Frank Butler. 'Come 'ere you Scotch twat.'

'I'm comin',' said Jim, 'but this staircase is covered in rubbish.'

Jim clambered over a fallen pilaster and tripped over an upturned chair. When he looked up he found Frank standing in the middle of a large room, covered in thick red carpet. It had begun to blacken with rot at the far end where one of the large windows was smashed in. The last occupants had tried to block the stairwell by pushing all the furniture down it – the furniture that Jim and Frank had just clambered over to get into the rooms above. A large mahogany table stood in the middle of the floor. One of its legs had been broken in the middle, causing it to bow forward as if it was bending one knee in a curtsey.

'You see?' said Frank. 'Didn't I tell you?'

'It's big,' said Jim. 'But you can hardly get up here.'

'That's the whole point,' said Frank. 'That's why it's still here. Look at all this prime wood and not one fucking Kraut's touched it.' He rubbed his hand swiftly over the thick dust on the table revealing the shining, varnished surface underneath.

The smuts of white skipped up into the air and floated down behind Frank as he marched forward.

'What d'ya want to do with it?'

Frank put his hands on his hips and shrugged. 'I dunno. Anything. We could do anything with it. Have a knees up. Get a few gals in, y'know – attract the boys, make some money.'

'That sounds like a brothel. I'm not running a brothel.' The room smelt damp and he couldn't imagine making a prostitute clamber over the river of debris that flowed down the stairs like vomit. 'It stinks, pal,' said Jim.

'Well, it's not the fucking Ritz mate, but it's a big room to ourselves.'

'But if we clear all of this, won't someone else just find it? Strip all the wood out and everything?'

'No, she said it was protected, like.'

'And you trust her?'

'Got no reason not to.'

'Except that you've never met her.'

'Met her kids, her twins.'

'You don't think that's a bit strange? Not at all?'

'She's getting half of anything we make off it – it's hardly charity.'

'Why isn't she just running it?'

'With all the stuff she's involved in? Jesus Jim – this is exciting mate. It's a discovery – don't be such a miserable cunt your whole life.' Frank laughed. 'It's gonna be brilliant.' He blew hard on the table and a spray of white dust curled up into the air and jumped up around him like flakes in a snow globe.

Jim wandered to the window and looked down into the street. A group of German women were standing around a bike arguing and two British soldiers were inspecting a camera – some new black market purchase. 'What'll we call it?' said Jim.

'Call what?'

'This. Our club,' he said turning.

'That's more like it,' said Frank almost running towards him from the other side of the table. 'We'll call it . . . I dunno. Jim and Frank's. Or Scotch 'n' Soda.'

'Then you're not in there.'

'I'll be "Soda". New nickname.'

'Soda eh? Is that because you're a bit "bubbly",' he said, prodding Frank in the sides. 'Because you're a bit "fruity".'

'Hey,' said Frank, knocking his hand away, angry, taking a few steps back. 'That's fucking out of order. You shouldn't take the piss. Especially you.'

'Ah, it was a joke. Come on. You're the RAF's finest.'

'Fuck you,' said Frank.

Jim grabbed his belt and pulled him towards him. He put his arms round his waist and pulled him in tightly. Frank stared grumpily down at Jim's red moustache. 'Why don't we keep it private, eh?' said Jim. 'Why don't we keep it for us?'

'Maybe,' said Frank. 'Won't last long. Nothing does.'

'Now who's being miserable?'

Frank shrugged and Jim kissed him on the head and then on the mouth. Frank pulled away and said softly, 'Do you think it's safe enough for, you know . . . '

Jim looked down into the street. The soldiers were gone. 'I don't know.'

'Maybe just a hand job,' said Frank.

'Maybe,' said Jim, but as if in answer there was a crack of furniture from outside the door. They sprang apart and ran towards the door. Jim got there first, but couldn't see anyone – the staircase was dark and the mass of detritus that tumbled down it made it hard to pick out a human shape.

'Hello?' said Jim. His voice echoed around the marble of the columns and balustrade in the grand entrance.

'Maybe it was just the furniture shifting.'

'Hello!' called Jim again. Something fell and bounced onto the floor near the side door they'd come in through.

'Shit,' said Frank.

'They can't have seen anything. Wait here.' Jim took out his gun and picked his way down the steps, over the upturned chairs, cabinets, papers and tables. He kept his balance by holding onto the thick stone banister with his left hand, his right hand holding his pistol. The metal drawer of a filing cabinet was set loose and slid down away from him hitting the floor at the bottom with a crash.

'You all right?' called Frank.

'Fine!' Jim called back.

Frank watched him edge down into the darkness. He shaded his eyes from the little light coming from a window high up on the ceiling above him, trying to follow Jim's progress through the precarious landscape. He squinted and managed to pick out Jim when the dim light from the crack in the door at the bottom of the stairs lit his profile momentarily.

'Anything there?' Frank called down and Jim turned to him and shrugged. There was a flash of light and then Frank heard the crack of a gun, followed by a scream and then a second series of bangs that rang out in rapid succession, echoing up the staircase and around the giant empty room.

'Jim?' shouted Frank. 'Fuck! Jim?'

His eyes searched the bottom of the stairs, but Jim was gone.

'Jim!' he shouted. He thought he'd run out of the door, that he'd run after someone. But then, in the bay of white light, he saw Jim lying at the foot of the stairs. 'Jim!' shouted Frank. 'What's happened. Don't worry I'm coming.'

He ran into the rubbish on the staircase and forced himself down towards the light of the door. He kept losing his balance and was thrown over to the side of the staircase, then on top of a filing cabinet, cutting his head on a sharp corner.

He pushed on and furniture came loose and began to roll down with him until he arrived groaning at the bottom where he found Jim against a pillar, his eyes open, his face white. He scrambled up towards his friend, his feet sticking on the floor in water, no, in blood. Frank knelt down, a stool tumbled from the wreckage and came to rest by his side; a ream of paper slipped out from underneath a broken desk, the blank sheets spinning past him and settling again like autumn leaves, drawing the dark blood into their fibres. He screamed, grabbed at his hair and screamed. Jim turned. 'Jim?' said Frank desperately. 'Oh God, Jim,' he said, feeling around his body for a wound, but finding none, just feeling Jim's shaking limbs.

'A girl,' said Jim. 'She tried to shoot. She had a gun. I swear she had a gun.'

Frank turned. A girl lay by the half open door on her back. She was small and pretty with black hair, cropped short like a boy's. Her skirt had folded up exposing her knees and there was an ugly black wound in her head that poured blood. Frank cradled Jim's head. 'It's all right,' he said, as her blood soaked into the knees of his trousers. 'It'll be all right.'

A BOTTLE OF BRANDY

There were lights on in three of the flats in Frau Beckmann's block, including Frau Beckmann's own. It shone dimly onto the small balcony that led into the living room. There was a girl standing on the balcony, but her face was obscured by the darkness of the street. Kasper watched the girl for some time from the safety of the doorway opposite. The house that the doorway had once belonged to had no back to it. A breeze blew through the empty rooms and onto the back of Kasper's head, cutting through the nascent warmth of the spring evening.

His leg shook – he wanted to run into the house screaming, grab her and flee into the night with her. But he felt the twins on him, the rubble women dragging him down to the floor, Frau Beckmann putting a foot on his chest and aiming a gun at his head. That wasn't the way, he thought, but until he had found his chance, he would wait and watch and stop her getting her justice. He hoped briefly, joyfully, that Heinrich was lying, that he was playing tricks on Kasper; that this was all just some black market game, that Eva was safe, in control, indifferent.

He took another large swig of brandy from the bottle in his hand, but almost choked as it ran from the bottle far quicker than he had expected. He rubbed his chest and breathed in slowly as the alcohol burnt in his throat, then he stepped out into the street drunk, afraid and lost.

It was then that Eva appeared beside the girl on the balcony. Kasper froze. She said something, but Kasper was too far away to hear it, and the girl stood up straight. It was the girl from the rubble group with the large port-wine stain that curled down from her eye, over her cheek, ending at her throat. The girl nodded and Eva put her arm round her. He saw the shadow of a woman appear briefly at the window and the two girls nodded and moved away into the living room. Then another girl came out onto the balcony – the taller woman with the crooked nose – and flicked her cigarette over the edge before going back inside.

Kasper moved across the street quietly, past the still-glowing cigarette butt that had just fallen from the woman's hands. He pushed himself up against the wall, the smell of burning tobacco irritating his nose, and tried to listen in to the conversation through the open window, but the window was too high up.

The building to the left of Frau Beckmann's was just a shell, its windows missing. He picked up the cigarette butt and smoked the last of it as he walked into the front hall, sucked hard at it and threw the stub hissing into the standing water at his feet. He looked up the staircase – it smelt strongly of charcoal and damp. He made his way up slowly, testing the wooden steps in the dark as he went, with his heavy drunken feet. The wood creaked and cracked beneath his feet and when he reached out his hand to grab the banister he found a gut-churning void.

When Kasper reached the third floor he was angry to find that the flat adjacent to Eva's still had a locked front door. Although he was sure no one lived inside, he still put his ear to the door and when he heard nothing he knocked gently a few times. His stomach gurgled. No one answered the door. He pushed at it with his shoulder with a rocking motion and when it didn't give he took the small knife from his pocket and worked the keyhole with his pick and nail file until he was able to pop the latch.

The apartment was blacker than the staircase and he flicked the light switch out of habit, but nothing happened. He walked carefully into the hall and waited until his eyes became accustomed to the small amount of grey light that dribbled in through the open windows.

The flat had been stripped of all its furniture except for a mirror that hung incongruously on the wall a little way down the hall. He stopped briefly by it and staring at his own face he realised how drunk he was. He looked sadly at the thin white head and the white eye, which, in the dark of the apartment, seemed to be made from the same skin as that on his face. *You look tired old man.*

He walked into the living room. Smoke had poured up into the ceiling and down towards the floor and from below the soft, sooty border emerged the large vegetal leaves of a heavy, floral wallpaper. The furniture remained here too, un-blackened beneath the tide mark, a large sofa, with wide arms, covered in striped silk, iridescent even in the meagre light, a coffee table, a cup still on it, an abandoned newspaper by its side, weighted down with a child's doll. Beneath the doll's plaited braids he could make out the mask of the Führer from the black sockets and the blurred square smeared beneath his nose.

A gust of wind showered the damp carpet with flakes of charred wood from the windows, the leaves of the paper lifted and rustled, like the tail feathers of a peacock. He turned away and moved towards the gap where the window had once been. He put his hand on the sill and the crisp, burnt wood crunched beneath his fingertips. Moving towards the side of the window he was able to hear the conversation in Frau Beckmann's apartment quite clearly.

As he approached a woman stopped talking. There was then a period of quiet in which he could hear the creak of people moving on chairs and the sound of a girl crying softly.

'Come on, Frieda,' someone said. 'Come on.' Frieda didn't stop – it was muffled as if she was crying into her hands.

'Where is she then, Silke?' Frieda said. 'What's happened to her?'

'She'll have run away. Not done the job.' From her voice he recognised Silke as the tall woman with the crooked nose.

'What are you talking about? She'd have come back. I know she would. She's dead. They got her, I'm telling you. They got her. Don't do it. Eva – don't do it. Don't let her make you.'

'No one's making anyone do anything,' Silke said. 'No one has to do anything. You're here by your own free will and you can go if you like.'

Frieda started to sob loudly.

'Oh, Frieda, come now. You're all done now. Soon we'll be done and gone too.'

'We should all just go now.'

'Keep your voice down. We can't go now. We're not all done.'

'Why can't we just scare them?' Frieda wept, 'Just say something to them?'

'You think they're going to be scared by some woman threatening them? They've been shot at all over Europe. They'll just laugh at us. You came here because you wanted justice done, didn't you?' The girl didn't answer.

'What if Eva doesn't come back?'

'I'll come back,' said Eva.

'Aren't you afraid?'

There was a pause. Frieda seemed to be holding her breath.

Kasper closed his eyes. 'I need my justice,' said Eva, quietly, and the resignation of it, the determination of it made his blood run cold.

Frieda began to cry again, short breaths turning into sobs. 'She's dead, I know she is. And now we've done these things, now we know what we've all done, we can't get out, can we? We're trapped. Because she's always got something on us, she'll always know what we did.'

'Frau Beckmann isn't interested in blackmailing us.'

'How do we know that for sure?' she said to Silke. 'You're the only one who ever seems to see her. How do we even know she's telling you all her plans?'

'Frieda, you're being hysterical. I think you need some fresh air.'

'I don't need any fresh air, I want to . . .' The girl's voice broke down and she disappeared from the room.

Kasper heard someone coming towards the door and he moved back. A woman stepped onto the balcony and Kasper saw a hand on its plastered edge – Eva's hand. He saw the sleeve of her beige shirt. There were little lines of dirt beneath her nails, in the broken skin of her bitten fingers. Kasper reached out to her. He wanted to grab her, pull her into the strange, half drawing room, and run into the streets with her, flee the city, flee the country.

'Eva!' someone called from inside the room and Kasper snapped his hand back inside.

Eva's fingers tensed on the stucco. He heard her take a breath, pause and then confidently say, 'Yes, I'm coming!' She didn't move away immediately though. She seemed to be staring into the street, waiting for someone, and then she disappeared from sight and he listened as the door was pulled shut.

Kasper rested his head on the broken plaster, to cool it down. It was too horrible surely, he thought. *You've seen far worse.*

Perhaps he had misunderstood what was happening. *No, you've understood perfectly.* Perhaps he was too drunk to be of any use. He tried to imagine Eva shooting somebody – her holding a gun up and killing somebody. Yes, it was surprisingly easy to piece together into an image, blood spraying into her face, traces remaining on her cheek, behind her ears.

Kasper crept back out of the building, crossed the street with an eye on Frau Beckmann's front door and waited in the shadows. Unexpected hot tears filled his eyes and he hit the wall hard with his elbow in an attempt to allay them. The other lights in the apartment had now been extinguished and it was only Frau Beckmann's that remained on. Kasper was still drunk and his mouth very dry. He realised that he'd left his bottle of brandy in the room upstairs. He considered going back to get it when someone appeared on the balcony again, but he couldn't make out if it was Eva or not. She looked both ways down the street, then disappeared into the apartment. The lights went out.

The door of Frau Beckmann's building opened and the girl with the port-wine stain from the rubble group appeared from the gloom of the front door. She stopped and snivelled into a handkerchief, then took a deep breath, checked the street and disappeared down it hugging close to the buildings. A few minutes later another woman appeared. She was wearing a headscarf, a dark trench coat, tied around the waist with the collar up, her head hung low. She seemed too tall to be Eva. Kasper squinted, trying to see her face, trying to see if it was Eva, but the woman was too fast. He looked up at the balcony and saw someone standing there again, watching her in the dark. He wanted Eva to come out onto the balcony, to know she was safe in the apartment, to look over at him and give him some sort of sign; tell him somehow what he should do. The woman in the trench coat turned the corner and the girl on the balcony looked over the street once more and closed the French windows.

Kasper scuttled out into the street and walked swiftly to the road that the woman in the trench coat had turned down – she was gone. If he got a look at her, he thought, and could be sure it wasn't Eva, he could go back and take up watch in Sybelstraße, sure that Eva was inside. He walked on, checking each turning until he heard the woman's soft tread and saw her disappearing around a distant corner. He followed her down two dark streets before they briefly broke onto the Ku'damm, then pitched into another road the other side of the avenue. He had her comfortably in sight.

PYOTR FEDOTOV

Pyotr Fedotov had brought three records with him all the way from St. Petersburg. They had accompanied him to Stalingrad, through Königsberg to Auschwitz where he had watched the skeletons of men and women wandering the complex like ghosts, the smell of death so strong that it had rendered him speechless. When he had played them again he was amazed that they hadn't been changed; that the horror of the camps hadn't somehow wiped away the beauty of the music, or at least made it somehow ugly and terrifying.

One was a recording of old Russian folk songs that his mother had given him, the second was of various Soviet hymns, and the third – the one that he played every day – was a recording of Borodin's Symphonies One and Two that crackled badly after being hauled around in his trunk for three years. He wound up his record player and put the record on the spindle, then left it tensed, ready to play while he wrote a letter to his wife.

Dear Anoushka,
A year of peace. It is quite a thing. There is still so much to do here, so I don't suppose we'll be coming home soon, but

my leave in July has been confirmed and I count the days until I am back with you and the children – give them a kiss from their Papa.

Pyotr paused and then put his pen down. On the desk in front of him lay the letter from his wife, long and rambling, that detailed their daily lives in Moscow, how well their son was doing at school and how their eldest daughter was now able to say a few sentences. Then she described the twins to him – two girls conceived the last time that he had been on leave and who he'd never seen. She talked about her gossipy neighbours, the difficulties she had finding bread, the cold of the winter and her fears for the heat of summer. She complained about the pain in her back and her knee that became inflamed when it was damp. She said she loved him and that she missed him and she described how empty her bed was without him.

He wanted to write her letters deserving of those that she had sent, but he couldn't tell her what he did every day, what he saw. He had become sick of writing about the success of the Red Army and how well things were coming along, though he did believe these things. She encouraged him, asking him to describe his day, to tell her what the weather was like in Berlin, to tell her what he did when he wasn't working, but what could he say? That he'd organised the patrols around the Brandenburg Gates and they'd found five dead children hidden under a bed in a cellar; that he'd seen a woman who'd gone mad defecating in the street; that he had organised the shooting of one of his soldiers, because he'd been fraternising with the enemy and trading on the black market, even though everyone was doing that and this soldier had just been chosen as an example. Should he say that this soldier had cried and clung onto his jacket and told him that he wanted to go home? Should he say that the boy had to be tied onto a chair, because he kept trying to run away and it was dangerous for the other men? Should he say that this soldier pissed himself as he shook in his chair with a bag over his head? Should he say that this soldier was only nineteen and that he reminded him of their Konstantin?

He left the letter on the desk and put the needle of the record player down at a point around a third of the way to the centre of the disc, so that it started playing part three. He had marked it by scratching a thin line into the side of the groove. The little wind-up gramophone crackled and the strings began to yawn and he lay down on his little camp bed.

He closed his eyes – the tent smelt of waxed canvas and he could smell the hair oil on his pillow. As the music streamed along he imagined himself arriving back from war. He imagined he was on a horse, with his soldiers behind him, also on horseback. They were in a meadow, filled with long grass and wild flowers and the sun was just beginning to rise over Moscow, the city as it was before the war, and their faces were stained pink-orange in the morning light. Their horses slowed to a gentle walk when they saw a crowd of people running through the meadow towards them, to greet them. It was a group of women and children waving white handkerchiefs above their heads and laughing and shouting. At the front of the mass of people was Anoushka, surrounded by their children. She was holding flowers. She had let her hair down and it tumbled golden around her face, which was rosy and healthy. He dismounted his horse and someone took the reins from him and she ran into his arms and she was soft and wonderful and she smelt of fresh air and grass.

Pyotr fell asleep and when he woke up he scrambled to find his watch and saw that it was nine o'clock; he'd promised to meet some of the other officers at the cinema that had been set up in Mitte near the old Gestapo building. He was tired and he wanted desperately to put the record back on and fall asleep again dreaming about home. He took the record from the spindle and slipped it into its brown paper sleeve, then laid it gently in his trunk, with the gramophone that folded down into a small blue case of its own. He locked the trunk and left his tent, nodding at comrade Vasilyev who sat with his gun on a seat outside Pyotr's tent at night. As he passed another set of soldiers at the gate to the main road he made a mental note to talk to comrade Vasilyev about his personal hygiene – the boy had become putrid and Pyotr was sure that the smell crept into the tent at night. Though it seemed unlikely, he had a notion that it had been responsible for making Nina Portnova, one of the tank drivers, sick.

He stopped at a street corner near Hackescher Markt to light a cigarette. He searched around for his lighter and then a woman's voice said, '*Match*,' in Russian.

He looked up. The woman was handsome in the light – though her crooked nose stopped her from being pretty – and she wore a man's navy-blue trench coat, accentuating her height.

'Thank you,' he said. She struck the match and lit the end of his cigarette. In the brief orange flame her face was lit up and he saw that she had dark hair and a bony lump on her long nose.

The woman smiled. 'Where are you walking?' said Pyotr. The woman scrunched up her face in incomprehension. '*Wohin gehen Sie?*' he said.

'*Sie sprechen Deutsch!*' she said.

'No,' he said, '*Nein. Ein bißchen.*'

The woman shrugged. He smiled and began to walk away from her, but she followed. '*Ich komme mit,*' she said. He didn't understand what she'd said, but he let her walk along beside him. They didn't speak, but he looked at her and smiled every now and again. She seemed nice. The memory of the woman he'd raped came back to him as it had done every day since he'd arrived in Berlin, especially when he met German women. He

328

found it easier to block out the other horrors, but she wouldn't leave him. There had been many other opportunities, but he'd never taken one – he was no monster. They had been drunk and they had talked about the women raped in Russia and Poland. Someone had talked about rape and duty. He couldn't quite connect these things, so he didn't try. They had burst into a cellar and the other soldiers had dragged some women out – he did the same and grabbed a girl by the door and pulled her out into the courtyard. He was surprised by how slender her wrist was. The women that the other men had picked were screaming and he thought he'd been lucky and for a brief moment, when he led her into the stairwell, he thought she wouldn't mind and he thought he'd be gentle with her, but then, when he'd gripped her by the shoulders, he looked into her face he saw that her eyes were wet and he realised how young she was. He didn't understand what she said to him, but he could guess that it was – '*Please don't. Please don't. Please don't.*' He paused, but then he heard a shriek from the other side of the courtyard and he pushed her onto her back on the staircase and pulled off her pants. She didn't scream then either, but she never took her eyes off him.

'*Ich will Ihnen etwas zeigen – kommen Sie, bitte. Kommen Sie mit,*' said the woman with the match and held out her hand.

'I don't understand what you're saying,' said Pyotr.

'*Kommen Sie mit,*' she said.

He took her hand and she led him into the hallway of an abandoned building, but he pulled away. He didn't want to do it again – whether it was conceded or not. Not on a stairwell in another dark ruin.

'*Bett,*' she said, seeming to understand his concern. She pointed up the staircase and said, '*Bett.*'

'Bed?' he said and began to follow her up the stairs, still unsure.

She turned to him and smiled and said again, '*Bett.*'

They walked higher and higher and Pyotr's legs became tired – he hadn't exercised since the end of the campaign and got out of breath easily. They reached the top floor and the woman pushed open the door. It revealed a wide attic space, lit by the dim light from a few windows that studded the roof. He could make out the form of a mattress on the floor.

The woman kissed him – it took him by surprise. She kissed him hard holding onto the lapels of his jacket. She took off her coat and threw it onto the floor. He took off his jacket too and came back to kiss her, but she laughed and mimed undressing then pointed at him and pointed at the bed. She smiled again and did the same mime and he gathered that she wanted him to undress. He took off his shirt, but she kept on signalling for him to take his clothes off. He shook his head. She laughed and did the mime again.

He sat on the edge of the mattress and took off his vest and then his boots. She unbuttoned the top of her blouse by a few buttons as a concession, but then gestured at him again. He frowned, but he had an erection now and he did want sex and he knew he would keep performing for her until he got it. He took off his trousers, tugging them down and then throwing them onto the pile of clothes that were gathering near his feet. She gestured again, but he shook his head and signalled for her to come nearer. She shook hers and then, just as he thought she was becoming stubborn, she slipped off her shoes and then, he was surprised and elated to see, her stockings. She dropped them lightly on the floor by her handbag and motioned again. She unbuttoned the rest of her blouse and the sight of her bra was enough to get Pyotr to remove his underpants, so that he was completely naked. She smiled at him and he began to stroke his penis, gesturing her to come over to him. She bit her lip and smiled and reached into her handbag. He lay on his back watching her and began to masturbate quicker. 'Come,' he said in Russian, 'Come to me.'

The woman pulled a small pistol from the purse and laughed.

Pyotr went for the gun under his clothes, but she shot into the pile and he fell onto his back with his hands in the air like a shamed dog. Dust kicked up by the bullet spun briefly around in the air beside him, spraying into his eyes. She walked round to the end of the mattress, so that she was looking up between his legs, up his body. His erection shrank away.

She stayed where she was, tracing the contours of his body with the barrel of the gun. He said, 'Please don't. I'll give you anything you want. I have a lot of things you'll want. I have food. Bread. Tins and tins of meat. *Fleisch*,' he said in German. '*Ich habe Fleisch. Brot. Kartoffeln.*'

She fired at his genitals. The bullet missed and buried itself in his groin. He screamed and grabbed his crotch. Blood poured out from underneath his hands and the mattress turned red and then crimson as it soaked into the material. Pyotr gasped and rolled onto his side. In the dark of the doorway, peeping up above the top step of the staircase, he thought he saw a man with one white eye. At first he thought it was the devil or one of the devil's helpers – the head of an army of demons waiting to creep forward and drag him down the staircase, which would dissolve into a dank fiery pit. But as he began to feel faint, as the blood ran so fast through his fingers that he could smell it, that it made his hands slippery, he thought he saw a worldly pity in the man's eyes, a sadness that could only mean he was a crippled angel, one of his fallen comrades waiting to bear him to heaven where he could wait for his Anoushka.

The woman followed his gaze and squinted into the dark. Seeing the same one-eyed man, she fired two shots quickly into Pyotr's head and ran onto the staircase. She tried to shoot at the man as he rushed down the stairs, but she missed and the bullet cracked through the wood of the banister below. She ran back into the room, slipped on her shoes, gathered up her things and descended the stairs rapidly, her gun held out in front of her. As she burst out of the building onto the street she saw him some thirty feet away, running, his skinny legs pounding the ground. She took aim and shot three times. She heard him yelp, but he only stumbled, without breaking his stride, and by the time the white flash from the gun had stopped flashing in her vision he had disappeared into a distant side street.

A NEEDLE AND THREAD

Kasper knocked at Dr Hoffmann's door. He heard nothing, but knew that by now the doctor would be behind it with his eye to the spy hole and a gun pointing at him. 'It's Herr Meier,' said Kasper.

There was another pause and then he heard a single knock – the pistol against the wood of the door. It meant he had to step backwards and show his hands. Kasper was only able to do this with one hand; the other he lifted weakly halfway and there was a heavy pat-patting as blood from his shoulder, that had soaked through the material of his jacket, pooled at his elbow and dropped onto the floor.

The door opened slightly and Kasper walked towards it slowly. He pushed it open with his healthy shoulder and walked inside. The wizened doctor was standing in the dark at the end of the corridor still pointing his gun at Kasper – his small round spectacles glinted with the dim light from a kerosene lamp shining from a room at the end of the hall.

The old doctor didn't put the gun down until Kasper had dutifully pushed the door shut and locked it.

*

Kasper sat in the dimly lit room with his shirt off, the smell of kerosene almost overpowering the murky smell of dry blood and illegal medication. The doctor investigated the dirty wound on Kasper's shoulder. 'How did you do it?'

'A rusty nail,' said Kasper.

'I get a lot of those,' said the doctor.

'There are a lot of them about.'

'How are you going to pay for it?'

Kasper reached into his pocket and pulled out a slim bottle of Canadian whisky, which he put on the table – the top inch had already been drunk. The doctor smiled and shouted something that Kasper didn't understand. A woman wearing a cotton blouse and a woollen skirt to her knees came into the room holding a napkin. Although her bearing and clothing suggested that she was young, her face looked dark and wasted and already suggested the face of an old woman, with its sagging skin and sunken, blackened eyes. The doctor took the napkin from her and threw it over the bottle. 'You will have to take that away with you.'

'What's wrong with it?'

The doctor stood up and his thin fingers tripped through the glass jars that sat on the turntable of an old gramophone, missing its trumpet. The jars clattered together gently like water. 'It's Passover, my friend.'

'And you can't drink Canadian whisky?'

The doctor laughed and selected a small bottle and a grubby looking rag. 'Not quite,' he said, 'nothing fermented.'

He sat down next to Kasper and put something from the bottle on a tiny bit of rag and dabbed it on the wound. Kasper sucked a quick breath in through his teeth as the astringent touched the raw flesh. 'I'm going to need to stitch it up,' said the doctor. 'I only have sewing needles and I've no anaesthetic. If we leave it open though it'll become infected.'

'Do it,' said Kasper.

Dr Hoffmann shouted to the woman again and she called back to him.

'You'll need to pay with something though Herr Meier – it's all hard to come by – even the sewing needles.'

'I know, I know,' said Kasper. He put his good hand into his side pocket and pulled out a watch.

'Do you have anything I can use?'

'What do you need?'

'Well, some of that penicillin that I organised Frau Hannover to give to your contact – some of that would have been a help.'

'Yes,' said Kasper. 'I'm sorry. There was none left over.' He pulled out a second watch – the one with the ugly Art Deco letters that Eva had given him. 'I'll leave you these and I'll get anything you want. I will come back, but you'll know that if I don't you can swap these with the Russians. They're both Swiss.'

'Can you get me morphine as well?' said the old man.

'Yes,' said Kasper. 'And I have papers.'

'Papers?'

'Yes.'

'What kind of papers?'

'To get you out, to get you to Hamburg on a boat. To America. Or you could get to Palestine from there, if that's what you want,' said Kasper. 'I'm sure.'

The woman came in carrying a small pan of steaming water. She put it on a broken piece of marble that sat on the little wooden table beside the two men and retreated to the kitchen. The doctor got up and followed her. Kasper heard water splashing and then the doctor returned wiping his hands.

'It's quite easy for us to get those sorts of tickets.'

'Then why don't you go? Why don't you leave? You must hate the Germans now.'

'But we are Germans.'

Kasper bowed his head. 'Yes, of course.'

The doctor used tweezers to take a thick sewing needle out of the hot water. He waved it in the air to cool it then held it between his fingers and picked a thin black thread out of the water. 'It's real medical thread,' said Dr Hoffmann.

'Write down what you need.'

The doctor nodded. 'We will probably go somewhere, for my daughter. But ... as I said, we can get papers. We don't have any relatives in America, like some do. My family's all from Brandenburg. Well they were. Nathalie was born two streets away.'

He held Kasper's shoulders firmly with his bony fingers then lifted the needle and pressed it against his arm. It was blunt and there was a slight pop as it punctured the skin. Kasper swallowed hard and squeezed his eyes shut as the needle pierced the skin on the other side of the wound and he felt the thread pulling through, beneath the hot pain. 'Do you want a slug of something?' said the doctor.

'No,' said Kasper, his voice broken and dry. 'Just finish it quickly.'

The doctor nodded and tied and cut the first stitch.

'Talk about something,' said Kasper shuddering.

'Talk about what?'

'You can't eat anything with yeast?' said Kasper.

'Nothing fermented,' said the doctor.

'What about bread?' said Kasper.

'Unleavened bread.'

'Is that easy to get?'

'We make it.'

'Must be tough.'

The doctor laughed as he tied off the second stitch. 'This isn't tough, Herr Meier,' said the old man. 'Having food at all isn't tough. Having my daughter here isn't tough,' he said, nodding his head towards the kitchen.

The doctor put the third stitch in.

'Where were you?'

'Do you really want to talk about this?'

'Anything,' said Kasper. He looked down at the doctor's arms, at the small blue numbers tattooed beneath the long grey hairs.

'Why don't you cut it off – your number? You could do it, couldn't you?'

The doctor tied off the third stitch and put in the fourth. 'Just two more to go,' said the doctor. 'I could cut it off I suppose, but it won't help me forget.'

'I want to forget everything,' Kasper said. 'I want to forget it all. I wish I could. I wish I could drink it away, but I can't even do that.'

'And what use are you to anyone then?' The doctor had to pull the fourth stitch particularly tight to close a large gap in the wound. 'What use are you?'

'None,' said Kasper as the final stitch went in. 'None at all.'

Kasper pulled his bloody jacket on. The doctor helped him with it. 'I'll get that morphine,' said Kasper.

'It would be appreciated,' said the doctor and then, 'but if you can't – if it's impossible, then iodine's fine.'

'I'll get the morphine,' said Kasper. The doctor nodded.

Kasper put his hand on the door handle and the doctor moved back in the hallway and took out his gun to aim at the door while it was briefly open. Kasper turned back to him and said, 'I had friends there.'

'Where?'

'In Sachsenhausen.'

'Friends?'

'Yes,' said Kasper. 'Friends.'

'Why are you telling me, Herr Meier?'

'I don't know. They all died – all the ones that were taken –

337

all but one. I think it was probably bad for them in the camp. Because of why they were arrested.'

The doctor put his gun down by his side. 'I understand what you're saying Herr Meier, but you need to leave before you say anything else.' Kasper looked up. He could see the old man's eyes beneath his glasses – they were watery, perhaps just with age. 'You understand why, don't you? If you tell me what you might be telling me – about your friend, about you – and I don't tell the authorities, I'm implicit. You understand, don't you? We've had enough trouble, Herr Meier.'

'Yes,' said Kasper, 'I understand.' He turned the handle and opened the door. The doctor lifted his gun again.

'Herr Meier.' Kasper turned. 'Don't forget it – what's happened to you. You'll be no use to anyone then. Yourself or your friends.'

Kasper nodded and pulled the door shut behind him. He heard the locks click slowly into place as he descended the stairs.

A PISTOL

Kasper's father walked into the kitchen. 'You made a hell of a noise crashing in like that.'

Kasper turned to him, looked at his withered frame, the damp yellow whites of his eyes. The old man looked down at Kasper's hand, at a stack of dollar bills and cigarettes.

'What are you up to?'

'It's Eva Hirsch.'

'What about her?'

'She's in trouble.'

'What are you doing with all that? What's wrong? And why are you holding your arm like that?'

Kasper looked down at the notes again. 'I've got to buy a gun. I don't know what else to do,' he said.

'Kasper. Make some sense.'

'I've got to stop something. I've got to try tonight. Someone might come for me. A woman maybe – Frau Beckmann.' Kasper saw her eyes catching him as he stood on the stairs, as she shot into the Russian soldier, barely pausing to take aim, and came for him. 'Or she'll send the twins.'

'Twins?'

'Yes. Or – if it goes wrong – I suppose the police or soldiers maybe. These people – they might say I did things I didn't do, but you have to trust me that I didn't.'

The old man came closer. He leant heavily on the counter top and put his arm on Kasper's back. 'Kasper, I've known you all your life. I'm not stupid. I know why you never remarried. I understand. And if this has come out somehow – well, I can vouch for you, can't I? We can say that Fräulein Hirsch is your ... I don't know, lover can't we? I don't think she wants to go through with this at all. Let's just talk to her.'

A rush of blood flooded into Kasper's face. He stood open-mouthed staring at the water stains on the cheap wood of the kitchen counter. He felt as if the last physical vestiges of his known world were falling away; as if he was standing naked in front of his father, his kind eyes impossible to bear. He put his hand on the edge of the counter, felt the rough wood with his fingertips, desperate to know that the room was still real, that he was still in it.

'Kasper? We can sort this out.'

Kasper swallowed heavily. He felt the rims of his eyelids stinging and his cheeks became hotter. He wanted to say something profound. To acknowledge what his father had said. More than this he wanted to comprehend what it meant. But all he could see were the dirty stains on the counter top, and all he could feel was the paper of the notes becoming damp beneath his finger tips and a deep cavernous sickness, a dark unfathomable hollow.

'It's not that,' said Kasper. 'Not what you think.' He tried to look at his father, but could only get as far as the buttons on his waistcoat, before he had to look back down again. His father's hand stayed on his back though – wide and surprisingly heavy. 'Eva's in a lot of trouble. I've got to try and sort it out.'

'Is this to do with this pilot?'

Kasper slowly shook his head from side to side and bit down on his lip. 'Yes,' he said eventually. 'Someone's making Eva do something terrible. But I think I can stop it. I have to try. And I wanted to stay here,' said Kasper, his voice breaking badly. 'I wanted to look after you as long as I could. And I know I'm bad at it. I know I'm a bad son. But now there's nothing I can do. They'll come for me anyway now, you see. One of them saw me. They know I'm making trouble, and this way . . .'

The old man put his hand on Kasper's arm and nodded. They stood quietly for a few seconds and then his father led him to his own room. He opened a drawer in the dresser and took out a slim battered box made of thick cardboard, tied with string. He undid the bow, struggling a little with the knot, and then took off the lid. There were two guns inside, nestling together on tissue paper.

'They're not so old,' said the old man.

'Where did you get them?'

'I bought them on the black market just before you brought me here. I had to barter some of your mother's jewellery for it. I knew you'd never carry a gun. And I remember your friend – Phillip. I remember what happened to him and I thought you . . . I thought there may still be a danger.' He looked up at Kasper. 'You were never alone Kasper. I can't say I never wished it was different. That I approved. But I always understood.'

His father held up the box and Kasper took out a gun. It was cold and heavy, like stone.

'Do you understand what I'm saying, Kasper?'

Kasper nodded, staring at the pistol in his hand.

'Go.'

He managed to bring his eyes up to meet his father's. 'The box that I put in your mattress,' said Kasper. 'They're papers. If I don't come back . . .'

'You'll come back.'

'If something happened, they're tickets. Passes. You could use them – get away, you understand.'

'Where am I going to go?'

'Or you could sell them – for good money.'

The old man went to his mattress, inserted his hand into a little slit in its side and removed the box. 'Why don't you take them with you? Hide them somewhere in the building or outside of the flat.'

'You won't be able to get to it.'

'If anyone really does come and search the place, well, I'll only be in trouble, won't I? It's better that you know where they are.'

The old man handed him the box. Kasper took it. 'Perhaps,' he said. 'I'll hide it in the burnt-out barbers by the synagogue on Pestalozzistraße.'

'I know it,' said the old man.

'You'll be able to find it if you need it?'

'Yes, yes.'

Kasper moved forward to embrace his father, but the old man said, 'No, no. I'm going to expect you home this evening. I'm going to read my book, have some sleep, and I'll expect you home. Not too late. It's better that way. And don't wake me when you come in.'

Kasper nodded again. He opened his mouth to say something, but his father shushed him. He put his hand up, squeezed Kasper's shoulder and then grabbed the back of his head, his fingers through his hair, and held it firm, the thumb and little finger of his giant hand almost touching Kasper's ears. 'I'm going to read my book,' he said again, in a dry whisper. 'Not too late, you hear.' The old man let him go. Kasper felt the firm imprint of his hand on the back of his head, listened to the old man settle down on his mattress and the apartment fall silent.

*

342

A gusty wind blew down Sybelstraße, picking up dust from the dry ground, spraying it against the standing walls like sand among ancient ruins. It carried a sheet of waxed paper across the street in front of him, spinning and spinning, scratching at the uneven cobblestones beneath it. It blew Kasper's hair away from his face, then over it, then threw dust in his eyes. He spluttered and rubbed his eyes and mouth on the sleeve of his jacket. He spat out the dirt and felt the terrible weight of his life, in the dust in his eyes, the aching pain in his raw wound, his monstrous fatigue.

He looked up at the apartment again. Still no lights on.

He crossed the road, squinting into the stinging wind, until he had reached the door of Eva's apartment block. The lock of the building's front door had been turned, so that it rested ajar on the bolt. Kasper pushed the door open – it creaked and shuddered in its hinges – and he slipped into the black space.

He waited in the darkness. A window in the door to the courtyard and another on the landing of the staircase formed grey rectangles in the black. There was no sound other than the wind outside, which intruded on the interior space only in the movement of the door, tapping the bolt against the side of its brass housing.

Kasper moved to the staircase and slipped up the side, keeping one hand on the dado rail. As he turned the curve in the stair, he was met with a wave of terror, seeing the door to Eva's apartment open, a little bluish light emanating from it into the corridor.

He listened. There was no sound. He took two more steps and then stopped. He felt his blood pulsing in the wound on his shoulder, heard it in his ears, but nothing else. He looked up the staircase and shivered. There was no sound in the whole building, just the wind outside.

He climbed the final steps and arrived at the open doorway,

through which he moved, without touching the frame or the door's edge. He took out the gun from his pocket and pulled at the safety catch, the click echoing off the parquet floor. He listened to the echo die, then passed the bathroom and turned right into the second reception room. The beds were still lined up against the wall, but the bedding, mattresses and duffel bags were gone.

He walked into the second bedroom – it was as empty as the first – there were no papers behind the washstand.

He walked quickly back through the two rooms and into the living room. It was exactly as it had been before, except for the photographs that had stood on the side table in the corner of the room. They had been replaced by a single photograph, framed in a cheap, wooden frame with a thin border. He walked over and grabbed it. In the dim light he could make out a man standing with two children. He took it to the window and angled it, to make the best of the little light afforded by the overcast night sky. He felt the cold on his face emanating from the window-pane and he saw, in his hands, a picture of Hans and Lena Beckmann standing either side of someone in the black market at Berlin Zoo. The children were smiling.

A match struck. Kasper turned, but the flame was already out. A small orange circle glowed hot in the dark corner to the right of the door.

Kasper threw the picture onto the sofa and raised the gun. 'Frau Beckmann?'

He heard a high laugh. 'Close,' said the man's voice.

'Where's Eva?'

'You're too late for Eva.'

'I've got a gun.'

The man walked out of the shadows. Kasper squinted as he came forward, until he could make out the stout form of Heinrich Neustadt.

'Jesus Christ,' said Kasper. 'You bloody idiot. What did she offer you? Where's Beckmann?'

'She's here,' said Heinrich.

Kasper searched the corners of the room, but could make out nothing. 'Where's Eva?' he said, holding up the gun. 'I'll shoot you both.'

'Oh Kasper,' said Heinrich. 'That would be counterproductive.'

'What did she offer you?'

'Let me explain.'

'Heinrich, you don't understand what's going on. She's not getting other people to kill the soldiers, it's the girls who are killing them. Killing the soldiers who raped them.'

'She's not forcing them – they want to do it. They're desperate for it.'

'You . . . how much do you know? What do you know about this?'

'Put the gun down, Kasper.'

'Where is she?'

Kasper fired two shots into the corner of the room, away from Heinrich. The gun kicked back and Kasper saw the room in two flashes, empty of faces, except for Heinrich's shocked, white expression.

'Jesus, Kasper!' said Heinrich, coming forward.

Kasper lashed out, catching Heinrich on the shoulder, causing him to fall to his knees on the floor. Kasper scuttled away, into the corner he had shot at, pushing his back into the wall, and holding up the gun in his shaking hand.

Heinrich groped around until he found the sofa, then pulled himself onto it and sat silhouetted against the window. His cigarette glowed on the floor between them, the smell of tobacco mixing with the stink of old gunpowder and sweat on gun metal.

'Where's Eva?' cried Kasper and shot into the ceiling. Beneath the sound of plaster dust falling onto the floor, he heard Heinrich's high, whispered laughter again.

'Kasper, Kasper, Kasper. You've already saved Eva.'

Kasper's finger squeezed onto the trigger of the gun until it reached its bite point.

'Eva will get her man – the pilot you found for us. A particularly nasty piece of work. He's not to be mourned. Really. I know you've become rather attached to each other – it's sweet. I almost thought she'd turned you.' He laughed again.

'I don't . . . I . . . Why are you doing this?'

'No one's a loser here, Kasper. The girls we find, they don't have families or husbands. They don't have any prospects. They've all been raped – countless times, some of them. And they want a bit of revenge, a bit of justice. That's all.'

'You can't do that to them. Turn them into murderers. You can't. That's not helping anyone.'

'Well, that's where you're wrong. For a start they're helping me. Take your pilot – he tried to stiff me over a few used blankets, of all things.'

'Blankets?'

'Care packets, military rations, guns. Come on Kasper, we're on the same page here, aren't we? It's all black market, except I'm trading with people who have enough to give, unlike you. And I'm turning a profit.'

'With rapists?'

'No.' Heinrich retrieved another cigarette from his pocket and struck a match. The flame lit up his face briefly – healthy, round, calm. 'They're not rapists. I mean, they probably are rapists. All the Russians were doing for the first few weeks was fucking our girls. And our other international friends have their vices too. I mean, I don't imagine we did a lot better on the way to Stalingrad.'

Kasper's body melted with relief. 'So they didn't rape these girls,' he said, his eyes stinging. 'This pilot – he didn't rape Eva?'

'Oh don't get your hopes up – gosh, you've become quite the soft egg, haven't you? Of course she's been raped. They all have. I only let them do one or two, then I let them go – if they behave well. I tell them they're doing one of the other girl's rapists – that they can't do their own for their own protection, and they swallow it. They're so desperate for it they never know their rapists could never be found. Because let me tell you, I can't make them do it. They have to be desperate for it – desperate for revenge. Your Eva Hirsch – she was begging Silke to know when her time would come.'

Kasper wiped the sweat of his brow with the back of his hand. His tongue was dry and his head ached. He shook his head. 'I . . .' he said, but there was nothing to say.

'It's a perfect cover. Do you know what the punishments are like for the sort of scams I'm running? You're small fry, Kasper. I've been thinking big, you see. The girls do the killings, if I need killings done. It's not as often as you think, but sometimes there aren't any other options. And you need to do enough to get people scared, to get some respect. They're nice girls, no records, no nothing. Young, unassuming. And the best thing is, they get someone else to do the snooping around for them. Someone who would have a tough time explaining to the authorities why they were being blackmailed. Layers and layers of separation. I've been dying to tell you about it Kasper. Dying to share it all with someone. Dying to make you really see me. Because you could have been part of all this with me, don't you see? I didn't find you to use you like this, not at first. I wanted us to be a team.'

'A team?'

'Yes, a team. And there were other offers: Spielmann begged my girls to get a piece of what I've created, but I was never

347

interested in Spielmann, that trumped-up little Nazi. Half his toes frozen off in Stalingrad, and had he learnt a single iota of humility? Not a jot. He was as slippery as he ever was, marching about in his shiny boots all day and soliciting boys in your bar. He was just another route to you. But you couldn't, could you? And why? Because you enjoy your misery, you enjoy mourning your little fancy man, because it makes you feel like it was important, like you were important. But you're not, I'm afraid. Not quite. I think it could have worked out for us, but once you stopped caring, well, you were just another opportunity. That's what we deal in, isn't it? Opportunities. You turn them to your advantage. I did worry about it, Kasper. Honestly. And it was good of you to try and look after the girl. She was fond of you, I know she was. I'm assuming the friend escaping off on a ship was you, was it? You and the girl? I was almost moved – honestly, I was almost moved by it. Rather sweet. But needs must and you were both too useful to me to let you both off the hook, just because I was getting a bit sentimental. Things are getting big for me now, you see. Really big.'

'Please Heinrich, I . . . ' Kasper tried to swallow, tried to think, but he was so tired and he ached and he was sick and he was terrified. 'Eva's not like the other girls.'

'You don't know the other girls.'

Kasper pushed his head back against the wall. 'If you let her off, I can give you something. I have connections. Just tell me what you want.'

'What could you give me?'

'This girl's a good one. She has a future and . . . '

'They're all good ones, Kasper.'

'Then,' he said, 'Then . . . If you let her off, maybe you and me, I don't know . . . Maybe we could . . . '

Heinrich stood up. The orange of his cigarette flushed yellow. 'Stop begging, Kasper. You're starting to disgust me. You made it perfectly clear how you feel about me. I gave you chance after idiotic chance.'

'You're just a fool!' shouted Kasper, surprised by the volume of his own voice in the empty room. 'I knew this blackmail was fishy right from the start. It barely took me a day to find out Eva's story was horseshit. I know it's you. I know you're Frau Beckmann.'

Heinrich whooped with laughter. He looked out of the window. 'Oh, someone coming to spoil all the fun,' he said.

Kasper heard the door opening and someone on the stairs. He pointed his gun towards the sitting-room door.

'Don't you see Kasper,' said Heinrich. 'I'm not Frau Beckmann. It's much better than that. You're Frau Beckmann.'

Sweat began to run off Kasper's forehead, stinging his eyes. 'What are you ... What are you talking about?'

'And when the authorities investigate it,' continued Heinrich, 'they'll see that you've been snooping around in military business, making deals with soldiers for information. Asking questions all over Berlin. And they'll find things Kasper – whistles, pipes, St. Christopher medallions – trinkets, taken from the soldiers' bodies. They'll find them in your flat. Why, I suspect they're there as we speak. You would have traded the expensive items, wouldn't you? Spreading like cancer across the city.'

'Hello!' shouted someone in the hall. 'Police!'

'The evidence just stacks up, Kasper,' said Heinrich.

Suddenly an electric light went on. Kasper squinted, but kept the gun raised. The room opened up in an instant, half empty, the sparse items of furniture like theatre props. Heinrich stood in front of the green sofa, a plume of white smoke rising from his cigarette, the other on the floor burning a little black mark on the varnished wood. Two policeman, including the man that Kasper had already met in the same apartment that week, came through the door. They looked gingerly first at Heinrich and then turned, startled, to Kasper.

'Put the gun down,' said the young policeman.

'He won't shoot,' said Heinrich.

'I'm going to put the gun down by my side,' said Kasper, lowering it. 'I don't want to shoot anyone, but you have to listen to me. This man has been getting women to kill people. From this house. There's a woman, I won't say her name, but I need to help her, to stop her.'

'Officers,' said Heinrich. 'We should perhaps take this down to the station, no? Beckmann?'

'You stay where you are,' said Kasper, lifting the gun again. 'Listen, I'm not Beckmann. Do you understand?'

Heinrich lifted up his hands.

'Herr Beckmann. Sir,' said the policeman. 'Can you put the gun down on the floor?'

'No. Listen,' said Kasper. 'This man has been forcing women to kill soldiers. It sounds insane. It is insane. Do you see? He's set this all up. The apartment, you coming here, the last time too.'

'My name's Neustadt,' said Heinrich. 'I just heard there'd been a disturbance in this flat. I own the block. This man's been renting the apartment, under the name of Beckmann.'

'I'm not Beckmann. This is not my flat.'

'But I've seen you here,' said the policeman. 'You told me your name was Beckmann.'

'Because someone called you, because he'd planned it,' cried Kasper.

'Daddy?'

Kasper looked towards the sitting-room door, where the policemen stood. Hans Beckmann walked through the door, wearing an all-in-one, rubbing his face, followed by Lena in a heavy cotton nightdress. 'Why are they shouting, Daddy?'

'Kasper,' said Heinrich, lifting up the picture from the sofa, turning it towards him. 'It's time to give up. For the sake of your children.' Kasper stared down at the frame in his hand. Hans and Lena stood either side of Kasper, his face shocked, the blurry back of the cobbler's head visible at the front of the picture.

Kasper roared, lifted the gun and shot repeatedly at the ceiling, until the light exploded into a tinkling burst of glass. He ran at the door. One of the policemen, grabbed at him, but he ducked down, and the man caught his hair, ripping a tuft painfully from his scalp. 'Daddy!' One of the children's hands grabbed at his arm, another caught the wound at the top, a finger forcing its way in. He screamed and skidded to the floor, the gun spinning out of his hand. He scrabbled forward, found the handle of it again, and pushed himself towards the doorway, as a blow hit him on the shoulder.

But he was out of the door. He was on the stairs.

'You can't run, Herr Beckmann,' shouted Heinrich. 'You're a wanted man now!'

Kasper was on the street. The wind blew hard against him. He heard footsteps behind him and fired a warning shot backwards and heard it ricocheting off stone and the footsteps clammering together, stopping. His body was suffused with a terrible freezing dread, but his legs moved almost without effort and the pain in his body became like a thing that he carried, without concern. He ran, unaware of the streets around him, unaware of anything except for the wind and the tears that it elicited from his eyes, which streamed out in thin lines, just above his cheeks.

He saw police, soldiers emptying his apartment, dragging his father onto the street. He saw Eva shooting at a soldier, naked on a mattress, blood spraying into her face. His father shivering in hospital, appalled by his son, by every mental, emotional, physical element of his son. Eva, in front of a court martial. His father dead in the rubble, his body rotting into the dirt. The rush after the trapdoor opened, as Eva plunged down, hooded, beneath the gallows.

MALCOLM BUTLER

Eva stood in the shadows of a buckled tram stop that rose up behind and over her like a rusting wave. She reached up and touched the sharp corroding edge in front of her, unafraid that it might cut her, completely unafraid that the whole structure might topple over and kill her.

Malcolm Butler came out of the British Army cinema with a friend, almost leapt out – a slim athletic man, animated and unbearably alive. The nausea she felt when she saw him was like a pain; it throbbed in her lips, her limbs and her extremities; it ached in her cheeks, in her back, in her fingertips which were touching the knurled metal handle of the pistol in the pocket of her woollen skirt.

He stopped to light a cigarette. The smoke rose up towards the electric lamp, clamped temporarily over the entrance, showing up the thick, swirling lines of the hastily painted black door and Malcolm Butler's fox-red hair and white, white skin.

She imagined his lifeless body, but was unable to comprehend what would be gone. This would be gone though, she thought. This loud laughter that echoed across the road, the nervously tapping foot, the ring finger that constantly beat the edge of his cigarette.

He laughed again, and tossed his head back, joyfully, arrogantly. Yes, she thought, her fingers so tight now on the gun and the rusted metal that all the pain in her flowed there now, ached there in her knuckles and her fingertips, yes, she could imagine him doing it. For so long she had stared at soldiers in the streets thinking, could you have done it? Could you have held a woman down, your forearms and the whole weight of you pinning down her shoulders as you fucked her, as you spat in her face? And so often she had thought, no, it couldn't possibly be. Not with that sweet, anxious smile, the peach fuzz on those cheeks, the nervous laugh and boyish gappy teeth. But this one, yes, she could imagine it, couldn't she? That white skin bared, that wiry strength.

Malcolm Butler moved off, but the friend went with him. She left the shelter and followed him silently, rusty fragments imprinted onto her fingertips. As they moved through the streets, through the grey darkness, she felt her body again: the ache in her feet, her heart thumping at her throat, her dry mouth and chapped lips. And yet she did not feel frail, she was moving behind him like a ghost in her soft, flat shoes, without conscious effort, patiently waiting until he was alone.

He walked, she followed. She was waiting to feel unsure, but she hadn't felt it yet. She would kill him. She said it in her head: I will kill him, and she felt nothing but resolve. It was only the thought of Kasper that caused her eyelids to tremble, her mouth to open as if to call out and then close again. Whatever happened tonight, he would find out what she had done and he would be appalled. He wouldn't forgive her – he was too good, but he would think it was because he was too bad. She wanted him to find her again, but as she ran the thought through her head she saw that it was impossible for her and for him. She must never be found.

Butler's laugh rose again and Kasper's concerned face was replaced with an image of the pilot striking Silke across the face, the hollow sound of his fist punching her throat, his hands shaking her like an animal, the sound of her choking as he bore down on her. She loved Kasper, but how could he ever understand?

As they came near the Kurfürstendamm, she felt anxious for the first time, afraid that no chance would present itself. The friend had not left Butler's side and now they were entering a road separated from the boulevard by a series of collapsed houses and were heading to the entrance of Yvonne's, a basement bar the note had said he frequented, but always alone. She stopped and watched helplessly as the men approached the squat entrance, where a crippled old doorman sat on a dented chrome chair that had been nailed onto the wall with strips of metal. The man looked up as Butler and his companion came close. Seeing their uniforms, he moved his stick away from the door and ignored them as they pushed it open and descended the steps into the belly of the building.

Eva stood on the corner of the street frowning, muddled. She had imagined the moment often – following the pilot until he was alone in an empty street and then raising the gun and pulling the trigger. It was meant to be one shot and he would be dead. She wasn't stupid – she had prepared to miss, to fire again, to chase him down briefly, to have to finish him off, to be numb, thrilled or appalled, for her reaction to be nothing like she'd thought it would be, but she had not imagined him with a friend or in a crowd. She had thought that her situation was hopeless, but she realised now that she hadn't given up the hope of escape completely. If she was shot or caught she would think, yes, this was inevitable. But she saw that she only wanted to fire if there was a chance, a possibility that she might make it out somehow, to something.

She considered waiting, but in a few hours it would be morning, and then she considered coming back the next day, but the thought made her sick. She couldn't bring herself here again, she couldn't try to sleep again, try to drag herself out of bed once more knowing what was coming. She would have to go in, she would have to get him.

She approached the entrance. The old man didn't hear her coming and didn't notice her in the dark street. 'Hello!' she said.

He looked up – he was younger than she had expected. His eyes were surprised and then sad. She opened her mouth to talk her way past, but she heard a scrape and realised that it was the man's wooden stick being drawn away.

Eva half nodded her thanks and then pushed the door open to find herself in an enclosed staircase that was filled with an impossible blackness as the door clunked shut behind her. For a second she was still and terrified, but realising there must be another door at the bottom, she felt her way down the concrete steps, the mutter of voices building as she descended. She found a door and then a handle and turning it she fell into a mass of hot bodies, loud voices and low orange light. The air was thick and the smoke hung in strings beneath the dim lamps, stinging her throat. There was a strangely domestic smell beneath the scent of men's sweat, damp wool and cigarettes, of talcum powder sprinkled on the rough floor so that the German girls and British soldiers could slide along as they danced. And there was already dancing, but Eva couldn't see the dancers; she was only aware of a swaying in a distant corner and the sound of shoes scraping the floor, beneath the shouting of men and the laughter of women.

Someone said, 'Butler!' and she pushed herself forward towards the voice, towards the bar. She had no idea what she would do when she got to him, but she would do something, and as she was bustled left and right, was pushed and tripped, and began to sweat beneath her woollen coat, she thought, perhaps she could just shoot him here after all – press the gun into his back and shoot him. And what if someone did notice? Just to let the gun drop, to stagger away onto the floor and lie there waiting for someone to take her away, to deal with her – that would be something. Just to close her eyes and sleep.

She caught sight of Butler and his friend at the bar and manoeuvred herself into position nearby. Butler, waiting to order, stared down at the bar and for a second she imagined that he was haunted by the thought of what was about to happen to him, but then, as if in response, he smiled.

A tall, sour-smelling woman with black hair, rolled up into a large puffed fringe, pushed roughly past her to the bar and shouted out an order of schnapps over Butler's head. Malcolm turned to her angrily, but the black-haired woman leant sideways on the bar and said in English, '*I've seen you here before, I think?*'

'*Maybe*,' said Butler. '*What of it?*' He turned his back on his friend who took the cue and moved away. As they flirted Eva lost track of their English, which the woman spoke loudly and apparently fluently. Butler smiled at the woman, or leered at her – Eva found it suddenly impossible to tell. He nodded at something she'd said and stroked the back of his index finger from her waist, down over her thigh.

The barmaid passed the woman a glass with a thin layer of clear liquid in the bottom. She swirled it round a few times, then knocked it back. Butler seemed to invite her somewhere, but then he moved off and Eva realised he was going to the toilet. The woman raised her glass to him as he left and leant her back up against the bar.

Moving again, without knowing what she was going to do, Eva found herself standing next to the woman. 'Excuse me,' she said. The woman was lighting a cigarette and either hadn't heard her or was ignoring her. 'Excuse me,' said Eva again.

The woman looked down at her, her face instantly taking on an air of disgust. 'What do you want?'

'Your pilot,' said Eva.

'My what?'

'The British pilot – the man you were talking to. He sent me to tell you he's waiting outside for you, behind the tram stop.' Eva realised immediately with a sinking horror that there was no tram stop in the street. 'I mean,' she said, 'I'm sorry, I realised what he meant now, not tram stop, but courtyard. He's out back, in the courtyard. It was his English.'

Eva seemed to be falling backwards, fainting. She had ruined everything, when all she had to do was stop and think about what she was going to say. Just to plan it. The woman let out a puff of derision, but then, incredibly, she frowned. 'Why did he send you?' she said, apparently undeterred.

'I didn't really understand,' said Eva. 'I don't speak enough English. Just "quick" and "money", something about the cash being ready or something.'

The woman looked down at Eva open-mouthed, her tongue investigating her upper molars. Eva tried to think of something else to embellish her story, aware of the painful possibility that Butler would appear at their side at any moment, that the woman would shove Eva to the floor and tear out a clump of her hair. But the woman pushed herself off the bar, elbowed Eva out of the way and marched to the back door, which closed behind her just as Butler reappeared by Eva's side.

'*Shit!*' he said, the tone expressing offence rather than disappointment.

Eva looked up at him and said, '*She send me. Your friend.*' She put her hand on her chest and said, '*Fräulein Hirsch.*'

Butler looked down at her and sighed. He grimaced as if she

stank. Eva smiled and touched her curling hair, trying to make her nervous smile seem naive and girlish.

'*I suppose you're pretty enough,*' he said. '*You got any money on you?*'

Eva frowned. She couldn't understand what he was saying.

'*Any money?*' he said. He rubbed his fingers together in front of her. She shook her head.

'*Well then,*' he said. '*I suppose we better go somewhere then. Have you got somewhere to go?*'

'*Yes,*' said Eva, '*Somewhere.*'

She took his hand. It was cool and smooth like waxed paper. She wrapped her fingers around it and pulled him towards the door. He resisted at first, but when she tugged at his hand again he came with her and she was able to lead him out of the building and into the cool air of the street.

Butler turned to the man at the door and said, '*What was that?*' The crippled man didn't move. '*Nothing,*' said Eva. '*He speak nothing.*'

Butler ignored her, but Eva tugged again at his hand, and again he loosened and followed her. Someone shouted, 'Slut!' from one of the dark windows above them, but Eva acted as if she hadn't heard and only let his hand go as they turned the corner and she was sure that he would keep on moving, keep on following her.

The rubble opened up into a dark, loamy space on one side of them. She stumbled over a stone or brick and he caught her, his grip tight on her arm, righting her again. She held up a hand as a signal, to show him she was fine and walked on.

Her flat shoes sunk into softer earth. All traces of the city had petered out, as large dark banks of earth, newly made, rose up around them like the steep sides of a valley.

'*Where the fuck are we?*' said Malcolm. Eva reached back and took his hand again, the feel and grip of which had already become familiar. She turned to smile at him, but he had turned also and was looking back, as he stumbled on, at the rippling bank of broken buildings behind him, like the spines on a lizard's back. '*I thought you had a room,*' he said, but not crossly.

The earth bank to their left began to dip and she knew that it was signalling the end. It must happen now, she thought. For a second she felt herself trying to analyse her actions, to think them over, but it was impossible. She had thought about it all so many times and decided she must kill him. Now was the time for action and the simplicity of it all was suddenly chilling. The bank dropped away sharply revealing a patch of clear land. This is the place, she thought, and felt afraid, but also surprised by the clarity of her thinking, by the quietness of their feet on the soft earth in the echoless space.

She let go of his hand and walked a little way off. She heard him stop and nodded to herself, before pulling out the gun and turning, lifting it up so that it was aimed squarely at his head, which now floated like a pale mask in the grey darkness in front of her. There it is, the gun in my hand. It will only need one shot. Yes, she was afraid now, she thought, as she heard her heart throbbing in her ears and felt her blood, sweat and saliva retract into her body, leaving her cold and dry. But that numb help-lessness – that impossible feeling that nothing could be done with all her fear and all her pain – that was all gone. She saw snatches of her rapists – a pomaded fringe hanging down over her, a dirty rolled-up sleeve, bitten fingernails, stained, broken teeth – she felt the pressure of a thumb on her throat, heard the angry grunts, could smell the dust of the floorboards and tasted blood and the dryness of her mouth, and then her hatred over-whelmed her and she let it come and she enjoyed it like biting down on an aching tooth.

Butler put his hands together and began to play with his thumb. '*All right then,*' he said quietly, not noticing the gun aimed at the space between his eyes. He looked around at the little clearing in the dark, like a boy waiting for his mother. She imagined his family sitting around at that moment in some English living room, listening to the radio. His father laying down his book, proud that his boy had fought as he had fought, his mother stubbing out a cigarette and lighting another, awash with that overwhelming happiness that comes from thinking of a once great threat now completely disappeared.

She felt her breathing becoming shallow and her arm ache. He looked at her and smiled. The smile was warm, sweet. And then he frowned and said, '*What are you doing?*' He stepped towards her. '*Are you getting your fucking knickers off, or what?*'

'*Back!*' she shouted.

Only now did he see the gun. He lifted his hands up automatically, but barely above waist height. He stared at the gun and then up at her face. And then he laughed. '*What are you? Some kind of crazed Nazi?*' he said. '*The war's over love – stop playing silly buggers.*'

'*No joke,*' said Eva. '*Rape!*'

'*Rape?*' said Malcolm, turning his ear towards her as if he'd misheard. He laughed again and put his hands cautiously on his hips. '*Excuse me, it was you that dragged me here!*'

'*No, you rape. You rape friend,*' said Eva.

'*I haven't raped anyone, darling,*' he said moving towards her. '*Put the gun down.*' She fired a shot into the ground at his feet.

'*Shit!*' he said, '*Fuck! What are you doing? Put the gun down. Help! Help!*' he cried and then, '*Don't shoot. Help! This is Flying Officer Malcolm Butler. Help! You know they'll be coming, don't you? They're coming. Someone will have heard the shots. You can't escape.*'

He stared into her eyes. She could hear shouting from the road. This is the moment, she thought. And it wasn't that she didn't want to kill him – it was that despite everything she'd seen she still couldn't quite fathom the change she was about to bring about. This man alive and in an instant he would be dead – the weight of it was suddenly overwhelming.

'*There's no point,*' Malcolm said to Eva. '*There's no point. Come on.*'

There were voices calling.

She saw a man up high with a gun to her right and it jolted her awake. She turned back to the pilot. No, she thought, she had seen this before – men, women, children she had known, her mother, her father, so alive and then so dead. She tightened her finger on the trigger, but she heard her voice being shouted – 'Eva!' The man ran down the earth slope towards them.

'*I'm here!*' cried Butler. '*Shoot her, man!*'

'Eva!' cried the man and she saw it was Kasper. Her frown faded. 'Oh Kasper,' she thought, 'It's too late,' and as he turned to the pilot she pulled the trigger and shot.

Kasper stood in the dark street holding a copy he had made of Marta's note, listing the hangouts of the red-haired pilot. He had been pushed around Willie's by angry British soldiers, stared frantically at the flickering white faces in the cinema and stood for an hour outside a whorehouse near Berlin Zoo, but she never came. And now both the prospect of finding or not finding Eva at Yvonne's – the name tightly written at the bottom of the list – terrified him, yet he launched himself forward, forcing a bundle of Marks into the crippled man's hand when he tried to protest.

A few minutes later he came back out onto the street, sweating and breathing heavily and looking up and down the empty street exhausted and lost. There was a coolness in the breeze as it dried the sweat on his forehead. His heart beat so hard that he thought it might seize up and stop, like a cramping muscle.

He looked directly in front of him at the blackened wasteland there, at the rising hills of rubble and turned earth and he saw that he had failed. Square miles of people once there and now gone. Streets and streets of activity, trams, shops, schools, churches. Lives led with their small tragedies, minor successes and failures, all now empty space, black soil and worms, churning the earth, breaking up the dead. And somewhere Eva and her pilot, a spark, a blemish that would go unnoticed and unremarked, not even recalled by a grandchild or a niece. And his father – just the body of an old man who had died when the authorities had handled him too roughly, just another corpse to dispose of.

'Kasper?'

Kasper turned and looked at the crippled old man at the door. The man's face was turned towards him and he was holding himself up on his stick. But the face belied the broken state of the man's body. It was clearer, only lightly wrinkled with a few deep lines on his forehead. And there was something familiar in the square skull, barely hidden by its skin and flesh. Something that had once been broad and masculine. Something that had once smiled and laughed and drunk in Kasper's bar.

'Joachim?' said Kasper. 'Joachim . . .' but he had never known his surname. A regular, a tram driver, from Hamburg, with a Belgian wife that he never mentioned, but everyone knew about.

'Kasper Meier.'

'Yes,' said Kasper.

'How are you?' said the man.

Kasper looked at his large brown eyes, the tufts of stubble around his face, shaven some time ago with a blunt razor. He stared at him open-mouthed, unable to offer any sort of response to his question.

'You're looking for someone?'

'Yes,' said Kasper. 'A girl. A German girl, about ... she's nineteen. Looks a bit older maybe. Blonde. Pretty. She would have been with a British pilot. Tall with ginger hair.'

'Yes,' said the old man. 'They were here, Kasper.' The man pushed himself up on his stick and came closer to him. He was bent over, his back arching up behind him, like a hyena.

'Where did they go?'

Joachim pointed towards the black hills, silhouetted against the black-grey sky. 'She led him in there.'

'Thank you,' said Kasper.

As he went to run Joachim caught him by the elbow. 'I think about your bar Kasper. I think about it often. I replay those evenings in my head, sitting here. They're such wonderful visions Kasper. I think of you and Phillip. I replay whole evenings, from the moment I left my apartment to the walk home – those wonderful walks in the morning air. That wonderful blue.'

Kasper touched his arm. 'Thank you,' he said.

'You must go,' said Joachim.

'Yes,' said Kasper and began to run.

'Thank you!' cried Joachim as Kasper reached the other side of the street and disappeared into the rubble.

Kasper tried to run, but it was so dark and there were small walls and large lumps of cement and concrete. He picked his way through, listening out for voices, but he heard none. The ground beneath his feet yielded and he felt that he was walking on soft earth, newly turned. Banks of earth rose up around him and he stopped to listen, but all sound was swallowed up by his own strained panting.

Then there was a shot and a light flash in the dark. Kasper's stomach lurched and he turned and ran up one of the banks. He heard shouting. First an English-speaking voice close by and then responses further off. He had shot her, of course. Of course he would do it first. Kasper would come over the ridge of the mound and find her in a heap, the pilot moving her body with his foot like a hunter with his kill. But as he reached the summit, after becoming briefly aware of being high up, of seeing the city and its meagre lights straining through the darkness around him, he looked down and saw two figures both alive, one of them a young woman holding a gun. The wind was not strong, but it battered his ears noisily until he began to run down the slope, stumbling as he went, his legs threatening to buckle beneath him. The two figures looked up at him, straining to see who it was in the dark. The male figure who had had his hands in the air in front of him, dropped them to his side and came towards him expectantly. 'Eva!' Kasper cried.

'*I'm here,*' cried the pilot. '*Shoot her, man!*' And as Kasper came near, Eva raised her gun again and Kasper shouted 'Eva!' He tripped, but managed to lift his gun as he fell forward. There were two shots, like echoes of each other. The gun jumped in Kasper's hand. Eva screamed and stepped backwards. The man stumbled as Kasper fell onto his knees and steadied himself with his free hand, the pain from his gunshot wound rippling down towards the ground. The pilot remained on his feet for what seemed to be an impossible amount of time, but as Kasper cocked the pistol and Eva raised her gun again, the pilot crumpled down dead, disappearing into the darkness, down to the floor.

Kasper heard nothing, just the echoless air of the wasteland, but could smell his own sweat, the gunpowder, the metal of the gun, the sweet blackness of the earth.

'Kasper?' Eva said it in a whisper.

Kasper got to his feet and went to her. He put his arm around her and she leant into him and put her head on his shoulder. He took the gun from her hand and threw it over to where the body of the pilot lay.

'What have we done?'

'It's over now.'

'They're coming.'

Kasper turned his head and listened. He heard the footsteps. They were close. He took her hand, and pulled her up and over the embankment.

TICKETS

They sat side by side on a narrow beer-garden bench in a ruined cellar. A grey rectangle of light was reflected on the glossy centimetre of water on the ground beneath them, shining dimly through the floor above their heads, open to the night sky. The partial space felt grotto-like to Kasper, filled with the comforting, earthy smell of stale water, peaty and damp.

Eva's head was on Kasper's chest, his arms around her, across her forearms, her hands up by her face, her fingers worrying her lips. 'What happened?' she said. The question was whispered, expecting no answer. Kasper rocked her, put his lips to the crown of her head, shushed her.

Water was dripping in an awkward, broken rhythm. Kasper was aware of his continued terror, of his heart beating hard, of his pulse throbbing in his wrists, at his temples; but rising above it, this lightness. As he lifted his feet clear of the wet ground again, as he felt the water seeping into the toes of his shoes, the emptiness overwhelmed him and he wasn't sure if its result would be his weeping, his fainting, his vomiting. But then Eva moved, rubbed her elbow against her side, scratched at herself through her coat, her cardigan and her blouse, and Kasper could smell the antiseptic soap on her skin and he felt alive again in the dampness of the cellar.

'We have to go back for my father,' he said.

'Is he all right? Will she come for him?'

'Who?' said Kasper.

'Beckmann.'

'Frau Beckmann's . . . she's not real. She's no one. She's nothing.'

Kasper heard a grumbling, a high droning whir. He looked up at the large hole above them – the broken edges of the floorboards turned white in a car's headlights. As it passed it reflected enough light onto them that Eva's face emerged grey from the darkness. Her mouth was small, her hair wild, having escaped from its clips and pins as they had run from the pilot, her eyes fixed onto the floor, tired and unmoved.

The sound dissipated. The darkness returned.

'You knew?' said Kasper.

'I wondered,' she said. 'How could I not wonder? But by then it was too late.'

'But you never met her.'

'She would send notes. Via Silke or the twins, but . . . ' She paused. 'Who was it?'

'Neustadt.'

'Ha,' she said, loud enough that it echoed off the damp cellar wall in front of them. 'Makes sense, I suppose.'

'You're not appalled? About what he made you do? What he made you all do?'

'Oh Kasper,' she said. 'He didn't make us do anything.'

Kasper squinted up at the grey sky. He felt a pressure in his throat. 'What about that girl crying in your apartment last night?'

Her head moved on his shoulder – she was looking up at him. 'You were there?'

'I was close,' he whispered, 'I was always close.'

She shook her head. 'She was just worried about Hilda, because they were friends. She wasn't crying last week after she'd shot some Ami soldier.'

Kasper heard tiny animal feet pit-a-pattering in the shallow water. 'How did you ... I mean, why did you ... ?'

'After my parents, after the hospital,' she said, 'I had nowhere to go. I slept in ruined buildings for a week – I was fine then. But I was hungry. Then I met a woman – Frau Tischler – at the water pump. She'd been widowed. She was doing some sewing, mostly for the soldiers – black market. I didn't get anything for it, but I could sleep in their bathroom – they had a bathroom – and I got a little food. The second night some soldiers came – she opened the door to them. There were five of them, but ... only one of them raped me. The others just watched. Afterwards Frau Tischler said it was par for the course. And then I met Silke. She knew the house – she knew what was happening. She followed me one day, told me about this woman – Frau Beckmann – told me how to get on the rubble group, told me about the better rations, and said there was somewhere to live. I mean, what was the worst that could happen? That she'd murder me? I didn't think that would've been so bad then. I don't think I even thought about it. And I got my bed and my work. There were rules, funny rules about how we had to keep the apartment, that we had to be out in the day – but it was a bed, and there was food and it was safe. And then Silke started talking about how I could get my justice.'

'You knew they wanted you to kill them?'

'Not straight away. But, yes, of course, later I knew. I want to tell you I was terrified when I understood, but when I realised what getting my justice meant, I was elated.'

Kasper winced. She held tight onto his arm.

'I know, it sounds terrible, doesn't it? But imagine – you've dreamed of killing someone for so long, thought of so many terrible deaths for those men and felt numb with helplessness . . . And then someone presses a gun into your hand, gives you a name. I mean, it's not that simple, but . . . ' They heard a distant shout, like someone calling a dog. 'No, it was that simple,' she said. 'Yes, I was elated. Desperate to do it. Some said no. Three girls who were there with me said no straight away. They were just asked to leave – nothing violent. They knew they had to keep their mouths shut.'

'And this man, this pilot? He . . . ?'

'No, you never kill your own one – it's like a deal you make with the other girls. If you faced your own, it might – well, so many things could go wrong.'

'Did someone kill yours?'

'Yes,' she said, in an exulted whisper. 'My Elka.'

Kasper shifted on the bench. He felt the dryness in his blind eye. 'How did you know it was yours?'

'We don't sort that out – Beckmann, or whoever, sorted that out. We got a token.'

'A token?'

He felt Eva extricate her arm from his embrace. She searched around in a pocket and then held out her hand. A brass button caught the dull light of the cellar.

'Could be anyone's,' said Kasper.

'I suppose,' said Eva. 'But there's a chance – a good chance.'

Kasper nodded, unwilling to correct her. 'And the pilot tonight?'

'He raped Silke. Repeatedly.'

'How long did it go on for?'

'They only met once.' She put the button back into her pocket. 'Why?'

'I don't know,' said Kasper. 'So that I can try and understand.'

'You don't understand?' Eva said. 'But either of us might've killed him. Or both of us. Didn't you want to kill him?'

'Yes,' said Kasper. 'I wanted to kill him. Because it was too late. Because I wanted to save you. Because I wanted to save myself.'

'Well,' said Eva. 'There you are. And it's done now, I suppose.'

The light in the cellar darkened and a sharp crackling was quickly followed by a wall of sound, a huge cold hush of rain that fell into the cellar and pummelled the stagnant water on the floor, creating a silvery spray that drifted up and wet their faces. Kasper wanted to say something to her, to explain to her what she had done, what he had done. But instead he heard himself saying, 'Can you come with me? For my father.'

He felt Eva's hand on his wrist. She pulled at it and he lifted it up, freeing his hand. She sat up and held it, intertwining her fingers with his.

They climbed out, into the rain. Eva let out a gasp at the shock of the cold water hitting her scalp. Kasper bent his head down and pushed forward.

Beneath the veil of rain pouring from the brim of his hat, the city had become a landscape of broken brown shapes lining the grey river of the road. Kasper felt his suit jacket, his shirt and trousers, his underwear pulling down as they drew in the rain, until the cotton of his clothes was glossy with water, which ran down his arm, out from his sleeves, and over Eva and Kasper's hands.

Kasper heard nothing but the rain and their footsteps. He understood that he had saved no one from anything. That at best he had won a stay of execution for Eva, for his father, for himself, and one that was probably going to be short-lived. But holding Eva's hand, walking with her in the dark, he had found someone again who knew him, who he knew. He saw Phillip in the snow, descending the steps towards him, reaching his hand out to him, touching his frozen skin. And as they approached Windscheidstraße, passed the ruined tank, bent over double, he felt briefly triumphant.

'Kasper,' he heard.

He raised his head.

'Kasper,' said Eva.

He squinted.

'Look.'

In the distance, around the door of his apartment block, a group of people had gathered. The number of dark shapes was impossible to count, but they could make out some sort of large vehicle – military or police. It stood ominously behind the crowd – a dark bulky box.

'They've really come for me.'

'Yes,' said Eva.

They stopped walking. 'Papa,' he said. He felt his father's fingers on the back of his head, heard him calling, his voice vibrating through the walls of their house, his laughter, that enormous rolling laughter. He saw him frightened, hiding beneath his sheets as someone kicked in the door; he saw him hiding behind a curtain, a gun in his hand.

A woman in the crowd shrugged and disappeared into the night. Someone held up a hand, the arm straight, the palm flat. It dropped away. Someone whistled. Someone coughed. The crowd moved, changed shape, moved again. A form separated from it, resolving into a man wearing a long leather coat, a white policeman's band around his arm.

'Shall we run?' whispered Eva.

'It's too late – he's already seen us,' said Kasper.

'What shall we do?'

'Stay still.'

They lowered their heads. The policeman looked up at them

and nodded as he walked by. 'Nothing to see here,' he called to them as he passed. 'Move on.' They didn't move. Kasper's skin was so cold from the rain, his body so wet that he hardly seemed to be there at all. They heard the policeman stop.

'Excuse me,' he called back. Kasper let go of Eva's hand and they turned slowly.

'Do you know who lives there?'

'No,' said Kasper.

'What's happened?' said Eva.

Kasper turned to her and shook his head.

'Another suicide,' said the policeman. He kicked a stone on the ground – it pinged against something metal. The rain poured off his hat. 'Old guy – you wonder what the point is at that age. Tommies have just turned up though, so maybe he was important. Some old Nazi or something.' The policeman studied Kasper's face. His eyes narrowed, but in the dark, in that heavy rain he couldn't see that there were tears pouring from his eyes, couldn't see that the girl was weeping as well, would think that their lips and chins were shaking with cold. 'You're not a member of the family or anything?'

'Family!' said Kasper, choking the word out, trying to feign shock. He took Eva's hand again, squeezed it, because he couldn't utter another word.

'Why,' said Eva, her own words strange and stilted, 'We don't even live here.'

The policeman nodded. 'Well, you better get to wherever you're going,' he said. 'It's past curfew and there are soldiers around.' He tipped his hat and they watched him disappear into the dark.

Eva turned to Kasper. Her hair lay flat to her head and hung down around it like a cap. Her eyes sparkled, black in the dark. Her lips were wide and soft. She took in a breath, a gasp. Kasper knelt, his hand in the water, his fingertips on the concrete. Eva knelt down too. She leant into him, her head resting on his shoulder. He grabbed her hand and pressed his face into it. Rain poured from the brim of his hat onto his exposed neck, down his collar, onto his back. The rain came on harder, it began to spray back onto them, began to cling to the fabric of his hat, run over his cheeks and fill his mouth.

HEINRICH NEUSTADT

Heinrich Neustadt leant against one of the huge, cylindrical washing drums, still warm from the hot water that had been churning around in it all day.

'You'll need to keep a look out,' said Heinrich. 'Just an hour.'

'I've got to get home,' said the laundry woman, frowning, her arms crossed beneath her breasts. 'I've got mouths to feed.'

Heinrich reached down into a large canvas bag at his feet and took out a full bag of flour, placing it on the large table between him and the laundry worker. Her eyes widened and she slowly moved forward and squeezed the thick paper, feeling the softness of the flour beneath it.

'The whole bag?' she said.

'The whole bag,' said Heinrich. 'This week,' he added.

'I could get sacked for letting you use this room. You might take something.'

'I don't want to take anything. I just need a neutral space. For a meeting. I'm just setting something up. There's no harm in that,' he said, gently placing a bar of soap on the table, by the bag of flour.

The woman looked at it, hypnotised. 'Who are you meeting?'

'It'll be a soldier in mess uniform. Nothing seedy – just a meeting.' The woman looked up suspiciously. 'You can peep through the windows if you like,' he said.

'Just an hour?' she said.

'Probably less.'

The woman gathered up her treasures. 'I'll have to turn off the main lights, else someone will see,' she said, not taking her eyes off the goods in her arms.

'Fine,' said Heinrich. 'As long as I can see something.'

The woman nodded, and turned, then disappeared immediately between two of the sheets that hung in great rows across the room like sails. He heard her padding towards the door in her soft, rubber-soled shoes and heard the clunk of a switch as the large lights went off overhead. The room around him was suddenly transformed into a dim mass of abstract shadows, lit from behind by the weak lights at the side entrance through which the woman had left. They shone on the vast ceiling and walls above the sheets, covered in smooth white ceramic, and in the pools of drying water on the hexagonal tiles at his feet.

Heinrich lit a cigarette and looked down at the shiny toes of his shoes. He heard a distant, echoing scream from somewhere else in the hospital above him. He looked up at the ceiling, breathed in the warm soapy air and picked over his last meeting with Kasper again. He took pleasure in the slow revelation. Kasper had been genuinely shocked, he could feel it. And he punctured his spasm of pity by thinking of Kasper's coldness in Sybelstraße, that morning at his flat. He was annoyed that he had escaped the policeman, but not surprised, since they had become so feckless and useless since the end of the war – unarmed, nervous children.

And then Kasper was dead – he had killed himself, they said at his apartment block; no, it didn't make sense. Not that hard-nosed, sentimental bastard with his rubble girl and his father. He didn't believe it – Kasper had already had too many chances to give in. Heinrich had worried about it for days until he finally went down to the mortuary and paid off Göthe, the porter, to let him see the body – such a drunkard that he only needed a quarter of a bottle of bad corn schnapps. And Heinrich found, not Kasper, but the withered body of his old father, his eye shot out in an attempt, he supposed, to fool the authorities, to fool Heinrich himself when he came looking. He had been disgusted by that old body, how needlessly devoted it all was.

He had wanted Kasper to have been taken, that night in Sybelstraße; that's how he had foreseen it. He would have been killed certainly, but organising to have him killed himself, so directly as he would now have to, that upset him. Because there could have been something with Kasper. He could have saved him, if Kasper Meier had known how to love anybody. Because Heinrich had loved him. He really had.

Something metal hit the floor and tinkled along the ground.

Heinrich took his cigarette out of his mouth. 'Hello?' he said. 'Peters? You're early?'

He stood up and pushed himself up on his toes, but couldn't get high enough to see over the lines of drying bedding.

'Frau Köper?'

He felt a breeze cutting through the warm air of the vast, basement laundry and the sheets around him rose together, then fell, as if breathing.

'Who's there?' he said. He saw a shadow, a figure. He pulled at the sheet in front of him, which fell down around his feet, and revealed more sheets, more shadows. Then he heard a girl sniggering.

'You little buggers!' he cried. 'You scared the shit out of me.'

Heinrich pulled aside another sheet. 'How did you get in here?' He tried to sound fatherly, afraid he had scared them.

'Through a window,' came Hans' voice. 'What did you think?'

Heinrich was angry, but said, 'Like a pair of little monkeys.' Heinrich pulled aside another sheet. 'I said I was coming to see you tomorrow. Is something wrong? Something at the flat?'

'It's our mother,' said Lena.

'What about your mother?'

'You said you'd have found her by now.'

'You keep fobbing us off.'

'"Fobbing." That's a grown-up word.' There was no answer. 'Look,' said Heinrich, 'I've got people looking. It's ongoing.'

'Which people?'

'What's this really about?' said Heinrich. 'Come out so we can talk properly. He saw a shadow moving and pulled down another sheet – it revealed a coat-stand beneath a high window. He turned back. He had a good mind to spank them stupid once he caught them. 'Listen,' he said. 'I wanted to talk to you anyway. Another job – something fun. Kasper Meier's still alive. Can you believe it? After all that palaver. He's somewhere in Berlin. If this is all getting a bit too much for you, he could be your last find for a while. Maybe you could have a little break, do something a bit more, I don't know, child-friendly. Something fun. Would you like that? We'll sort out Kasper Meier, then something fun. Whatever you want.'

'We've been waiting for a year,' said Hans.

Heinrich kicked over the coat-stand and shouted, 'You've got a bloody cheek you know, talking to me like this, after everything I've done. You don't realise how bloody lucky you are. Your own room, food, water. There are children starving to death in this city as we speak – do you hear me? And you two are living it up like pigs in shit. And all I hear is you bloody moaning about your mother. How old are you now? Twelve? Thirteen? It's pathetic.'

He put his hands on his hips and looked around him. He heard nothing except the low electric hum from the lights by the exit. He was on the verge of shouting at them again, telling them he was done with them, telling them that he'd seen their mother's body with his own eyes. And then he heard Lena's voice, just metres away: 'You've let us down Neustadt.'

Heinrich lunged at her, pulling at sheets, kicking over buckets and large baskets of dry laundry, knocking into empty washing machines that rang like low church bells. He turned, panting, and saw a shadow, and beneath the shadow he saw the toes of shoes poking out beneath the hanging sheet. 'Ha,' he cried and ripped the sheet away. But behind the sheet stood Frieda, the large port-wine stain tumbling across her cheek, down her neck and into her blouse. 'What the fuck are you doing here?' said Heinrich. He saw that she was holding a gun, her hand shaking.

'They said you're Beckmann.'

'Who,' said Heinrich laughing. 'Those children?'

'Are you?'

'Beckmann's helping you.'

'They said those men didn't rape anyone.'

'You're listening to children?'

The girl looked confused. Her hand sunk and Heinrich made a grab for the gun, pulling her arm down, hearing her scream, hearing a whooping cry and punch in his gut. He stumbled backwards. The girl stood in front of him, her mouth wide open, her face pale. He heard sniggering, heard his blood splashing onto the terracotta tiles, felt the lights shrinking then widening as he fell backwards.

Frieda let the gun drop to her side. How foul the smell of gunpowder and blood was, she thought, and how familiar. Her hand shook and she felt nauseous. She put the sleeve of her coat up to her face and breathed in the smell of old damp wool and camphor.

The twins came out from behind the sheets; Hans held onto the line that they hung off, pulling it down so that blood began to soak into the corner of one. Lena played with the edge of another sheet and they both stared down at the body, their faces betraying nothing more than the vague interest they may have given to a dead bird.

The door behind Frieda opened. The twins looked up.

'What are you all staring at it for?' Silke shouted. 'And get that sheet up out of the blood – do you want to get caught?'

Hans let go of the line and it sprang back up, the sheets settling like the skirt of a dress.

Silke was at Frieda's side and took the gun from her, dropping it into a large, leather handbag. She threw two military duffel bags onto the tiled floor and said to the children, 'You two gather up as many sheets as you can. You've got five minutes.'

They stared at her with bored derision.

'You can have a tube of sugar each if you get more than forty.'

'Can we have his watch?' Lena said.

'Or his shoes?' said Hans.

Silke sighed and said quietly, 'Dear God!' They stared at her and she shook her head. 'I don't want to know what you take from him, just try not to get any blood on yourselves, if you know what's good for you. But forty sheets!' she shouted, as they went for him. 'Then take what you like. You've got five minutes.'

Silke gripped Frieda's hand and led her outside. 'You're shaking,' she said, looking at her with genuine concern.

'I know,' said Frieda. 'This one feels strange. Didn't we owe him something?'

'He was never interested in us, Frieda. That I can assure you.'

'Mmm,' she murmured, 'I suppose.'

Frieda became aware of an armed man in khaki standing in

a doorway and she stopped dead. 'Silke,' she whispered, her eyes filling with tears. 'They've come for us.'

Silke pulled at her hand, 'Keep moving,' she said.

'There's someone here – watching us.'

She looked up at Silke. 'They know what we did,' she said.

The soldier left the darkness of the doorway and walked swiftly and silently away from them towards the door of the laundry room. Silke turned to her as another soldier moved past them and then another. 'We didn't do anything,' Silke said. 'Do you understand?'

Frieda shook her head. 'When did you ... ? What ... ?'

'Don't be a dummy,' Silke said. 'We need to get out of here.'

Silke walked on and Frieda followed. She thought about the children and waited, terrified, to hear a shot. But there was no shot.

They walked onto the road, past a row of military vehicles parked in the dark. There was a soldier standing by the final wagon smoking a cigarette. When they reached the place where he'd been standing the smell of tobacco was strong, but the man was gone. Silke gripped Frieda's shoulder and took off her shoe; she shook it and a slip of yellow paper fell apparently unnoticed from it – she continued to search inside as if for a stone. She shrugged and put the shoe back on. Frieda stared at the slip of paper, a yellow blur on the dark road. 'Come along,' Silke said, 'We've got work to do.'

RUNNING WATER

The dog was barking and Kasper's father ran along the street, the tails of his dress coat flapping and as the street dropped away he fell and rolled, laughing, throwing out his hands, his hat coming loose, flying off, spinning. The smoke of the city shrank away. He called to Kasper, 'Run, my boy!' Phillip dived over him, a shadow against the sun, his arms widening as he dived, and Kasper, breathless, jumped up and fell down onto concrete, onto grass, rolling, cart-wheeling down and down. A girl's voice formed foreign words, she appeared at his side, on a train, Eva, staring at him, Kasper frowning in confusion. She fell silent. He felt a finger poking his side. He was cold and pulled up the blanket around him, felt the tight canvas of a deck chair beneath him.

'Kasper,' whispered Eva. 'Look.'

Kasper moved and felt a strange sensation, of pitching forward, of being supported in air. He turned his head to the side, then up, then opened his eyes. He saw Eva's face, smiling, and smelt the sea in the wind that whipped around his head, felt the residual happiness from his dream. She was holding a battered book, a book of English plays that she'd been reading from, trying to make sense of the words, forming them slowly and deliberately as he drifted off.

Eva took his hand. 'Look.'

She pointed up at the cloudless sky. As on many nights before, the stars were indescribable on their black bed. So many stars that it made Kasper dizzy – giants like blue diamonds, yellow suns and pinky nebulas.

'I was sleeping,' said Kasper.

'I know,' said Eva.

'Was I snoring?'

'No. You don't make a sound when you sleep.'

Kasper sat up, letting the blanket fall down around him.

'I think I need my bed.'

'Yes,' said Eva. 'Let's sleep.'

Kasper stood unsteadily at first, but then regained his balance as they made their way down the narrow deck. The air was cold and the deck virtually empty save for one of the American shipmen who was putting away the last of the deck chairs.

'Is that that man from breakfast?' said Eva.

Kasper looked up – some way down the ship, silhouetted in front of an electric light at the bow, a man was standing at the railings without a coat. His features were completely in shadow, the electric lighting creating an aureole of his hair. He seemed to turn to them and then moved through a doorway into the ship.

'Was it him?' said Eva.

'I don't know,' said Kasper. 'Did you like him?'

'No, you idiot,' she said. 'I just noticed him earlier.'

As they approached the door, it opened and a young drunken couple stumbled out. The woman put her gloved hand up to her mouth in exaggerated embarrassment and the man pulled himself up straight, and hid the bottle he was carrying behind his back.

'*Sorry*,' said the woman in English.

'*It's fine*,' said Kasper.

'You're speaking German,' said the man, also in German.

'Yes,' said Kasper. 'So are you.'

The man frowned and tried to steady himself. 'I learn some there. I am soldier. Where you from?'

'The Sudetenland,' said Kasper.

The man nodded. '*Czechoslovakia*,' said the man to the woman.

She nodded.

'What are you reading?' the man said to Eva, pointing at her hand.

She held up the battered book. 'Trying to learn a bit of English. We found it in the library.'

The man read the title out loud: '*English Restoration Drama*. You're going to learn some pretty funny English from that,' he said.

Eva smiled and nodded. A gust of freezing wind blew at them briefly, causing the woman's hat to come off. It spun past them, dancing along the railings for a few hopeful seconds then disappeared, whirring into the blackness. '*Oh*,' the woman said simply, and looked terribly sad.

'How miserable,' said Eva and pulled in the sides of her cardigan against the wind, crossing her arms. Kasper pulled at the sleeve of the cardigan, so that it covered her bare shoulder.

The four of them turned back to one another, frowned and made sad faces, spending a few seconds in silence until the loss of the hat seemed to have been duly observed.

'Well, goodnight,' said Eva, at last.

'Yes,' said the American soldier. 'Goodnight.'

They descended into the close, oily air of the corridor leading down to the third-class cabins, deep within the bowels of the ship. Through the door they heard children – both laughing and crying – men muttering, bottles clinking, a woman singing. They moved down the narrow corridor, still smiling. Kasper put a hand on Eva's arm and moved her in front of him, out of the way of a young man in shirt sleeves, who nodded his thanks and took a brief second glance at Eva, who had hung her head, when she saw him coming.

In the cabin they began the simple ritual that had developed naturally over the preceding weeks. They turned away from each other as they undressed and got into their night things. Kasper used the washbasin first, cleaning his teeth and washing his face from the weak stream of water. Then he ascended into the top bunk while Eva spent a minute or so in front of the sink, letting the tap run the whole time for the novelty of it.

She went to the door and turned the light off, holding onto the metal bar of their bunks in the total blackness. She heard Kasper roll onto his side, and she ascended the bunks, climbed into Kasper's bed and held him, her arms under his arms. She put her cheek against his back, in between his shoulder blades, and she began to describe their apartment in New York, what they would eat for dinner, where they would drink. She described the music to him, the sound of the city, the trips to beaches, to cinemas, to bookshops, and she held him until eventually he stopped crying and fell asleep.

Then she returned to her own bunk. She lay awake in the dark, not knowing if her eyes were open or closed. A door slammed and a group of giggling women ran past their door, drunk and happy. And the ship groaned gently, rising and falling, rolling softly in the icy black water.

ACKNOWLEDGEMENTS

I would like to thank the many early readers of the book, including Shaun Levin and Maggie Hamand who both gave invaluable feedback and encouragement on early drafts. Special thanks also go to the *harter Kern* of my Berlin writers' group (most importantly Meg Alderson) who read early sections and shared the ups and downs of the publishing process with me. A huge thank you also to my most committed reader – my mother, Loraine Fergusson – who has read every draft of every novel that I have written, including the first three that I never published. And thanks also to my final readers: my agent, Karolina Sutton at Curtis Brown, and editor, Clare Smith at Little, Brown, for their invaluable input and support throughout the long road to publication. Thanks are also due to the whole team at Little, Brown, in particular Nick Castle, Helena Doree, Kate Hibbert, Rhiannon Smith and Hollie Smyth, for their hard work on every aspect of the book.

I would also like to thank my family – be they Fergussons (Colin, Loraine, Sam, Jegsy, Tamsin, Eve), Whitlocks (Katie-Jane, David, Scarlett, Huxley), Falkensteins (Hans-Peter, Gudrun,

Valeska, Arthur, Ada), Sauers (Robbie) or Trubys (Chris) – for their constant support, enthusiasm and belief over the years, and also my friends who have offered help and advice along the way, especially Toby Garfath who helped me submit the manuscript in the first place.

Most importantly, I would like to thank my partner, Tom, who not only read draft after draft, but introduced me to Germany and Berlin and is thus wholly responsible for this book. I also want to thank him for putting up with countless lost weekends, evenings, mornings and holidays over the years and for always believing that I'd get there in the end. *Mensch, Tommy, ich hab's endlich geschafft!*